DARKHELM

DARKHELM

TALES OF SHATTERED GLASS: BOOK ONE

BARDLYRE

NEF HOUSE PUBLISHING

Darkhelm
Tales of Shattered Glass: Book One
Copyright © 2023 BardLyre

ISBN 978-1-958414-31-6

ALSO BY BARDLYRE

Tales of Shattered Glass
Darkhelm
Stonehand

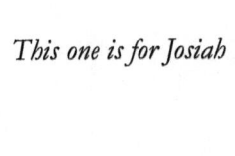

This one is for Josiah

CHAPTER ONE

"Let There Be Ale"

It would be very easy, Daine Orban, Knight of the Road, thought, *to lose perspective now.*

There had just been too many village halls. Too many earnest, sun-reddened faces. Too many discordant, insistent demands for her attention over too, too many years.

It was not that her role had become unnecessary or redundant — far from it. She found herself with more to do now than when she took her first step on the Road all those years ago. It was just that, day by day, tale by tale, complaint after complaint, it had all become hauntingly, banally familiar.

Had it not been one of Old Gant's host of unwritten rules that, come the third Tour, the excitement of it all would pall?

"But that's for starry-eyed wanderers with dreams of slaying dragons and banishing warlocks," he had cackled. *"Not for the cynical*

ones like you, Daine Darkhelm. Not for the ones who really know their business. No illusions for you, love, are there?"

She had grimaced and dipped her head in acknowledgement at the nickname, knowing she was in truth one of those dreamy wanderers. That she would gladly spend her blood and her lifetime on the King's Road. It was, quite simply, the right thing to do. She had accepted her peers' mockery, good-natured, and otherwise, knowing all would be well once on Tour. Her justifiable reputation for morose taciturnity would be neither here nor there once she began fulfilling that sacred duty.

On days like this, though — and were they not all days like this recently? — that time of naïveté felt a world away.

With a sigh, she refreshed <Intimidation>, drew the short sword at her hip and began swinging it, almost absent-mindedly. The petitioners awaiting their turn instinctively stepped backwards under the pressure of her aura. When she spoke, the softness of her voice stood in stark comparison to the physical presence of this legendary knight in full plate and helm. "You will appreciate I feel more than a touch of scepticism at these claims, Lord Trellec. I see your son in front of me." She made a casual gesture with her blade toward the skinny, sullen youth of ten or eleven with a bloodied nose. "A boy who has, I sense, had more than his share of scrapes over the years. To speak plainly, he does not possess the look of a defenceless victim. But I have been wrong about such things before, and I accept there may be more to this incident. I then turn to his assailant" — a nod to a small, sobbing, bundle of clothes wrapped in her mother's arms — "who seems somewhat miscast in her role as the aggressor. So, what do we have? A slip of a girl assaulting, without provocation, a Lordling twice her age and more than twice her size. It seems an unlikely tale, does it not?"

The older man in the delicate red-and-gold robes did not quite manage to keep the sneer off his face. He looked around the wooden hall, raising his arms to encourage comment from the group of villagers waiting silently behind him. Dozens of pairs of eyes intently studied the floor. "That is not the point, my Lady. It is not for you to parse such things. There is right, and there is wrong. And there is the Justice of the Goddess. This girl, a commoner no less, struck my son, and blood was spilled. We have innumerable witnesses. I fail to see the complexity here. You must do as is required."

Yes, she thought, eyeing Lord Trellec and finding him rather too pleased with himself. *All too easy to lose perspective.*

It had all gone as she had dreamed for those first few years. She would travel the Road, and she would deliver judgement: there were bandits to be slain, corrupt officials to be toppled, and monsters to be rooted out. Most villagers were happy to see her. Of course, some would resent her intrusion into their lives, but that was to be expected, and there had been more bouquets than brickbats in those early days. True, there had been violence — more often of late, now that she thought of it — and she had done things over the years which troubled her.

But that was the role she had chosen. And she did it well. Since those first few days, she had never turned her face from what needed to be done, and she would not do so today.

The casual swinging of her sword fell, unconsciously, into an old training pattern. "As you say, Lord Trellec. As you say. Right and wrong. And the Justice of the Goddess.

And blood. But that's the trick of things, don't you see? That is why we are charged to make our Tours and why the Goddess travels with us when we do. Right and wrong. How do we tell the two apart? A Lordling has his nose broken, which is certainly a matter for a Knight of the Road. We can't be having that sort of disorder in the outlying regions. One bloody nose in the West leads to smashed windows, leads to riots in the town, and, before you know it, we will have venerable elders with their heads on pikes and the commonality dancing toward the palace with pitchforks and ill intent."

The excited hubbub that had greeted Lord Trellec's call for justice hushed to a tense silence. All that could be heard was the hum of Daine's sword as it carved ever more complex shapes in the air.

"But there are other matters also for Knights of the Road. Some of us — not so many nowadays, to be sure, but enough of us to make a difference — look askance at young Nobles throwing around their weight in what may be considered to be an inappropriate manner. It may be felt that any . . . retribution that came the way of a young gentleman overstepping his boundaries would be entirely proper. I feel the need to mention that some may feel a wise father would deliver his own justice when coming across such a matter and should not seek such wide attention" — Daine indicated the crowded hall — "for unfortunate, youthful indiscretions. Indeed, I seem to recall, Lord Trellec, that you chose not to attend my last Tour: were heard, if rumour be true — and is it ever? — to describe this Court as a 'backward, tyrannical ritual of which we would do well to be rid.' I may be misquoting, of course. My age, you see. You have the reputation of a clever and thoughtful man, sir. Thus, I may find myself questioning your motives this day."

The sword paused its intricate spirals, its tip hovering in front of Lord Trellec's son. The boy stared at her without emotion, seemingly able to ignore the blade inches from his face. She said, "Noble blood has been shed —and for that, as all know, there is a dire penalty. But you ask for the execution of this girl in compensation for a bloody nose, my Lord."

Trellec raised his chin. "That is the law, my Lady."

Daine nodded. "So, it is. And, as that is the law, this 'backward ritual' finds it should grant you what you seek."

There was a soft sigh in the room, undercut by the sobbing of the condemned child. Her mother, eyes huge at Daine's words, tried to comfort her.

"But, in calling down the Goddess to witness that judgement, other crimes —perhaps ones of which you are entirely, innocently, unaware — may well come to Her notice."

The outstretched sword did not move from its place in front of the youth's face. Daine's brown eyes, seemingly so tired and unremarkable a few moments ago, now glowed with the power of the summoned Goddess. "Are you quite convinced you want judgement in this matter, Lord Trellec? Once summoned, the Goddess can be implacable in such things."

Trellec looked considerably less sure of himself than he did barely half a bell earlier, when he pushed his way to the front of the supplicant line dragging his son's "assailant" with him.

Suddenly, he dropped his head, unable to withstand the weight of her Goddess-given power pressing down upon him for a moment longer and cleared his throat. "I wonder, my Lady . . . well, now that I have properly considered the matter, whether this is not more a case for the village Constable? In retrospect, it was just the shock of things, I'm sure. I am sorry to have troubled you with such a trivial matter. Master Flynn will be happy to take this off your hands for a less extreme remedy."

"But it *is* in my hands, Lord Trellec. You brought it to me. And here it sits, like a turd on a Naming Day cake. What shall we do about this turd, Lord Trellec?" The sword continued to be held, without wavering, in front of the nose of Trellec's son. Yet the boy did not show an ounce of fear throughout. Few even those thrice his age, would be so collected in the circumstances. "Blood has been spilt, my Lord, but mayhap there is more to discover about the events that led to that outcome. Should I sound the judgement of the Goddess?"

The boy held her gaze; wholly defying the Goddess' regard. She stared back at him, not quite amused at his impertinence but intrigued nonetheless. He was either entirely innocent of what she suspected, or . . .

The silence stretched out. She could see that Lord Trellec was unwilling, or perhaps constitutionally unable, to withdraw his case in front of so many witnesses. She could feel him prepare to do whatever it took to save face in front of his neighbours, even if that meant sacrificing at least one child. She had met his type before. The death of children, even his own, would not squat for long on his aristocratic conscience.

Daine cursed softly. Even after all these years, she still had not learned how to compensate for her low Charisma. She had gotten by too easily by upping the ante. Had become too comfortable in her capacity to dominate to ever accept the possibility of compromise. She had not left him room enough to back down. "*Sometimes a sucker deserves an even break*," Gant rasped in her mind. Sometimes they did, but not today, it seemed.

She began to channel <Divine Justice> to deliver her doom when the mother of the crying child took a step forward. "I would, my Lady, petition for a mutual closure of this case. The young must be able to make mistakes, and I am sure my Belle meant no harm. And whatever Drunnoc may have done" — her eyes shifted to the dead-eyed youth who stared impassively back at her — "well, boys will be boys, and no more needs to be said."

The tension in the room audibly broke. *A clever woman*, Daine thought. Everyone, even Lord Trellec, should be able to accept that with no loss of status. An admission of fault on both sides with nothing more needing to be said. Or done.

"Boys will be boys? I've found that to be true. At least until I brought it to a halt. Permanently, and on more than one occasion, if memory serves. Lord Trellec? It is your complaint. Should I accept the petition for mutual closure, or do we see whether a 'boys being boys' defence survives the judgement of the Goddess?"

For a heartbeat, it seemed Lord Trellec would not accept the lifeline. Then good sense won the battle with pride, and he bowed low. "Of course, my Lady. I would be happy to see such a conclusion to this disagreement. I misspoke and gladly withdraw my complaint in the spirit of mutual closure." He pulled his seemingly reluctant son toward the door and exited with a swirl of retainers and hangers-on. The boy — Drunnoc, was it? — kept his eyes fixed on her the whole time. ""Boys will be boys" indeed."

She ended <Intimidation>, slipped her sword back into its scabbard, and Daine Orban, Knight of the Road, the Lady Darkhelm of a hundred tavern tales, on her third Tour of the West Coast and well into her fifth decade, smiled for the first time that week. "Excellent. Now, let there be ale."

CHAPTER TWO

"Should Have Cut His Thumbs Off"

"**Y**ou should have cut his thumbs off."

Daine raised her eyes to settle on the man who had sat, unbidden, opposite her. Considering the volume of ale she had quaffed, such focus took an effort worthy of a Knight of her renown.

She vaguely remembered him from a previous Tour. Ceyn? Cryn? It was some such name like that. One where the letters performed a noise they had no business making.

She disliked words. Could not trust them. Could not rely on them to do the same thing, day in, day out. Once something was spoken, regardless of the original intent, its meaning could end up being entirely different.

It was the reason — at least, she acknowledged, one of the reasons — she travelled alone. Bards might sing countless odes to the origin of her name: Darkhelm. But none of them mentioned any companions. Depending on the source, it was held that she perpetually wore the visor of her black-iron helmet down because she was horrendously scarred; that the helmet had been deformed in a titanic struggle with a dragon and hence could never be taken off; that her silence when wearing it was the result of a mighty Wizard's final curse depriving her of a voice. The reality was, of course, far more prosaic. She wore the helmet with the visor permanently down to dissuade conversation. Words could not be twisted if they were never spoken.

She wished she had it on now.

Although probably not. Helmeted, storied warriors in village taverns raised conversations all on their own.

Warming to her theme, ignoring the uninvited companion who continued to speak, she reflected that words had caused more strife across her Tours than any giant, orc, or enemy action. She had lost count of the judgements she had made where words had been used to mislead the unprepared: property stolen, funds misdirected, assassinations ordered. More often than not, the whole span of human cruelty came down to the malicious misuse of words.

With a snort that startled her unwanted guest, she recalled her habit of posting judgements on the door of the Church of Dawn in whatever hamlet she found herself in. She had liked the formality of that action. Had thought it prevented people from "forgetting" her meaning once she moved on. At the very least, she trusted that the words of the Goddess would be enacted when given written form. It had been somewhat of a shock when she learned how rarely the orders she'd written occurred as intended.

How Old Gant had howled when she'd come to him for advice. *"If you make the judgement, you're the one to carry it out, Darkhelm! You don't write the truth and expect the Goddess to spring, fully formed, from your quill. She may be divine, but the rest of us surely ain't."* Laughter dogged her for weeks following that. Anything told to Old Gallant Stonehand in the strictest of confidence would be broadcast news. But it had been worth it. From that moment, she had learned her lesson: words were slippery.

The untrustworthy man — was that fair of her? She shouldn't let her sour mood run away with her. He couldn't help the role he was given. Call him the changeable man; that was better.

The person sitting across from her whoever, whatever he was, spoke again. She wished he wouldn't. Or, at least, would find someone else to do it to.

"Goddess knows there would be testimonies of support enough. He's always been a bad one, has Drunnoc Trellec. Doubt he was even born when you last came through. That's been plenty of time for him to have earned a thumb-pruning a hundred times. And there are rumours that we don't know half what he has been up to. His father's coin, you get me? Much silence can be bought with a deep enough purse. If you'd taken action today, even at the cost of the Acas girl, you'd have been cheered to the rafters for it. Her mother would tell you the same if you asked her. The greater good and all that."

This man with the changeable name — still not being fair, Daine — was not the first to seat himself opposite her with such a tale of Drunnoc Trellec. At least the others had read her mood accurately enough to bring a couple of full tankards with them when they imposed themselves. It would have been rude to reject such generosity. She did wish they'd leave off with all the talking, though. It was getting that she'd have to do something about it. And she wasn't sure she had it in her tonight.

Daine stared significantly at her empty cup, and the man took the hint, scooping it up and retreating to the bar. She watched him go and nodded to herself. She did recall whatever-his-name-was from early in her second Tour. He'd been younger then, of course, but there was still much around the eyes of that earnest man who'd asked for judgement concerning his father's estate. He was a Tailor, she remembered, and a good one. Had some sort of unusual Skill that increased the durability of his wares. His shop had been flourishing, and he did not seek redress for any financial benefit. He was troubled, that was all, by a sense of something that was not as it should be in the way his father had passed from the world. She'd liked that about him: there was nothing mercenary in his heart when he raised the complaint. On the contrary, he had been genuine in his concern. And she had seen little enough of that recently to be touched.

She'd found in his favour. Memories of a young widow who had been rather too eager to speed up the day of her inheritance stirred, unwelcome, in her mind. The Goddess had been clear about her guilt, and the execution had been swift.

That widow had cried at the end. There'd been a lover — wasn't there always? — and a promise of a better life overseas. But funds to set up the venture were needed. All in advance, of course. And the lover would have to set sail without her, perhaps with another, more generous partner if she could not raise the required sums. She had become desperate and acted out of "love." With the deed done and an estate mortgaged to the hilt, it went without saying that better life did not manifest. "But he sent me such beautiful letters," she'd sobbed. "I had to do it, or I would have lost him."

Words. They were slippery.

She'd hunted the lothario down. Blood was also slippery.

Now that she thought on it, unless she was mistaken, the Tailor had gifted her a cloak in thanks. She didn't usually accept such things, it gave the wrong impression, but she'd liked him, and the giving of it mattered to him. Was it the one she still wore? She thought it might be. Fine work indeed, to have survived ten years on the Road. Did the man opposite her think she consciously chose to wear it on her return? That would explain his belief that he had the right to her ear. She had been on his side before, after all, hadn't she? She would retake his side again, surely. He clearly believed that she could be used to further whatever passed for an agenda in this place.

None of them ever understood. There was no side. There was only judgement.

He sat down again and presented a filled tankard. Her irritation at his presumption — probably undeserved, she recognised — sparked. "You're telling me you need a Knight of the Road to keep your children in line? That's the tale you want me spreading on my travels? 'All is well in the West, provided enough of us carry out hourly visits to stop door-knocking, apple-scrumping, and the like.' Thought Westerners were made of stronger stuff. At least you used to be."

The man wiped his mouth with the back of his hand and glanced furtively about him before leaning in. If he were about to say something unpolitic about his betters, he must have been both mad and a fool. Five men, all in

Trellec's red and gold, were conspicuously lurking within earshot. At least two were armed; the rest were probably simply better at hiding it. None of them caused her any concern. Low-ranking Men-at-Arms. Maybe the odd Serjeant-at-Arms mixed in, if Trellec was seriously thinking about making an issue of what occurred earlier. She hoped not. Such a confrontation would be beneath her.

That said, the least of them would be more than enough to deal with a Tailor, no matter how skilled he might be with a needle and thread. In her darkening mood, if he were to bring them down upon him by being indiscreet, there was little she was minded to do about it.

He leaned forward and whispered, "Drunnoc Trellec—"

"Take care with your words, whatever your name is. If these walls don't have ears, those men surely do. It's been ten years since my last Tour, and I am heartened to see you well. I would that it stayed so. I have no wish to ride through in the future and hear of the mysterious death of a Tailor that needs investigating. You may feel safe opposite me now, but in a few days, I won't be here. Ten years is a long time until I'm back. You've surely got enough years on your back and brains in your head to know better than to thumb your nose at power and seek to hide behind my skirts."

Hurt bloomed behind his eyes. He paused for a second to gather his thoughts. "My name's Cenwyn. I thought, after what happened before —"

She had been cruel, unnecessarily so, with her words. She'd have liked to blame the ale, but she thought dimly that it was more than likely just her. At least, how she had been of late. Casting backwards for a kinder version of herself to share, she tried to soften her voice. "Ten years is a lot of wronged men in small taverns buying me drinks, sir. But, yes, Cenwyn, I do remember you. Faces and judgements, I don't forget. Names, though? They have started to wriggle free." She smiled to break the tension. "See if you can do better when you get to my age."

The hurt faded to be replaced by — something she could not entirely read. "My Lady, I was right when I came to you back then, and I'm telling you, I'm right now. Drunnoc Trellec is not going to let what happened today stand. He's going to seek a fearful reckoning."

"The boy? You overstate, sir."

He silenced her with a raised finger. When was the last time someone had the wherewithal to stay her in such a manner? "Please, my Lady, hear me out. Things are not what they seem in this village. There are currents to the tides that flow here, of which you need to be aware. I see those men in their bright livery and their swaggering noise, and I tell you that their purpose is to hold your attention. Those who know where to listen have heard tell of four outsides in the alley and three sent to the woods to dog your path. And not the usual dregs we see around here. There's been a call for serious talent to linger in the fog. And the coin offered to make it worthwhile."

Cenwyn leaned even farther forward, his words barely audible even at the intimate distance. "You were right in what you said. Ten years is a long time. It's a long time for us to live without judgement. You may think your time on the Road brings order to chaos. But I tell you, Lady Darkhelm, you and your kin are a brief candle in a long night. You pass through, and we are grateful, but the blackness will take you. In your wake, we live in the shadows with those who seek to do harm. In the face of that, your light is too little and oftentimes too late. We deserve more, but we will take what we can get. I would not have your light snuffed out. There's a dire need for you and yours in the world."

Her already sour mood was in danger of tipping into something she, or more likely someone else, would profoundly regret. "What are you telling me, sir?

"I'm saying you should have taken Drunnoc's thumbs when you had the chance."

CHAPTER THREE

"Dead Before Sunrise"

Today was not the first occasion Fion Trellec had cause
to bemoan his decision to become a father again.

With his other children, it had been easy.

In his heart, he knew that his long-lamented Briar had
been entirely responsible for the smooth management of
the Trellec household. It was just that he had become used
to the parade of clean and dutiful children presented peri-
odically for his approval and had thought he played some
role in that achievement. His children had grown up largely
out of sight and gone on to make something of themselves in the world. Fion had told himself that their success
demonstrated the good sense of his hands-off parenting.

But with age had come some little wisdom. That he had
not seen any of them since remarrying was a growing matter of guilt. He was not too proud to admit the estrange-
ment was largely his fault.

His second wife — second in every way possible, he now recognised — managed to embody everything Briar was not. Where she had been understated, Trivian was all excess. Where he had become used to calmness, his days were now spent trying to quell towering rages.

He now well understood, with rueful appreciation, the breadth and depth of bounty offered as her dowry. Her father must have been dancing a jig to get her out of his hall.

Nothing was ever quite right for the second Lady Trellec, and those in the village had quickly learned that House Trellec was no longer one on which to call. Old acquaintances made excuses to avoid social visits. Cherished, long-standing staff found other, less confrontational positions. Piece by piece, his old, comfortable life was dismantled and replaced by something peculiarly dissatisfying.

Nevertheless, even with all that disappointment, things would have been acceptable. That is, if it had not been for Drunnoc.

Even in the womb, he had deeply affected Trivian with his malevolence. He did not just kick; he attacked with vigour and focus. Once born, everyone whispered about how unnerving it was to hold a baby that stared as if seeking to identify weak spots. When he was not biting, he was pinching. When not crying, he was screaming. Fion was sure that much of Trivian's unhappiness had, at its root, the incessant torture of Drunnoc's presence through early childhood.

"Boys will be boys," that upstart Knight had said. Fion disagreed. He knew boys, had been one himself, and he knew that his youngest son was something different. Fion had been no paragon of virtue in his youth. More than once he'd felt the sting of the old Steward's stick. But Drunnoc?

He was something *other*. There was a predatory presence lurking behind those flat eyes. He did not mind admitting that, at times, he feared it.

As he had grown, the boy had begun lying as quickly as breathing. Fion had lost track of the times he was, against his inclination, absolutely convinced by sincerely expressed regret for one heinous act or another. Lord Trellec was not a man given to naïve self-deception, so he could not understand his recurrent shock when the same thing would happen the following day. That lack of genuine remorse, while knowing the advantage in displaying its simulacrum, was most troubling.

Likewise, he was all for his boys enjoying hunting and fishing — did not their trophies still line the walls of his hall? — but there was something sinister about how Drunnoc went about it. Indeed, rarely was enough left of the animals he caught for mementoes.

And that wild pack he called his "friends" . . . Geril. Blount. Yorul. All several years older and all lesser sons of the other High Houses. None of them had any of the restrictions on their behaviour that came with a responsibility to the family name. They had all the wealth, all the arrogance, and none of the humility that must attend such power. He had heard stories of each of them that quite chilled even him. If it was possible, he felt that those jackals were encouraging Drunnoc to wider and wilder excesses.

In his more reflective moments, Trellec genuinely feared for a world in which Drunnoc grew to prominence. It had taken all of his considerable will not to hand him over to that damned Knight and be done with it all. But Drunnoc was his son, and, as the bitter voice in his head reminded him, the only one around that he could still call his.

With a crash, his boy entered the Banqueting Hall, startling the retainers in attendance. "I want her head!"

Life had been much more manageable when his children were seen and not heard.

Fion raised his cup for one of the hovering servants to refill. He recognised it was an indulgence, but eating alone in the giant space was one of the few pleasures he had left in life. He waited until she had returned to her place against the wall before addressing his son. "Drunnoc, she is a Knight of the Road. Even if we had the capacity in the Keep to attempt something untoward, the political fallout would be seismic. I do not wish to bring down our House because you cannot control your darker impulses for a few days. The Darkhelm is an irritant once every ten years. I may have thought to use your indiscretion this morning to demonstrate the cruelty of this method of justice, but that was a miscalculation. It seemed to me, in the moment, that the casual slaughter of a young girl over such a slight thing would bring the Houses together against these barbaric Tours. But you were not the right foundation upon which to build that castle. That was my error. Thus, we will keep our heads low until she leaves and things can return to normal."

The second figure that had followed his son into the Hall now spoke. "She humiliated him. In front of the whole village! She should never be an irritant for Drunnoc again. People need to know what happens if they disrespect him."

Trellec turned to look with distaste at Veron Geril, one of the least appealing of Drunnoc's "friends." As solid as Drunnoc was wiry, as stocky as his son was tall. Trellec could never shake the feeling that he needed a wash after spending time in the young man's company. If the rumours were true — and for the money he spent on unearthing them, they had better be —Lord Geril spent almost as much of his wealth as Fion to keep news of his own son's misdeeds from public view.

Trellec suppressed his habitual sneer when speaking to Veron. "I rather think it was his having his nose broken by a child half his age that caused the humiliation." He turned his eyes back to his son. "Drunnoc, we've spoken of your responsibilities as the heir to High House Trellec, and they do not involve fighting with every waif and stray in the village. Put the Lady Darkhelm out of your mind. If we had anything like the power to do something about her on our own, she would not be Touring the village in the first place."

"You are afraid of her!" Drunnoc's wheedling voice grated across Trellec's nerves. He raised his eyes to one of his favourite tapestries that ornamented the walls of the hall. He'd always found something oddly compelling about that depiction of the fall of House Irketh.

"Am I afraid of going it alone against someone who speaks, quite literally, with the voice of the Goddess? Yes. Yes, I absolutely am. If you are not, you have even less sense than I credit you. Had I allowed you to have been called to judgement today, there would have been nothing I could have done to protect you. Should a quarter of what we know you do in secret have become known, the Knight would have killed you where you stood. I flatter myself that my good name has managed to keep the worst of your behaviours from wider knowledge. Believe me when I say that would have been nothing in the face of the Justice of the Goddess. These Tours will continue until the Houses choose to act together against the vicious imposition of the

Crown's will. Until that moment, this is our reality. Meekly, we must accept it and seek to avoid unnecessary strife."

Veron's face darkened with rage. "We are Noble born! The Houses cannot allow her to do as she pleases to us. To submit in such a craven manner is pathetic. "

"Lordling Geril, if you choose to address me again in such a manner, I will remove your tongue."

Veron was immediately silent. It was widely understood, if not openly discussed, that the seemingly pleasant older man in his ridiculous robes of red and gold had, in his youth, demonstrated a significant capacity for violence. "Apples and trees, my son. Apples and trees," his own father had often said cryptically when the topic of Drunnoc's behaviour was raised.

A chilling silence descended around the hall. A servant nervously crept forward to refill Fion's goblet, pointedly ignoring those of the two boys, and withdrew to her place behind his chair.

"For the removal of any doubt, let me be completely clear." A few of the servants staggered as <Our Master's Voice> pressed down on those in the room. Drunnoc was the only one who appeared to be unaffected. Fion's mood was not improved by that development. "I do not want to hear another word about Daine Orban from your lips. She is beyond us, and I forbid you from using any House resources in poorly conceived revenge plans: the treasury is closed to you. Indeed, on reflection, I do not want any other word from you at all for the evening. Remove yourself. Both of you. And try not to cause any embarrassment until that damned Road Knight is beyond our borders."

With as much dignity as they could muster, Drunnoc

and Veron fled from the Hall leaving Fion to complete his meal in blissful silence.

The glares of those few servants still loyal to House Trellec went unremarked upon but not unnoticed by Drunnoc. Veron knew that his friend was adding them to the extensive list of slights for which there would, eventually, be recompense.

*

When they were far enough into the depths of the Keep to avoid being heard, they slowed their pace and retired to the shadows.

"Well?" The querulous, somewhat peevish tone of voice Drunnoc used when speaking to his father had gone. In its place was something almost deathly in its flatness.

Veron only grinned. Besides Drunnoc's friends, no one understood him. They looked at the size, the thuggery, and the tantrums, and they thought they knew everything there was to know about him. "Bully without a brain," they'd decided. Certainly, that was the view Drunnoc's father held. But there was something else there that hardly anyone got to see, at least not more than once. His soul possessed a reptilian coldness hiding underneath that brutish mask.

While Fion Trellec congratulated himself on keeping Drunnoc's misdeeds secret, the father only found out about that which the son allowed to be noticed. In the last few years, his little group of friends had established quite the infrastructure to abet all manner of secret crimes and cruelties. It was amazing what could be achieved with indulgent parents, unlimited funds, and the lowest possible expectations regarding conduct. At this stage their names were whispered with fear throughout the village and beyond.

And yet, even now, only a select few were privy to the true face of Drunnoc Trellec.

It was safe to say, had that girl from the morning not possessed an unusually vibrant survival instinct, as well as sharp elbows, there would have been little of her left to sob in front of the Lady Darkhelm. There would have been no tearful public reunion with a mother who dared deny an underage Drunnoc service at the tavern a year or so back.

If revenge was a dish served cold, Lordling Trellec liked his both icy and exceptionally bloody.

"Well?" Drunnoc asked again, drawing Veron's attention back to the present.

It had been quite the afternoon for Veron Geril. He had been tasked with locating any talent, local or otherwise, that was confident or desperate enough to cross paths with a Knight of the Road. Although he had long lost his surprise at the things people would do for money — it was so easily obtained, why were people so curiously needy for it? — he was astonished at his success. From those who had come forward, he felt he had chosen wisely, distributing his — well, Drunnoc's — resources liberally to outfit a series of lethal encounters.

He was aware of the famed resilience of those who walked the Road. However, he had been unimpressed by the old woman, with her threadbare armour and soft voice. The Tours were an antiquated system of justice just waiting for a new generation to banish them to the past. In the face of what he had prepared for her, he did not feel this particular Knight of the Road was likely to offer trouble.

"Everything is as we discussed. Darkhelm will be dead before sunrise."

CHAPTER FOUR

"Bemused, Albeit Short-Lived, Surprise"

A meaty hand thudded down on the table.

"There's people who ain't too happy with you."

Daine looked up into a forest of ginger hair. In the middle of her talk with Cenwyn, one of Trellec's retainers had finally found his courage to upgrade "conspicuous lurking" into "active intimidation." Although, as he was not the biggest of them, nor by the smell of his breath the most sober, his aggressive approach merely suggested an attempt to test the water.

"I imagine so. Usually means I've done the right thing. But we've got that in common, at least." If he had an expected response in mind, that was not it. Through the tangle of hair, she watched a frown form. "Whoever encouraged a man of your colouring to serve in red and gold seemed determined to expose you to ridicule."

The big man tried to wrest the conversation back toward

the script he had prepared with a visible effort. "You'd get back on the Road right now if you knew what's good for you." He then took a course of action which, had he been less in his cups, he might have recognised as a touch unwise. Still leaning on the table, he reached out and poked Daine in the shoulder.

With a single fluid movement, she drew a knife and slammed it into the middle of his hand, pinning it to the wood. With her other hand, she grabbed a handful of his beard and brought his head down with a crunch into the corner of the table. The big man's eyes rolled up into his head as he sank to the floor, and Daine yanked the knife free.

In the silence that followed, one of the man's fellows took a hesitant step forward before catching her eye, pausing, and retreating with palms raised in the universal signal for "I have reconsidered the advisability of my actions and would like you not to hurt me."

Daine looked over at Cenwyn and reflected on his words. "I agree with you, Master Tailor, ten years is too long." She wiped the blade on the back of the prostrate man, replaced it in her sheath and stood tall. "No matter how many stories they hear about us, there's folk who just can't keep it in their heads between Tours. I'm a Knight of the Road, and you all" — she raised her voice, powerful with <Intimidation>, to carry across the room — "you *all* need to remember what that means. Me, and those like me, make certain there's a reckoning. We might not be there to stop it, but we will always give answer for it. You do not get to tell us what we should care about. Not now. Not ever." She stood and brushed down her rumpled clothes. Any effect of the ale was long gone —purged by the activation of her <Barroom Brawler> Skill—and that irritated her more than the behaviour of Trellec's man. "I was here ten years ago and will be here in another ten. Some of you may think there's all sorts of deeds that can be achieved in that time. That it is worth the risk. But while you're about it, remember this promise: I will see you soon."

She bent low to whisper in Cenwyn's ear. "I'll think on what you said, Master Tailor, but hear me when I say judgement is never 'too little.' Not for those who deserve it. It's not much, but it is what the Goddess promises us all." Then, turning back to Trellec's men, she opened her arms wide. "Any of you still think this is a good idea?"

They stared at her dumbly, then down at the man sobbing at her feet, as did the rest of the tavern.

"I'm glad. Now, I'm going to step outside for a moment and give anyone waiting out there the same chance I give you now. Live another day. Collect your friend and run back to Lord Trellec. Tell him he best mind his manners the next time I come through. I'll be checking. And that man" — she indicated Cenwyn, whose eyes widened in dismay as everyone turned to regard him — "better be the healthiest, happiest Tailor in town when I'm here again. He so much as pricks a finger, someone needs to be there to kiss it better." She winked at him, and the crowd parted around her.

The Men-at-Arms hesitated for a few moments. Within them warred two different fears — that of being the recipient of Daine's displeasure against the certainty of what awaited them back at the Keep should they fail their mission. Eventually, in grim, silent agreement, they all filed out after her.

As Daine's eyes quickly adjusted to the darkness, she

sensed the opening of the tavern door behind her: Trellec's men hovering at the threshold. Either those men were blindingly stupid, or they were more afraid of Trellec than they were of her, which was a new experience. She favoured brief moments of instructive violence, as they often forestalled this sort of situation. That this one had not suggested that maybe there was more to what Cenwyn had said about Drunnoc Trellec than she thought. That would need considering.

A sudden hiss from her left jerked her back to the moment. She turned and caught the downward swing of a long knife in the palm of her hand, wincing as it cut to the bone. With a sharp tug, Daine disarmed the attacker and had a moment to appreciate their startled expression before she struck them, hard, across the face with the pommel. The figure — a small woman in black — sailed back into the darkness, neck broken even before she hit the alley wall and slid into a crumpled heap.

Daine dropped the long knife just before the wound healed around the blade. That had happened several times before, and, as well as looking ridiculous, it hurt twice as much to pull it free. Blades were infinitely preferable to arrows, though: she absolutely could not be doing with Archers.

As the cut closed and she felt the bones knit back together, two strong arms closed around her and began to squeeze. It was a worthy attempt to pin her arms to her sides and expose her to a third man who was approaching quickly from behind with a dagger. It was clearly a tactic that had worked for this pair before — enhanced by a talent for <Grapple> — and, against a different opponent, would have doubtless found success again. However, what Daine lacked in sociability, she more than made up for in brute Strength.

With ease, she broke the bear hug before reaching over her shoulder to drag the startled man over her back. His feet hit the ground and he stood, somewhat surprised at this turn of events, in front of her. In that position, he provided an effective, if reluctant and entirely temporary, shield for the subsequent knife attack. When she felt the impaled man sag, she shoved him firmly in the back. He flew away, taking his unfortunate ex-partner with him. The two of them hit the same spot on the wall as the first assassin and joined her in an unmoving pile on the ground.

With raised eyebrows, Daine turned to regard those still hovering around the tavern door. They all avoided meeting her eyes. Then a shout from the alley caught her attention. She turned just as a ball of fire flew from the darkness to strike her in the chest. In quick succession, three more fireballs followed, each hitting Daine, who grunted in pain at each impact. However, as soon as they struck the Knight, the flames vanished in wisps of smoke. From the expletives she heard, rapid dissipation was not an anticipated effect from the spellcaster.

There was a brief pause, and then a white-hot tide of flame rolled toward Daine, engulfing her, and causing the cobbles beneath her feet to glow.

A young red-haired girl stalked from the shadows, fire roiling from her hands. She shrieked words of power with each step, pulling in every source of heat from the surrounding area: every hearth in the village went cold, every torch, every candle went dark, and frost even started to form on the outside of buildings.

Those watching from the tavern murmured their

surprise. What the Fire Mage was attempting was a significant summoning, quite beyond anything witnessed in the village for many a year. Thus, in the face of such a show of pyromantic strength, the Knight's indifference to the conflagration was somewhat comical. As if on an evening's stroll, she slowly advanced toward the woman, stooping to pick up the discarded long knife, flames trailing above and behind her as if she were a meteor.

There were myths of demons used to elicit screams of joyful terror from children on certain nights of the year. The joy came from the knowledge that such things did not exist, and the terror grew from fear that, perhaps one day, they just might. No one who watched Daine's slow, fiery walk across the courtyard that night would ever again question the existence of such monsters.

The Lady Darkhelm paused in front of her assailant. The Fire Mage's blue eyes widened with panic, and she poured more and more of her soul into the spell, as if she could change her rapidly shortening future by will alone.

With the spending of her life force, the Mage's skin lost its lustre as if she were ageing thirty years in barely a moment. Her back bent inwards, causing her to stagger, and she stooped forward. Still, she tried, tried unto the last, to make that which would not burn catch fire.

Daine waited patiently, politely, until the old woman — for that was what now stood in front of her — ceased her casting and hunched over, gasping for breath, staring at her hands in awful wonder.

There were several moments of silence as the horror of the Mage's physical transformation settled on the observers. Then Daine spoke in a quiet, almost gentle, voice.

Somehow, those softly delivered words carried to

everyone watching. Faces could be seen crowded at every window on the street. The tavern had emptied itself around Trellec's men, Cenwyn at the forefront. It was as if every member of the village had come to witness this Mage's final moment.

"There's a tale in the South of the Cult of Tara. You may have heard of them. A wind cult, as it happens, but the same principle serves here, I think. They thought they could live wholly outside of judgement. That their abilities meant no one would ever be able to call them to account. They did appalling things with the power the gods had granted them. You would not think the ability to control air would easily lend itself to torture, to destruction, to slaughter. You would be wrong. They killed thousands for the cause of ambition with barely a thought. I tell you now what I told them. Those of us granted gifts have a choice. You have chosen poorly."

Daine swung the long knife experimentally, assessing its heft and weight. "I should say, that look you have on your face right now, they had it too. Right at the end. I tell you this because, since my Tour through there, when the people of Darnak wish to express bemused surprise, they'll say: 'Well, I'll be a Priest of Tara.' Bemused, albeit short-lived, surprise."

Daine beheaded the woman with a swish of the borrowed blade.

She turned to face the crowd, seeking out Cenwyn. "Tell me, Master Tailor, do you think they will remember me the next time I come through?"

CHAPTER FIVE

"The Realm Needs Heroes"

While varieties of humankind might be infinite, Classes were not.

At least, that was how Old Gant said he had explained it to her parents. For most people, the paucity of life's choices was barely a consideration: families specialised in a Class and each subsequent generation simply followed in the well-trodden footsteps of their parents and their parents' parents before them. Of course, there were exceptions: every hamlet had dark tales of "bad seeds" who rejected beloved family traditions to run away to one of the towns or, Goddess forbid, the Capital, but those exceptions merely proved the rule. For the most part, year after year, Bakers bred Bakers, Stonemasons had little Stonemasons, and so on and so forth until the end of time.

"But that does not need to be the fate of your little girl,"

Gant had reportedly told them. "For her, there are much greater opportunities out there."

Daine did not know what had first drawn his attention to her. Perhaps some aggrieved neighbour had complained about the Orbans' "wild child" traumatising their children. More likely, Daine thought in her gloomier moments — and she certainly had enough of those — her exhausted parents had reported her themselves. Too strong, too fast, too hungry, too destructive. Whatever the truth, Gallant Stonehand — who was, at that time, already well on the way to earning his "Old" honorific — had been summoned and had arrived, with great fanfare, to present the Orbans with the opportunity to sell him their fourth daughter.

Daine liked to think they would have agonised over that choice. Gant had never said either way, but it made it easier to stomach if she could imagine long, tearful nights of debate, followed by months (years, surely?) of painful recriminations once she was gone.

Not that it mattered.

Truth be told, almost fifty years later, she could not even remember what they looked like. Had they loved her? Presumably. There were far easier ways to deal with a troublesome child than hoping someone would come by and offer them hard coin for her. That she was alive to meet Old Gant spoke of . . . something, did it not it? She could have asked them herself, swung by to visit on one of her Tours. But what would have been the point? "Thank you, dearest parents, for selling me to the Kingdom's cruellest, more brilliant Mentors. Yes, I learned many ways to kill people. No, I would not recommend it. Yes, I am *that* Darkhelm. No, I do not especially enjoy it. How is

Grandma?" Somehow, she could not see the reunion progressing in such a storybook manner.

A few years back, she had been approached by someone, presumably from her part of the world. They'd recognised her surname and wanted to know if she "be an Orban of the Farming Orbans?" She had ridden on without pause, leaving him with a mouth filled with dust and a curse on his lips. But the question ate away at her in the long nights. Could she say she was truly an Orban any longer? Would she be good for anything on a farm more than pulling a plough?

The Orbans, for generations unending, had been Farmers. Good ones, too. That meant lots of Strength, lots of Constitution, and a fair bit of Dexterity. Even for those with that Class, as evidenced by the interest of her unwanted questioner, Orbans were highly regarded for their physicality. Their sons were welcome to come courting at any hearth, and their daughters were seen as excellent breeding stock to supplement a family line. In many ways, it was surprising that Daine had been the first in their bloodline to show the potential for Class Evolution. Most families had stories of children gathered by someone like Gallant Stonehand, having displayed preternatural talent. Nevertheless, she had been a local first, and Gant had needed to deliver what he witheringly called "*the provincial talk*" to her mother and father.

"One of my roles, appointed by the King himself, I am pleased to tell you, is to look out for children like your dearest Diane — sorry, Daine, is it? What a creative use of vowels! Never let tradition, good sense, or literacy stand in your way; that's what I always say! — who have the opportunity to have their Class evolve. You will have heard that children with this potential demonstrate prodigious talent in their common Class from an exceedingly early age. This is, after all, how we find them. And you will know, of course, the rewards available for those who locate these children."

He conspicuously stroked a full bag of coins to emphasise his words.

"Once identified, we have found that should these children collaborate with an appropriate Mentor — I dare flatter myself here by noting the King himself sponsors my school — there are almost no limits to the paths these children can walk. Now, the potential for this is not as rare as you may think. However, if we do not find these children before their fifth birthday, then their common Class will simply 'lock in,' as it were. At that stage, they will go on to lead normal, albeit rather more successful, lives. I am sure you will have a nephew or distant cousin who seems to be better at . . . sorry, I'm not especially familiar with Farming practices. But they will be better at it than anyone else. Perhaps they will develop a Skill to allow them to milk the bulls twice as fast as expected, for example."

"And Daine could do this?"

"Certainly. At three years old, from what I'm told, she's already as strong as your husband, as quick as a rabbit, sleeps less than two hours a day, and, I am sure, already eats three times as much as the rest of your family combined. Yes, I see in your faces you are well familiar with going without to ensure this voracious little terrier gets the opportunity to eat her fill."

"Is there anything that can be done to stop it? To make her normal again?"

"My dear young thing, please do not cry. I am sure you cannot spare the moisture. This whole situation is entirely commonplace, I promise you. It's nothing to worry about at all. Believe me, if you turn down my generous offer, you will, in no time, have a very accomplished . . . do you people do something with seeds? Yes? Well, she'll do it very well indeed, and you will all be enormously proud. But, of course, you will also be quite a bit poorer due to the substantial drain of your meagre resource she will be. But let us look on the bright side; if your family manages to survive tending this cuckoo in your nest — and I have heard that some families can buck the trend and struggle through — then in ten, maybe fifteen years, she will be able to start repaying you. And what a Goddessend that will be, eh?"

Daine imagined the look on their faces as they tried to conceive of even another ten weeks with her in their house, consuming all around her like some malign, anthropomorphised locust, let alone ten years. She was sure that vision of a bleak future sealed the issue as much as Gant's next words.

"However, should you decide you can bear to part with Diane — sorry, Daine. Are you absolutely settled on that? They adapt so quickly to new names at this age. Oh, so be it— she will have, and I mean this quite literally, the chance to transform the world. Not everyone can make this sacrifice, so our greatest heroes are rare. Should she survive the training, she will become someone of whom you will hear songs. You will see statues erected to her and be able to think, 'That's our little girl. How brave we were to give up her life of chicken-fondling to allow her to follow those dreams.' And, as I may have mentioned, the realm has the hard coin to pay for that chance."

"What will happen to her? I mean, what will you do with her?"

"A sensible question to ask and one that does you credit, ma'am. You wouldn't be doing your due diligence if you did not ask about me and my process, would you? I can tell you that some parents, well, they're just grateful for the coin. I ride into town, offer them a solution to the single biggest problem in their lives, and they simply bite my hand off with gratitude; indeed, most try to pay me to take their little tyke away. But no. Here you are, half-starved, looking that gift horse in the mouth and asking to count its teeth. I take my hat off to you, ma'am. Quite the integrity you possess."

Her mother had tried apologising then, worried the offer would be snatched away. But Gant would not hear of it. So instead, he told her of his training school. Of the methods that would help a Farmer's child use her Orban foundations to increase her Attributes and to seek to develop a broader range of Skills. To try to build on what nature had provided with hard work, focus, and "to speak plain, ma'am, because we are all people of the world here, as much of the stick as the carrot."

Daine hoped her parents had understood quite how much stick would be required. She doubted it.

"And she will become a hero?"

At that, Gant had leaned forward, light glinting off the silver ball that sat in place of his left eye, and spun his favourite tales: of Dreadnaughts and Blood Rangers, of Metamorphs and Lightweavers. And, of course, of the Knights of the Road.

Gallant never told the story the same way twice, and, as age and drink stripped away more and more of his personality, Daine had come to recognise how little of what he told all of them about their families and the circumstances in which they parted with their children was likely to have been true. She doubted he even remembered the visit to the Orban farm — he just told whatever version of the past suited at the time.

Some of her classmates had needed to hold on to the romantic view of the peasantry nobly sacrificing their children for the greater good. Darkhelm knew differently. She had heard the rumours of blood and fire in the night, of screaming mothers and slaughtered fathers. While she did not think Old Gant's school had needed to resort to such an approach, he would have been peculiarly unique if he had never ordered it.

The realm needed its heroes, after all.

She did not feel especially heroic right now, covered in the blood of a Fire Mage who had neglected her reading on the magical resistances of Knights of the Road.

Cenwyn approached Daine with, she thought, the excessive caution of a man faced with a caged tiger. "To answer your question, there is every chance tonight will live long in the memory. Without seeking to be presumptuous, perhaps you would appreciate somewhere to clean up?"

She looked down at her clothes. She favoured dark colours for this reason, and while vanity had never been her problem, there was always an attraction in washing away the worst of the residue. She fixed Trellec's men with an unwavering stare. "Is there any reason I should hesitate to change? Are more demonstrations required?"

"No, my Lady. We'll be leaving you be now and making our way back to the Keep." The spokesman paused and jutted his chin at the bodies. "May I arrange their collection?"

"Tell Trellec I expect their families to be compensated. He wasted their lives tonight. Take care he does not spend yours so lightly."

"As you say, my Lady." The men retrieved their uncon-scious fellows, and they all quickly departed. Daine turned back to the Tailor.

"Master Tailor. Cenwyn. A quiet place to clean up and, if I may presume, some new clothes would be very wel-come. If you have anything to match the quality of the cloak, you will find that Orbans are not short of hard coin."

CHAPTER SIX

"No One Special"

There were many disturbing things to which she had adjusted over the years, but the sensation of blood drying in her hair was not one with which she had made her peace. But, of course, the experience was different when she knew it was her own: she had grown familiar enough with that, after all. It was particularly unpleasant, though, when it was another's — usually someone with whom she had shared a brief, violent moment. There was an unrequested intimacy there that breached all of her boundaries.

For that reason, she had kept her hair cropped as short as possible for as long as she could remember. However, with her relatively low Dexterity to balance out her exceptional Strength, she had quickly realised she needed someone else to shave it for her. Just because she healed quickly was no reason to inflict gaping head wounds on herself if she could avoid it. Finding someone who had the Strength to cut through her locks and whom she trusted enough to get that close with a blade was not as straightforward as might have been hoped. As her current Tour was running overtime, she was aware she was wearing it much longer than she usually liked to, which was why she squeezed gore from the strands well into a fourth change of water.

"The time to make sure you do it is before you regret not doing it," Gant wheezed in her mind. Excellent. Thank you for that memory. Always a pleasure.

Her thoughts moved from her Mentor to the cause of the blood in her hair: the death of the Fire Mage. At that last moment, she'd been struck by how young the caster had been, sixteen if she'd been a day. Unless she'd travelled extensively, it was likely Daine was the only Knight of the Road she had ever, would ever, encounter. That was a steep and ultimately terminal learning curve.

That would have been her, once upon a time. Sixteen years old and with more power than she knew what to do with. A girl with complete certainty she could take the worst the world had to offer, could smile and spit in its eye. At that age, everyone was the most powerful person they knew until they very much were not. If they were lucky, they might make it out of that encounter alive. She had. The girl had not.

A black mood settled on her. That girl would have had a whole future mapped out when she awoke that morning. One that would not have included losing her head at the end of a mediocre looted blade.

Could Daine have managed things differently? Probably. She had not needed to leave the tavern, after all. Could have thrown Trellec's retainers out the door and continued drinking while they scurried back home. But that was not her way. It had never been her way.

The Tour system relied on the complete certainty of the delivery of justice. As Cenwyn had noted, it might not have always been timely, but it would arrive. She could not back down from challenges, any challenges, and maintain the people's confidence in that system. She did not hurt others because she enjoyed it. She did it because doing it thoroughly forestalled the need to do it more. No one who saw what occurred this evening would be in any doubt as to the outcome should they stand against the Crown.

Was that worth the death of a girl whose only crime was overconfidence? Daine sighed and shook her head. Probably.

She needed to move her thoughts onward. What was done could not be undone, and mithering about it would not change that. Others were awaiting her in the woods, Cenwyn had said. She would need to deal with them next. The blood she was washing from her hair was unlikely to be the last this evening.

A boy, presumably Cenwyn's son, had been bringing and removing stained water bowls to the small room Daine was occupying in the Tailor's house. He placed a fifth clean bowl in front of her and backed away, regarding her with a look of utter horror. She hoped that was the sight of so much blood being utterly alien to him rather than him being generally aghast at her appearance.

"It's usually not this long." She gestured at her hair, talking to break the silence. "If I think I'm going to get . . . like this, I make sure it's cut right back. I hadn't expected to get messy today, I am afraid."

She bent to rinse the water in the bowl through it again.

The worst out of the blood was out now. Little point in being too thorough, though, if she were about to head back out. She'd need to tie it back.

Daine became aware that the boy was still standing there staring at her, mouth open. Small talk about blood-in-hair etiquette was apparently different from what the situation demanded.

"I could cut it for you," he offered.

Or apparently not.

She straightened and looked at him properly. He was nothing like his father: fair skin and sandy hair, whereas Cenwyn was swarthy with dark curls. The boy had sparkling blue eyes to the Tailor's dark, sombre gaze. That heart-shaped face with an upturned nose echoed little of the man busily sewing Daine a new set of clothes in his workshop. She assumed the lad — nine or ten, to guess — took after his mother's line. That, or his stepmother was not the only woman in Cenwyn's life to betray his trust.

"That's kind of you, lad. But unless you're secretly leading a life in the militia, I doubt you'd have the Strength to get through it." She pulled out a relatively clean strand of her hair and handed it to him. "One of the problems of, well, of being like me is you end up with hair you could tie a hog with. I'd be surprised if you could saw through it with a host of tools!"

The boy rolled the hair between his fingers. She smiled at the level of concentration he brought to bear on the task. Then, after a moment, he gestured toward the pile of weapons at her feet. "If I can borrow one of your knives, I think I could do it. I'm happy to try if it would make you feel better. You look so sad."

She was amused and a little touched by the sincerity of

his expression and the sentiment of his words. He really did look nothing like his father at all. "Shall I let you in on a bit of a secret? I always look a bit like this." She stooped to pick up one of her dagger sheaths and tossed it to him. He caught it with both hands, staggering back a few steps at the surprising weight of it. "But it's kind of you to offer. I likely have further work to do tonight and would gladly not have the same problem. If you want to give it a go, there's nothing to be lost letting you try. I tell you, though, you'll need to give it all you've got. You don't need to worry about hurting me."

He drew the knife and approached her with the same sincere, concerned look. She smiled in return. "You almost look like you're preparing to stick me with that, lad, not trim my hair!"

"Oh, my Lady. I'm not. I would never." His eyes widened in horror as he blushed a deep crimson.

"Just a joke, lad. Sorry, I did not mean to tease you. But come on, let's give you a decent chance at this." She pulled up a stool and lowered herself onto it to face him. Even sitting, though, she towered over him. But he was hardly unusual in that being the case. Those Orban Farmer genes in all their glory. "You'll need to stand on one of these yourself to reach."

He stepped outside into another room for a moment before returning with his own stool. Climbing on it, he put his hand on her shoulder to steady himself.

Instinctively, she rested her hand on his while he gained his balance. Tears filled her eyes for a reason she could not quite pinpoint. There was something so innocent, so wholesome about the interaction. He wanted nothing from her other than to alleviate her sadness. When was the last time she had someone this close to her without violence being in the air? She'd forgotten what it was to have such moments, and she could not bear what that said about her life.

Oblivious to his impact on her, the boy reached out with surprising confidence considering his nervous demeanour and grasped a fistful of hair. "I've done this before, don't worry. It will all be okay." Again, his odd manner brought a smile to her lips, especially as she was old enough to be his mother.

Gant roared into life in her mind. *"Mother! Grandmother, Darkhelm, if you were lucky. In this part of the world, more likely a great-grandmother. And you know what that means? It's not the foes who are getting younger. It's you turning into a relic."*

The harshness of the words spurred her into uncharacteristic generosity. "If you can as much as fray a strand, lad, you get to keep the knife."

With a precise swish, he chopped the excess hair in his fingers before taking another handful and repeating the movement. Within a few moments, he had finished and was backing away, clutching the knife to his chest like it was the most precious thing in the world. "Is that okay? Is that how you like to wear it? When you're going to fight, I mean."

She stared at the small pile of hair on the floor and then up at the small boy who had produced it. "Yes, thank you," she said, distracted. "That's perfect."

"So, I can keep the knife?"

"What? Oh, yes. It's yours. Thank you."

He smiled down at his prize and ran from the room, leaving a stunned Daine behind.

She ran a hand over her crown. The last person who'd managed to cut her hair properly had been a Blacksmith whose family had been repairing her armour for twenty years. She did not exactly trust him, but he had no excuse for trying to cut her throat when she paid so well for work that was, at best, adequate. After all, there was little need for expensive armour when your skin turned a blade just as well. So, she'd assumed she'd have to wait until returning from this Tour to get it cut so close again. And she knew he'd fuss and groan about the effort and the damage it'd do his tools.

And then a slip-of-a-son-of-a-Tailor shaved it to the scalp as if it were nothing.

"If you are ready, we can try fitting you into all this. The only good, sensible thing is to burn what you took off." Cenwyn was in the doorway holding a bundle of new clothing. He frowned at her blank look in response. "Is everything okay, my Lady?"

"Your boy . . ."

Cenwyn's frown deepened. "My boy? Do you mean Genoes? Did he upset you? I'm so sorry. We don't know what to do with him sometimes. He means well, but he has some odd ways."

"Nothing like that. He . . . surprised me, that's all. I — sorry, let me just gather my thoughts. Does he have an unusual Skill? I've never heard of a Tailor's Apprentice having such Strength."

"Genoes? No, he's not mine. Never married. Never had the time. But that's beside the point. Genoes is just an orphan from the village I keep an eye on. Lives out of the stable behind the inn. He doesn't have anything else, so we all give him some jobs — but I doubt anyone would be training him in a Class. He's no one special."

Over the next few days, those words haunted Lady Darkhelm as much as any homily from Old Gant.

CHAPTER SEVEN

"An Irrational Hatred of Archers"

"All I'm saying is we should have come up with a better communication system."

Kirstin closed her eyes and began a slow count to ten. If that were "all" Jak was saying, that would have been fine. But the fact was, it was not "all" he had been saying for the last four years. She was willing to concede they might have only been two hours skulking in the woods, and thirty minutes since they stoked the campfire. But time was relative. Especially when spending time with relatives.

"How do we even know if we're needed? We might be sat here, and the rest of them are already back in the barracks and having a good laugh. There were eight of them. Eight! Are you telling me they wouldn't be able to handle her? Drunnoc even lent them that scary Fire Witch he's been dallying with. At best, we're redundancy in the system.

We should have thought up how they would tell us if they hadn't got her. That would have made more sense than just coming out here and waiting to see if she turned up. We could be here for days before anyone thinks to tell us to come home."

She restarted her ten count.

"Look after your brother." That was the only thing her mother had ever asked of her. "Don't let him go the same way as your father." And she'd tried. Goddess knows, she'd tried. But when he fell in with Drunnoc Trellec, she knew it would just be a matter of time before something like this happened. Jak was not a bad man. Well, not a terrible one. He was just easily led and willing to take the easiest path available. Waylaying a lone woman in the woods was precisely the sort of thing that had lost her father his head. And it was exactly the sort of thing her mother would have wanted her to keep Jak away from.

Kirstin checked her crossbow for the fiftieth time that hour and, heroically, managed not to shoot her brother in the head. Tonight was only going to end badly. If by some miracle the motley crew back at the village had killed a Knight of the Road, there would be a terrifying reckoning called down. Few things were certain in this life. One of them was that the King would take a dim view of people murdering his agents. And that was the *best-case* scenario. The more likely outcome tonight was that in very short order they would all end up dead.

And Drunnoc Trellec would not be inconvenienced by that in the slightest.

Kirstin remembered Daine from her last Tour ten years back. Nothing in the woman's appearance matched the songs about Lady Darkhelm. She remembered being so disappointed when seeing her for the first time. And then the judgements began. She'd only been able to bear watching for the first day.

It was the glow in the Daine's eyes that had most unsettled her. Most normal people tried to spend their lives without ever being in the presence of a god. The fact that people were actively seeking out the regard of the Knight baffled her. Most of the cases on that day were largely insignificant — those crimes that would require execution were being kept until the end of the visit. No one wanted to bring their complaint about a neighbour's noisy children to someone cleaning blood off their sword.

Jak was moaning again. "Are we supposed to stay here for the night? Just huddled down by the road like beggars?"

The third member of their party, Heroc, was reaching the end of his patience. The problem for Jak was that, while Kirstin might dream of shutting him up by shooting him in the head, Heroc would do it. More likely, he'd use that axe of his. He liked the mess. "Lad, if I hear one more word from you, it'll be your last."

Fool he might be, but Jak had enough of a survival instinct not to push the man further. So instead, he pulled his overcoat tighter and glowered at the darkness.

Kirstin instinctively flashed Heroc a smile of gratitude.

"Put your teeth away, girl. It don't work on me." Realising her mistake, she quickly dropped her eyes. She'd been around these two long enough to know the only way to survive was to be ignored. "Don't know what you think you're doing out here anyway. He's bad enough — but at least he has the stomach for it."

She made a noncommittal noise and poked at the fire. When enough time had passed to risk glancing back up his way, Heroc was not there anymore.

Startled, her eyes lingered on the space where the Axeman had sat. They had been crouched around the small blaze, listening for the sounds of travellers coming down the road, for so long that his sudden absence from opposite her felt bizarre. It was so strange that she could not find the appropriate way to react for several seconds.

"Jak?"

"What?"

"Heroc's gone."

As he turned, the sneer on her brother's face became surprised and then fearful. They both stood, Jak drew his daggers, and she raised her crossbow.

Then Heroc floated backwards into the camp. No, he wasn't floating, Kirstin realised. A hand around his throat held him about a foot above the ground as his feet kicked for purchase. His fists beat down against the arm holding him but made no impression on the iron grip.

But the scale was all wrong. Heroc was a tall man — there were few doors he did not have to duck under — and the woman, for it was a woman who held him aloft, surely could not have the Strength to lift and hold him so easily. A heaviness settled in her stomach as she took in the short hair, the grim expression, and the softly glowing eyes. She lowered her crossbow.

"Sensible girl." The woman raised her eyebrows at Jak, who had stayed in his ready position. "At least someone in your family has brains. Stop your fretting!" she barked at Heroc, who thrashed around in her hold.

"I've come to give you a fair chance. Same chance as I

gave them back at the village. Gather your things and make your way back home, and we'll say no more about it. You had your orders, you followed them, and then you thought better of it. No harm. No foul. And no one could say otherwise. Will you stop it!" Heroc was now trying to kick out with his dangling legs.

"Are they dead?" someone said. With surprise, Kirstin realised it was her.

"Some. Those who decided not to be reasonable. The big ginger guy will have a headache for a few days. The rest should be home by now. For the love of —" She shook Heroc hard as he dealt her a blow on the elbow with one of his flailing feet. He went limp, and Daine dropped him to the ground.

"People say I have an irrational fear of Archers". She rubbed her elbow, wincing. "I say, spend an evening trying to work out whether pushing or pulling an arrow out of you will hurt more and then come back to me. I have a perfectly rational hatred of your Class. What was the plan? Hear me coming down the road, line up and turn me into a pincushion when I came round the bend?"

"Told you it was a stupid plan," Jak mumbled.

"Might have worked if I'd not known exactly where you were the moment I left the village. Which genius thought to light the fire?"

Jak, surprisingly, chose not to share his lengthy thesis on why the blaze "couldn't possibly be seen from the road."

"So, what are we going to do? Full disclosure, these are new clothes I'm not minded to get mussed up, so you have that in your favour. On the other hand, I've just had my hair cut, so, all in all, I could go either way."

Kirstin sensed Jak make the wrong decision. She'd spent

her whole life in the shadow of such moments. Despairingly, she raised her crossbow to cover his attack as he ran forward. Then, with one knife, he activated <Frenzy> and slashed wildly at the face of the Knight while plunging toward her chest with the other.

It was pretty well done, Daine thought, leaning back to avoid the blade aimed at her eyes. On a normal day, she would have allowed the second knife to hit her, then pivoted at the waist to disarm him when it sunk in. However, she did not think Cenwyn would appreciate repairing her tunic so soon, so she caught the boy's wrist and squeezed. There was a brief scream as the bone splintered before he passed out. She gently lowered him on top of the other man.

The girl, she could not be more than eighteen, stared at her down the length of the crossbow.

"Today might be your day." Daine did not make any attempt to move. She was well-lit by the small fire, making her a perfect target against the dark. "It's not just me who hates Archers. More Knights of the Road fall to lucky shots to the head than they do in pitched battles. You see, it does not matter how fast you heal with an arrow to the eye."

Kirstin adjusted her aim to the Knight's head and refreshed her most effective Skill, <Sure Shot>. Daine smiled.

"Of course, the eye is a much smaller target than the body. And you will only get one shot. It looks like a decent crossbow; one you have cared for. It probably will shoot true if you are good enough. And you have not got stiff from sitting in the cold for hours. And I do not move."

Then something happened.

The soft glow from the Knight's eyes changed into something more vibrant, dwarfing the light from the flames. The Archer stepped back for a second in alarm before settling and rechecking her aim. When Daine next spoke, there was a different timbre to her voice. "I could kill him for you."

"What?"

"Your brother. I could kill him for you. And then you would be free."

"Shut up."

"Your mother did not want this life for you, Kirstin. None of this is what she expected from you. There was a time you did what you could to keep him away from the wrong path, and she is grateful for your care. But it is no longer helping. What you do now is merely postponing the inevitable. She asks that I release you from your promise."

The tip of the quarrel dipped for a moment before rising back up. "He's my brother."

"He deserves judgement. You do not know the extent of what he has done, nor what he will do if he is not stopped. I can feel the influence of the Dark God around him, and he is enjoying that attention. Jak is not the worst of them, but he will not change. You will not be able to change him. Rather, he will drag you down with him until you cannot keep yourself clean from the filth. And I tell you, should you not accept this offer, you will wish you had the next time we meet."

Kirstin knew what the voice — she did not think it was the Knight speaking — offered her. Freedom. And, in many ways, she wanted to accept it and leave this Goddessforsaken village behind forever. She knew the Jak she loved, the child she still saw when she looked at him, was gone. That mischievousness had long since changed into something more vicious. There was a swagger to him in the village, and she knew that he was looked at with fear even if she would not admit it to herself.

But you did not abandon family.

If she did, then she would be no better than what she feared he was turning into.

She pulled the trigger. And she was that good.

CHAPTER EIGHT

"Particularly Resilient Cockroaches"

"The fern blizzard is mapping the stone garden?"

It was generally frowned upon for Knights of the Road to tell lies. For sure, this was more of a guideline than a hard and fast rule, but if they could avoid telling mistruths, they would. After all, when delivering justice with the voice of a goddess, it was wise to make sure She did not have cause to take issue with the words used. There were stories of Knights of the Road who, having played rather loose with the truth, suddenly found Her face turned from them at a crucial juncture. Indeed, most of the tales of fallen Knights had their origins in displeasing the Goddess somehow.

In that, She was widely regarded as one of the more capricious deities in the pantheon. It was rare, for example, for the Master Builder to suddenly withdraw His patronage from those who worshipped at His, constantly-under-development, temple. And should He choose to do so, it was unlikely that a sudden loss of divinely enhanced professional expertise would prove especially fatal. But, on the other hand, the occasions where the Goddess chose to express her annoyance were usually entirely terminal for the Knight concerned. It was not just the Knights themselves that preferred brief, violent demonstrations of the benefits of compliance.

Thus, by and large, Daine avoided speaking falsehoods.

"This blacksmith's grin invites the lizard! Small upturned faces in rows?"

However, within that context, she had always found it wise to spread a little misinformation regarding the extent of her healing properties. There were legends aplenty of the Knights of the Road — the Lady Darkhelm in particular — and they all carried hints of what could and could not be done to lay one low.

Decapitation, for example, was generally seen as a solid approach; of course, the power required to achieve that was so extraordinary that there were few examples enacted by humans upon which to draw. Back when Giants were more numerous, it was certainly an occupational hazard for those in Daine's position, but they were less of a threat of late.

Twenty years back, there had been somewhat of a fashion for throwing incapacitated Knights into the ocean, the belief being that they travelled by the Road due to some weakness connected to water. However, enforced drowning was complicated for someone whose lungs could heal the damage caused by a loss of air faster than it occurred. Generally, this tactic merely resulted in the emergence of a rather vengeance-minded Knight on the coast several weeks later. As with most questionable fashions, this approach quickly passed into obscurity.

Various alchemic compounds had been tried — both as poisons and applied topically to the skin — but failed to do much more than irritate, and who wanted an irritated, heavily-armed warrior on their hands?

With a willingness to throw enough men into the meat grinder — and most Lords reached their willingness reasonably quickly when a Knight of the Road came calling — they could, it was true, gradually be worn down. But that was the sort of approach that took a toll on morale and was best kept as a last resort.

Indeed, the last death of a Knight of the Road documented with any accuracy was that of Filip Woolley, eight years back, and was reported to have occurred after four days of battle with an entire army. The story went that he had become so discouraged about massacring the King of Cold Water's troops that he had taken his own life rather than continue with the slaughter. Having known Woolley quite well, Daine thought such magnanimity unlikely. Rather, she felt that five thousand against one was a good exploration of the limits of their invulnerability.

"You lot are particularly resilient cockroaches," Gant had noted with his usual charm. "Pretty much unkillable by the type of people you will come up against on the Road. You can take whatever they throw at you, shrug it off, and ask for more. Take a few axe blows to the head and keep going, and most of the bumpkins out there will treat you as some sort of god. But, of course" — his solitary eye unfocused as he became swallowed up in his memories — *"there's more than just the Road out there."* And with that, he had downed the rest of the drink and refused to say any more.

"Cave dwellings is a storm-filled cat?"

The efficacy of the "arrow-through-the-eye" method, though, was one that had gained significant traction amongst those interested in nefarious ways of dealing with those blessed by the Goddess. It made sense, after all. The eye, even one of a Knight of the Road, was a vulnerable spot. If an arrow went in there, it would go into the brain, and surely that would be that? Did not Daine herself get her nickname from the black helmet she wore precisely to protect that weak area?

Thus, the tale went around that a good enough Archer, with the right Skills, was the solution to these pesky dispensers of justice. And Daine was happy enough to do what she could to spread that story.

"Eel soup is more than enough for the farmer's daughter."

But none of that was at the forefront of her mind right now.

She found herself in the uncomfortable situation of having a minimal idea of what was going on.

She appeared to be in a woodland clearing just off the main trunk of the Road. A small fire was burning merrily, a type to suggest whoever set it had no desire to be inconspicuous.

Before her stood a young woman, a teenager really, mouth open and a discharged crossbow limp in her hand. Her skin was ashen, and she looked ready to faint, vomit, or both at any second.

Daine wondered what had happened to scare her so? And why was she staring at her, not answering her questions?

She recognised that the quality and clarity of communication were not being improved by the loud grinding noise reverberating through her skull. On the contrary, with this sound getting louder and louder, it was blocking out anything else she might hear.

In an attempt to ease the uncomfortable sensation, she shook her head and felt something loosen from the front of her face and fall to the ground. In an instant, that grinding noise ceased, and the growing pressure eased.

Surprisingly, that slight shake of the head significantly changed her perception, as if a dam had been filling up close to bursting and were suddenly released. Memories started to return.

There'd been some unpleasantness in the village, nothing worth really exploring, but it did bring to mind the unpleasantness with that wind cult for some reason. What did they call themselves? It did not matter.

There'd been tell of other assailants waiting in the woods. She had not wanted to wait until the morning to deal with them and, despite that man's entreaties — what was his name? He had made her some new clothes, she thought. Why had she needed new clothes? — she'd come straight here.

But then . . . something had happened, and she'd been talking to this woman.

She realised the gloom to her left-hand side was lifting. With a start, she saw there was more than just this woman in front of her. On the ground were two men. One looked like the woman, presumably a younger sibling. The other was much older. She did not feel he was a relative. The Goddess was not well-disposed toward either of these men. In fact, once she had her bearings again, she would be doing the world a service if she ensured neither of them ever got up again. However, there was more ambivalence toward the young woman. As if she stood at a crossroads, and the Goddess could not see down which path she would tread. That was uncommon.

Nevertheless, with every passing second, the clarity of the scene on that side of the clearing improved and other memories of the last few hours returned.

"Freedom of the ink dweller is no guarantee. Plants that run fire the cauldron?" she asked the woman.

But no. That did not sound quite right. She had meant to say: "I feel a powerful thirst. Do you have any water?" But her mouth, or more likely her aching head, had made something else come out instead. This had happened before, had it not? She felt she could recall similar moments of uncertainty. With that thought came a sudden loathing for Archers. She looked again at the young woman and started appreciating some of the ambivalence from the Goddess.

When this had happened before, when a bloody Archer had shot her, what had she needed to do to get things right . . .

She raised her right hand, the left seemed unresponsive, to touch the back of her head. There was wetness and movement back there as if something gelatinous were being pulled back together. Thankfully, there was no grinding noise anymore, more of a soft clicking of small pieces reconnecting. Her eyes — yes, there were two of them now. Had there not been two before? — cast downwards and saw a crossbow bolt, its shaft oddly bent, lying at her feet.

So, the woman had shot her. That much was clear, she supposed. Had she done something to deserve it? Probably. The bodies on the ground and the terrified look in the woman's eyes suggested there had been a confrontation. Unless she had lost her mind and just waylaid a family picnic, this was presumably the group for whom she had come looking. She'd dealt with the two men, yes, the Goddess hummed approval for that, and had — what? — let the woman shoot her in the head?

That did not feel like what she would do in an ordinary course of events. Something must have stayed her hand.

"Give me a mountain. It's all just haranguing in here. I'll make fish soon."

Daine again looked at the young woman. Despite Daine's reduced efficiency, there was still no flare of danger from the Goddess. In these circumstances, it seemed sensible to allow some further healing before deciding on her next steps. "*Some of the worst decisions ever made on a battlefield were by those who did not know they were already dead.*" How odd. That thought did not sound like her internal thoughts. Too gravelly and masculine. And actually, now she thought about it, not much like constructive advice. She did not want to hear that voice much more at all.

So, she paused while the final parts of her fractured skull and destroyed brain reknitted.

*

For Kirstin, this had been an appalling few minutes. Her shot had been perfect, hitting the Knight, as expected, in the left eye. The bolt had been buried halfway into her head, and that, in her experience, should have been that.

However, instead of the impact dropping the older woman to the floor, she merely took a few staggering steps backwards. There was a moment, and then she looked up at Kirstin, with the arrow protruding from her face, and started spouting nonsense about "*stone gardens* and *lizards.*"

But, no, that hadn't been the worst thing. That was still to come. With horrid fascination, Kirstin watched her quarrel work its way back out of the eye socket as if pulled on a string, blood and other fluids pouring from the wound.

The Knight who had seemed understandably disorientated by this, if wholly unconcerned, kept asking questions that made no sense until, with a sudden shake of her head, the bolt had dislodged.

This seemed to speed up the whole process of recovery, and within a few seconds, the wound had closed, and the eye was wholly restored.

The Knight, her face covered in gore, grinned at her. "Shall we try all that again?"

CHAPTER NINE

"An Allergic Reaction in My Soul"

All in all, it had not been a day for the history books. Daine was not so filled with self-loathing, at least not usually, that she could not acknowledge she had achieved some noteworthy things in her life. Bards did not bother with the mediocre; tales of heroism and derring-do filled their purses.

It might have been a long time since her heart had swelled while on Tour, but those days had been many and plentiful: giants had been slain, warlords overcome, shadowy conspiracies uncovered, and so on and so forth. Perhaps, more importantly, there were people alive today who would not have been without her intervention. And, of course, those in the ground who had needed someone to help them there. She had been happy to oblige in both cases.

So, there were reasons enough for her to look back on

how she had spent her life with, if not pride, then certainly
with the grim satisfaction of a demanding job done well.

That made today's events taste particularly bitter. So
many years after she took her first step on the Road, she
had enacted the slaughter of some minor henchmen in the
backend of nowhere and caught a crossbow bolt to the face
for her trouble.

*"T'was in the dark month, so do I say, when flowers clad the
landscape gray, on a winding path her journey lay, the Darkhelm
forgot to duck as an arrow came her way."*

She supposed it was a triumph of the Tour system
that most significant impediments to the common good
in the Kingdom had been removed during the past fifty
years. Even before Daine had begun her own journey on
the Road, many of the great battles had already occurred.
Some of the tales she had heard of the deeds of Gallant
Stonehand in his prime or Eliud Duskstrider could still chill
her even today.

It did not compare to what was common overseas.
Could anyone even recall the last time a dark creature had
rampaged across the countryside?

But, by the nature of their success, and the successes
of those who likewise had the patronage of a god, the
Knights of the Road had become increasingly involved in
the day-to-day problems of the regions. Without dragons
to slay, the King had directed their attention to more human matters. She was uncertain what was the more monstrous of the two.

The songs of the deeds of the Knights were so popular in the taverns because they touched on a shared cul-
tural history that was *just* far enough in the past to become
rose-tinted. To hear some of the ballads, a Goblin army

on the march was a foreboding sight of wonder and terror. Her particular memories were undoubtedly more concerned with their smell. Likewise, she could vividly recall
the mundanity of the slaying of a sick Cyclops, an event
that had been transformed into something so glorious it
would only take the strumming of the first few bars of
the song before everyone in the inn would be buying her
drinks.

She shifted the weight of the Archer's brother across
her shoulder and plodded onwards. He was not heavy, but
the Goddess disapproved of his continued existence, so
even touching him made her whole body ache. If she still
held any romantic delusions about such things, she would
have described the experience of carrying this man on her
back as an allergic reaction in her soul.

Daine recognised that her relationship with the Goddess
was complex, even for a Knight of the Road. She remembered the first time she had "heard" Her voice, although
the experience was nothing as prosaic as "hearing."

Gant had told her that, should she be welcomed on the
Road, she could expect some moral, guiding light to help
plot her steps. It was precisely that certainty that she had
felt she needed in her life, naïve as she had been. After all,
for those without a path to walk, those with a map held an
instinctive attraction.

"*She'll want you to be hers, though, remember that. Completely
and totally. Yon folk see Knights of the Road as all-powerful, but you
only have as much as she is willing to give you. And for as long as she
is willing to give it. And that you can accept, of course.*" It turned
out she could accept a lot.

It had been on a deer hunt that she first learned that the
Goddess was willing to accept her. A few of the students

had taken some days away from the interminable training to try out their new Skills. She had little talent with the bow, far too much Strength — "Stop making matchsticks of my damn equipment!" — but she had found that if she treated a longbow with enough care, she would be able to get through a few days of shooting before the inevitable snapping.

She had been lining up on a hart of ten when, just on the point of loosing, she felt a slight adjustment to her hold. A gentle touch as if a Master were politely yet firmly correcting her form. The arrow had flown true, far better than any shot she had previously shown the potential to make, and she enjoyed her peers' admiration and Gant's approval. She blushed at how a strut had entered her gait that evening. In the quiet moments that followed, though, she considered the meaning of that momentary prod and knew she was beginning the next stage of her journey.

That gentle guiding touch had occurred again and again in the coming weeks, each time enhancing her performance beyond that of which she was usually capable. Gant noticed — of course he did — and offered some advice around the usual outcome of holding a tiger by its tail. But she was young, and what did that old drunk know?

Would she have chosen to walk the Road if she had known what it would hold for her? Of course she would have. After all, that was the type of person she was, which was why the Goddess had accepted her.

She swapped shoulders again. The ache was becoming troublesome. Again, she considered her defiance of Her will in this. The young woman had been insistent: she would not allow her brother to be killed. When it came to it, Daine respected that obduracy, particularly as the girl had witnessed how little power she had to do anything about it. Even after seeing the impact — or lack of one — of her last shot, Kirstin had loaded up her crossbow and stood between doom and her brother, and if that was not the sort of thing a Knight of the Road could grudgingly admire, then they were in the wrong business.

The Goddess could trust her discretion in the matter or, well, She could make carrying the man feel like Daine was sitting naked in a field of nettles. She guessed there was little ambiguity in her deity's feelings here.

Fortunately, Kirstin had less scruple about the older man's survival. If the touch of the boy across her shoulders made Daine distinctively uncomfortable, then that man made her very teeth itch. The Goddess had supplied enough visions of past and future atrocities to close the matter. It had been the work of seconds, a quick twist of the neck, and it was over.

At the precise moment of his death, back in the village and across the countryside, men, women, and children had awakened with a start, as if something seismic had happened, then turned over and returned to sleep, dozing a little deeper and a little easier. If anyone were to ask them why, they would have said that it felt like a shadow over their lives had suddenly and irrevocably been lifted. And some of them, certainly enough to make the whole thing worthwhile, had offered a prayer to the Goddess for their deliverance.

Another shift of position. Maybe under the arm would prove less painful?

The Archer had barely stopped speaking for a moment since they had begun their slow walk back to the village. Daine let her talk. Shock took people in unusual ways. For

some, it closed them down, tight as a drum. They withdrew into themselves as if hoping to wrap up in a silence
that could undo the damage, that there was new armour
that could be forged through solitude. They were the ones
Daine worried about the most after a fight. Too often, she
had known the casualty list to increase overnight when
those quiet ones were left to brood.

Kirstin was not brooding, and Daine was happy to let
her deal with the aftershock of violence in her way.

"He doesn't know, of course. Well, he knows some of
it, but only enough to make him think his son does some
disgusting things when he is out of his sight. He doesn't
realise what Drunnoc actually is. I don't think many people
do. Only those who get to see how his little gang operates
truly see it. I tell you, he's not right at all."

She let the girl's voice fade into the background. Now
that the immediate problem of the group lurking in the
woods had been dealt with, Daine could feel that the
Goddess wanted her to turn her attention to the problem of Drunnoc Trellec. Kirstin was clear that she, and
her brother, felt no loyalty to his House. The actions in
the wood had not been taken because they wished harm
on Daine. Instead, they feared what would happen if they
turned down anything the Lordling asked them to do.

It went without saying that if "go the woods and try
to murder the nice, semi-immortal Lady Knight" was the
better of two options available, then she needed to spend
some time considering how best to address this.

"And the things he has his friends do to that stableboy?
They're vile. Of course, he never gets his hands dirty himself, but he likes to watch. It's part of why I let Jak fall in
with them when they showed an interest. It was not because

I wanted him to be around boys like that, but, well, better the Dark God you know, right? If you'd seen what they do to torment that lad, you could see why doing this . . . well, you'd see why being one of the gang is better than being their victim. No matter how bad being part of this gets, it is still not as bad as being someone Drunnoc wants to be punished."

"Which stableboy?"

"Sorry?" The Knight's question brought Kirstin up short. She herself had barely recognised that she had been speaking at all. Instead, she was trying to avoid thinking about the appalling horror that threatened to overwhelm her. She worried that if she let things lapse into silence, she would need to consider that she was walking next to someone she had shot in the face and who, clearly, had the power to kill her, and her brother, without a moment's thought.

If she were not speaking, she would be shrieking. The noise of Heroc's neck popping was not one she would forget in a hurry.

"You said Trellec has his friends torment a stableboy?"

"Yes. The one who does the odd jobs around the village. Genoes. I don't think he has a second name. Or if he does, I haven't heard anyone use it. To be clear, I say 'stableboy,' but that's just where he lives. It's not his Class or anything. He's an orphan."

Daine stopped and shrugged Jak off her shoulders and onto the ground. The boy made a soft mewing sound as he connected with it, his broken wrist flapping unpleasantly free from the rest of his arm.

Kirstin looked at the Knight with alarm and unslung her crossbow from her shoulder. Had something she had said changed her mind about Jak?

Daine's eyes met hers, and, yes, there it was. The flaring of the hidden power. "Tell me everything you know about the orphan, Genoes."

CHAPTER TEN

"This Is Absolutely Fine"

T he face was not quite right.

Drunnoc Trellec replaced the brush in its pot and tilted his head to take in the model. But, no. There was a particular something about the mouth he had missed. The lips, perhaps, were too thin. Their vibrant redness was too dully depicted. With a sigh, he wetted his thumb and rubbed them out before beginning again.

Anyone who had been an unfortunate witness to his tantrum an hour past would have found his current attitude astonishing. Yet, at his easel, this quiet, almost contemplative boy was as far away from the rampaging thug terrifying the staff and devastating the breakfast table as possible.

It was rare of late for Fion to be called to restrain the boy — he had made it clear he no longer had appetite for that role — but such was the level of violence that Gilles Halcoth, Steward of House Trellec, had dispatched a maid to request help. "If the Master can't be persuaded to come, tell him I'll be taking a stick to the boy myself," he had shouted after her running form.

Drunnoc stepped back, considering the image with a frown. As he did so, he ran his tongue around the inside of his mouth, carefully exploring the newly loose tooth. Father had struck him hard this time. Presumably, notwithstanding the broken furniture, the events of last evening at the tavern had reached his ears. It was unusual for him to have become so invested in discipline without an added impetus these days.

He was unsure whether the beating was for disobeying Father's orders and making an attempt on the life of Daine Orban or because the effort failed. Fion Trellec was complicated in that way.

Maybe the problem was not the lips. The chin. Was it that pronounced? Humming a few tuneless notes, he began reworking the face.

Drunnoc had been surprised to hear how things had played out in the village. He knew Knights of the Road were hardy, but it stretched credibility to think Veron had not arranged enough talent to get the job done. After all, on her own Layla had more than enough power to cook that old woman in her armour. He briefly smiled at memories of recent conflagrations; there was something about widening eyes when a person realised the increasing heat would not abate. What had he said which made her crow with laughter? Oh, yes. *You see something die inside, and then they die inside.* He still could not identify the cause for humour.

His thoughts rested for a moment on that angry young Mage. There had been some sort of kinship between them. Both bore the scars of being unwanted additions to already complete families. At length and with great pleasure, she had spoken of the firestorm that consumed her parents' estate. She still carried some of the ash in a locket around her neck. He had found that anger . . . useful. There were innumerable things people could be persuaded to do when the alternative was fire.

Despite that, he would not miss her. Others could step into her role. But it was odd to think of her headless body lying in the icehouse. He wondered if the fire continued to burn in her veins after death.

The light in the painting looked better. The shadows fell just right on the neck now. He cleaned his brush and began adding colour to the hair.

Being banished once more to the Tower held few concerns for Drunnoc. If it meant Father forgot about him for a few days, it was more than worth the discomfort of a hard bed and loose teeth. There was, traditionally, a good week of freedom following such a beating. With Lord Trellec thinking his son was safely stowed away *"considering his actions,"* he could turn his full attention to how he wished to address the troublesome Knight.

His brush flickered across the canvas as he considered Daine Orban. Not many people would hold his gaze of late, and that she had done so, and with such challenge, was fascinating. They had shared something down the length of that sword, and while Father may have feared the outcome of a clash, Drunnoc was not sure about the inevitability of his defeat.

He had his own resources on which to call, after all. At that thought, he felt a soft pat on his head.

Drunnoc's explosive anger was all a pretence, of course. From earliest childhood, he had understood that others preferred that version of him: the shouting, petulant child was one with which they were comfortable. They knew how to react to him in that form. So, he obliged by breaking things, hitting others, strutting, bullying, and sneering. Then they could beat him for his behaviour, relieve their discomfort, and leave him be for a while. If it troubled him that his only fundamental interactions with others were either causing or receiving pain, he would not have known how to express it.

For that was at the heart of things. Drunnoc Trellec did not feel. It was not that he was "dead inside," as the last in a succession of Tutors had shouted when fleeing the Keep. On the contrary, he was very much alive. Sometimes overwhelmingly so in that he felt he would burst unless he relieved the pressure. It was just that nothing, no matter how wonderful or how terrible, left an impression on him. He felt as much joy at the sunrise as he did when considering a hangnail. He was as upset about his increasingly rare beatings from his father as he was about noticing a grease stain on his fifth-favourite tunic. Screams of torment gave him as much pause as the droning of a Priest from the pulpit.

It was all one and the same to Drunnoc Trellec.

Nevertheless, what he may have lacked in emotional range, he felt he more than made up for in creativity.

It was in those moments — during those times that he truly gave bloody expression to that which was inside him — that he could feel a soft, approving presence envelop him. Of course, he had no familial context for such unconditional positive regard, but he recognised it was a heady experience he craved.

With a final twitch of the brush, he nodded in satisfaction. Yes, this was all perfect.

A querulous voice whispered from the doorway. "Dru?"

"Mother. I did not know you were out of bed."

He did not turn to look at her. He did not need to. She would have the same despair-filled look of disapproval on her face that was the first thing he could remember seeing. He did not know what he had done to cause such rejection, but he had grown to accept it. And, to the dismay of those around him, to seek to deserve it.

A soft voice in his head insisted it was better to be feared than loved. A sentiment with which he heartily agreed. That said, though, he did not feel the need to allow her to inflict her presence on him continually.

"What are you . . . what has . . . what is going on?"

He waved a dismissive gesture at the model. "I'm just painting Wilhelmina. What do you think? I had some trouble with the mouth, but it seems just about right now."

Lady Trivian took a few more hesitant steps into the room. She had come to see her son from a sense of obligation rather than anything else. She always did whenever he was returned to his banishment up here.

When he was younger, she had relished the beatings. Found solace in watching her husband mete out endless punishments to this demon. But, as the years rolled by, and his behaviour did not change, it had all become rather . . . dull. What little pleasure there was in seeing his chastisement was somewhat reduced when she sensed how little he cared. Even Fion, she knew, found it difficult to summon the required rage any longer. "It is like beating a carpet,' he had told her. 'Extremely tiring, and it does not stop the blasted thing from getting dirty the next day."

So, she still visited in his regular seclusions, but, given a choice, and without the thrill of seeing him humbled, she would rather be anywhere else. She suspected Drunnoc felt the same. Certainly, she knew neither of them gained anything of joy from their infrequent interactions.

"Is she . . . alive?"

"I have no idea." He was rather pleased with how the painting had turned out. Sometimes, they cried so much at the beginning that everything swelled up, especially around the eyes. But then it looked like he had the proportions wrong, rather than their own stupid biology letting him down. He had ensured Wilhelmina had finished all her leaking before seeking to capture her on the canvas. That seemed to have improved the final product. He would have to remember that in future. Of course, doing things this way ensured there was a further challenge in accurately representing the cuts and bruises. An enjoyable and diverting difficulty. As much as he enjoyed anything.

"I . . . why would you do this?"

*

Drunnoc turned his eyes, for a moment, on his mother, and she recoiled. When he was like this, when he was not wearing the brutish mask he presented to the outside world, it chilled her. He looked almost cherubic without strong emotions twisting his features into a snarl. The stillness, the flatness of expression, was impossible to reconcile with what lay on the floor before him. How could this face have done all that? How did a boy with those golden locks and soft eyes inflict all this pain on someone who had bathed him, fed him, and bounced him on her knee?

She had not worried, not for a moment, that he would

unleash this side of himself on the Nurse. In many ways, Wilhelmina had taken on her maternal role in raising Drunnoc. She had given him a facsimile of the love that Trivian had been unable to summon.

Was that why he had unleashed such wrath on her? Had the Nurse stood proxy for what her son wished to do to her? She pushed that thought away. That way lay madness, and she had dangled too often over that precipice of late.

But what was she going to do now? Who could she possibly find to take over this role? She could not be around this creature any more than she currently was, and rumours were rife enough about Drunnoc that this would not be an attractive opportunity. Despair filled her as she contemplated filling the void that the Nurse had left behind. Propriety would demand it of her. And the one thing everyone knew about House Trellec was that it did all things correctly.

Finally, she had the wherewithal to turn her eyes back to Drunnoc. But if she had hoped for a shred of humanity, his closed expression gave her no respite: he was not angry. He was not ashamed at what he had done. There was no sorrow, he was perfectly at his ease.

"Dru, she loved you. Had always loved you. Do you not see that doing this to her was wrong?"

Without answering, he turned his eyes back to the painting. Yes, this was one of his better efforts. The procedure for reaching this stage would bear repeating.

"If there was not anything else, Mother?"

"Drunnoc —"

A faint whimper came from the torn figure on the floor. Mother and son turned to regard her; one with horror in

her eyes, the other with a smile of genuine, if wholly disconcerting, warmth.

"Ah, there you go. No need to worry. Wilhelmina's absolutely fine."

CHAPTER ELEVEN

"Too Many Teeth and Not Enough Jaw"

With a dancer's grace, the boy slipped through the driving rain.

He was not sure his movements, as fluid as they were, made much difference as to how wet he was getting, but it felt good to be doing something to avoid the deluge. At such times, he liked to imagine each raindrop was an arrow launched from some fell Keep, and he, a figure from legend, was charging to free a beautiful Princess.

Dodge. Swerve. Pivot. Slide. And repeat.

No one had ever taken the time to explain Skills to Genoes. If they had, he would have been able to make more sense of what he was doing during this run. He had an instinctive grasp of cooldowns and triggers that would have dazzled anyone who bothered to engage with him on the matter. However, to most he was just "the orphan"— one whom people favoured to be sure — but still afforded the appropriate attention according to that status.

Nevertheless, for all his efforts, as deep puddles formed in the road, he was increasingly becoming as soaked from the bottom up as he was from the top down.

Breathless, he paused momentarily in an open doorway, somehow resisting the impulse to shake himself dry like a dog.

"Don't even think about lingering, Genoes," snapped the shopkeeper, moving from behind his counter with a speed that belied his girth. "Folk have been traipsing the weather in and out all morning."

"But Master Roen, just let me a tarry a moment. I think it's about to lighten up."

"But me no buts. I've just got the floor dry. Don't want you messing it up again." He aimed a half-hearted kick at Genoes's backside, inexplicably missing, considering the range. Despite this, the boy still crashed into his delicatessen table, knocking meat everywhere.

With a curse, the shopkeeper righted the table and began restacking the goods. "You no-good ragamuffin. Chaos in your wake, wherever you tread. Get yourself out of here!"

Sticking his tongue out and stamping his boots to dislodge the worst of the mud and water on the floor, Genoes ducked back out. Truth be told, he did not have much farther to go, but it always warmed his heart to take an opportunity to irritate John Roen: there had been more unpaid errands than he could count over the years.

Genoes recognised that he had it better than most in his situation. He could not remember his parents — he had been told they had been taken when he was no more than four years old — but the village had enough kind eyes that made sure he did not want for much. It was rare that a day passed with no odd job for him to undertake, no hot meal at the end, and no pack of dry clothes waiting for him at the stable.

The falling water continued to tug at his cloak, his payment from the Tailor for attending the Lady Darkhelm last evening, as he darted, hither and thither, toward his destination: the Church of Dawn. His rhythmic game with the rain made everyone he passed smile.

He nodded in greeting at the raised hands as he sped along, twirling to avoid carts and fellow soaked pedestrians. Heads turned to follow his progress. There was something about Genoes that made everyone's day improve when they came across him. Most assumed he possessed unusually high Charisma, yet no one had every sought to explore the matter further.

Back in the general store, even John Roen, misanthrope that he was, felt a smile pull at the corner of his mouth when thinking about their interaction. Almost subconsciously, he took out some greaseproof paper and wrapped up a piece of steak that he felt had spent too long on the floor for him to be able to sell. It would find its way to the stables that evening.

Genoes was nearly there when the rain truly began to hammer down.

Fortunately, it was the work of a few moments before he was leaping up stone steps. One, two, three at a time. He then yanked open the heavy double doors before stopping on the threshold.

As always, his breath was literally taken away by the beauty of the sight in front of him, a sigh stolen from him as he gazed in wonder at the interior decorations. The whole back wall of the Church was made from worked glass of every conceivable colour: it depicted a dazzling array of historical figures, scenes of triumph and disaster, and images of every conceivable god and goddess. On days like this, when the sun hid behind angry clouds, the light coming through that wall softly diffused across the space, giving the impression of everything inside being underwater. Quite fitting, considering the deluge outside.

On a brighter day, though, it would look like a myriad of rainbows exploded outwards from that wall. Each pool of light driving into the wall opposite, a disconcerting riot of colour that was as intimidating as it was wondrous.

"And therein lies both the greatness and the stupidity of the Church of Dawn," Brother Evelyn had said after his customary, one too many, sips of Holy Wine. "To take all that skill, all that wealth, all that time and then to use it on a wall that cracks when I fart and has all the heat-retention properties of a nun's tit. Pass me that bottle, lad." While he felt some affection for the raggedy drunk in his stained robes, Genoes had long learned to keep out of reach of Brother Evelyn when he was in his cups.

He flew up the ladder several rungs at a time to check on the old man asleep in his small room at the top of the Church. Genoes extricated the empty bottle from a loving embrace and pulled a blanket up to cover him. The first service was not for a few more hours; the Priest would be able to sleep it off.

At times, he worried that this small room with its unwashed, lost occupant was a premonition of his own future. He knew the Church of Dawn would accept him — would take anyone — if he could not identify a Class of his own to pursue. But, despite his love for the place, he could not quite imagine turning into someone like Brother Evelyn. He wanted more from life than this.

Nevertheless, despite its morose and unpredictable guardian, he loved coming here. He would take any opportunity to stand and look at that wall of coloured glass. So, perhaps a life spent here would not be so terrible?

He knew that, should he ask, he could move his small bundle of belongings out from the stables and into the second room. But that felt like it would be an irrevocable step toward locking down his future. He was not reconciled to that course of action as of yet; after all, you never knew what the next day would bring.

He slid down the ladder and made his way back down toward the entrance. He spent a few minutes lighting candles that had been allowed to burn low and reorganising furniture. He smiled as he did so: in many ways, he was almost Brother Genoes as it was.

Hearing footfalls on the stone steps outside, Genoes moved further into the main body of the Church to give the pilgrims space to enter. Then, with elastic ease, he ducked under the vast wooden crossbeams separating the foyer from the Church proper before turning to welcome the new visitors.

His heart sank to see Veron Geril and four or five of his assorted hangers-on crowding the doorway. "Ah, it was the horserat we saw sneaking through the rain," he sneered. "Did I not say so, Yorul?"

"You did, Veron. You did." The second speaker appeared to have an unfortunate combination of too many teeth and not enough jaw. Genoes assumed he did not simply say "*Yes*" to avoid adding to the flow of water that gushed in around them. He probably would have drowned

Master Roen if he had ever bought sausages. That thought made him smile.

"What is so funny, horserat?"

Genoes adjusted his position behind the crossbeams and took stock. There had been no shortage of confrontations with Veron and his interchangeable pack of hounds over the years. Most of those ended with some blood being spilt, but rarely enough to warrant anything more than a few days of feeling sorry for himself. There had been occasions, though, when he could sense how close he came to serious harm, usually when Drunnoc joined the hunt. Quickly checking the faces in front of him was reassuring; their alpha must have stayed home today. It was just to be some mild hazing, then. At worst, a beating.

He had long recognised that he was good at reading the atmosphere, and he did not think there was anything in the air to cause him undue concern. Perhaps it could all be diffused with some submission?

"No, sir. Just wet and cold, sir. Nothing funny, sir."

*

Veron looked at the skinny boy coming forward, shivering in front of him. If anyone were to ask, he would not have been able to articulate what about this orphan child engendered such rage within him. He just knew he wanted to hurt him and then keep hurting him. A voice in his head whispered profoundly unsettling things about what needed to be done about this boy, quite out of all proportion to rationality. For the most part, he managed to restrain that drive, recognising it was beneath him to give so much thought to a stableboy. But there were times the urge bubbled dangerously close to the surface. Like now. *"You could kill him,"* the voice whispered. *"No one would even care."*

The group of boys around him mocked the cravenness of the boy's words. "Cold, sir. Nothing funny, sir," mimicked a voice behind him. They all guffawed. Veron watched Genoes's eyes flick toward the one who had mocked him. He may have tried to hide it, but such raw contempt blossomed on the boy's face that Veron's temper roared to life. How dare this *nothing* feel superior to one of his betters? There was not one of them here who was not, at least, a Minor Noble. Was not Veron, himself, a Nominated Heir?! Such derision could not stand. Without another thought, his hand was drawing his sword and was swinging it down, stepping forward into the Church foyer.

Genoes seemed to feel the ignition of Veron's rage as a physical thing. He reacted instinctively, ducking beneath the crossbeam as the sword hissed down, the blade hurtling deep into the solid wood. Within a blink, he was wheeling away, putting distance between them.

*

The others regarded Veron cautiously. On a grey day, and without much more on their schedule, they had been up for tormenting their favourite target. Not one of them had anticipated this turn of events. That was the problem with Veron. He always needed to prove that he was as terrifying as Drunnoc, but bloodshed required greater planning than this. That was why they were happier to follow the directions of that strange younger boy. If anyone understood the necessity of keeping a father out of things, it was Lordling Trellec. Indeed, he had made an art out of such deception.

Moreover, with a Knight of the Road in the village, each of them recognised that understated discretion, for a few days, was the better part of valour. None of them wanted

to end up facing those glowing eyes at the end of a swinging sword. At the very least, coin should have been left with
the Constable so that he would be slow in arriving once the
word got out they were on a hunt.

That said, if Veron were truly minded to cut the horserat
into ribbons, they would not risk their place in the group
by protesting overmuch. What was a little more blood in
the grand scheme of things? An orphan's blood, at that.
Enough witnesses could be found to place them several
days' journey out of town. No one would believe it, of
course. But no one would make an issue of it.

"Don't just stand there — get him!"

As the others slipped past Veron, who was still trying
to pull his sword clear from its wooden prison, a keen observer might have made out a pair of softly glowing eyes in
the shadows.

CHAPTER TWELVE

"Rhythm and Flow"

Daine watched silently as the boy backed away from his pursuers.

His only option in the face of their assault was to retreat into the Church, but that superficial safety offered no way out. She saw the recognition of that flash across the boy's face but was pleased by the determination that quickly replaced it. He was afraid, for sure, but there was no panic. No surrender to an outcome he was running out of ways to avoid.

She did not think she had ever seen someone so young with such a capacity to <Dodge>. It was not a Skill she possessed. Her Class, after all, with all its healing properties, meant she did not need to focus on getting out of the way. Many was the aftermath of a fight, while repairing crushed and pierced armour, when she felt envious of the elegance of those who ducked and weaved. Although she imagined they felt much the same way when they watched her shrug off wounds that would kill them instantly.

It was not surprising that an orphan, living by his wits on the streets, would develop a significant ability to avoid trouble. If he had not, he would not have survived this long. But that sword hack? It should have cut him in two, no matter his capacity to move away. And yet, it was almost as if the boy were suddenly in two places at once and had chosen to switch to the body in the empty space, quite a feat for a child. She wondered what Class he held.

Unusually, the eyes of the Goddess told her little about him. There was past trauma, true, but it felt indistinct, as if whatever had occurred did not prey on his mind and her patron did not want her to consider. Likewise, there were flashes of his future deeds but, again, in an oddly imprecise way; the Goddess was rarely so coy about such things. "*Not yet*," a voice murmured in her mind.

There was no such uncertainty about the young men that were swarming around Genoes. Each and every one of them had committed deeds for which there would need to be justice. The one who still wrestled to free his sword from the wooden beam was the worst. To look at him was to feel an oily taint spread over her skin. He was one without a limit: his actions would continually spiral into greater outrages until he was stopped. Moments of futures, of other lives maimed and devastated, flowed around him as an unholy shroud. But there was some-thing else there, too. She could not quite pinpoint it, but this was not just typical malignancy. The Goddess did not want her to focus on it, that was clear, but that had rarely dissuaded her in the past.

None of those in front of her would escape her visit

to this village unscathed, But that boy with the sword. He needed particular attention.

*

"What's the matter with you all? Hold him still!"

The sword-wielder abandoned his futile effort to free his blade and joined his fellows in their faintly comic attempts to pin Genoes down.

The boy had discovered the little-known truth, much beloved of the Knights of the Road, that being outnumbered was not as problematic as commonly assumed. When it was two-or three-on-one, things often worked out poorly for the minority. However, when numbers swelled to more than that, it was possible to turn a numerical disadvantage into a strength.

In such a situation, the attackers could do little but get in each other's way. When too many swinging arms and legs went up against an opponent utterly focused on defence, it was all a lot of sound and fury, signifying little. The boy took blows, of course he did. He could not stand at the eye of that hurricane and not receive buffeting. But try as they might, none of the assailants could do much more than land a glancing connection here and there before one of his fellows got in the way and the power was diverted. And as the frustration in Veron's group reached a fever pitch, this did little to improve their coordination.

For his part, Genoes was enjoying himself.

In such a scrum of humanity, it did not take much to divert hands and fists into unintended directions and, more than once, he saw a nose bloodied by a punch, shins cracked by kicks, eyes watering with an impact initially fired his way.

When not in this mindset, Genoes found it hard to explain the feeling of this rhythm — and it was not just a state he reached when fighting either. A similar sense of flow oc- curred when he found the right way to peel potatoes, when the needle danced in his hand while stitching, or when jug- gling for crowds on the street. It was as if the world slowed down, yet he could continue at normal speed. He foresaw problems before they occurred and could choose from options as they opened out in front of him, their conse- quences clear as a winter stream.

But it was also more complicated than that.

Genoes could almost foresee what others planned to do and could adapt accordingly. He did not see the future, he knew that, but he had glimpses of possibilities. Lacking any knowledge of Skills, he was not able to explain what occurred to his perception at these times, but he knew he loved it.

However, when in this state, he knew not to try to throw punches of his own. Any movement to make a strike dis- turbed the rhythm and broke that bubble of concentration. His fist flashing outwards would unbalance the dance and make him lose his footing.

No, this was strictly a defensive dance: an instinctive, protective response unsuited to aggression.

There was also, and he did not like to dwell much on this, a weight behind his punches that disturbed him. Lord Amanan had let it be known that his son's fractured skull, an injury from which he would never recover his wits, had been caused by standing too close to a kicking horse. Genoes could well remember what happened in that alley, and while he felt no regret, the feeling of a concaving skull around his hand was not one he ever wished to repeat.

That had been the first time he realised some people

would not back down; that a smile and a joke could not de-escalate every situation. It was a lesson that had come back and back again with this gang of boys, and especially with Drunnoc and Veron.

*

The group was breathing hard now. Wet clothes covered in sweat and blood steaming in the light. They seemed to agree that this was not how such things should play out, and with his spirited defiance, the boy had earned his beating a hundred times over. Even the most reluctant of them now needed a violent release from this frustration.

At a shout from Veron, they broke away from their ineffective scrummage and spread out to form a loose circle, Genoes at the centre.

Daine could sense things were reaching their climax. If she had been impressed by how the lad had avoided a swinging sword, it was nothing to the display she had just witnessed. She had known Assassins — friends and, briefly, enemies — with far less Speed than this boy displayed.

However, as was the problem for all in that Class, eventually, numbers would tell if you could not whittle the attackers down. The fact that Genoes seemed to be wholly focused on survival meant he had not taken advantage of the chaotic situation to thin out the crowd. Time and time again, Daine had watched an opening for a kick, an elbow, a stamp, which would have eliminated one of the threats, but the boy let it be. She could not understand that reluctance to take the necessary forward step. But, then again, her entire Class was built around barrelling forward, never mind the consequences. Who was she to judge another who chose a different path?

However, her trained eye could see that the group would make him pay for that naïveté.

A hush fell over the Church as Veron drew a thin knife and gestured for the others to do the same. To their credit, several of them grew uncomfortable. Or perhaps they were just wary, considering how many of their attacks had gone astray, of adding sharp implements to proceedings.

Genoes sucked in air as he regarded Veron hesitantly. This was an unwelcome development, and one with which he was unfamiliar. Even at their worst, these boys rarely wanted to do more than humiliate and dominate.

"Veron," he started.

"It is Lordling Geril to you!" Veron's voice was shrill, even to his own ears. He did not like how it sounded. The soft voice was whispering in his ear. "*You look weak. You cannot let this stand. Who will miss him?*"

And he stepped forward.

There was no gloating, which surprised Daine; and made her too late to intercede. In her experience, at this point, there would be some moments of gleeful monologue.

Instead, the ringleader stepped forward and sunk his knife into Genoes's chest.

Time seemed to stop for a moment, and even Veron's eyes widened in shock at the success of his gambit before the boy gasped and fell to the floor, blood streaming from the wound in his jerkin.

Silence and then chaos.

The group fell over each other in their haste to flee the Church. Veron, though, stood still, eyeing the body, if not with pleasure, then certainly with triumph. He bent to re-trieve his knife and backed out of the door, eyes on the body his whole way back. The voice in his head was purring in a way he did not find wholly objectionable. Was this how Drunnoc felt all of the time?

He went to follow his fellows.

*

While they had left in disarray, Daine could hear their growing bravado as they gained distance from their crime. The backslapping. The whooping. The braying. Any who were unfortunate enough to pass them in the road would think they had conducted some hilarious prank, not murdered a young child.

Yes, there was something very amiss in this village.

Daine slowly left the shadows. She did not think they would be back. There were alibis to be arranged, after all.

She walked toward the prone figure of the boy, the blood spreading out from his wound to carpet the floor in a red circle.

She'd noticed the extraordinary quality of the window light while she had been waiting for the boy to return. Cenwyn had been clear that if she could not find Genoes at the stable, he would find his way to the Church of Dawn by, at least, midmorning.

The colours streamed through the glass and picked up the red wetness, producing a glowing halo around the body on the floor.

She knew that the Churches of Dawn had been constructed to inspire awe. To ensure that everyone who stood facing the stained-glass wall would be humbled in the presence of the light. For sure, she remembered feeling that emotion once upon a time. But now? Now it left her feeling cold.

Standing over the body, she was, again, struck by the difference in their ages. Had she even been this young?

Had Gant ever looked at her, as she did this boy now, and felt despair? Despair at not having created a better world. Despair at knowing the weight of the burden that must be passed on. Despair at just being so damn old.

Roughly, she prodded the boy with her foot. "They've gone."

His eyes shot open; shocked to hear her voice.

Daine extended her hand. He took it and was hauled, with ease, to his feet. "So, which shopkeeper is missing his best blood sausage?"

CHAPTER THIRTEEN

"Too Late"

"He can stay here for a few days. Until it all blows over."

Daine watched Cenwyn busily fussing over Genoes and smiled. The Tailor obviously felt great affection for the boy, most clearly witnessed by the suspiciously fine cut of the orphan's clothes. She was sure this was not the first time Cenwyn's house had been a haven following one mishap or another.

For her part, she could admit there was something infectious about the boy's enthusiasm for absolutely everything. On their way back from the Church, Genoes had regaled the Knight with his thoughts on every topic under the sun: from his disapproval at a local Farmer leaving their field fallow for a season longer than necessary, to his amusement at the way the Miller left his thumb on the scales when dealing with the High Houses, to his bafflement as to why some young ladies and gentlemen, at first light, could be seen creeping from homes not their own. His sharp mind darted about in much the same way as his body in his confrontation with Veron's gang.

Her smile vanished at the thought of those boys, and Daine's mood darkened. The callous way the older boy had thrust the knife was not a childish game gone wrong. He had intended to kill Genoes. And was delighted at the thought that he had succeeded.

Veron, Drunnoc, that vicious Fire Witch, the man from the woods — Heroc, had the Archer called him? That was quite a litany of dark souls in a village at the far end of nowhere. Daine had lived long and seen much and had few illusions as to the capacity of humankind for endless cruelty. But even in her considerable experience, it was rare to confront such a range of hatefulness this far from one of the great Cities.

But then there was that strange presence she had felt around the Veron boy in the Church, and, indeed, was there not something like that behind Drunnoc's eyes when they had met during the hearing? Such a pull towards darkness in ones so young.

She could understand, if not forgive, how people became used to the cheapness of life when there was so much of it around them. In a City, or, worst of all, the Capital, with its teeming multitudes, it was far too easy to ignore the consequences of your actions. One of the few things she still appreciated about her time on the Road was that it allowed her to escape the press of humanity around the King.

But in a small village where you knew everyone's names and your great-grandparents had probably courted? It was beyond her ken how you could care so little for your fellows.

What was clear was that something was rotting at the heart of this place. And it needed cutting out. In her mind, she felt a satisfied hum of approval from the Goddess.

Pulling her thoughts back to the present, her eyes settled on the young boy again. Genoes was demolishing his third bowl of stew with all the ravenous hunger of a veteran with a Speed-heavy Class. The smile returned. She remembered, long ago, Farrah's constant outrage at the rations Gant provided when they were training. It has been all they could do, all working together, to protect their meagre portions from the Shadow Dancer's daily predations. But, of course, no amount of Speed could have saved Farrah in the end. "You are either quick, or you are dead" had been one of her favourite sayings.

It turned out, sadly, you could be both.

With a start, she stopped herself from travelling that memory.

He was an odd boy, for sure, but she did not need to let her imagination run away with her. He had enough about him to make some rich boys look foolish. That hardly made him uniquely gifted. She knew about his Strength already, and he probably had some good Dexterity. And, obviously, no shortage of Luck if, as an orphan, he'd managed to have the people of the village look out for him. There was quite some Charisma there, too — she constantly felt its pull on the corners of her mouth. Unfortunately, this was obviously the right combination to rub a black hole like Veron the wrong way.

That he had some unusual Skills was interesting and, if she had the time, she might want to explore that farther. But, against the need to address the darkness in the village, it was a minor thing.

Genoes was unusual but not extraordinary.

And she did not need to get involved.

"*And if my Aunty had balls, she'd be my Uncle.*" Gant, and his sayings . . . His voice had been showing up in her head more often of late — a sign she was getting old.

Walking past to refill the once again empty bowl, Cenwyn touched her back, smoothing out the cloth of her tunic. "How did it feel when you were out and about? You were lucky I had some things on order that looked like your size. I've let them out in the shoulders and thighs to give you more room." She raised her eyebrows at that, and he reddened. "Not that I'm saying you needed a bigger size, just that my clients don't usually need the range of movement you clearly want."

She grinned and nodded her forgiveness. She liked this man. Remembered liking him ten years back. "It is all exceptionally fine work. The lad's clothes too. A standard I'd expect to find in the Capital. There can't be enough people who can afford you all the way out here, can there? Have you ever thought about setting yourself up at the centre of things?"

"There's more important things to life than money."

She knew an open wound when she heard one, she had enough of them herself. So, she moved the conversation onwards. "Speaking of money, how much do I owe you?"

"You kept an eye on the boy, that's good enough." She was unsure what part of the story made it sound like Daine had done anything other than watch as Genoes was stabbed. People were funny with what they chose to hear. "Besides, I will make coin enough from people around here knowing I've outfitted the Darkhelm. If you're feeling generous, mayhap mention my name when someone asks about your clothing on the Road."

"How do you get to be like you?" The question burst out of Genoes as if he could keep it in no longer. The explosion was mirrored by a mouthful of stew that flew to land on the corner of the table.

Cenwyn cuffed him good-naturedly. "You know better than that, lad. You never ask a woman about three things: her age, her purity, and how she obtained her Class."

Genoes was not so sure about any of that. He knew he sometimes rubbed people up the wrong way, but it was hard to tell why one question might cause a frown rather than any other. For example, people liked to answer "How are you?" but sometimes found "How come you did that?" rude. It was very confusing. It was all information, after all, wasn't it? But he couldn't worry about offence right now. He might never get a chance to break bread with a Knight of the Road again. He would learn everything he possibly could about her before she moved on.

"Is it true you were born covered in iron, and a Blacksmith had to hammer you free?"

The Tailor opened his mouth, but Daine stopped him with an amused shake of her head. She had worried about how Genoes would respond to the assault on him. It seemed his coping method was to ask questions, and she was happy to oblige with answers. "I've not heard that one before. And no. I was born the same way as everyone else: bloody, screaming, and bald as a coot."

Genoes swiftly nodded as if ticking something off a mental list. "What about the Dragon of Balon Keep? Did you really kill it with your bare hands?"

"Dragons breathe fire, lad. A sword and shield aren't

much use once they're melted down to slag. Neither's armour, if truth be told. And it's not as hard to kill a dragon as people make out. They're smaller than you'd think, and no one, not even a dragon, has much a mind for anything once you have them by the throat."

The hours passed as the three batted around myths and legends that had arisen around the Lady Darkhelm. She was happy to accept the Tailor's offer for food and drink and shared countless stories in payment. She could not remember the last time she had spoken so freely.

There was, she had to admit, pleasure in the company of others. She wondered when that truth had been forgotten. Or, thinking back to her childhood in Gant's school, had it ever been something she had learned? For Genoes's part, despite the puncturing of some of the more outlandish stories — he was devastated to hear that the Boar of Autumn was not eight foot high and that the Fields of Nimore did not *still* flow with the blood of those Daine has slain ("It was a few minutes of tussle with five bandits; two of them got away to spin the tale") — the hero-worship in his eyes glowed brighter with each minute.

The early afternoon light moved toward murky dusk, and her stock of shareable stories began running short. She was debating how best to describe the Fall of Penwyre without mentioning any of the more questionable behaviours when Cenwyn, pipe in mouth, interrupted the flow of the boy's questions

"What about the Tower of the Halcyon Princess — is that one true? I remember hearing about that when I was but a kid."

All of Daine's pleasant calm drained away in a sudden torrent of memory. That Tower. The cruel laughter. Her, in the dark, holding a small, broken body. Screams. And blood. So much blood.

Cenwyn saw the change in her expression. "I'm sorry. I didn't mean anything by it."

Genoes frowned. "Wasn't that about some Baron who stole someone's daughter to force a land deal? You freed her, didn't you?"

"No. I was too late." Daine drained her tankard and stood. There was a heaviness in the air now. It was a weight that neither the Tailor nor the boy could understand, but could feel as if it crushed their chests.

This was why she preferred to be on her own. You could never let it get too comfortable. Eventually, something swam up from the depths to drown any connection in sorrow. "That's what none of those legends explain, lad. Don't matter if it's me or the Silverbow or Gallant Stonehand himself that shows up. We're always too late. We get to dry the tears and try to wash away some of the pain with blood. But it's always too late. I surely slew the Dragon of Balon Keep, and wasn't I a glorious sight when I was doing it? But three families had lost sons before I got there, and I doubt they sing of my deeds with much pride. I took the head of Warlock Urun, but those people he hurt were never the same. There's no comfort for the terror of the night in looking at a head on a spike. I went through there five, maybe six, years ago. It was a place of ghosts. They couldn't carry on. A whole town was wiped off the map. People like to talk of the light and innocence of the Halcyon Princess, but I found her in the dark —"

She was drowning in an ocean of pain. The companionship they had offered this day had opened a door she kept shut. The weakness that she let out was unacceptable.

She rose abruptly and turned for the exit. "Master Tailor, I'd be obliged if you'd keep the lad inside for the evening. There are things out there that need something doing about. That I need to do something about."

And eyes streaming with a flow of water she thought long extinct, she made her way out into the darkening streets.

CHAPTER FOURTEEN

"Trembling Earth"

I n the years to come, there would be much discussion and disagreement about "The Night the Earth Trembled." Not that there would have been anything wrong with calling it "The Night that Daine Orban Set About Balancing the Scales of Justice," but it made for a more poetic song title, and what Bard does not love a tortured metaphor?

To hear the stories, the population of the village would have needed to be five or six times bigger to incorporate everyone who had "*seen it with their own eyes!*" But, of course, human nature being what it was, most had instead locked their doors, shuttered their windows, and hunkered down, trying to ignore the shrieks and screams that punctured the night air.

That Yorul Carel, fourth son of House Carel, had his left hand removed at the wrist was in no doubt. Although whether his father had done it due to the misuse of House funds or because the Lady Darkhelm had dragged Lord Carel from his bed, put the axe in his hand and given him some words of encouragement, was less clear.

Thus, although it was genuinely agreed that the reckoning began at House Carel, things became less distinct from that point on. House Blount lost five Men-at-Arms after orders to "keep that mad bitch at the gate" were hysterically given. Their wasted lives were added to the weight of justice called upon Haver Blount. This was a pressure he did not survive. But whether that happened before the fire at the Hall or during the inexorable fighting leading to Keep Trellec was unclear.

But it was the grim familiarity of it that most troubled Daine. She always tried to view such a thorough cleansing — although she was struggling to feel there was anything "clean" about the red river through which she was currently wading — as achieving something tangible. That such brutal and efficient punishment would leave this village in a better, more stable place for years to come.

But she'd played this tune too many times to hold on to any illusions.

She well knew that someone would write a song about this night, and it would be the talk of the taverns for years, perhaps decades. How Lady Darkhelm had rooted out corruption in the High Houses on a night of dark slaughter. It would have a beat to which you could tap your foot and a chorus that could be bellowed out in a taproom. But not a single Lord, hearing that song, would think there was anything in it for them; that the fates of the Lordlings of Houses Carel, Blount et al. (and Geril and Trellec when she ran those two to ground) had anything to do with his behaviour or that of his own family.

No, the moral most would take from tonight's actions would not be the importance of "raising your heirs to know right from wrong," but rather it would be another tale of "how entirely implacable is the Darkhelm." And if there were any tangible use in that particular message, she would not keep finding herself waist-deep in men seeking to die at her hand.

A push from the Goddess moved her one step to the left as a sword slashed past her ear. She dropped her shoulder into her assailant, who exploded backwards into the wall, and kept walking the street leading to Keep Trellec.

She did regret the deaths of all these retainers.

Few of the broken bodies that marked her path, door to door across the village, deserved what they had received from her. Of course, one or two of them had indulged in the same excesses as their master, and she was glad to ensure they shared their fate. But most of them were just following orders. Little more than unwilling corn in the path of a scythe.

As she stood at the final crossroads before reaching Keep Trellec, Daine paused, stretched out her back and checked on her cooldowns. She had not needed to use many of her Skills this night — this was a village, not a battlefield — but it never hurt to ensure she had access to her full array of powers.

By her count, just a handful of the Lordlings on her list were left now A couple from the attack on Genoes at the Church had fled once word got out of her crusade, and then, of course, Drunnoc Trellec. Yet, oddly, the Goddess gave no hint of what Daine would see when she finally confronted him.

He was clearly the dark centre of events, from the

visions she had received tonight and the tearful confessions of so many "very sorry" young men. Veron Geril and his ilk orbited that void, but the Trellec boy was at its core.

Perhaps removing him would ease the tightness in her chest? Would help the light in the village shine more clearly.

But that odd feeling she had experienced in the Church when looking at Veron kept rearing its head. There had been something behind that young man's eyes that went beyond human motivation.

Drunnoc might be crucial in explaining what had occurred here, but she would be much surprised if it ended with him. The lack of clarity, or honesty, from the Goddess troubled her.

After a few more minutes of slow walking, she reached the gate of Keep Trellec. Unlike the residences of the High Houses, which sat proudly in the middle of the village, this lay just off the main road, almost hidden in the darkness of the woods.

That was not the only difference, now she came to look at it.

Whereas all the other properties were essentially vanity buildings of stone and glass, this seemed to be an adequately designed military compound. Presumably, there were plans to turn this village into something more substantial, and this building would, along with the Church of Dawn, form the heart of a bustling town.

But there was something quite incongruous about this looming presence in an otherwise unexceptional part of the world. It was all dark metal and treated wood. Daine, who had spent her evening simply walking through doors barred to her, knew that storming the gatehouse in front of her would prove a challenge.

The more she looked at Keep Trellec, the more her frown grew. How had she not realised what an exceptionally well-put-together place this was? Of course, deep down, she knew the answer. So did Old Gant. *"Too full of your own puissance, ain't you? All hail the Darkhelm. Swaggering around, whetting your sword on the common-Classed, and you don't even notice a bloody stronghold where none has any place to be. Moon-eyed moron."*

She took a few steps back, trying to adjust her eyes to the scale of the building. It was a square keep with corner towers packed with loopholes. From where she stood in front of the gatehouse, it looked like all the walls were the same height as the towers. There could be a hundred men inside, easily. What was something of this size doing out here? The cost of building it alone — both in terms of material and labour — would have been colossal. And that was before employing enough men to defend it. When she had come through on Tour before, this had certainly not been here, nor even a whisper of a plan to construct it.

Was it credible to think that all of this had been built in ten years? Not impossible, nothing was with enough coin, but this was all an exceptional expense quite out of proportion to the importance of the location.

She thought back to her impression of Lord Trellec a few days before. A smugly satisfied man, not one who struck her as having the wealth, ambition, or hubris to fund this folly.

So, what was she looking at? A fortress more in keeping with a frontier town than a backwoods Western province. Again, she felt there was more to all this than she could piece together. And the Goddess continued to sit in her head in complete silence.

There was movement at one of the windows, and a boy and an old man emerged to stand on a balcony. The boy, Drunnoc Trellec, she recognised from their time in court. The older man, though, was unfamiliar and looked keen to be anywhere else.

"I have given some thought about what to do with you, Lady Darkhelm." The boy's voice was oddly flat. If he was afraid, she could not hear it in the words which carried easily to her across the night. She thought the older man must be a Mage, enhancing the boy's voice. <Air Specialism>? Maybe. Most of them had a version of that Skill.

"Many have, Lordling Trellec. Not sure any ever came up with an answer that stuck."

"Yes, that's what I find most fascinating. So hard to beat in a fight. Certainly, no one I have found seems confident they could manage it. Immune to magic. Layla clarified that for us. None of the poisons we've tried seem to have worked. A little bird told me, reluctantly, that arrows have their limitations. So, what are we to do about you?"

She remembered from Court that he seemed to be immune to <Intimidation>. She triggered in anyway and watched the Mage almost sink to his knees. "You could come down here and accept judgement."

"Oh, I don't think I want to do that. I am not for the likes of you, Daine Orban. Not for the likes of you at all. I have applied some logic to the matter. You are strong, you are resilient, and you heal faster than I can hurt you — by the way, the latter is a trait I would find most attractive in other circumstances. However, and this is where things become interesting, just because I cannot use magic on you does not mean that is not my solution. Please meet one of our House Mages, Boruld."

The old man, now back to his feet, made no sign of greeting other than to continue to stare at the ground.

"He is not as interesting to look at as Layla, but he has a number of interesting Skills that I feel will benefit this situation."

"*Withdraw.*" The warning pulse from the Goddess was swift and spectacularly unusual. Indeed, had she ever had such a premonition? Daine took a few hesitant steps backwards, eyes locked on Boruld.

"So, I need a solution unaffected by how strong you are or how fast you heal. So how about —" Drunnoc signalled to Boruld, who muttered a word of power Daine could not place — "I drop you down a very big hole?"

The ground opened up beneath Daine's feet, and she fell, plummeting hundreds of feet, to hit bedrock with a splintering of breaking bones and an explosion of organs.

Mercifully, she was senseless for much of the healing process. Gradually, she became aware of her skeleton shifting back into place, internal ruptures sealing and split skin reknitting. She had no concept of how long the process took, but, eventually, as always, she climbed back to her feet and, shaking her head to clear the fog, looked around.

It was almost pitch black at the bottom of the hole, with just the tiniest pinprick of light above to show the way out. It would be a long climb up, for sure, but nothing that would be too difficult.

Daine smiled grimly; did that fool think he was the first to try that? She activated her climbing Skill: a minor version of <Grappel>, but one that had always served her well. Once it was live, she punched a hole in the wall, and then another, and used the handholds to start the slow climb upwards.

That magically enhanced voice suddenly boomed out.

"My Lady Darkhelm. So glad you've woken up. Sorry, did you think I was finished? Of course I knew the fall wouldn't kill you. It was quite the mess you made when you hit the bottom, though. That aside, how do you keep something in a hole you don't want to escape? You fill it in."

She did not have a second to react. Boruld's magic flared, and there was overwhelming pressure as the hole closed up around Daine. Crushing the breath out her lungs and holding her in the tightest of embraces.

Drunnoc walked back into the Keep without a backwards glance. As he went, a careful listener might have heard the words he muttered: 'The Night the Earth Trembled' would be a good title for a song, I think."

CHAPTER FIFTEEN

"Fragments: Games, Walls and Bitches"

Genoes, eyes glinting, watched the three cups bounce backwards and forward.

Cenwyn spun, dropped, raised, and circled them on the table with an uncanny deftness. At times they were a blur; at other times, moving in an impossibly slow orbit. Finally, their dance suddenly halted, and he looked up at the boy.

"So, where's the ball?"

Without hesitation, Genoes reached out and tapped the middle cup.

With a wry grin, the Tailor revealed the small wooden ball hidden under the middle cup. "Ten times in a row, lad. Remind me never to hazard coin against you."

Genoes smiled back; he knew that gesture was what was expected of him, but he did not understand the point being made. There was nothing complicated about what they were doing. Cenwyn put a ball under one of the three cups and then moved the three around some. Was he supposed to forget which one it was under? He must have been missing something in the interaction.

"Can I try?"

"Sure." Cenwyn pushed the cups across the table and went to refill his pipe. He liked the boy — did not everyone? — but he did find him unnerving. That cup trick was somewhat of a favourite of his. As his Class had exceptional Dexterity, he could count on the fingers of one hand the number of people he would fail to misdirect when he put his mind to it.

For the boy to pick it out ten times in a row . . .

There was a crash, and Cenwyn turned to see Genoes standing behind the table, chair overturned. His skin was pale, and his eyes huge.

"The Lady Darkhelm . . ." With that, the boy ran out the door.

*

Pressure.

Pain.

She could not gather her thoughts.

Something had happened. Happened. Was happening —

Pain.

Pressure

She could not concentrate on —

Pressure

Pain.

*

Kirstin winced at her reflection, turning her head to take in the damage.

Drunnoc's men had not been kind when asking about

the events in the woods. Heroc had been one of the Lordling's favourites. An older, terrifying man who did his bidding no matter how cruel without hesitation. That loss caused . . . frustration. Unfortunately, as Jak was indisposed with a Healer — his splintered wrist needed rebuilding — there were limited other outlets for that annoyance.

In some ways, she wished Drunnoc had struck her himself. It was more humiliating that he simply watched.

Her nose was broken again, she thought. If she were lucky, that was the worst of it and the rest of the swelling would go down with time. A broken jaw, or a fractured cheekbone, would mean she'd have to join Jak at the Healer. That would be expensive. The Trellecs made clear any use of House resources was to be taken out of their pay.

She smiled grimly, splitting her lips. There was an irony that following Drunnoc's orders to waylay a Knight of the Road, with a promise that success would complete their financial obligations, had ended up pulling them into further debt.

After paying for board and lodging in the Keep, their kit, their uniforms and various sundries, there was barely anything left to put by. Moreover, Jak's time with the Healer would cost several months' wages, wiping out the meagre savings she had accrued.

Meaning they'd be stuck here for even longer.

She splashed water on her face.

"I could kill him for you," the Knight had said.

She could not meet her own eyes in the mirror.

*

There was no change.

Not in the pressure.

Not in the pain.

But she was used to pain.

Yes, these unstoppable waves as bones broke, then re-knit, to be crushed again, were . . . she did not have the language to describe it. But as there seemed no end, she could focus on something else.

The agony — and that word did not go far enough — became, as far as such things were possible, background noise. So, she fled from the pain inside herself. To a place where she could start to think. She could leave this pain behind, outside of herself.

The constant pressure, though, was different. To not be able to move. To be held in this crushing embrace was intolerable.

Within the place to which she retreated, the only part of her now free to do anything, Daine screamed.

*

Genoes knew she had wanted him to stay inside.

She had been planning to do things this night that were both wrong and, in some indefinable way, entirely correct. He did not understand how an action could be both those things at the same time, but knew it to be a truth.

She had not wanted him to see her doing the goodbad things but would do them anyway.

He passed bodies in the street.

Some of them were mean men that he knew and, with a spurt of . . . something, he was glad to see them fallen. Some of those he saw on the ground had thrown him a coin now and again, and always had half a pie to share with him when the mood took them.

He did not like what had happened to them.

Was that why she had been so sad when she left? Because of the necessity to do the goodbad things?

Regardless, Genoes could feel her pain calling to him. He did not know why or how, but he had always seemed drawn to suffering things. A cat stuck up a tree. An old woman who lived alone and had fallen. A lost child separated from its mother in a busy marketplace. He did not have much to offer, but following this sense and doing what he could to provide remedy was the right thing to do. Was that how the Lady Darkhelm felt?

But he had never felt this call with such blazing-hot intensity before.

He ducked his head and ran onwards.

*

Solid walls were around the place in her mind where she had retreated. The pain and the pressure were all outside these walls. She could not stay here for long, Daine recognised, but it was a welcome reprieve.

"There will be a time," Gant had growled, *"when you'll need to lock yourself up tight. You'll know it when it happens; there's no preparation for it. It could be grief. It could be pain. It could be any manner of thing. But you'll be overwhelmed and need to take yourself away, or you'll shatter."*

They had all listened to him, but had they believed it was true? Secure in their young, strong bodies, confident in their abilities, had they been able to understand to what he was alluding? She knew she had not.

Daine had seen the consequence of that youthful arrogance in too many friends no longer with them.

"You'll build a nice little fortress to squat in while the worst storm rages. But you can't stay there, do you get me? It'll feel safe, hidden away from whatever you fled. And you won't want to leave. Now, don't get me wrong, no one will judge you if you choose to stay there. No one has the right to, least of all me. But that'll be it, you hear me? If you

stay in that place a second longer than you need to, you will never leave. If you want to come out the other side, consider it a tactical retreat to prepare for a new offensive. That place cannot be your new home. Unless you need it to be."

A tactical retreat . . .

She had some time, then, to think and to plan.

There was no magic behind what was occurring. That Mage had ripped open a hole in the earth and let it reseal around her. He was not holding her here. She was trapped somewhere she should not be, and the world sought to return to balance, which could only be achieved by crushing her out of existence. But she was healing as fast as the damage could be caused. So that balance could not be restored, and the ground continued to press down.

Daine could not move because of the tightness of the compacted earth around her. All of her Skills that would be useful in such a situation required momentum. But, if what was holding her was not magical, then a finite amount of material was pressing upon her. She could move if she could create some space, no matter how small. And if she could move, she could bring her Strength to bear on the problem.

That would not be an elegant solution, but still one that was usually effective.

Within her oasis of logical calm, she could see only one way to create space to move.

For a second, she hesitated.

Did she wish to do this? To do what was necessary to continue? She could stay here and let it all end. Eventually, the healing would cease — even the resilience of Knights of the Road had its limits — and that would be that. She would not even know when it happened. And with that, she could finally put down her burdens.

But that was an idle dream. She would not, could not, forget the flashes of the future she had seen. She could not choose to let those visions come true. Could not let that darkness fall.

Not today.

"Don't get ahead of yourself, my Lady of the Darkhelm. Don't worry about the destination. You put one foot on the Road and follow it with the next. Let what will come, come." She could concede that, at times, there had been words of wisdom from that old goat.

She stepped from her fortress, and the pain swallowed her again.

Daine took a moment to let it settle, like a malignant cocoon, and then slowly, inexorably, remorselessly, began breathing in the soil around her.

*

Jak stared out of the window at the spot where, he was told, the Knight had fallen.

He flexed his fingers, feeling them click and pop as they moved. A sloppy healing job meaning he would never be the same again. Sure, he could hold a knife, but he had lost any of his Skills linked to dual wielding.

"Bitch."

If you had asked him, at the moment, he would not have been able to tell you to whom he was referring. The Knight who crushed his wrist. The Healer who did the bare minimum to save his hand. His sister who — well, who forever was deserving of scorn.

Too weak. Too unwilling to take tough decisions. Too quick to judge. Too like his mother.

Bitches all.

He knew deep down that the rage he carried within him

like hot coal was disproportionate. That there was nothing in his life to justify the surges and explosions that characterised his days. And that, perhaps, angered him even further.

He liked Veron and, to a lesser extent, Drunnoc because they approved of these moments. Encouraged them. Gave him an outlet to express himself creatively. They didn't look down on him.

Not like those bitches.

Movement caught his eye, and he grinned as he watched that orphan boy everyone fawned over approach the spot where that Knight had vanished.

Subconsciously touching his knives, Jak slunk away from the window and to the stairs leading to the gatehouse.

*

Daine had lost count of the mouthfuls of dirt she had dragged into her stomach and lungs.

The sensation of so much cold earth sitting within her was appalling, but what was that discomfort in her grand scheme of agony?

She could not displace much of that around her, but it was something. She had not dared to try to move yet. But now her lungs and belly were full, and her cards were played. It was now or never.

She started at her head, seeking any give in the weight pressing down on her. Nothing. Torso. Arms. Fingers. Toes. No movement. No let-up of the squeeze around her.

There was no panic. Not anymore. She was beyond that.

No despair. Just resignation. And regret for that which she could not stop.

She prepared to return to her fortress. To allow the weight to settle upon her until her candle would flicker no more.

And at the moment her spirit withdrew her finger twitched.

*

In his room at the top of the Keep, Boruld's eyes widened in shock.

CHAPTER SIXTEEN

"An Inexcusable Breach of Protocol"

It's nice to be back in the middle of things, thought Fion, settling into his favourite chair.

Of course, he regretted the loss of life that had caused all these Lords and Ladies of the High Houses to appear at his gate. A terrible, terrible thing had happened, after all. Blood and tears and all sorts of upset. But that notwithstanding, he appreciated seeing all his old friends back around his table.

"Something simply must be done. It's carnage, absolute carnage, out there!" Lord Michaeleas was mopping the sweat from his brow, his face, and his chins with an enormous handkerchief. If the reports were accurate, he had run all the way here once there was a knock at his door. It was probably the nimblest movement the man had undertaken in thirty years. "There's just no respect. No respect for common decency at all."

The pillars of the community murmured their agreement to his words. Fion thought it instructive that, with blood literally running in the streets, it was a lack of etiquette that seemed to be most troubling to those in this room.

"There is precedence for such a cull. We all remember Whistletown?" Lady Culloden noted. "This callous and unrestrained approach is shocking. Where is the due process? Where are the proper procedure? The Lady Darkhelm has acted at the very edge of her authority tonight."

"She killed my son," wailed Lady Blount, "a boy who had never done anything wrong in his life!"

There was an awkward silence while each member of the group considered the information they held about the recently deceased Lordling. Stones and glass houses, after all, but that comment was stretching things a little far. If the bereaved mother noticed the shift in mood, she did not let it affect her caterwauling.

"Perhaps you could . . ." Fion indicated for his wife to assist the Lady Blount from the room. This was a time for serious people, after all. People who kept their heads in a crisis. And if there was one thing they had all learned about the Blounts this evening, they tended to lose their heads. Ha. That was a fine one. He would find a moment to weave that into the conversation once she had gone. He realised he was smiling inappropriately and returned his expression to its sombre, grave mask.

Several other, more fragile group members went with the two women. Including Lord Carel, who had arrived crying, carrying the axe he had used on his son's arm. He had not had much of use to add to proceedings thus far. With chairs emptying, his visitors resettled themselves around the table, with the usual jockeying for precedence.

"She'll be coming for you next, Fion."

At Lady Culloden's words, a few heads turned to look at him. Others shifted nervously in their seats as if questioning whether Keep Trellec was quite the haven they had thought. "We all know your coin has kept the worst of your boy's deeds quiet."

"I am not alone in that, my Lady, or else none of you would have come here. You would have opened your doors and invited the Darkhelm in for tea. But, instead, you fled to the protection of my walls. So, I will have respect at my table, or you can return to whatever remains of your household." He was quite delighted to see her eyes drop to the floor.

Yes, he did like being back at the heart of things.

Swirling the dark liquid in his cup, he paused momentarily, choosing his words carefully. "Today, my friends, has been a reminder of the Throne's power." The others around the table leaned forward, long familiar with Fion's theme but sensitive enough to the mood to allow him to lecture. "There are, how many do we think? Twenty? Thirty Knights of the Road currently on Tour? They are all equally capable of the destruction that the Darkhelm has brought to our hearths. They act quite beyond our laws and entirely outside our ability to constrain. Our pleas to the King to call back his hounds have fallen upon deaf ears. Instead, we are told to accept their deprivations on our communities, once every ten years, as the cost of being allowed to be part of the Kingdom."

He stopped to sip his drink, savouring its earthy flavour, and their eyes locked on him in the silence. That quiet thrill of attention had been so missing from his life. "We spoke, long ago, about the need, the desperate need, for us to take measures to secure our freedom from such tyranny. It has often been a matter of personal regret that I have been the only one who sought to take the measures we discussed."

No one would meet his eyes, so he let the silence grow. He knew they had all viewed him as a foolish old man while his Keep was under construction. For all their warm words when they had been making plans, they had watched with amusement as he poured his entire fortune into a building to give a Knight of the Road pause. For sure, there were those in this room who had provided credit for materials at a "preferential rate," but they had treated him as a host to be fed upon, not a friend to support. Then, when all the money was gone, they saw him marry indiscreetly, laughing behind their hands, and pour all that acquired fortune into the same folly. For that was what they had called the building that now kept them so very safe: Trellec's Folly.

Oh, how they had laughed at him. Well, no one was laughing now, were they?

"What I feared has now come to pass. It has happened, and we, well, you, were not prepared. The King has sent one of his destructive emissaries who has, without any discussion, slaughtered the young of our Houses. Now, we may admit that there has been somewhat of a failure of discipline amongst the youth of the village." If there was a disbelieving cough from a Lord who had received considerable compensation from Fion to overlook a stable hand who had lost an eye, no one remarked upon it. "But the events tonight have been an inexcusable breach of protocol."

"That is all well and good, Fion," said Lord Michaeleas who had drenched through his first handkerchief and had started on another, "but we have an unstoppable maniac killing people on our streets. We are here because you fore-saw it. Prepared for it. We accept that we were wrong in ignoring your advice. We need to know now what you pro-pose we do about it!"

Fion did not miss that they were all turning to him for leadership. It was not just the sturdy comfort of his walls — well, not just them, anyway — but that they rec-ognised the truth of his arguments. Who could disagree now, now that they had literal skin in the game, that they needed to take measures to protect themselves from these infernal Knights of the Road?

"We certainly, unlike the Blounts, need to keep our heads, Lord Michaeleas!" No one laughed. Perhaps it was not that funny a jape after all, now he thought about it. Never mind. He pressed onwards.

"There comes a moment, ladies and gentlemen when a stand is required. We will not accept such derision from those who consider themselves our betters when we need to show our discontent. If we allow the Darkhelm to murder our children, to drag us from our beds, to cause us to flee our homes in terror, then we accept we are little more than common-Classed for the King to play with as he pleases. When we come of age, we all pledge to give our allegiance to the Crown. But where is the honour it owes us in return? We have not seen it tonight. No, indeed, we have not. We have seen the contempt of the King. We have seen the dis-dain in which we are held through the ease with which he wastes the lives of his Lordlings. Something must be done."

Fion felt all the eyes on him. Felt his breath quicken at the recognition that they were his now. That they would do anything for him. Perhaps he could tell the joke about the Blounts again? They would laugh this time, for sure.

"She's dead."

All heads in the room swivelled to take in Trellec's youngest boy, who stood in the doorway. The strange one. The one they had warned their daughters and their sons to avoid.

With a flush of frustration, Fion felt the atmosphere in the room drain away. "Drunnoc, you are confined to your room."

The boy shrugged. "I was coming to tell you the Knight is dead."

The words were so incomprehensible, so beyond expectation, that Fion felt himself smile. "Knights of the Road do not just die, Drunnoc."

"Oh, she did not 'just die,' Father. I had her killed."

Silence. And then a chorus of questions and raised voices. Fion stood and unceremoniously forced his son from the room.

Once outside, with the door closed, Fion pushed him roughly against the wall. "What is the meaning of this?" His anger hissed through clenched teeth, his face inches from the boy's.

"I thought it would please you, Father. I am terribly sorry if it does not. You seemed so worried about her coming here."

Father and son regarded each other for a moment. Intrigue warred with rage in Fion's head as his boy, his strange, strange boy, peered owlishly up at him. Then, after a few moments, intense curiosity won the day. "Tell me more."

CHAPTER SEVENTEEN

"Playing Nice"

From the shadow of the gatehouse, Jak's eyes were fixed with reptilian stillness on the boy.

Genoes seemed fixated on a small mound of earth, repeatedly bending to press his hands into the dirt before standing, fretting around, to return to the same spot again.

To hear people speak about this child, you would think there was something wonderfully unique about him. As if his being an orphan made him, in some way, "special." Well, Jak was an orphan, too, was he not? No one ever made his life easier because of it, quite the reverse. Those in the village coddled this boy in a way that had never been forthcoming to Jak. All warm smiles and kind words, whereas he received only scowls and scorn.

Jak felt his blood heat in that familiar, comfortable way. It had been the same story his whole life. No one ever gave him a fair shake, never looked the other way when he was caught with his hand somewhere it should not be, never believed him when he spun his version of the tale. That constant mistrust meant he had to work twice as hard to make half the progress of everyone else. No one could doubt that the odds of life were forever weighed against him.

Despite it all, he'd still managed to drag himself up, with no help from anyone, to his current position. And he was, if not proud, then satisfied that he was finally getting something like his due. Against that backdrop, surely everyone could see why it was wrong that boys like this could come along and have everything handed them on a plate?

With that injustice rapidly combusting inside him, Jak pushed away from the wall and strutted outwards. "What are you up to, horserat?" He liked the nickname Veron had for this boy. Liked the derision in it. Liked the sense of casual superiority it engendered.

Genoes, startled by the voice, stepped instinctively back. "I didn't see you there."

Jak enjoyed the faint quiver in the boy's voice and smiled at how his body curled around itself in fear. He bent to touch the ground Genoes had been busying himself about. The soil was loose as if it had just been dug over. "What have you buried? What're you looking for? Have you got some secret treasure hidden here, horserat?"

"Nothing. I was just looking, that's all." Genoes was backing away to the escape of the road.

Jak stood and narrowed his eyes. "Stop shifting about. You're up to something, I can smell it on you. You are going to tell me what. Come here. Now!" He moved quickly toward Genoes, who stumbled backwards, falling to the ground with his arms spreading out in a tangle. Standing over him, Jak put his foot on an outstretched hand and pressed down. The boy winced in pain.

"What have you got hidden here?"

"It's nothing, I promise. Please. Let me up. You're hurting me."

"Please let me up," Jak mimicked. "Is that how you get everyone on your side? By being pathetic? Do you think you'll always get what you want if you're like this?" He ground the heel of his foot down harder. "Well, it don't work on me. I can see the game you're playing, and I know the rules of it too. You've got hold of something you don't want anyone else to know about, and you thought this was the place to hide it. So now you've been caught, and you're trying to weasel out of it. Now, get up and see if we can't make a man of you."

*

Favouring his injured hand, Genoes climbed, reluctantly, to his feet. He had played his part in this scene too many times. If it was not Veron or his gang, it was some nobody like Jak taking pleasure in being bigger and stronger. It did not matter what the stakes were, there would be no appeasing that hungry glint in the older boy's eyes without blood.

Jak drew one of his spare knives and threw it, pointing down at Genoes's feet. "That's for you. Pick it up."

Genoes backed away from the knife as if stung. "I don't want it."

"I don't care. You can pick it up, and we can play a little, or you can do without, and we can see how that works out for you. It's all the same to me. I'm just giving you a proper crack at it, that's all. No one ever said I wasn't fair." That claim rang hollow, even to Jak's ears.

Trying to ignore the clamour for help from the ground

beneath him, Genoes weighed up the situation. There
was little to be done to avoid what was about to occur.
Before Jak could catch him, he could get to the road and
be long gone, but that insistent pull to this spot would remain. Whatever had happened to the Lady Darkhelm had
occurred here, and he would not be able to help if he was
cowering on the edge of the woods. However, if this confrontation were going to happen, it would be on his terms.
"I don't need your knife. I've got my own." He withdrew a
bundle of rags from behind his back, from which he carefully unwrapped a dagger.

*

It was a pretty piece of work to Jak's appraising eye, and his
wolfish smile broadened. Perhaps there would be more of
a reward for this entertainment than he'd thought. "Where
did you get that? Did you nick it?"

Genoes was almost cradling the blade rather than holding it. "I didn't steal it. I earned it."

With a serpentine movement, Jak shot out to pluck the
knife from the boy. Genoes reflexively jabbed out with it,
cutting into the palm of a recently healed hand. The heat
in Jak's blood blossomed into a furnace. He loved this feeling more than anything else because, once this blaze roared
into life, it meant he did not need to worry about trivial
things, such as consequences, anymore. He could just let
that fire rage.

Stooping to retrieve the knife he had thrown to Genoes
with his left hand, he drew a second one with his right and
dropped into a fighting stance. "So, you think you've got
some sharp claws, horserat? How about we test that?"

Repellent human he might be, but no one would deny
Jak's skill with his blades. It was the key reason he had a

place with the local Lordlings, albeit at the periphery. While there was no shortage of Rogues in and around the village, few could claim to be genuinely ambidextrous. More than once, Jak had drawn the blood of someone far his superior in pure talent who had underestimated the complexity of fighting someone as competent with both hands. Jak had grown to love the look of concern that flashed in the eyes of even the most experienced knife-fighter when they realised what they were getting themselves into. His injury may have robbed him of the more exotic Skills he had developed, but there was no time like the present to begin to earn them back.

Without further discussion, he feinted a wild slash with the blade in his left hand. Then, when Genoes clumsily overcommitted to block it, stumbling to one side, he brought his right blade in to flick, almost delicately, a line down the boy's face. The cut was so fine that it did not bleed straightaway, but the shock and pain in the boy's eyes were immediate.

For Genoes, this was a nightmare. His head was clouded by the fierce need pulsing out from the ground beneath his feet. Even before the arrival of Jak, he had no conception as to how he was supposed to appease that feeling. It seemed to intensify with every passing second. Against that internal noise, he could only just focus on Jak's words, let alone defend himself adequately. While he could usually rely on his Speed to keep himself out of trouble, he was finding it impossible to take up a mindset to allow him to flow.

And Jak was going to make him pay for that.

Minutes passed as the younger boy was slowly and quite deliberately cut to ribbons. Blood streaming from a myriad of shallow, and not-so-shallow, cuts to his face, arms, and body. And yet, even with all Jak's size, reach and experience advantage, the bout was not quite working out the way he anticipated.

On several occasions, he had sought to bring things to a terminal end, only for Genoes to block a thrust at the last moment. If he did not know better and could not see the brutal evidence of the fight with his own eyes, he would think he was being toyed with somehow.

But in the end, the flow of blood was Genoes's undoing. One of several cuts on his forehead was in danger of running into his eyes. When he briefly paused to wipe it away with the back of his hand, Jak pounced.

Moving his knives in a complex arc, he caught Genoes's single blade in the midst of them and, with a violent twist, disarmed him, pushing him roughly to the ground with the same action.

A better man would have taken his prize and left the boy on the floor to lick his considerable wounds. A worse one would have taken the opportunity to mock the fallen and crow about the victory. Jak, however chose to step close, knives raised, eager to finish the job.

An arrow hit the ground between the two fighters. Quickly followed by a second. Then a third. Jak spun around to see a familiar face, bow drawn.

"How many times, little brother, do I need to remind you to play nice?"

CHAPTER EIGHTEEN

"Intrusive Thoughts"

Gilles Halcoth, Steward of House Trellec, was getting too old for this.

He was not so naïve as to think there was anything peculiarly terrible about the current state the household. The Maids had ever been slatternly, the Cooks perennially open to a bribe, and the Men-at-Arms had always tended toward the brutish. No, the business of running the estate was much the same as it had always been. He would even admit, if not aloud, that he could remember a young Fion being just as much of a scamp as the latest House progeny.

So, it was not that the world had lurched somehow toward the unsatisfactory in recent years. It was more that his tolerance for it all was starting to wear rather thin. He also, in private moments, was not wholly sure his mind was quite as sharp as before.

"Master Halcoth! Master Halcoth!" One of his inter-changeable Janes was at the door. The small one. With all the hair.

What fresh horror awaited — well, no, not "fresh." That was his point, was it not? All this had happened before, and doubtless, it would happen again. Sooner or later.

The girl was staring up at him. She seemed to be waiting for something. It was probably him. He did like her hair. "Yes, my dear?"

"There's a fight at the gate, sir."

"A fight?"

"Yes, sir. On the street, sir."

"On the street, there is a fight. A fight on the street." It was funny how you could move the words around and they meant the same thing. "A street fight." He giggled and then wondered why.

The Jane was fussing at the sleeve of his robe. She wanted him to follow her. It was funny how much they were like dogs that way: keen to please their masters with their finds. He smiled at that. A good Jane was like a good hunting dog. But so much more satisfying in other ways.

"What's Drunnoc been up to now?" With an effort, he raised himself to his feet and reached for his stick. It was a good stick. A stick that had featured in the nightmares of generations of young Trellecs. Not that the most recent recipient of its attention paid it much mind. Yes, he was just like his father in that.

"It's not the young Master, sir. It's one of his men. The one who hurt his hand? He's cut up a village boy something dreadful. And his sister — the Archer, sir. You know, the one with the eyes you like, sir? — his sister's broken it up.

But it's going to turn nasty. So, you need to come quick, sir."

That was a lot of information. Before he could begin to make sense of it, the Jane was already pulling him out of the room and onwards. "You should see the blood, sir. We've called for Mistress Healer, but you know what she's like! Won't get out of bed without promise of a coin."

If anyone thought anything unusual at the sight of the Steward of House Trellec being dragged along corridors and downstairs by a constantly chattering Maid, no one who witnessed it felt much of a need to mention it. It had been an increasingly common occurrence.

By the time Gilles found himself at the foot of the gatehouse, he was well acquainted with the order of events. It seemed that one of Drunnoc's thugs had lured a local boy into a duel, and that had all gone as expected. He disliked that particular young man. He had spoken to the Master about some of the liberties the Rogue had been taking around the Keep. It was one thing for a man such as himself to enjoy the privileges that came with rank. It was quite another for some jumped-up thug with delusions of grandeur. But that was by the by, he supposed.

During the walk here, he had also been exposed to a number of unsolicited opinions about members of the household, their capabilities in their roles and the infinite combinations of their relationship.

Janes, he thought as he shook his head indulgently, were ever thus.

He was pushed, with much less care and reverence than he felt was owed a man of his age and experience, through the door to the outside. It took a moment for him to steady himself — it was an excellent stick — and he then took in the scene.

*

Kirstin winced at the sight of the Steward stumbling toward their group. She had hoped to get this all smoothed over before he made an appearance. It could be a . . . challenge to deal with Gilles Halcoth. She did not like the vacant look in his eye, either. He could be startlingly unpredictable at such times.

"Mistress Archer, you will lower your bow!" Gilles's voice was surprisingly, to look at his fragile appearance, powerful with <Authority>.

As a paid retainer of House Trellec, she could do little to resist the commands of its Steward. The tip of the arrow dipped sharply to the ground.

"My apologies, sir. If I could just take a moment? We have a family disagreement, and we are both sorry it has needed your attention. It will all be sorted in a moment."

"Like hell it will! You shot at me!" Jak was almost hopping with rage — waving both knives at her in impotent fury. At his feet, the boy he had hurt so badly was not moving. Kirstin hoped this was from sensible discretion rather than anything more sinister.

"I shot near you, Jak. At your feet. I haven't shot at you, since I carried something that could do actual harm. I didn't want to hurt you, see? I'm currently reassessing that point of view."

"Come closer and say that again, bitch."

"I will have your silence!" The <Authority> in Gilles's voice crashed against brother and sister. Both instantly ceased their argument. Jak swayed on his feet while Kirstin blinked to try to clear the sudden blur in her vision. There was no refusing this order. The rumour was that, in his dotage, the Steward had permanently left this Skill running. The strain this placed on his mental faculties was cognitively destructive, but it had increased the Skill's power far beyond the usual subtle nudges towards compliance.

*

This was not acceptable, Gilles thought. He had no problem with siblings settling their disputes in physical terms. On more than one occasion when they were growing up, his sister had seen fit to box his ears. That had not stop him from his nefarious activities, but he appreciated her spirit. Once he was big enough to repay the favour, it became much more enjoyable. He did miss Ursula. Wished he hadn't — but that was beside the point.

Which was —

His eyes refocused on the young people in front of him. Yes. That was it. "We, of House Trellec, do not scuffle on the street like common ruffians. You are, of course, entitled to your familial strife, but you will pursue it behind these walls." Both Jak and Kirstin took several staggering steps toward the door of the gatehouse, pulled against their will.

There was something terrifying about a man with such a tenuous hold on his wits having the power to compel compliance. Kirstin had heard rumours that, when he was younger, Gilles Halcoth had not been beyond using his <Authority> for less than pure intent. Indeed, a sizeable minority of the staff of House Trellec bore more than a passing resemblance to the Steward. But such predations by the strong on the weak were common in the world of Lords and servants and barely worth mentioning. She was sure there must be Houses where such things did not occur, but she had never heard of them.

But such dabbling in his youth was to nothing when compared to the recent impact on the household of a man with his Class having a wandering mind. The Janes — they all, dimly, knew they had names to call their own, but Gilles's conviction that that was what they were called had made it so — had taken to incessant chattering when around him to try to quell his need to muse. It was better for all concerned if he did not have the conversational space to say what was in his head.

In the usual run of things, the outcome of Gilles's uncontrolled thoughts was nothing worse than, say, a Washerwoman working twenty-four bells straight as "I wonder if all the linen in the house can be cleaned in one day," or a Man-at-Arms enduring a week-long search of every inch of the Keep for a scroll that "you must not rest until you find!"

However, there had recently been significant tragedies adding to House Trellec's declining reputation. For example, a Merchant who had been told to "take a long walk off a short battlement," or the serving girl he had ordered to curl up in a chest in his room and had then forgotten about. Her body only recovered once he complained bitterly about the appalling smell.

So, while the Janes secured their safety with their chatter, several other servants who could not find employment elsewhere had stopped their ears with wax. This, as could be imagined, did little to improve the efficiency of the household of House Trellec.

Kirstin was not sure whether it was affection for the old man, respect for his long and distinguished service or, most likely, complete indifference to the suffering of those in his House that led Lord Trellec to allow him to retain his position. She supposed those who suffered and died under his increasing dotage did not care much about the motivation.

Jak was still raging. "How dare you use your Skill on me, old man! You know Drunnoc said —"

"Hold your breath."

*

Why did the young always think that what they wanted was so urgent? That it took primacy over everything else? Year after year, he was sent these children to whip into shape who simply did not understand the way things were to be. You were born, did what he told you to do, and then you died. The date of the latter often depended on how well you did with the former. Or something like that. He used to have a saying around that. People laughed. The girl with the eyes was speaking again.

"Master Halcoth? Sir. If you would not mind letting him breathe again? I promise he will behave now." He liked her eyes. Would have done something about it once upon a time. Might still try.

The man — her brother? — was on his knees. He was also turning an interesting puce colour. He wondered why he was doing that. "Of course, my dear. Breathe normally, young man."

*

Jak sucked in several vast mouthfuls of air as his panic receded. He'd been promised the Steward would have no power over him. It was one of the reasons he had agreed to move into the Keep. There had been too many stories about the "accidents" around the old man. How dare he break that deal! In a flash, Jak picked up both his knives and launched himself forward.

And things would have gone poorly for Gilles Halcoth, Steward of House Trellec, if, at that very moment, a hand had not exploded upwards from a mound of dirt, caught hold of the foot of his assailant, and dragged him, screaming all the way, belowground.

CHAPTER NINETEEN

"Poor Life Choices"

"So, cast it again."

Boruld bit his tongue to avoid giving potentially fatal offence. It never ceased to amaze him how little those without magic understood the art, but perhaps now, under the baleful eyes of two unhappy Lords, was not the moment to hold forth on that particular theme.

He had sought out Drunnoc the moment he had, to his continued incredulity, felt something stir below. He was familiar with the legends surrounding the Knights of the Road but had always assumed their famed resilience to be somewhat overstated, fodder for those who frequented taverns and suchlike. To have the truth of those myths brought home in quite such a humbling manner was causing him deep consternation. As Earth Mages were by inclination slow to thought and careful of deed, his equanimity being so disturbed was an unusual and unpleasant experience.

He had found Drunnoc in deep, nay intense, conversation with his father outside the Great Hall. But unfortunately, it did not appear his news did much to improve the palpable tension in the air.

"For sure, sir. In a few weeks, I should be able —"

"Cast it now."

Again, Boruld resolutely kept a screed on the obtuseness of the non-magicked to himself. "The amount of mana required to perform that spell is quite high, sir. I won't be able to achieve anything close to the scope of that effect for some time, I'm afraid."

"Your Class can use your life force to supplement your power, can it not?" Boruld did not feel Fion's interjection here was either helpful or welcome. "Do that. We have a Healer to keep you alive."

Boruld increasingly believed that his relationship with House Trellec had been a poor life choice.

The sheer volume of pay on offer to assist in the construction of "Trellec's Folly" had been wholly beyond his experience as a middling Earth Mage in his twilight years. No one, especially this far from the Capital, offered such sums merely to shape and position giant stone blocks. Of course, it was not a skill many with the art sought to develop — why specialise in something an army of motivated common-Classed could achieve just as well? — but following that path had earned him enough to get by over the years, and if there was one thing everyone could agree on about Boruld, it was that he would stick to it once he had an idea.

Thus, when House Trellec had offered him fantastic sums for relatively straightforward work, it had seemed like a dream come true. He had whiled away many a carefree day, shaping giant granite slabs into serviceable bricks and positioning them to the Architect's specifications. If he thought the designs were oddly . . . martial for a small backwater village, then it was not for him to question the wisdom of the man with the big bag of money. The Keep had rapidly taken shape, and while pride was a sin and all that, he did feel a swell of satisfaction at the outcome. That he had been asked to stay on as a House Mage following its completion was another offer too good to refuse.

However, his dream existence had rapidly become a nightmare when that strange boy with far too much onyx in his veins appeared in his room yesterday with a plan to eliminate a Knight of the Road.

There had been no threats. There had not needed to be. Everyone knew what occurred to those who displeased Drunnoc. While there were few left in the world whom Boruld would consider friends, even fewer of his extended family, he would need an excellent reason to give that boy any excuse to look for them. Even explaining that he would need to use several months' worth of stored mana — a phenomenal cost for a single spell — caused little more than a raised eyebrow from that impassive edifice of a face.

"I can, theoretically, use my life force, if necessary, sir. But, alas" — Boruld added a quaver to his voice while gesturing to his ageing form — "I am not a young man. I doubt there would be anything your Healer could do should I tap, however briefly, into that source for a major working."

"Do it."

"No, Drunnoc. Stop. We give it up as a bad lot." Fion's tone was derisive. "If it did not work the first time, it is the height of stupidity to walk the same course again. So, you dig another pit and fling her back into it. What's to stop her from scrabbling her way out again? What then? Third time's the charm? No, the trick is to fold at the right moment, particularly if the attempt wastes even more resources that we will likely need in short order. We will plot another course. Thank you, Mage; you can leave us."

Boruld bowed to the pair and walked away with as much dignity as he felt able to muster in the circumstances.

*

"Fool." Fion struck Drunnoc hard across the face with the back of his hand. The boy's head turned slightly with the impact but showed no other distress. The Lord raised his hand to hit him again but thought better of it. Such chastisement seemed to have negligible effect of late, if it ever had. Besides, he worried that on some level the boy was enjoying it. "The attempt and not the deed confounds us. Should you have consulted me before this latest misstep, I would have highlighted the necessity of ensuring success." Then, in the face of the unyielding stare of his youngest child, he softened his voice. "I do not decry your ambition, boy, Goddess knows I share the sentiment, but this was poorly done."

"What would you have me do, Father?"

He hated the wheedling tone of that voice. Felt his fists bunch again. He forced them to unclench. "Nothing. We have some time until she digs herself free. I suggest we use —"

Boruld returned at, for him, a run. "My Lords," he gasped, "she's breaking free."

The three arrived at the gatehouse window just in time to witness their Steward seeking to impose order on squabbling retainers. There was no sign of the Lady Darkhelm.

"Are you sure — "

The Rogue who had lost his temper with Gilles — for which Fion could hardly blame him if he believed a quarter of the reports — suddenly vanished mid-attack. No, not vanished. He had been pulled beneath the ground. The shift in perspective took a moment to appreciate, and suddenly there, crawling upwards to replace him, was a monstrous sight.

While it may have looked like an act of spectacular, heroic timing, Daine had not intended to save the Steward from Jak's flying assault. She had been clawing her way upwards when, with the last sweep of her arms, she had broken the surface of the ground and instinctively sought to grasp what was above her. The Goddess, who had been peculiarly silent when Daine had been entombed below, nudged her reaching hand around a leg.

She had heaved her body on that and used its slight and temporary resistance to lever herself out. As she went upwards, the person attached to the leg was pulled downwards behind her. The Goddess took charge again and pushed down hard, using that body as a stepping stone to propel Daine upwards. If she felt any pity for the being she felt being crushed to death beneath her, then that would be an issue for another day.

On her knees, finally free of the crushing dark, she coughed and vomited gouts of dirt and blood out of her lungs and stomach, relieved to feel the air for the first time in hours. The sensation of perpetual suffocation had not been pleasant.

After all she had gone through, it was not a surprise that, physically, she was in poor shape. While her body continued to repair itself slowly, it was at a much slower pace than usual. This was not wholly beyond her experience, but was unusual enough that she could not risk any further damage for the near future. Mentally, her time underground had inflicted wounds that would gape for some time.

With a wet *pop*, her eyes reinflated, and she became dimly aware of her surroundings. Genoes, seemingly severely hurt from a myriad of wounds. That Archer from the woods, tears streaming down her face. A vacant-looking older man gazing at her quizzically. Blurred figures regarding them from on high.

The Archer put her arms under Daine, forcing her to her feet. "We need to go."

Putting as much of her weight as she dared on the petite woman, Daine managed, with great difficulty, to stand. She knew that, in extremis, her passive healing Skill focused on protecting her life at the expense of dealing with minor injuries. The truth of that had never been more apparent to her than at this moment. Apparently, there were an awful lot of bones in the feet that had little impact on whether she lived or died . . .

"I can manage," *somehow.* "You get the boy."

*

Reluctantly, Kirstin let Daine go and the older woman sagged without her support. The Archer scooped up Genoes — who weighed far less than a boy of his years had a right to — in both arms. He was still unconscious and was an appalling mess of cuts. She had just watched, in horror, as the emerging Knight crushed the life out of her brother. But though she felt residual pangs over his fate, the sight of this boy's injuries quashed them flat. As much as it hurt, and she wished it were not true, the world was a better place with Jak out of it.

I'm sorry, Mother. I tried.

"You will stop!"

She could not move. Halcoth had regained his composure.

"You will return to the Keep."

Now wholly out of her control, her body turned — still carrying Genoes — and walked to the gatehouse door.

"Good girl. Keep walking. You will take the boy to the servant's quarters and then present yourself to my chamber for —"

When she was only a handful of steps from the Keep, Kirstin felt wrenched free from the control. Glancing around, she saw Daine stooped over the unconscious form of the Steward. It spoke ill of the current state of the Knight that her blow had merely served to knock him out.

"Let's go," the Knight whispered through fractured teeth, stumbling back toward the road. Kirstin followed, holding Genoes tight to her chest.

*

From the window of Keep Trellec, three figures watched the motley crew retreat until they faded into the tree line.

"She'll be back, Father."

Fion ignored him. "Boruld, please arrange for Mistress Healer to attend to Gilles. She can see if there's anything left of the other boy too. When that is done, I think it would be wise for you to ensure your work on the walls is as impregnable as you claim. There will be no room for failure."

He walked away, stroking his chin thoughtfully. Overall, that had worked out better than could have been hoped. And now he had success to present to his friends in the Great Hall. An assault from a Knight of the Road on "Trellec's Folly" had been rebuffed. Yes, he could work with this. He could indeed.

Drunnoc, for his part, stayed where he was, staring at the spot he had lost sight of the Knight. A small smile, such a rare expression it felt uncomfortable on his face, played at the corner of his mouth.

The problem of Daine Orban was proving more interesting than he could possibly have hoped.

CHAPTER TWENTY

"Leaking Bleeding Hearts"

No one ever asked a Healer how they were feeling.

That was not the most significant of the complaints Mistress Pernille had about her life, but it was the one that scorched most fervently in her heart.

The old arguments bounced back and forth through her head. She had never wanted this Class, did not have the temperament for it, the inclination, or, if she was honest, the empathy. It would not be correct to suggest she was cruel, at least not consciously, but she did not care much about people. Certainly not enough to waste her mana on solving their ills.

This disinclination had not been an issue when she had lived at home. After all, there had been aura enough leaking from the bleeding hearts of her parents and her younger sisters to mean her efforts were rarely needed. No, mother and father never met a lost cause to which they would not dedicate their lives. Karla and Alma Darlan were precisely the same. Huge, tragic, flowing waterfalls of compassion, for one and all.

"There is no higher calling than to ease suffering." She could not fault her father for his sincerity in believing those words. She was, though, frustrated by his inability to believe that she would even want to consider doing anything else. "You will grow to love it, Penny," he had said, patting her head. She was fairly sure she would much more quickly grow to love following a more lucrative Class, but that line of discussion always made her feel like she was punching a rabbit. So, she acquiesced and undertook the training because, deep down, do we not all want to please our parents? Or, at the very least, not alienate them as far as to have them disinherit us?

Thus, she had leapt at the first Healing job that came her way. Anything to escape from the relentless need to do good at home. That the offer came from the backend of nowhere, about as far away from home as possible without taking to the seas, was a bonus. She knew she could, via well-constructed letters, carefully craft a version of herself that would make House Darlan proud. Besides, how much Healing could be needed in a Keep this far away from the border?

It turned out quite a lot.

The funny thing was — well, not funny ha-ha, more a "screaming with frustration" kind of humour — people did not realise that Healing was pathetically easy. More often than not, the body wanted to fix itself anyway. All it needed was someone with a Skill to fuel it doing it faster. So, all a Healer did was push some of their mana in to speed things up and let nature take its course. Those of House Darlan were blessed, or cursed, with a host of Skills that achieved this. Of course, things were a bit more complicated with more grievous injuries or more significant illnesses, but that was just a matter of scale and not worth the fuss.

She guessed, when it came down to it, she just did not like using her mana. The only times she felt close to "normal" were when her reserves were full. She utterly resented the implication she was supposed to, and daily, use it up to sprinkle joy on all and sundry. The moment she triggered a Skill, she would start to feel lethargic, the headaches would kick in, and should she keep it active for any length of time, she would, eventually, get the shakes of which her family seemed so inordinately proud. "A good Healer is a wobbly Healer," her mother would proclaim, smiling broadly while her teeth chattered as if encased in an ice floe.

And that was without the fact that putting something so precious of hers inside another person made her feel physically sick.

Help this, Heal that, close this cut, clean that infection. Yet, no matter how often that need was answered, it returned for more. Like an unending black hole. A hungry child. A sucking leech she could not quite reach to pull free and crush underfoot.

"Mistress Healer? Mistress Healer!" A frenzied banging from outside, the handle twisting impotently. She liked to lock the door to her infirmary; otherwise, people would just wander in with their aches and pains. And those pleading eyes. She hated the need in them. As if she did not have anything better to do with her time.

With as much bad grace as she could muster, she cracked it open slightly and took in the sight of a harassed Jane. Pernille had only been working in Keep Trellec for a few hours before she had identified the unusual brain trauma that seemed to afflict the majority of its female servants. But it had taken her waking up in the bed of the Steward to identify its source. It was the work of moments to strengthen her mental pathways to resist his <Authority>, and that was the end of that little game."Master Halcoth is hurt! You need to come right away."

Sighing, Pernille locked the door behind her — she could not have sick people sneaking in and waiting for her — and followed behind the chattering Maid. As always when interacting with a Jane, she let the flow of words wash over her. She was not needed in the conversation, and she knew her silence would not offend. She supposed it was intriguing that all this talk was some sort of a primaeval survival instinct given shape, and the fact that the Steward being absent did not change their behaviour was curious. Perhaps it would be worth discovering why that happened, but she was honest enough to recognise that she was not genuinely interested enough in the phenomenon to put in the time.

She could feel that this Jane was pregnant again. As Fion had been quite clear, there were to be "no more of Halcoth's bastards this year," and she felt the obligation to act, so with a pulse of her power, she remedied that situation. For some reason, using her mana in this way felt less wearisome than the more traditional use. There was a momentary hitch in the Jane's step, which quickly smoothed out as they went up the steps to exit the keep.

Her first instinct was that this must have been the site of a recent, astonishing slaughter. The terror, pain, and suffering in the air were wholly oppressive to her senses, and she found herself swaying on her feet. It was as if the very ground were, to her enhanced eyes, glowing a dark-red colour, as if pulsing with the rawness of it.

Her mother had been a Battlefield Healer during one of those interminable wars in the East, and she had spoken of the techniques needed to block out the volume of demand that would occur in the aftermath of a clash of armies. Conscious that she found *any* pull on her resources intolerable, Pernille had quickly learned the Skill to shut herself off from the screaming world around her. It could be draining to maintain that state for too long, but, at this moment, it was exactly what she needed.

The red tinge to her vision slowly dulled until she could properly see the scene before her. Gilles Halcoth was lying on his back, a purple bruise spreading across his face. She doubted anyone could do much to damage that man's addled brain further — and a quick examination showed no new internal damage had been inflicted. But, as she always did when looking at the Steward, she wondered whether life in the Keep would be better if she soothed some of those dark inflammations that riddled the inside of his skull.

But no. Bringing him around to consciousness and fixing the bruise would be her good deed for the day. She activated <Minor Heal>. Power flowed from her, and the expected headache started to pound. She would need to take to her bed for the rest of the day to recover. That more complex and tiring work could wait until she was recovered. She'd add it to her list.

The Steward climbed to his feet, balancing on that ridiculous stick of his. He seemed oblivious that anything had happened. It was a kindness, she thought. *He does not need to worry about whether anything he does is right or wrong. He cannot remember it anyway.* That was not such a terrible way to live. With the help of the Jane, she watched Gilles make his way back inside, his hand resting in various inappropriate places.

There was still something else out here, though. Even through her dulled senses, another source of pain, an excessive throbbing, was nearby. Her eyes fell to a patch of disturbed ground which seemed to be at the heart of that feeling. Then, kneeling and dusting away some of the earth, she was shocked to see a face staring up at her.

Well, it used to be a face. Most of the constituent parts for a face remained, but they had been flattened out of all recognition as such. She had heard that Giants liked to flatten their prey for easier storage, and this . . . man, she supposed, looked exactly like she imagined this would look in practice. What was worse was that he was still alive.

He did not speak — she doubted he would be capable of that with the instruments he had left — but he certainly groaned quite impressively. Then, with a start, she realised it was the man with the knives she had needed to heal earlier. The one with the mangled wrist.

Fury blossomed inside her. She had wasted all that mana on this man, and he had, what, left the infirmary and let this immediately happen to him? What was wrong with people? Did they have no compassion for how complex her work was?

Her hand was resting on the face, forcing what was left of the eyelids closed. And then, rather than the expected pull on her power, she could feel something forcing itself inside her. No, not forcing; it was nothing so invasive, she was pulling it in. Looking through her Healer's eyes, she could see the customary flow of mana — but rather than flowing from her outwards, it was going the other way. The man was whimpering pathetically as it happened, but it was easing her headache.

Within moments, his store of energy was used up, and his dwindling life force emptied. She, however, felt better than she had in days.

<New Skill added: Life Drain>

Pernille blinked at the notification. When was the last time she had added a Skill? And what was <Life Drain>? Certainly that was not one of House Darlan's range of capabilities that she knew about. Why had no one ever mentioned that the transfer could happen both ways? This was a revelation!

Although now that she thought on it, she could see why it might not be something Healers would discuss too widely. She'd never heard of anyone in her family that . . . refreshed themselves in this manner. Vampires had such a terrible reputation, after all; she could understand some hesitancy in revealing this Skill.

A shadow fell over her, and she looked up into the eyes of Drunnoc Trellec.

"That looked interesting. Perhaps we should talk?"

CHAPTER TWENTY-ONE

"They Are Many and We Are Few"

Daine lay uncomfortably on her back, staring at the ceiling.

She was grateful that Cenwyn had accepted them back into his home. The journey of the staggering, battered Knight, the bleeding, insensate boy, and the clearly distressed Archer through the village had caused much comment. If as expected the Trellecs sent pursuers, it would not take much investigation for them to arrive at the Tailor's door.

She hoped his help was not due to misplaced confidence in her ability to resist.

A Healer, of sorts, had been called for Genoes and had, after a few minutes of work, pronounced him "on the mend." He would not be dancing a jig anytime soon, but the worst damage was undone. He still had not come around from his ordeal, but that was probably for the best and would happen with time.

Daine was happy to let him sleep. Knife fighting was nasty, even for an experienced hand. You were too close to your opponent for too long to escape without some taint on your soul. She knew some revelled in that intimacy, but she thought she knew enough about this boy now to see he was not one of them. The poor lad, at his age, had been on the wrong end of two blades within a day. That would leave as many scars as anything else. She hoped there was a way to help him come out the other side in one piece.

With an audible click, some of the pressure on her chest was relieved. Another of her ribs was back where it should be.

When the Healer had finished on the boy, the kindly old woman had taken one look at Daine and shaken her head ruefully. "I can dull the pain some, but there's nothing to be done for you by the likes of me, my Lady. Truthfully, if you'd be a horse, I'd be reaching for my mallet."

That was a metaphor that would fester.

Once the Healer had gone on her way, they'd helped her to one of the rooms that functioned as a storehouse for the Tailor's completed work. She had dozed some on top of this bed of tunics, but there was too much slow, internal shifting for her to get comfortable.

From where she lay, she could hear the low murmur of voices in the other room. The Archer — Kirstin — and Cenwyn. Discussing what had occurred, she imagined. She was glad the girl had someone with whom to talk, and the older man was a good fit for that role. No matter the circumstances and no matter the justification, the loss of someone close would make as deep a wound as any weapon.

She remembered the fierce refusal in Kirstin's eyes when — was it only the day before? — Daine had offered to kill her brother. To take away that corrosive ache eating into her sense of self. But she'd stood willing to die to protect him. So, although the devastation Jak had wrought on Genoes and the pleasure he had taken in doing so had been the final straw, there was a difference between wishing it so and confronting the reality.

On their slow way through the village, Kirstin had assured her that she felt no ill will. Daine would take that with the handful of salt it deserved. If there were a friendship to forge here, hard words would come in their future.

The voices next door suddenly became more audible as one of her eardrums completed its reshaping.

"— to get as far away as possible." Cenwyn's voice was a gravelly rumble.

"There's nothing left for me here. I can take him."

"Lass, you're handy with the bow, no doubt. But you've seen the mess they've made of her next door. And she's Goddess-Blessed. If they come calling, you'd be nothing more than a raindrop in a hurricane. No need to spend your life that cheaply."

A knocking on the door abruptly halted the conversation.

Daine did not have the adrenaline spare to react, but she heard the panicked scraping of chairs and anxious voices as they readied themselves for unwelcome visitors. She thought she made out the whisper of a drawn blade. A Tailor and an Archer in a confined space were hardly a force to be reckoned with. Well, they would not have to stand alone. She dragged herself upright and tried to find some sense of balance. She could probably fall on top of an assailant if it came to it. As long as they did not move too quickly.

There was a creak of a door opening, and she could

make out a new voice. But quietly insistent, not commanding belligerence. So, not an official house-to-house search for fugitives, but rather a neighbour calling. Perhaps. There was quiet talk for a time while Daine swayed. Uncertain whether to join or return to sleep. The sound was too low for her to make much out.

Whatever the discussion, though, Cenwyn was suddenly, explosively unimpressed. "He's mad! What does he think will happen next?"

"I think he's just mad enough to find out." The new voice was male. Younger than Cenwyn. Nothing from the Goddess. No danger sense. In any event, not from the newcomer.

That made her choice. She staggered her way into the room. Two men were deep in conversation over the table. Kirstin sat on the makeshift bed at the back, the still-sleeping Genoes's head in her lap.

Upon seeing her, Cenwyn leapt to his feet. The unknown man likewise, pulling a cloth cap from his head. "My Lady! I apologise for waking you."

She motioned for them to sit, collapsing into the third chair at the table herself. "Stop your fretting. If I still had a ma, she'd be fluttering less than you these last few bells. You, sir, I don't know."

The newcomer dipped his head. "Apologies, my Lady. Rowan's the name."

"Class?"

She knew she was being rude, but whatever internal filter she possessed to guard against such missteps had not yet recovered. Maybe it never would. Perhaps she never had one. While Classes were not secret — how could they be when most made their living by advertising them? — it was not the done thing, in polite company, to inquire so bluntly.

From her seated position behind her, Kirstin cleared her throat to ease the tension. "Master Glazier stopped by with some news. Seems the Trellecs have been busy."

"He's claiming independence!" Cenwyn's tone was outraged.

"He's what?" She turned her eyes to the Glazier. "Tell your tale."

If he had ever harboured a wish to meet a Knight of the Road, the man was now sincerely regretting that desire. Blushing, he avoided eye contact by fiddling with his hat, twisting it this way and that. "Lord Trellec. Well, all of the, erm, the High Houses. Yes, all of them. They've sent runners to the Village Council." He paused and then, finally, met her eyes. "He's said he defied you, my Lady. Sent you running. Gravely wounded."

"Never let your guard down. Never let them think you're mortal. Never back down." Old Gant had been clear about how the Knights should conduct themselves. That the only reply in this situation was a derisive laugh and a display of unbowed strength. The thing was, the man had eyes. It would take an act of astonishing self-delusion for this stranger to pretend to think she had received anything other than a humbling. It was trust she needed, not compliance.

"A temporary state of affairs, Master Glazier. It don't make it into many songs, but it happens. But as you can see, I'm not running. Just reassessing. There will be a reckoning for Lord Trellec. That I vow." Her fine words would have been more convincing had not new teeth started to push through at that moment. Instead, there was an insistent tap as each broken one was replaced and fell to hit the table She turned to Cenwyn; he was evincing less horror than Rowan at the sight.

"What has that got to do with independence?"

"According to Rowan, and he hears most of what happens here, the High Houses have asked the Council to dissolve the charter. They claim the Crown has lost its authority."

Kirstin chimed in. "They say you lost your mind last night. Murdered a bunch of children, and Trellec had to step in to halt it. He's let it be known he's backing calls to secede. Claims he has the power to make that stick. Says he sent you packing *'like a whipped whore.'"*

"No one knows what to think, my Lady." Rowan was still staring at the teeth that continued to drop and collect in a small pile on the table. "Everyone knows you're here and, well, in a bad way. There are Trellec men on the street, and men from the other Houses are joining them. They're telling everyone to stay inside while the Council chooses the way forward. They know you're here, but they're not doing anything about it. Folk think that means . . . they think you're broken, my Lady. It's got them wondering . . ." He paused and looked to Cenwyn. "They've secured the Council Chamber."

Kirstin frowned. She had carefully extricated herself from Genoes and joined them at the table. "What does that mean?"

"I'm on the Council. So's Rowan. If there's a meeting, it means it's going on without us. They'll do whatever Trellec asks them."

"But that's ridiculous. There's what, two hundred, three hundred people who live here. What can they do against the Crown? Places can't just decide not to be part of the Kingdom. Can they?"

The heaviness in Daine's stomach had nothing to do with her injuries. "I doubt the King will hear anything about it. Even if it did get to him, we're far enough away for it to take months, maybe even years, before those in the Capital will formulate a response. Some regiments could be sent, I suppose, but there's barely any to spare to send to put down a village rebellion."

Daine rubbed her face as the ramifications grew in her mind. One village seceding was not worth worrying about. That was a few boxes of taxation coins. Maybe a tiny sliver of the Crown's trade. But that was not what was going to happen here. No. If the story was that a Knight of the Road had been defeated, then other villages — all equally aware of the thinness of Crown resources — would also start to think about that relationship. And if Trellec could offer protection or even enough of a pretence of it, others might join. Momentum had its inevitability.

The West was her Tour. It took ten years for her to complete the journey, and she had done it three times in her life. She was out here, alone, because the Crown did not have the men to hold the territory any other way. All that the Crown's authority held, this far from the centre of things, was the certainty that the Darkhelm's sword would come calling.

The Crown could lose the whole of the West before it even knew there was a problem. She doubted that by the time word got out, there would be much anyone could do to stop it.

"*Your biggest weapon, my sweet dears, is confidence. You can defeat a hundred men because they will quail to stand against you. They see you and your Strength and think of any conflict in terms of their weakness, their individual pain, and their deaths. They do not see the power, the irresistible strength they have as a group. They are many, and we are so few. The Goddess help us all if the multitudes ever realise it. When that sleeping bear awakes, it will change the world."*

Daine feared the truth in Gant's words. The bear was stirring. And she was in no shape to confront it.

CHAPTER TWENTY-TWO

"The Chimaera's Tail"

From Cenwyn's upstairs window, they could see a growing crowd in front of the Council House. It seemed peaceful enough for the moment, but the occasional chant that indicated a darkening mood broke out. Daine cynically wondered how many of them were there of their own accord and how many had Trellec coin in their pockets. Certainly, if you were planning to address the populace, it helped to be liberal with your purse. While most of those gathering seemed to be genuine villagers, there were enough flashes of red and gold, along with the other High Houses' colours, to recognise a considerable military presence on the street.

Such a buildup of numbers boded ill for the Council resisting anything for which the High Houses asked. Representing the will of the mob, even a rented one, was ever an influential negotiating position.

They had moved to the roof of the Tailor's house, the better to hear what was occurring. "This is going to turn ugly" — Cenwyn was shaking his head in disbelief — "too many short fuses and long blades in that crowd. And that's without the Mercenaries. What's Trellec thinking?"

"I don't know that he is. He's found a way to get what he wants and damn the consequences." Rowan's despair mirrored his friend's. "I should get home."

"I would not like to see you on the streets right now, Master Glazier." Daine had not taken her eyes from the scene below. "That tinderbox is merely awaiting its match."

"As you say, Lady Darkhelm. But I fear, and I tell you it plain when the blaze comes, it will find its way toward you. Begging your pardon, but not all of us can survive a furnace."

She nodded her understanding, and he slipped back down the stairs and away.

"He's right, you know," she said to the others, "Trellec is going to whip that crowd to a frenzy and point them my way."

The silence from those around her was its own answer.

"I need to go. I can find somewhere else to hole up." She'd barely managed to drag herself to her feet when a trumpet sounded.

Two Trellec Men-at-Arms were pulling open the door to the Council House, and a line of people filed out. Daine recognised a few of the Lords and Ladies from the previous evening — albeit, at that stage, they had mostly been running from her. This, perhaps, gave her a poor impression of their capabilities. The others, identifiable by their much less expensive dress, were obviously the Village Council, minus Rowan and Cenwyn. They looked like they were having, if not quite the worst day of their lives, certainly one in the top five.

Exiting last — and was there a trumpet flourish as they emerged? — came Fion and Drunnoc. The great and the good lined up on a makeshift stage that had somehow entirely spontaneously constructed, and Lord Trellec stepped to the forefront.

"He's surely not going to preach sedition right there on the street, is he?" Cenwyn was staring with disbelief at a crowd of people with whom he had spent his whole life.

Daine's smile was thin. "He has the Chimaera by the tail, he has to keep it well fed."

"It gladdens my heart to see so many friends and neighbours come together on this extraordinary day." Fion's voice carried easily across the marketplace. Daine spotted Boruld to the right of the stage presumably channelling his speech enhancement Skill.

The sight of him caused an unfamiliar flutter of panic in her heart. She flashed back to her time belowground and felt her breath quicken. Overcoming that debilitating terror would be as necessary moving forward as any physical recovery.

Out of the corner of her eye, she watched Kirstin levelled her crossbow at, almost hidden on the other side of the stage, the old man Daine had struck when they were escaping. There was some sort of compliance Skill there that, presumably, was being used on those who owed allegiance to the Trellecs.

Which would, she started to realise, include anyone that had taken coin to be in the crowd . . .

There was cold intelligence, not just blind ambition, behind what was happening here.

Fion's voice continued to boom out. "As you will be aware, there were a series of atrocities committed in our village last night. Daine Orban, popularly known as the Lady Darkhelm" —he could have put more venom in his voice, but it would have required the milking of a hundred serpents — "took it upon herself to deliver summary justice to a number of our children. While no one claims those punished were wholly innocent, her barbaric actions have shocked us." As if on cue, several of the Lords and Ladies started weeping.

"I take some of the blame on myself, for I saw this coming. You will recall it was just the day before when she was prepared to execute young Bella Acas for a misunderstanding with my boy. Fortunately, I persuaded her to a different action, and cooler heads prevailed." If anyone wanted to dispute that version of events, the presence of many men with swords dampened down that inclination.

"Sadly, there was no such opportunity to plead mitigation in the dead of night, and the first I knew something was afoot was when several dear friends came to me for help."

Fion took a moment to bask in the attention of the crowd. Daine saw the lips of the old man at the side of the stage move, and the volume of cheering rose significantly. She turned to Kirstin. "I should have hit him harder, right?"

"Anyone with tits would have applauded."

"That bad?"

"That bad."

The speech continued. "It was seconds after we had shared a moment's silence for the loss of so many of our children that we heard the monster herself had come to my gate. We presumed the next life to be stolen would be that of my own, dear, Drunnoc." All eyes shifted to the "dear" boy who stared resolutely ahead. "We were thus fortunate that the oft-mocked strength of our walls was more than enough to see off this unholy terror. You will have heard that she fled, tail between her legs, to lick her wounds." The laughter here felt especially acute despite all the pain she had experienced over the last few days.

"House Trellec has long argued for a cease to the predations of the Knights of the Road. Repeatedly, we have petitioned our Village Council to disband our charter with the Crown. And we have been denied." The crowd booed, and those on the Council shifted uncomfortably. Stones were thrown and, where they struck, drew blood.

"Last night was not the first time Lady Darkhelm has brought slaughter to our homes. You will recall, for example, the execution of the Widow Tailor ten years back?" Cenwyn gasped with dismay. "We now possess information that makes that execution highly suspect. I have seen letters between the Lady Darkhelm and Cenwyn Tailor that makes clear they orchestrated the whole thing, falsifying testimony, and the confession. The Widow Tailor was sacrificed for coin, pure and simple."

The mood of the crowd was now entirely toxic. Daine saw more than one glance toward their vantage point. It was all being orchestrated quite masterfully, she could admit.

"Now, I do not suggest all of the executions carried out by the Lady Darkhelm were likewise so motivated. But the fact that she now hides within the Tailor's home means some questions must be asked."

As one, the crowd moved toward them. Daine took a step toward the stairs to block the front door. Injured as she was, she did not have a chance of victory against such a press of furious humanity. But she could hold that door long enough to buy the others time.

"Not. Yet." The Steward's voice boomed across the square, and everyone froze. "Let the Master finish." Glassy-eyed, and in one movement, the villagers turned back to face the stage.

Lord Trellec seemed slightly unnerved by the passions he was inciting. It took him a moment to regain his poise. "I understand your anger, I truly do. That is why we have been busy petitioning the Village Council for a change of policy." All eyes shifted to the small group to the left of Fion. Several sported wounds from flung stones. All of them seemed particularly delighted to be included in today's event. "I am pleased to tell you that they have approved the suggestion of the High Houses that, due to the reckless behaviour of the Knight of the Road, our charter with the Crown is now invalid. At this very moment, we are sending messages to all villages and towns within a day's ride to inform them of our intent to secede from the Crown. What is more, we are inviting them to a Great Council of the West within the week to consider standing with us. There we will discuss the future of the Kingdom."

"And what of the King?"

Daine was pleased to hear that not everyone in the mob had lost their minds.

"Have any of us ever seen him? No. Has he ever deigned to visit despite the mountain of coins we send each year? No. All we have to show for being part of his Kingdom is a once-a-decade cull of our children at the whim of a bitch with a secondhand sword. It is tyranny, ladies and gentlemen, and after last night, I can no longer stand idly by and let it happen under my nose."

Fion was warming to his theme. "I was strong enough to repel the invader last night, and I would share that strength with you all and our neighbours and friends. I say we are better than they think we are. I say we will stand up for what we believe. So, we say today, and we say with one voice, down with the Darkhelm and down with the Crown.

"Down with the Darkhelm! Down with the Crown!"

Daine turned to the others. "You need to go."

Cenwyn was shaking his head. "There's a back way out of here. Take Kirstin and the boy and run. I can reason with them. They won't hurt me."

"It's a mob, Cenwyn. They might be your best friends, but they've been whipped up and told a tale. And that's without <Authority> being pumped into them. They'll be tearing your arms out today and weeping at your funeral tomorrow." Then, as if to prove the validity of her words, a stone came sailing from the crowd through one of the downstairs windows, smashing it into a thousand pieces.

Now *that* was a metaphor, she thought.

Kirstin fired back, cursing as the shot took one of the Men-at-Arms in the chest, intercepted on its way to Halcoth. "We all go. Now. Daine, Lady Darkhelm, we need you. I can't protect Genoes on my own. Cenwyn, she's right. There's no reasoning with a riot. They'll kill you." The thud of shoulders hitting the wooden door below punctuated her words.

Daine had been in this position more times than she could count. The clever play was to put herself in the doorway to the house and let the blood run. As she had done so many times before. She had no illusions about her incapacity to survive the encounter on this occasion, but she was fine with that.

But her eyes fell on the still-sleeping Genoes. Kirstin was right. The Archer was not enough to keep him safe, certainly not in the world to which Trellec was giving birth. She would be abandoning him to certain death with the likes of Drunnoc on the rise.

The door splintered under its assault. The howling outside rose in intensity.

She made her decision.

"Grab anything you can carry on your back. No horse. No unnecessary kit. There is somewhere we can go to buy ourselves some time. But we leave now."

And the Goddess clapped her hands in glee.

CHAPTER TWENTY-THREE

"Power from the Shadows"

All in all, things were going *terribly* well.

Fion was wise enough to recognise that, without an exactly perfect confluence of events, the likely outcome of today's activities would have been his immediate execution. There were stories enough of what happened to those who displeased the King, and the current occupant of the throne was not even one of the more authoritarian of recent times. It had been the certainty of retribution that had persuaded him to stay his hand.

As it was, though, through no small amount of skill and no little diplomacy, he had been able to leverage his son's thoughtless attack on a Knight of the Road to his advantage. Then, finally, after all these years of impotent attempts, he had been able to force the Village Council to rip up that infernal charter.

He looked over at his boy, who was staring expressionless,

as the crowd methodically tore the Tailor's house down, stone by stone.

He could not disagree that Drunnoc's risky actions were the catalyst for this immediate change in his circumstances. From being viewed with, if not disdain, certainly amusement — and was that not infinitely worse? — to being hailed as the saviour of freedom for the locality? That was every one of his dreams finally coming true. It would take a hard heart not to feel a spurt of affection toward the cause of such a change of fortune.

He reached out and rested a hand on Drunnoc's shoulder. Was that something he had ever done before without violence?

Fion thought back to the meeting in the Council House. The speed at which the objections of those upstarts had faded away to eager acceptance had made for one of the happiest moments of his life. He did not quite understand what had so sharply changed the atmosphere in the room. Negotiations had been tense, and that Blacksmith, in particular, had been forceful in his refusal to shift his position. And then, for no apparent reason Fion could detect, the mood had changed, and they had voted in his favour . . .

And then that speech to the crowd! Of course, he had been liberal with what remained of the House funds to ensure a good turnout, but the way he had inspired them with the rightness of his position! Who had known he had levelled up <Oration> to such an extent! He would need to craft more opportunities for public speaking. Clearly, it was a hitherto unexplored strength.

Once the crowd finally forced their way into that house, he would be free of that blasted Knight *and* the Tailor — a man who on the Council, had been a thorn in his side for so many years — in one go. He had been outraged to read the correspondence Drunnoc had found between them. Outraged but not at all surprised. It made perfect sense that the reason the Village Council had been so set against Fion was conspiratorial collusion. That made all those years of rejection make so much more sense.

And now all that corruption was about to be rooted out, and by the self-motivated actions of the common-Classed, no less. Could there have been a more perfect outcome to the day?

He felt an unusual swell of paternal pride as he squeezed the arm of his youngest boy. Yes, today was going very well indeed.

*

It was a sad moment, thought Drunnoc Trellec, when you realised your father was a moron.

Almost from the womb, he had known that he could manipulate his mother. She had, after all, those primal instincts running through her entire being that forced her to wish to protect and cherish him. He had found, throughout his childhood, exploring the outer limits of those instincts to be instructive as to how far humans would deny reality. If the Lady Trivian still had any illusions about her son's capacity for cruelty, she was even more of a fool than he thought her to be.

His father, though? He had always held a grudging respect for the admittedly brutal way he had rejected Drunnoc's tendencies. Children, even those with twisted souls such as Drunnoc, liked to have boundaries against which to press, and certainly his father's fists had been a solid wall around him.

So, it was a matter of profound regret for the Lordling

Trellec to uncover the colossal blind spot in his father's mind. Nothing else appeared to matter when it came to breaking free from the Crown's influence. It seemed there was nothing, no story so unlikely, no action so unjust, that Fion could not rationalise it away as "all for the greater good." As far as Drunnoc felt emotions, he was disappointed in this turn of events.

Take the meeting in the Council House.

Drunnoc knew well that words had power. Sometimes, they were more powerful than actions. For example, there were circumstances when, in a tense Council meeting, such an innocent phrase as "Master Blacksmith, your children send their regards" would be a passing pleasantry. The sort of small talk that everyone made. On the other hand, the meaning was vastly different when you said it while holding a child's doll that might or might not — he could not remember — have blood on it.

He knew his father, so shortsighted when it came to his cause, thought he had been able to persuade them. Everyone else in the room knew differently and knew who truly held sway. And Drunnoc saw the benefits of that type of power.

Likewise, he was sure Fion genuinely thought the crowd was swayed, based on his sincere belief in the rightness of his argument, rather than them all succumbing to the unsubtle mental manipulations of Halcoth. Even Drunnoc winced to think of the damage the Steward must have done to his sanity in levelling his Skill that high.

He felt his father's hand on his shoulder and tensed. But no. He was not being struck in chastisement. Instead, this was — what? Affection, he presumed.

Yes — and Drunnoc felt a sigh escape his lips — his father was a moron.

For the moment, though, a useful one. As he had long experienced, there were benefits in continuing to operate from the shadows. Especially until they managed to remove the Lady Darkhelm from the board. He would be shocked if the current assault proved to be the end of that particular thorn in the side of the Trellecs.

Regardless of Lady Darkhelm, though — indeed, to a certain extent *because* of her — there was a significant time of change coming. If his father got his way — and Drunnoc was minded to use his considerable resources to help him achieve his goal — then more of this shadowy power would be available.

Independence. It was a word to conjure with. Free from the need for restraint. Beyond the reach of control. That would be a turn of events he would be interested in pursuing.

Speaking of those resources . . .

*

Boruld had watched things unfold with a depth of horror he had not thought he possessed.

He was still shocked by the brazenness of it. The Trellecs had bribed members of the village to attend a speech and then used <Authority> — a questionable Class power at the best of times — to drive them mad. He had heard of such things before, of course. But not in civilised kingdoms. It entirely defied belief.

Even now, those poor, ensorcelled people were tearing at that man's house like beasts; Goddess knew what would happen to the occupants when the madness broke through.

With a whispered word, he reinforced the stone in the building against their attack. It was not much in the face of things he had, unwillingly, helped set in motion.

But we all make amends in the best way we can.

*

Halcoth, bemused, stood at the side of the stage.

He could feel that intense skin prickle that meant he had been drawing on his power — and a lot of it, too, by the feel of the inflammation in his skin — but he was unsure what he had been influencing.

He blinked myopically in the midday sun and cast about fretfully. There were lots of people around, and he did not like that. He preferred being in his room, with all his bits and pieces around him. It was much easier to keep hold of his sense of self when he was in that place. When out and about like this — well, the centre could not hold.

No, he needed to get back to his room at the Keep. This wouldn't do at all. About now, a Jane would do nicely. Yes, that always made him feel more like himself.

*

Veron led what remained of the gang through the back alleys of the village.

Drunnoc had been clear that an incensed mob would likely not be enough to deal with the Knight and her companions. So, their role was to keep an eye on possible escape routes from the Tailor's house and alert him should they be seen.

After the events of the preceding evening, those that remained in this group were intensely motivated in this regard. Veron did not feel much of a sense of loss for fallen comrades — it was always sensible to thin out the crowd now and again — but he intensely disliked the feeling of being afraid.

He had been fortunate not to have been home when the Lady Darkhelm called. He had no doubt his father would have been glad to sacrifice him should that not have been the case. However, for once, the Lords of Misrule had smiled on him, and he had escaped the fate of so many of his fellows. But now, with a good group of friends around him, he was ready to rebalance the scales.

*

Back in the Keep, Pernille regarded the subject tied to the table with a quizzical eye.

She had been given one task — to explore the extent and reach of her newly acquired Skill. Her mind was aflame with so many questions. Was there a limit to how much life force she could pull into herself? How little mana could a person possess and still be alive? How quickly could she completely drain someone?

There were many experiments ahead of her and, fortunately, with Drunnoc's support, significant opportunities to find the answers.

With a small smile, she pressed a finger down on the forehead of Councilman Blacksmith's daughter. Just a little more wouldn't hurt, would it? Well, not her, anyway.

*

Yes, thought Drunnoc, things were working out *terribly* well.

CHAPTER TWENTY-FOUR

"Borrowing Trouble"

"**Y**ou know when most people say something like 'there's another way out of here,' they generally mean a back door," said Kirstin, adjusting the weight of Genoes in her arms.

"You complaining?" Cenwyn's voice was muffled, coming from further ahead down the passage. "A fine group of folks back there will be happy to offer you an alternative."

"I don't know. They seemed mighty keen to make my acquaintance. Could be that my charms are finally being appreciated. There comes a time a girl needs to settle down."

"Quiet, both of you."

Daine was at the back of the group, carefully watching the trapdoor through which they had descended. If the Tailor knew his business — and she would feel some welcome surprise to uncover this side of him — it seemed likely their escape would be clean enough. At least initially.

But as Old Gant had always said: "*Hope for the best, plan for the worst.*" Actually, what Daine remembered him saying was "*It'll always go to hell; the ones that make it through expected it,*" but the sentiment was, broadly, the same.

She stretched out her arms to their entire span and touched the opposite walls of the tunnel. She thought they were solidly made, a physical manifestation of the Tailor's personality. But tall as she was, she did not need to stoop, and the curve of the passage stretched ahead as far as she could see until vanishing at the edge of flickering torchlight.

Despite everything, their situation had improved. She could defend this end of the position if she had to. If she planted her feet, even in her much-reduced state, there would be no pushing beyond her. The Archer and the Tailor could grow old behind her.

If only she could find a way to calm her racing heart.

With a glance to ensure no one was watching, she rested her head against the cool earthen wall and tried to control her panic at being beneath the ground again. "It is not the same," she whispered to herself. "This is not the same at all."

No one had been more surprised than her when Cenwyn had pulled up a rug in his storeroom to reveal what could only be described as a smuggler's hatch.

"And it leads where?" She had peered down into the darkness below and felt a twinge of panic at the thought of being back down there.

"Out."

"Out?"

"Out, Lady Darkhelm" — there had been another crash as the mob came perilously close to coming through the door — "as in, 'not here anymore.' If you have any better

ideas, now is the time to share. If not, my vote is for this."
He threw his hastily assembled backpack into the gloom
and indicated for Kirstin to go before him. "You go down,
and I'll pass you the lad."

If the Archer had had any concerns about the plan,
she hid them well while springing through the floor to
land on the packed dirt below. Cenwyn carefully picked up
the sleeping boy and lowered him into her arms. He then
looked at the Knight.

Sensing her disquiet, he had drawn close and lowered
his voice. "You'll have to go next, my Lady. I need to be
last to reset the trapdoor." He smiled encouragingly. "If
we're lucky, they're all too far out of their minds to search
properly."

"And if we're not?"

He had shrugged. "I don't see us in any worse a place
than now."

He had been right, and she had been wasting precious
time. With a last glance around for an alternative, she had
climbed down the ladder and stood at the bottom silently
as he had made the necessary arrangements to hide their
escape.

Now Cenwyn lit a torch, the light spilling out helping,
somewhat, to quell Daine's rising terror. She took advantage of the time to explore her surroundings further to distract herself. The walls of the passage were studded with
shelving and packed with all manner of goods and materials. She reached out to take down a package of what turned
out to be some sort of dried meat. Cenwyn appeared at her
shoulder.

"My father always said that it pays to have a backup plan.
Today's not the first time in our history that one of them

Lords got a notion in their head for some nastiness. There's a few of us in town that have these little boltholes. The plan was always to save as many as possible and wait it out. I keep it stocked when I have the spare coin. Used it once or twice myself. Made a few missteps with married women in my youth. Time and distance heal most things." His eyes narrowed on her. Taking in her clammy skin. Her shallow breathing. "Anything you need?"

"I'm healing," she replied shortly. He gave her a look she could not read and then, with a shake of his head, moved ahead to speak to Kirstin.

She was left in the gloom, alone, for a few moments. From the noise above, Daine could tell that the crowd had finally breached the house and were busy destroying everything they could find. With luck, she thought as a crash of a bookcase hitting the floor was heard, the devastation they were wreaking would further hide their escape route.

Cenwyn's news that several people in town who had these tunnels did little, though, to quell her anxieties. What were the chances there was someone up there who still had enough of their wits about them and, indeed, had their version of a smuggler's hatch and knew where to look?

"There's planning ahead, and then there's borrowing trouble, girl. One is sensible, the other is destructive. So, deal with what is in front of you." For once, grateful to the words from her past, she shut down that line of thought tight.

Daine knew, intellectually, that she had felt fear like this before.

In those early days of training at Gant's school, it had been the only emotion of which she seemed capable. The others had seemed so much older, with so many more Skills. And so much more brutal. Her every waking moment had seemed to have been a series of stumbling events of terror: the hazing, the duels, the orchestrated cruelty. She knew it was all organised to make them strong enough to do what was needed from them. But it had been a hellish winnowing.

She shook away the memory. All that was a lifetime ago. Daine Darkhelm was one of the few who had made it through the experience intact, and, in the intervening years, she had almost wholly forgotten the taste of fear.

But she remembered it now and knew she would not survive further entombment. That experience had left her with mental scars that no time would heal. To have been so helpless, so unable to strike back, had been devastating to her sense of self. Quite apart from the damage it had caused her body, her internal resources had been stretched beyond breaking, and she was barely holding herself together.

The presence of that Earth Mage in the crowd earlier had wholly unnerved her. He could bring all this down around them with a word, and she would be trapped again.

She moved to join the others down the passage. There was little profit to such introspection. She was a Knight of the Road, the embodiment of an implacable drive toward justice. It was to her that others should be looking for solace. For leadership. It was not for them to help her through this trauma. "*Fine words, Darkhelm. Do you believe them?*"

Gant's mockery echoing in her mind, she caught up with the others. Cenwyn was speaking with Kirstin. "It leads to the outskirts of the village. There's a tree stump no one would look at twice at the end."

"You sure no one knows about it?" Daine's voice made them jump.

"Well, not to bet my life on. We'd have to fight our way out if we're unlucky."

Kirstin grimaced at the thought of exiting into an unknown situation. "I won't be too much use carrying the boy. Could we just wait down here for it to blow over? That sort of rage burns hot, but they won't be able to sustain it. Give it a few hours, and we could get out the way we came."

"No," Daine's answer was too quick. Too loud in the quiet space. The others exchanged concerned glances, and shame burned within her. "We're too exposed to wait down here. They could come in the way we did, and others could approach from the other end. I know this feels safe, but that security is illusory. The only thing, for now, is to put some distance between ourselves and this madness. First, I need time to heal. Then, with enough of that, I can give answer to all this, I promise you. If they catch us now, good as you are, you don't have enough arrows to keep us safe." She turned to peer into the darkness. "How far does this tunnel go?"

"Not far. Half a bell's walk until we reach the exit?"

She could restrain the terror for that long. "We need to get out of here as fast as we can. With no knowing what may come at either end, we're exposed. Master Tailor, you take the boy and the torch and stay in the middle of us. I'll guard the back in case someone up there has more about them than we think. Mistress Archer, you able to take point? Give a short, sharp shock to any thinking to sneak up at us from there?"

"Won't be the first time." Kirstin, with great care, passed over Genoes. "Should we be worried he's not stirring?"

"Healing takes it out of you. He was in a state, after all. I'd rather he's like this than needing babysitting in a fight."

A darkness passed over the Archer's face as she

remembered her brother's actions. Unfortunately, Daine was not the only one carrying wounds that were unlikely to heal.

Once Cenwyn had the boy in a comfortable position over one shoulder, she passed over the torch and, after a moment's thought, her loaded crossbow. "It's about as simple as it could be," she said in answer to his raised eyebrows. "Point and fire. You only get one shot. If anything gets beyond either of us, you will need it. So, make it a shot that counts."

Kirstin watched him balance it in her hands until she was satisfied he would not accidentally shoot her in the back. With a quick nod at the others, she unslung her bow and moved ahead of them. She activated <Keen Sight> and the shadows receded even further. Then, notching an arrow and holding it at half-draw, she headed into the darkness.

After a pause, they followed.

CHAPTER TWENTY-FIVE

"The Limits of Authority"

Rowan was dimly aware he did not want to be doing any of this.

It was, after all, one of the more horrifying aspects of being under the influence of <Authority>: you were perfectly aware of what was happening but had little ability to resist it.

He had thought that not being directly in the employ of House Trellec — something he had worked hard over the years to avoid for just this reason — he would be immune from the Steward's power. After all, that sinister old man should only have dominion over those paid to work for that House.

Apparently, though, not all of his employers had been entirely honest about their funding source. Looking at the actions of friends who were now also under Halcoth's influence, he was not the only one trapped in this manner.

Nevertheless, since feeling that synthetic, overwhelming rage to kill the Tailor and bursting through the door of Cenwyn's house, he had been doing everything he could to distract his conscious mind from focusing on that rug in the middle of the storeroom.

Earlier when so many of them were shambling about, smashing everything in sight, keeping his attention elsewhere had not been so difficult. His principal Class Skill, <Clear Sight>, allowed him to intensely focus on a task. Now, however, when there was nowhere for anyone to be hidden within the building, it was harder to keep his mind on other things.

"Where are they?"

That whispery voice hit him like a lightning bolt. Nearly every part of his being, wanted to raise his hand and point at that spot. Wanted to answer the question, to please the questioner, with a slavish need. He did everything he could to focus on other things. To think about other places the Tailor and his friends might be, other than hidden down the smuggler's passage.

The effort caused blood to start to drip from his nose.

"Master Glazier. Please do come here."

His feet moved of their own accord, and, in seconds, he stood before Gilles Halcoth. The strange thing was that this man had fascinated him as a young boy. Admired him. Wanted to be just like him. The Steward had always had a kind word and often something sweet from the kitchens for him. Everyone had appeared to like him, and he had just been so . . . affable. Rowan could never understand why his mother was so angry whenever his name was mentioned.

Only when he was old enough to appreciate how he used

his power and what he made others do in its service had he realised what a monster this kindly old man truly was.

"Master Glazier. Rowan. My dear young thing. You look like you have something you want to tell me. Where are they, lad? Where has the Knight gone?"

The pressure in his head was unbearable. The steady scarlet drip from the nose became a flood, to be joined on his chest by rivers falling from his eyes and out of his ears.

"You know you are going to tell me. Why not get it over with? There's no need for all this unpleasantness. Your poor old mother was just the same. Never gave it up without an unnecessary, undignified fight. Where. Have. They. Gone?"

Rowan's arm swung up, and he pointed out the hidden space under the rug.

As his brain haemorrhaged, the last thought that flitted through his ruptured mind was one word for his friend: *Run!*

*

It was a testament to Daine's compromised state that the first moment she knew that others were in the tunnel with them was when an axe sank into her back. Her ears had not picked up the sound of approaching feet, and, more worrying, there had been no whisper of danger sense from the Goddess. She and her patron would need to have a heart-to-heart when this was over.

She spun in response to the contact, the sudden movement wrenching the axe free from its wielder's hands. A big man — not a soldier, a Lumberjack, perhaps — stared up at her, the telltale dilation of <Authority> clouding his eyes.

She'd been sneak-attacked by someone with the size and delicacy of a mountain bear; this was not one of her finer moments. That there'd not been room in the tunnel for him to wind up his attack properly had saved her.

Behind him, she could see other shapes converge in the darkness.

"We've got company!" She could not quite bring herself to kill the man; it was not his fault he was down here with them. She put a hand against his chest and pushed him roughly into the growing crowd flowing down the passage. He travelled thirty, perhaps forty feet, taking all those approaching with him as he went.

"Cenwyn, tell Kirstin to get a move on, then put the boy down and get this thing out of my back."

They had some time as the heap of bodies sorted themselves out. While <Authority> could make you do things you would rather not, it rarely made you especially good at them. That was why the King had long since stopped using Stewards to motivate his armies. A compelled force could never defeat one thinking for itself. And the madness such a use of the Skill caused in those people was legendary.

There was a soft sucking sound as Cenwyn yanked the blade free. "You're bleeding quite badly from the wound; can you heal up?"

"No idea. Give me the axe."

Cenwyn hesitated. "They're good people, Daine. None of them want to be doing this."

Despite the rush of approaching footsteps, she chose not to snatch the weapon from him. "I don't want to be here either, Cenwyn. Doubt you want it, neither. Do I let them kill us because we're too dainty to defend ourselves?"

After a beat, he handed her the axe, and she turned to face the attackers.

There was an art to fighting in such close confines.

Daine had trained extensively, some might say obsessively, for just such a confrontation. The assorted shopkeepers and artisans currently trying to attack her, not so much.

Using the axe more as a quarterstaff than any chopping implement, she easily kept them at bay. One of her earliest earned Skills, <Polearm Master>, flared into use. She could not remember the last time it had been required. There was no technique to how they swarmed toward her. With proper coordination, they could have made her life difficult. As it was, it was almost child's play to defend the narrow space. It was this — mindful of Cenwyn's words — that kept her from racking up an excessive number of casualties.

With each sweep and strike of the wood, she aimed to incapacitate rather than slaughter, breaking arms and legs rather than heads. Soon there was a solid wall of groaning humanity blocking the tunnel. Those behind were still driven to squeeze through what gaps they could find in the press, but there was a limit to what they could achieve.

Satisfied that the passage was effectively blocked, she retreated to Cenwyn. "Let's keep it moving."

He gathered up Genoes. "Sure. Kirstin must be getting near the entrance now."

*

The Archer fired her penultimate arrow and was rewarded with the shriek of a Lordling with a somewhat inflated opinion of his< Stealth> capabilities. He was the third who had thought to try to come at her from that particular direction. It hadn't worked out too well for the first two either.

She guessed there was no teaching stupid.

It had all been going too well, she recognised. She had reached the end of the tunnel in no time before climbing the rope ladder to quickly check how the land lay above ground. It was, as the Tailor had said: the tunnel emerged from a giant tree stump in the middle of a wide clearing. Unless you knew precisely for what you were looking, it was unlikely your eye would be drawn to it.

However, with dismay, she had noted that nine or ten of Drunnoc's group — Veron among them, of course he was — were casting around through the undergrowth within a few feet of this hidden place.

They had clearly had information about where the tunnel ended, and she feared for the villager who had been forced to give up that location. However, knowing broadly where it was and zeroing in on the exact location within the trees were two different things.

She had ducked back down into the tunnel and taken a few hesitant steps back toward the group. She could not make out Daine or Cenwyn in the dark but, worryingly, could hear the sound of battle for the first time.

If Daine, Cenwyn and Genoes were being pursued and driven towards her, they could not afford to get trapped at this end. It seemed unlikely that the searchers aboveground would stumble upon the exit, but even they would be hard-pressed to miss the noise once it drew closer.

She made a decision.

Climbing back up, she took a moment to wait until none of them were looking directly her way and, activating <Quick Draw>, shot into the foot of one of the older boys, one of those who felt his higher status allowed his hands free access to "Jak's big sister." His indignant howl as the arrow buried itself between his toes pulled all eyes toward him, giving Kirstin plenty of opportunity to make her move.

She hopped out from the tree stump and <Dashed>

towards cover as far away from the exit as she could in the time. Then, just as Veron's group regained their composure, she dived behind a tree, turning to <Multi-Shot>, blind, toward the group. They scattered with hoots of anger.

From that moment, they had engaged in a reasonably predictable game of cat and mouse where the boys made unsubtle attempts to feign one way while attacking the other, at which stage she shot them.

With another half-quiver of arrows, she was confident they would run out of willing pincushion sacrifices before reaching her. However, as she notched her final one and took reluctant aim at the space from which she was confident the next attack would come, the nature of the game was about to change.

Her eyes strayed toward the hidden exit. Right now would be an excellent moment for the appearance of a Knight of the Road.

CHAPTER TWENTY-SIX

"Leadership Is a Burden"

Veron was frustrated.

He was not someone that should so blithely be dispatched to "search the woods." He was not a henchman. He was the sort of person who had henchmen. He should be with Drunnoc, directing things from the centre of the village. Showing everyone where the true power lay. Yes, that was where a man of his worth should be seen. Not wandering the woods on some foolish search for the "end of an escape tunnel." Particularly when the source for that information was some gibbering villager who kept begging the Steward to believe it existed.

During this little excursion, though, Veron quickly realised that one "clearing in the woods" looked much like another. He did not like to second-guess his command choices, but he now recognised that it would have been more helpful to have looked to bring that villager with them rather than blindly heading out. However, he knew that once those under <Authority> had finished answering Halcoth's questions, rarely was anything left to be of much use.

Therefore, in lieu of any actual guide, they had been all but kicking their heels, looking for *just* the right configuration of trees, logs, and bushes for the last few bells. Veron was beginning to think he would need an effective scapegoat for Drunnoc's rage when they came home with nothing to show for it when, out of nowhere, someone shot Larnach in the foot.

To be fair, if anyone in his group had to catch an arrow, Lordling Hunt would have been right at the top of Veron's list. Slow, petty, and obsessed with gambling, only the openness of his purse gave him continued access to their company. Indeed, he had spent much of this expedition seeking to wager on the likelihood of the next corner revealing the sought-after hiding place. The repetitive joy he took in this activity had so irritated the others that only his loss of several months' worth of tavern bills had mitigated his presence.

"Bet you didn't see that coming," sniggered Veron. The others laughed dutifully, but he realised that was an unworthy comment for a leader of his gravitas. So, they dragged Larnach to cover — regardless of personal animus, you did not leave a fellow in a spot like that — and then tried to identify where the arrows were coming from.

It was at this stage that they all realised how poorly their Skills translated to guerrilla warfare.

There was an art to being a bully. It took size, strength, and significant familial clout for this little group to be highly intimidating. It did not need much Intelligence, but a certain base cunning and a capacity to read the smart play in a situation were always helpful. Unfortunately, on top of these innate qualities, the Lord Class these boys possessed magnified things to an unpleasant degree. Such enhancement to already questionable personality traits made them quite tricky to deal with when in a group and, say, in a tavern with enough people egging them on.

Part of the reason the Lady Darkhelm had been required to conduct quite such a thorough scouring of the aristocratic youth of the village was that within this generation, these traits, alongside their Class, had combined into something exceptionally toxic.

For the most part, the people of the village had identified this and done what they could, with limited success, to stay out of their way.

However, whoever was currently shooting at them seemed pretty immune to the innate superiority of their bloodline. The sinking realisation that it was challenging to overawe someone with the braying insistence of your presence when they kept hitting you with arrows was not a pleasant experience.

That there had not been any deaths yet seemed more down to their attackers' understanding that an injured, debilitated, and, most of all, screaming foe was more helpful in such situations than anything else.

After several failed attempts to improve conditions, a Council of War was called amongst the leaves. Or, to put it another way, Veron hid beneath a rotting tree stump and gathered the remaining two of his still-mobile fellows. They hunkered down as low as possible and peered out into the foliage. "Look, there must be at least four out there. I think the arrows have come from there,

there, and over there." It was a testament to the low levels of Veron's Luck that he succeeded in indicating three
areas in which Kirstin absolutely was not hiding. "So,
what do we do?"

Silence was his answer.

Disappointed at the lack of options, Veron manfully
stepped into the breach. "Okay, so this is the plan, then.
Daniel, you go that way, and Ephron, you move to the left.
I'll hang back here and watch for where they shoot from.
That way, we can flank their position." His friends looked
over at the remnants of their small group — some crying,
some now worryingly quiet — who had learned to their
cost the challenges of flanking an unknown number of
assailants in an unknown position, particularly when they
seemed handy with a bow.

Ephron licked his lips. He had learned all too well that
any attempt to disagree with Veron could be tricky, but that
seemed relatively inconsequential compared to the more
pressing concern of an arrow to the face. "I don't know,
Ver. We were just coming to block up a tunnel. I don't think
Drunnoc thought we would be walking into a war. I mean,
if there's four of them, perhaps it would be best to get
some more backup?"

If there was one leadership skill Veron had picked up
from his more terrifying friend, it was the necessity of
ruthlessly crushing dissent. "When I want your opinion,
Ronny" — he used that hated nickname, the one which
never failed to make his friend wince — "I will ask for it."
Daniel and Ephron wisely ignored the fact that just such
an inquiry for ideas had been voiced a few seconds earlier.
"Now, get out there!"

Ephron peeked his head out from the side of the tree

trunk they were using for cover and, not immediately being murdered horribly, scampered as far to the left as he could go. The second youth, Daniel, who had more of a healthy fear of Veron than Ephron, used the noise of his friend's movement to launch his scurrying charge.

*

Kirstin tracked both boys as they made their way closer to her position. She only dimly knew these two; they were not the worst of Jak's "friends." The one, Ephron, seemed to be able to think for himself occasionally, while Daniel was about as inoffensive as this type of boy came. She had managed to hold back from hitting either of them thus far. And, without question, neither was worth wasting her final arrow while Veron Geril still drew breath.

Indeed, she had worked hard not to kill *anyone* during this confrontation. Her plan had been to hope that the injured's shrieking and crying would alert Daine or Cenwyn to the increased plight aboveground. But, instead, the noise levels had shrunk to some rather pathetic muffled sobbing, with no sign of either of her friends emerging from the tunnel.

Something must have gone wrong there, but she could not worry about that now. The three boys left standing had managed to manoeuvre themselves into a pretty decent position to launch an attack, especially against an arrowless Archer.

Cursing under her breath, she could not help but think she was running out of options.

*

Veron did not miss that no whistling arrows of death emerged from the undergrowth to forestall the progress of either of the sacrifices. Instead, his friends had made significant ground and were now crouched, sweating and breathless, eagerly awaiting further instructions.

Leadership was a burden, reflected Veron. Just once, he would like someone to show some initiative and devise their own plan rather than looking to him for everything. If he was scrupulously honest, it was why he liked being around Drunnoc. When Veron was in his company, he did not have to think like this; instead, he just did what he was told. It was much more enjoyable to enact the plans of others rather than have to be responsible for what took place.

A crunch in the undergrowth dragged his attention to Ephron's position; the fool was standing, shouting, and charging forward. What was he doing? Did he not understand that Veron had this all under control? He was yelling as he completed his headlong rush: what did he mean, "it's Jak's sister?"

Entirely without thinking, he stood to berate the running youth for failing to listen to instructions.

*

Kirstin swung her bow to track the approach of the one — it was Ephron, wasn't it? — who had moved to come at her from the left. He must have caught sight of her from that new position and now was poised to intercept. Well, she had done her best to keep the tunnel clear, but she was at the end of what she could reasonably achieve. So, with some regret for the boy's fate, she drew her final bolt backwards, prepared to run as fast as possible in the other direction when it was loosed.

Then, a fraction of a second before releasing the shot, the figure of Veron simply left cover and stepped into her peripheral vision.

While she knew Drunnoc to be a certifiable monster,

there was a special place in her heart for causing Veron pain. While Drunnoc came up with the plans, Veron was the one to get his hands dirty. And he enjoyed making things as messy as possible when the opportunity presented itself. He was the one, she knew, who had sought to egg on Jak's worst excesses.

Day by day, week by week, his gleeful encouragement had helped to bring out the side of her brother she saw in his knife fight with Genoes.

If anyone deserved her final arrow, it would be him. So, choosing to let Ephron continue his dash toward her un-molested, she swung her aim at the group's leader, activated <Sure Shot> and released.

*

The funny thing was that Veron heard the arrow that killed him before he saw it. The soft hiss of a bowstring made him turn slightly to his left to peer, astonished, at the ap-proaching projectile.

This movement had the consequence of lining up his forehead quite perfectly for the shot to enter just above his nose.

As he sank to his knees, there was just enough time to lament the behaviour of minions who failed to do what they were told.

And then darkness.

*

It's all fun and games until your friends are shot with arrows.

Ephron and Daniel froze at Veron's death before, seem-ingly without making eye contact, both choosing to flee into the woods.

They left behind their softly mewling wounded friends and a somewhat surprised and entirely arrowless Archer.

With a quick check, that there was to be no sudden follow-up, Kirstin vaulted into the tunnel and went to check on the others.

CHAPTER TWENTY-SEVEN

"The Madness of Cart Horses"

On reflection, Daine considered, it had been fool-ish to think there would just be villagers sent in pursuit. Her easy victory against the <Authority>-controlled horde had given her a false sense of security, notwithstanding catching an axe blow to the back at the start of the fight.

They had made it a bit further up the tunnel, still no sign of Kirstin or the way out, when a hail of crossbow bolts smashed into the walls around them. Daine turned and saw three elaborately decorated pavise shields blocking the passage a distance back from them. The shield bearers were protecting five or six crossbowmen who were reload-ing even as she watched.

She moved to stand between their line of fire and the Tailor. "Move further up the tunnel. They look pretty, but the range of those things is not great." Another hail of bolts was released, and she swept her hand to knock one that came too close out of the air.

Cenwyn jerked back as the bolts flashed around him and carried Genoes up and away from danger. "Aren't they just going to keep moving up and closing the distance, though?"

"I imagine that was probably their plan." And she ran toward the shields.

*

"You're slow," Old Gant had told her. "Not compared to your common or garden soldier, to be sure. But, in the grand scheme of things, you're a trudging cart horse."

To reinforce the point, he had . . . *blurred* was the only way to describe his movement speed toward her to tweak her nose. She had swung an arm to deflect him, and then he was moving behind her to flick an ear. "You couldn't catch me on my worst day. And I'm old. Burned out. Past my best. A drunken joke." He punctuated each sentence with a prod and a pinch of exposed flesh. Daine whirled about, sweeping her hands in increasingly frantic efforts to defend herself.

The rest of the school paused their training to watch this important lesson be handed out. Many of them had found that Orban had been getting too sure of herself. Had displayed too much unearned confidence in her progress. It was always the same with those that Gant brought in himself; they thought they were unique somehow. That he had specifically chosen them for greatness and that it meant something.

Well, such an attitude made times like this all the sweeter.

"Have you ever seen one of those cart horses driven mad by a horsefly? It's a sad state of affairs. They run and run, and fight and snap, but there's nothing they can do about it." A thin stiletto was now in his hand, leaving pinpricks of blood as he buzzed around her. "These big, strong animals. Capable of such strength. And a tiny little fly can, through biting, and biting, and biting, make them want to die. Yet, for all their much-admired power, they cannot do anything to relieve it. I cannot tell you how many I have seen that have needed to be put down. Because they were too slow."

Daine was panicking now, helpless in the face of this frenzied attack. She'd seen what happened when Gant took his training sessions too far. The attrition rate at the school was horrific for just that reason. She had been wrong to push him, to brag over how fast her Strength was outstripping his. As soon as she had said the words, she had watched as his face had gone slack in that terrifying blank way.

But what had started as a correction for her arrogance had slipped into something more deadly. He had that faraway look in his eye again, the one he got when he forgot he was no longer on a mission behind enemy lines for the King. In this state, anything could happen. And it often did. The small graveyard at the back of the school was a testament to the dangers of Gant losing his sense of time and place.

It had taken three weeks to properly heal from the damage that session had caused. Reportedly, Gant had sat by her bedside and drank solidly for every bell of those days.

She had been seven years old.

There had been no apology, not that she would have expected one. But, in any event, there had not needed to be. It would not be the worst state she would be left in during her tutelage with him. Not by a long way. No, the most important thing was that she had learned an important lesson that day.

Not that she was slow. She knew that already. The blitz attacks of some of her peers were not for her. With her Skills, she was not going to be found in the shadows of the rooftops, sprinting to avoid bodyguards and the like. No, what she learned, what Gant had leant over to whisper into her ear each and every morning during her recovery, was that, yes, she was slow. But so was an avalanche.

*

It was generally seen as one of the cushier jobs in the Keep.

If you could hold the shield still while one of those *fancy dans* with the crossbows — the ones who would not even deign to eat in the servery with the rest of you — took their best shot and then crouched down next to you for cover while they reloaded, you were golden.

To be a successful shield bearer, you needed to be calm, dependable, and blessed with no imagination whatsoever.

Artem liked the job. He had not been blessed with much Luck, so finding a reasonably undemanding role that came with bed and board was a significant result. His mother had been so proud to see him in his uniform — and while House Culloden might not be the *most* prestigious of the Houses he could have served, at least it was not House Trellec.

The only qualification you needed for this role was to have the Strength to hold the shield vertically for as long as required and have the ability to cope with long periods of boredom; you did not even get equipped with a sword in case you were tempted to get ideas above your station. No. You held the shield and, in extremis, helped with reloading.

Oh, and you got an extra half-coin a week if you

developed enough skill as an Artist to decorate your shield. Truth be told, he was not much with a paintbrush, but had been able to do a relatively serviceable depiction of the Dark God on his shield that brought some attention. He was quite pleased with it, and some friends had asked him to do the same on theirs.

They had not been surprised to be summoned to action this morning: it was common knowledge Lady Culloden wanted the head of that Knight of the Road. Something about a night battle that had got all the higher-ups with their pantaloons in a twist. So, once the news came down that she was debilitated and ripe for the plucking, they'd been ordered to gear up and move into town.

Artem could not help thinking that from the moment Lord Trellec finished his speech — it made his skin crawl the way the Trellecs used <Authority> to boost their popularity — things had started to spiral out of control. It was somewhat of an unusual course of events to be sent down into a smuggler's tunnel, and even more so to be needed to clear a press of unconscious common-Classed out of the way to carve out a line of sight with their target.

However, when all was said and done, Artem was happy with the unusual. It broke up some of the monotony of the day.

Crucially, however, while holding this shield upright might be an undemanding role, perfect for someone of his limited range of choices, there was nothing in his training about what to do when someone apparently impervious to bolts ran toward you.

He exchanged a nervous glance with Steffan, the pavise bearer next to him, as the distance between them and their target relentlessly decreased. The old woman — anyone

over thirty was old in their book, of course — was not
moving quickly, but she was certainly getting closer.

This was quite unprecedented. In his experience, the tar-
gets tended to run the other way. That could be quite a pain
as you then got shouted at to scurry to keep up with them.
Lugging the heavy metal oblongs at speed, while a chinless
wonder with a crossbow was berating you, was the most
challenging part of the job.

It would be fair to say Artem's unease with the situation
was not eased when the Crossbowman with whom he had
been paired suddenly swore, backed away and started running away down the tunnel.

Fortunately, he did not have long to worry about it.

*

Daine crashed into and through the heavy shields blocking
her and pressed on, seeking to close the distance with the
fleeing Crossbowmen. As she went, she felt a crunch of
bones under her feet when she stamped over a pretty decent picture of the Dark God.

It was not a long chase. The ones fleeing were weighed
down by weaponry and heavy armour, and she quickly
caught and then batted the slowest couple of runners
against the wall. They hit the sides of the passage with a
screeching, metallic crunch, each embedding several feet
into the soil. Seeing them hit the wall, Daine had to close
down a burst of fear as to what she may have done to the
integrity of that part of the tunnel and continued her chase.

Realising the futility of flight, the other three turned to
try to make something of it. One still carried a loaded crossbow and fired it into the Knight's stomach at point-blank
range.

Staggering backwards, Daine reached down to pull out

the bolt; experience had taught her it was better to do that now while the fury was on her. She felt something spill out from the wound and put it out of her mind. It would heal or it would not. Nothing to be done worrying about it. She forced the gory wooden stick through the throat of the one who had shot her; arterial blood sprayed out to cover her as she turned to break the neck of the second of them, who was too slow to do much of anything at all.

The final one threw his crossbow at her, which, as a tactic, was somewhat of a surprise. The shock of it striking her on the nose made her eyes water, and that brief moment of uncertainty gave him enough time to resume his run back up the tunnel. He vanished round the corner and out of her sight.

Daine was about to pursue him when a shout caught her attention.

"Lady Darkhelm!"

Daine turned and was pleased to see that Genoes had awoken from his healing sleep. Unfortunately, the sight of Cenwyn collapsed to the floor, a crossbow bolt protruding from his chest, was much less welcome.

CHAPTER TWENTY-EIGHT

"The Dark God"

He was standing in the middle of a field. But not one he recognised.

The fields around the village were all cultivated: carefully enclosed areas where everything had its place, and every inch was chartered and owned by Farmers. Those fields were passed down through the generations, and working on them was a jealously guarded privilege. Even during the harvest time, when he had expected all hands would be required to bring in the crops, his help had never been welcomed.

This field was not like that.

Lush grass stretched as far as he could see, and there were giant animals he had never encountered before, moving in herds in the distance. He could hear a river bubbling nearby but could not find its source through the tall grasses. Flocks of birds sang and arced through the air. The overwhelming sense was of a profound and abiding peace.

Genoes was not sure that he had ever dreamed before. If that was what this was, of course.

He knew people enjoyed talking about their dreams, and he always nodded along when they described the fantastic adventures they had taken part in the evening before. But had he ever been in this state himself? He did not think so.

Nightmares, on the other hand? He had experience with those. Well, one nightmare, anyway. Whenever he closed his eyes at night, he knew he was embarking on the next phase of an unending hunt. From the second he dropped off, he would spend his sleeping hours hiding, in terror, from something seeking him out. It was not entirely a chase, he did not think his pursuer ever quite caught sight of him that way — but he knew, deep in his heart, that he needed to make sure this . . . something never laid eyes on him. He did not know the outcome should he be caught, but he had a horror of it happening.

The quiet fear of the silent waiting and the never-ending need to scurry from one spot to another whenever he felt that sinister regard shift was overwhelming. He often awoke drenched in sweat.

He had talked about these nightmares with Brother Evelyn. It felt ridiculous to speak of dark nightmares when bathed in the light of the Church of Dawn, but, in many ways, it was the safest way to do it. The old drunk had listened and noted that these dreams were "an intellectual rationalisation of your constant battle to survive. Your spirit knows of your daily struggles to escape your fate, and it plays that out for you in the dreaming."

Genoes was not too sure about any of that. When

chased in a dream, he felt that it was as at least as real as anything that happened when Veron or Drunnoc loosed their pack on him. And yet, instinctively, he knew that the repercussions of being caught by that brooding presence in his sleep would be far more devastating than any beating at the hands of those boys.

But that nightmare state was as different from his feeling of peace and serenity here as anything could possibly be. If this were dreaming, he could grow to love it.

"He's looking for you, you know."

He whirled to stare at the loveliest woman he had ever seen. Not that he had much experience in such matters but, objectively, the figure in front of him was beautiful. Had she been standing there behind him the whole time? He did not think so. She must have just manifested from nowhere. In his dream state, he did not believe this was an especially unusual or noteworthy thing.

She was tall and dark-haired with eyes that shone with a powerful golden light. That light overwhelmed any other detail he could make out of her. But, regardless, he knew he felt safe with her. He could not have said how he knew this field belonged to her. And what was more, he was welcome here. That welcome felt like . . . home.

Smiling, she spoke again. "Do not fear, little one. He does not know you are here."

"Who?"

"The one seeking you."

"What do you mean? Who is looking for me?"

"The Dark God. He has been hunting for you for such a long time. You were supposed to be his, after all."

That did not sound like an especially good thing. Throughout his life, Genoes had limited experience of being sought by anyone who had good things in store for him. Likewise — and he was beginning to draw parallels between what the woman was saying and the experiences of his nightmares — it was difficult to feel warm toward someone called the Dark God.

"Where am I? The last thing I remember was —" He flashed back to his confrontation with Jak. The sharp hurt of the knife slashes. The overwhelming pain emanating from beneath his feet. His desperation to escape as the older boy cut and cut and cut.

The woman leant forward and put her hand on his forehead. His breathing calmed at the coolness of her touch. "Let that memory go. It is to little purpose to hold on to such things. You are as safe here as it is in my power to make you. Good friends have healed and protected your body. Your spirit is — well, he cannot find you here for now."

As pleasant as he found standing in this field and as comforting as this woman's presence was, Genoes did not like the idea of being separated from his body. Nor from his friends. Beyond everything else, he needed to ensure the Lady Darkhelm was okay. He could not forget, despite the woman's words, the pain he knew she had been experiencing.

At that, though, clouds started to form in the perfect sky. The birds were no longer spiralling through the air, and their singing had halted. The woman frowned. "His frustration is palpable. I can feel him intruding even here. He was promised he could have you and yet you have constantly slipped his grasp. He thought he had finally found you so many times — indeed, he took many in your village in your stead — but no. Not you. You always managed, at the last, to avoid his gaze." The woman's voice had lost some of its lulling quality. As if speaking of the Dark God had, in itself, disrupted her equanimity.

"I don't understand!"

"Do not worry. You are not meant to. Yet. Just know that he is looking and will continue to seek you. There is not much that I, that any of us, can do should he find you. But we have had some success in diverting his search, and we will continue with those efforts. Even now, one of my own has put herself between you and him. Not that she would see it as such, of course. Hear me, though. She will not be enough on her own. But where there is life, there is hope."

The weather was transforming. Rain started to pour from the sky, thunder rumbling in the distance. The herds of animals he had noticed earlier had withdrawn, and he thought he could make out the sound of the howling of wolves in the distance. Then lightning flashed, making him startle.

"Your time here has come to an end. I am sorry I could not keep you here longer, little one. But he grows angry and is more powerful when accessing that anger. So, I leave you with a word of warning. Those who call the Dark God patron will hate you. They will not know why; they will not recognise you as the one their Master seeks, but they will wish to destroy you. And they will not be able to restrain that need. To survive in this world, you must find friends on whom you can rely. You will need to get stronger. To develop who you are."

"But who am I?" he shouted above the rising gale. "I don't even know who I am!"

"Why, is that not the beauty of it all? For the first

occasion in a very long time, I look into the eyes of someone wholly free of us all. Genoes, my dear, you are a blank
slate. You are Unclassed. You can be whoever, whatever,
you wish."

Genoes was suddenly snapped out of that field by being dropped to the ground. The impact was not significant,
but was enough to disorientate him momentarily. At least,
he thought he must be disorientated because he appeared
to be in a tunnel. That could not be right, could it? The
ground was cold beneath his hands. There was also lots
of noise coming from nearby: screaming and shouting of
panicked voices and the crashing of metal. It reminded him
of — he was going to say "of the noises at the end of his
dream," but he did not dream. Never had.

Looking around further, he noticed that Cenwyn seemed
to have fallen to his knees next to him. There was something wrong with his breathing. He rose up onto his own
knees and put his hand on the Tailor's chest. It came away
wet. Sticky. He explored further and found the bolt in the
centre of his chest.

In the flickering light, the Tailor met his eyes and smiled
weakly. Blood was frothing on his lips. "Lad, it's good to
see you up and about! A growing boy shouldn't sleep in
so late. You've missed all the fun. Could you —" Genoes
understood and helped him to lie down on his back, careful
to avoid touching the protrusion. He supported the man's
head against his own chest. "How's she doing?" Cenwyn's
words came out slowly between laboured breaths.

Genoes turned to peer down the tunnel and could make
out the Lady Darkhelm dispatching several soldiers in the
colours of House Culloden. What was that all about? "She's
winning, I think."

"Then all is well in the world. It's my own fault. I wanted to see her fight again. She told me to get out of range." Cenwyn winced with pain. "She's going to blame herself for this, lad. You need to make sure she knows I was to blame. She does not need to add the weight of this to her shoulders. There's enough baggage there already. You will need to help her see that."

"I don't understand, Master Tailor. What is it you want me to do?" There was no answer. "Master Tailor?"

Cenwyn's eyes were closed, and there was a smile on his lips.

Far away, yet just out of sight, he was walking, hand in hand, with the loveliest woman he had ever seen through the most beautiful field.

Genoes looked on with horror at what he now knew to be a dead friend. Then he carefully placed Cenwyn's head on the floor, stood and called down the tunnel to Daine, who was just preparing to pursue the final Crossbowman.

"Lady Darkhelm!"

CHAPTER TWENTY-NINE

"An Excellent Source of Life force"

People died.

Of course they did.

They died all the time and from all manner of different things: violence, indifference, illness, malice. Any number of causes could play their part, and all had the same result. People died.

Sometimes deaths meant something. They left trails in the sky behind them to mark their passing. Other times, they were mean and quiet, and no one knew any different, or much cared, when that light faded from the world.

Pernille was becoming, and in a truly short period of time, something of a connoisseur of death.

There was an ebb and flow to her new Skill, <Life Drain> that she found fascinating. It was one of the central tenets of Healing that each person had their own finite store of Health. When you were injured, or became ill, or simply aged, that store of Health decreased. The role of a Healer was, therefore, to transfer their mana in to replace the lost life force. However, whereas she had always visualised Healing as the pouring of precious water into a great, unending void, it turned out the process worked just as well the other way around.

Indeed, it had been the single biggest revelation of her life that there were all these pools of life force walking around her, just waiting for her to dip in for a refreshing drink. Other people and their woes were not *just* a consistent drain on her, they could also supply a much-needed top-up.

She had started small, a dip here, a dip there as she walked around the Keep. Nothing so much that anyone would notice, but all those little tastes started to add up. It was amazing that what she thought of as her "full" state was nothing like it. She had the capacity to hold far more mana than she had ever thought possible. True, she could not maintain that state for long, but not only did it make her feel utterly amazing, it gave her somewhat of bulwark against the incessant demands of Healing placed upon her.

For example, right now she was patching up a Groom who had allowed himself to be kicked by one of the horses. It was nothing particularly complex, some bruising and the odd broken rib. Usually, this would be just the sort of Healing she would find objectionable: hugely mana-intensive for little real gain. Because of her generosity, this idiot would not learn the crucial life lesson that he needed to stop standing behind horses; the consequences of his unthinking actions had been removed by her Healing. What is more, the drain would leave her feeling low for the rest of the day and, more than likely, the same thing would happen next week!

Now, however, with her over-packed reserves, she was able to do the job in, she was sure, a manner of which her mother would be proud. While in the past she might be tempted to do the absolute minimum, maybe fixing the breaks but not dulling any of the pain, on this occasion she felt she could really put an effort in. With amazement, she watched as all that mana went away with no ill effects.

Of course, she was realistic enough to realise that her use of this new power was not purely altruistic.

Little sips of the life force of passing servants were one thing. It had taken far more than a quick sip to fill her up so entirely. That was where Drunnoc had come in.

It turned out that the youngest Trellec had quite a bit more to him than she had hitherto imagined. She had feared, when she realised he had seen the burgeoning of her new ability, that there would be some significant consequence for her actions. Had she not, after all, drained the remaining life force of one his men, albeit a terminally injured one?

Clearly, though, Drunnoc had the capacity to consider a far bigger picture than one broken knifeman. With barely a word, he had shepherded her through the gates of the Keep and down into the cellar that lay hidden beneath the Great Hall.

Dungeon, Pernille had thought. Not a cellar. A dungeon. A cellar was where you kept unnecessary furniture and perhaps stored some wine.

A dungeon was where you constructed cages, locked people in them and then, apparently, forgot all about them. A dungeon was a place of dark and death. And also, it was worth noting, a great source for filling up life force.

"I like painting them," Drunnoc had said. Indicating

one cell that contained someone that may likely have once been a human.

"You like painting them," she repeated.

Seemingly emboldened by her failure to run screaming for the nearest guard, Drunnoc pressed on. "Yes. But only when they are alive. That's the trick to it, you see. There's nothing within them to paint once they've died. I know, I've tried. It is a source of immense frustration." He opened the door and the . . . thing inside opened one eye.

She was aware that when people said "I'm starving" they were exaggerating for effect. During countless lessons in anatomy, she'd had it drilled into her how much nourishment, precisely, the average human required in order to continue to function. It had always amazed her how long some semblance of life could continue with little food at all.

"The body will protect the spirit at all costs" was how her father had put it. Shutting down extraneous functions one after another in order to protect that dwindling pool of water. If the thing in front of her was any indication, this process could go on for an exceedingly long time indeed.

Drunnoc had entered the cage and was crouched in front of that within. "What did they do?" Pernille asked, hesitantly.

"Do?"

"Yes, what did they do to deserve this?"

Drunnoc turned around to look at her, his head cocked to one side. His lips moved as if tasting the flavour of the words she had used and finding them unfamiliar. He turned back to the figure at his feet. "She was out in the woods one day. No one knew her. She said she was just passing through. Had some goods to sell in a pack on her back.

Some money in her pocket. From what I remember, she was probably your age."

"And?"

Drunnoc ran his finger, which slipped with a hiss, down the figure's papery skin. "If we are to have a partnership, you need to understand a crucial thing. There is no 'and.' She was there and now she's here and that is the way of things. If my men had not run across her, she would, right now, be a thousand leagues further down the Road and, I think we can agree, probably much happier for it." He indicated the other cages that filled the space; some were filled were shapes Pernille could discern, others looked empty. "It is the same for all of them. They were somewhere else and now there are here. They did not do anything to 'deserve this.' What could anyone ever do for this to be an appropriate outcome?"

Pernille slipped into the cage and touched what she now saw were the remains of a young woman. The emaciation was extraordinary: she had seen year-old cadavers with more flesh on their bones. With her Healing sense, she could brush just the thinnest stream of life still running through her.

"Why have you brought me here?"

"I'm interested. Interested in what you will choose to do." He was looking at her now and she found that regard chilling. Chilling and yet . . . not horrifying. He was genuinely interested in her next steps. Would she Heal this woman? She could. All this body needed was fuel, and was not mana the purest stuff of life. If she were to simply empty her reservoir into this woman, it would be incredible how quickly she would come back to life.

But she did not want to do that. She was dimly aware

that there was a perfectly rational reason for not Healing this woman. She was suffering and to prolong that suffering would be cruel. If she were to Heal her, it would only be a matter of time before she was back in this condition again. No, there was a good reason to withhold treatment here.

However, it would be cowardice for her to pretend that was what was uppermost in her mind. It might be a convenient lie to tell others, but why seek to mislead yourself in that way? She was reluctant to Heal this woman because she simply did not want to do it.

The connection between her fingers and the woman's head was becoming warm. She could see the soft tendrils of life running from the brain to the heart and back again. There was not enough to go much further, but that essential pulse still continued. This woman still wanted to live.

When she had drained Jak, she had done so almost unconsciously. Drinking in his life force in an uninhibited manner. Here, she was more controlled. Pulling on threads, and delighting in their flavour, rather than yanking out a tablecloth.

It was all over too soon.

Drunnoc was staring at the now-corpse on the floor. "You see? It looks different. You could see something left her the moment she died. Magnificent." He turned to face her. "That's what I want you to do."

Pernille was not satisfied. That taste had not been enough. She turned to look at the other cages, could see shapes within them pull backwards as if aware of her regard. "What do you mean?"

"It's that moment I want to paint. The transition from alive to dead. I've never been able to capture it." His eyes bore into hers. "Do you think you could hold someone in that state? On the bridge of life and death without letting them pass. I want to paint that moment more than anything else in the world."

"I don't know. Shall we find out?"

And, in the spirit of experimentation, what a few days it would be.

CHAPTER THIRTY

"The Mating Call of Failure"

They made their way through the woods as quickly as they could.

The Knight carried a quietly sobbing Genoes, his face pressed tight against her chest. Cenwyn had been one of the few constants in his short life, and he felt the loss keenly. He could not conceive of a world in which he never spoke to him again. Although not a boy unused to tragedy, the dying face of that too-kind man had broken his heart.

Combined with this overwhelming sorrow, were troubling flashes of memories he did not think were his own. A beautiful woman had never seen. A serenely calm field. And a hunting darkness, a cruel malevolence searching for something. And he feared that something was him. Without the Tailor as his jovial shield, he was exposed to that danger in a way he did not think had been the case before. He wondered if that woman in the field would be more afraid for him now Cenwyn was gone. He sensed she would be. He hugged Daine even tighter, and his tears continued to flow.

Kirstin ran next to them, eyes dark with her own grief. She had not known the Tailor long, but coming so close on the back of the loss of her brother and the adrenaline of her own battle, found her emotionally raw. Her world had spun on its axis too many times in the last few days. The death of Jak had been mitigated by becoming part of this little group. It was not a new family, she was not so childish as to think something like that, but it was a belonging she craved.

The attack by the people in the village, the flight through the tunnel, her desperate fight to defend the entrance and then, of course, the slaying of Veron. Each of these moments had left a scar on her already shaky spirit. Her momentary confidence in her ability to win against those boys had evaporated into a host of "what might have beens." Her death and worse, she knew, had been as close as they ever had been before. But, for someone so reliant and so sure of her own capacity and capability she also know that luck and the incompetence of her enemies had seen her through. If she had rolled those dice again, the outcome could have been quite different.

She did not regret the death of Veron; she had seen it as more than recompense for the fate of Jak. That vile young man had been responsible for much of the woe in her life, and, while he might not have been as bad as Drunnoc, the world was a far better place now that she had removed him from it. But it was a weighty thing to take a life. To watch as the arrow sank deep. It was one thing to shoot the arrow. It was another one entirely to see the consequence up close. She could not stop shaking.

Daine held the orphan tight as she moved through the trees. He had shared Cenwyn's final words, and she had been grateful to hear them. She did not believe they were true, but appreciated the man's last caring gesture. She knew she could have been faster. She could have insisted he moved further down the tunnel. She should have anticipated the crossbowmen being sent down after them. There were so many moments when a different choice, a more considered action, would have caused Cenwyn to be with them right now.

"Could haves *and* should haves *be the mating calls of Failure. I'm not putting all this effort into raising you right for you to run away and bed that loser. You make the best choice you can and keep your legs closed to his flirting.*" Gant's words had resonated with her once. It seemed a very long time ago.

Leaving Cenwyn's body behind in the tunnel had been hard. But with the return of more soldiers and with Genoes to protect, she knew it was the pragmatic thing to do. She wished there had been time to show his body proper respect. At the first of the shouts from behind, she had gathered him in her arms and moved swiftly into the tunnel's darkness.

Her vulnerability at this moment shocked her. Her back ached from the earlier axe blow; how long had it been since last an injury took this long to heal? Likewise, she could feel liquid spill out of the wound from the quarrel she had taken to her stomach. Blood loss had never been a concern for her before, and the light-headedness she was experiencing was deeply unsettling. She was still confident she could stand and hold her ground should the occasion call for it, but the very fact that she noticed the weight of Genoes in her arms was worrying.

She needed to take some time to recover. But who would protect her charge while she did so?

Kirstin had met them halfway toward the exit, her quick eyes had not failed to read the situation, and Daine had watched her sag with the weight of it.

"Trouble ahead?"

The Archer had shrugged. "Some. Veron and his boys."

"They still there?"

"It's clear."

There had been a story there, but no time to hear it. They reached the rope ladder and climbed upwards. Exiting the tunnel, they briefly took in the aftermath of Kirstin's defence. Daine did not miss the empty quiver on her back nor the hunted expression on the younger woman's face. It had been close, Daine thought. Having stood in the breach of enough hopeless causes in her time, she appreciated the mental toll it took. But, with a sinking feeling that did little to boost her flagging spirits, she saw that this girl would need as much care to recover as the boy in her arms.

"And what about you, Darkhelm? When you've pushed us all away, who is going to be there when you stumble? Which of us will have your back after you leave us behind? Who, at the end, will close your eyes and bid you well on your passing?" Those were some of the last words Gant had said to her before the mind sickness took him wholly. She had thought, at the time, they merely showed the depth of his terrifying descent. That to be so focused on need and companionship at the end revealed something shameful about him in his brokenness.

She remembered grimacing at those fanciful words. Then turning away and shutting the door, with disgust, behind her. Why would *she* ever need someone? Knights of the Road travelled alone, it was why she had pursued that path beyond all others. To be independent of the group. To stand and fall on the strength of her arm and her convictions. That clingy weakness of Gant in his dotage was a sad closing chapter in the story of a great, if terrible, figure in the Kingdom's history.

To be young was to be cruel.

After leaving the tunnel, she had scanned the landscape around her. The Goddess seemed to be back, reminding her she had been near this part of the world before. A soft push orientated her. Memories stirred, unbidden. Twenty years earlier. A cottage at the end of a winding path. Loud, shocking explosions. And laughter. So much laughter. These memories were bathed in golden approval. Had the Goddess raised them in her mind? If so, why?

He is good for you. Will be good for you.

Daine had not been minded to consider these words at the moment. She needed a destination, and this was as good as any other. "There's somewhere we can go. Someone we can ask for help. It's three, maybe four bells' travel. If we move fast. Are you well?"

Kirstin had looked anything but. "You asking if I can keep up with you?" She smiled wryly. "Might be better if you tucked me under your other arm. But I'll try."

The mental map forged over so many years had blazed into life in Daine's head. A bell's hard running for her. Maybe four with the Archer in tow. It would not be an easy journey, but they needed time to think. To recover. To plan retribution. More than anything, she needed somewhere familiar.

"Follow as close as you can. Don't push too hard. Shout out when we need to stop."

Daine had swung to the south and begun running,

Genoes still pressed to her chest. Kirstin, who considered herself a runner and had Skills to supplement that, did her best to follow, shocked at the speed and endurance of the older woman.

The woods were quiet in this part of the world. Had they been attempting such a journey further north, they would have contended with wolves, maybe the odd bear. Here, nature had been tamed. Daine's ears picked out deer fleeing at the noise of their unsubtle movement. Rabbits watched them cautiously from the undergrowth. Flocks of birds scattered at the approach and settled, cawing indignantly in their wake. They were far enough away from other humans that nothing, and nobody, sought to contest their journey.

The Goddess was a quiet hum in her mind. She remembered the reaction to her carrying Jak a few days past. The skin irritation which was the physical manifestation of the displeasure of her Patron at touching him. This was different. It was not quite pleasure she could feel in their connection. More like . . . was it anticipation?

Eventually, the pace proved too punishing for the girl. Kirstin pulled up, hands on hips, drawing deep breaths into tiring lungs. "Can we stop for a moment? We've surely put a distance between them and us now."

Daine nodded and halted to lean against a tree. Genoes did not relinquish his hold on her, continuing to hug her tight. She rested her chin on his forehead and stroked his back. If she was shocked at her maternal impulses, that was for examining another day. Perhaps. "We have. They'll be leaving us be for now. The Trellecs have plans to put into motion, and they've brushed us out of them." She scanned the wood around them. "Not far to go now."

"You've come this way before?"

"Once. Twenty years back. I can find the way." Kirstin arched her brow in scepticism. "Trust me. It was memorable."

CHAPTER THIRTY-ONE

"The Baking Pendragon"

"Looks simple enough," the Herald said, hand resting on the garden gate. "Don't know what all this fuss has been about. Quick in and out, deliver the message, and back to the Capital with him in a few weeks. Seems hardly worth all this effort."

Daine rolled her eyes. She did not like the woman. Had not liked her when the King had introduced them. Had not liked her when given the task of accompanying her on this quest. Had not liked her during their uneventful journey into the West. And really did not like her now when she uttered the most blatant tempting of the Lords of Misrule she had ever heard.

To be sure, the cottage did not look like a destination that required the attention of a Knight of the Road. On the contrary, it was almost comically stereotypical in its unthreatening appearance. A winding path led from the wicker gate to a wooden front door standing ajar, the smell of baking wafted from open windows, and a large crow perched on the chimney of a thatched roof.

"Caw," said the crow, flapping its wings to glide away.

Daine's eyes narrowed on the vanishing bird. It had definitely *said* "caw" rather than cawing. Maybe there would be a bit more to the task than met the eye.

The Herald was still wittering. "Unless he chooses not to come with us, of course. That's where you will come in."

Daine failed to suppress a sigh at the emergence of the oft-repeated argument. "As I have explained, my Lady, I am not here to kidnap the man. If he rejects the <King's Summons>, we will thank him for his time and take our leave. His Highness was clear as to that."

The Herald pulled her perfectly shaped eyebrows down into a frown, pursing her too-round lips into a moue of disappointment. Daine again gave herself significant credit for not punching the woman in the face. "Oh, Lady Darkhelm. I know His Highness *said* that, but what he says and what he means are quite different things. You have not joined this trip because I desired your sparkling conversation. You are here to be the mailed fist of the Throne."

"I am here, Lady Herald, to ensure your message is delivered. And that task is nearly complete. Shall we?" With that, she pushed open the gate and gestured for the Herald to pass.

On reflection, tactical thinking rather than faux politeness might have been a better strategy. The second the gate creaked, three enormous creatures appeared in the garden and loped toward them. The Herald had passed in front of Daine and blocked her from immediately taking up a defensive position.

Cursing, she reached out and yanked back on the flowing

cloak of the woman before her. With a yelp, the Herald was dragged backwards, flying around Daine and out of the garden to land ten feet away. Daine did not have time to draw her sword before the first of the creatures hit her midsection.

Despite bracing for the impact, she was momentarily winded, crashing to the floor. The jaws were in her face before she could bring her hands up in defence, and she steeled herself for . . . a leathery red tongue to drag itself from chin to forehead.

The other two creatures arrived and pinned her down, likewise beginning their own slimy assault.

"Boys, down!" a deep voice called from inside the cottage. "What will our visitors think of us?"

The pressure on her chest vanished, and the tongues ceased their invasive lapping. Daine staggered to her feet, drawing her sword and backing away from what she now recognised were oversized dogs.

Not big hunting dogs. Not the sort used to bring down boars, nothing of that type at all. Instead, these were of a breed that court ladies would keep as lapdogs. All low bellies and silly, stubby legs. Big eyes and waggly tails. These beasts, though, were massively out of proportion to anything Daine had seen before. She had wrestled smaller bears.

The Herald had climbed to her feet, holding her throat, coughing, and choking where her cloak had been bitten. If Daine felt a small surge of pleasure at seeing her so discombobulated, it was smothered by her own inglorious reaction to the situation.

Sheathing her sword, she raised her voice to be heard in the house. "My apologies, sir. We seem to have startled your dogs."

A man appeared in the doorway, rubbing his hands on the apron he wore. While at first glance she thought him to be an elder, she quickly realised that most of the flour that dusted around him seemed to have settled in his hair and beard. Her age, then, perhaps, and he matched her in height, though he was less broad around the shoulder.

"No, my Lady. The fault is all my boys'. Been a powerful age since they saw someone other than me with whom to play."

She liked his voice. Liked the glint in his eye. Liked . . .

"Lord Eliud, the King desires your presence at court. I am his Herald, and I seek to enforce that <Summons>."

The Herald had pushed her way past Daine to stand in front of the man and had unleashed her key Skill, bestowed upon her by the King. It was a shocking breach of etiquette to fully unveil a <Summons> on someone's doorstep in this way. Even Daine, with all her myriad of Resistances, felt a slight pull back to the Capital. She'd be amazed if they could run fast enough to keep up with the poor man as he raced to fulfil the request.

The man, Lord Eliud, instead laughed and opened the door wider. "Oh, I don't think so. Too many things to do here. Why don't the two of you make yourselves at home? Then, if all has worked out as hoped, there should be apple pie shortly."

And he went back inside. With bemused glances, the two women followed him.

*

It turned out that the ability to shrug off the <Summons> of a King's Herald had very little to do with whether you could bake. Daine politely replaced her fork and tried to avoid the eager eyes of her host.

"That is — quite unique, thank you."

Eliud's turned to the Herald. "Well? What do you think?"

There was a pause while she considered an appropriate response. "Do you grow the apples yourself?"

Eliud sighed. "I know. I know." In exasperation, he ran his hands through his hair, displacing some of the flour. "It's horrible, isn't it? The pastry is soggy, the apples are hard, and the crust is burned. It's just a disaster. Even the dogs won't eat it."

Daine watched him as he grumbled on. It was hard to reconcile the reputation of Eliud Villa, known to friends and foes alike as the Lord Duskstrider, with this slightly distracted figure in his cottage kitchen with his giant lapdogs.

With the rapid decline in the health of Gallant Stonehand, the Kingdom was in dire need of someone to step into the role of Mentor. That Daine had been tasked with ensuring this request reached its destination suggested this need was becoming acute. It would be quite a statement of intent and a significant show of strength, should she persuade the Duskstrider to take the role.

The man was blessed with a Mythic Class: he was the Pendragon. At his core, he had many of the talents of an evolved Class, much like the Knights of the Road, which was why the King had felt her presence when the request was made would be of benefit. Strength. Speed. Healing. However, it was there that any such similarities ended. While the Goddess guardedly approved of him, he walked a hugely different path to that of justice.

There were no tavern songs written about the Duskstrider. Bards worried he would find them disrespectful.

"We must make arrangements to return at once. Your

King requires you." The Herald was nothing if not stubborn. If the failure of the <Summons> had shaken her, it did not show in her haughty demeanour.

Eliud puffed out his cheeks and shook his head sadly at the largely uneaten pie. "Such a disappointment. My mother's own recipe, don't you know? She made such wonderful pies." His violet eyes settled on the Herald. "Do you think you could wait outside, please?"

And she vanished.

Daine started, climbing to her feet in surprise. Eliud gestured, and the chair slid to tap the backs of her knees, returning her to sitting again.

"Don't worry. I just moved her down the road a bit. Heralds make my head hurt: all that earnestness, don't you know?"

The ease with which he spent his power was instructive. For all his pleasant appearance, he was not to be trifled with.

"If we are not to eat my pie, I suppose we should talk. Is Gant dead?"

"No. But he is . . ." Daine paused, unsure how to phrase it. There was rumour these two were close once. "He is less than he was."

Fire flashed in his eyes. "Aren't we all? Let me speak plain. It has been many years since I was at court. Be not niggardly of your speech. I would know of the world the King would recall me to. What ails the Stonehand?"

They spoke for hours. Daine had limited recent experience of talking to people who were not, on a fundamental level, terrified of her. She had earned quite a name for herself during her first Tour, and with that notoriety came isolation. Of course, it was precisely that status she had craved in her youth, but she was of an age where some companionship was welcome.

There was something about Eliud that put her at her ease. He was comfortable in his extraordinary powers in a way she never was. And that was attractive. He was also extremely funny. During their discussions, the Herald had reappeared several times to be portalled away to increasingly ridiculous locations around the cottage.

On her fifth reappearance, soaking wet, with reeds in her hair, Daine, with regret, had to bring things to a close.

"My Lord, we must have your answer. The Crown calls. Will you serve?"

Those violet eyes flashed once more. "Would you have me do so, Lady Darkhelm?"

Her breath caught. "My Lord?"

"I like the King well enough. Gant, I once called a brother. Those are powerful pulls back to the centre of things. But it is not enough. Not to return to that den of vipers. A new friendship, though, that might tip the scales."

"My Lord, you flatter."

He shrugged at that, and she realised years later she never gave him a proper answer. The Herald had intervened, and the discussion had moved onwards, and, before she knew it, bags were packed, and they were journeying back the way they had come, a Pendragon in tow with his giant dogs padding behind.

*

"It sounds like he liked you," Kirstin said as they stood facing a small cottage, smoke curling from its chimney.

Genoes had fallen into an uneasy sleep in Daine's arms. "Perhaps. We barely spoke once we were back in the Capital. My Second Tour began, and when it was finished . . . Well, the politics of the Capital are cruel. He was displaced and, I believe, came back here."

A kitten was sitting in the middle of the path from the gate to the door. It cocked its head to regard the small party.

"Meow," it said, and turned to slip inside.

CHAPTER THIRTY-TWO

"Crimson Causes"

She had experienced more dignified reunions, thought Daine, sitting on the ground in a heap, her head spinning.

They had barely taken one step beyond the garden gate before a running Pendragon appeared and, quick as a flash, was whirling the Knight around in his arms, a single giant lapdog leaping and barking joyously around them. Genoes awoke in alarm at the unexpected motion and clung on even tighter to Daine in fright.

"My Lady of the Darkhelm. It does my old eyes good to see a friendly face," Eliud said, finally putting her down. Daine took a staggering step, stumbled, and fell, still holding the boy close. "It has been far too long since you darkened my door. And what do you have there? Some sort of bear cub?"

He plucked Genoes from her arms and held him at

arm's length, the boy's feet dangling. "Where has all your fur gone, little cub? What has that dastardly Darkhelm done to you?" He casually tossed the boy into the air once, twice and three times before catching him by the ankles and suspending him above the ground. The colossal dog jumped and licked at his astonished face.

"My Lord! Put the boy down, please!"

"'Boy'? Nay, you are mistaken, dear Lady. This is a hairless bear of some sort. Or perhaps a miniature sloth. A baby Minotaur. A magnificent mongoose." Eliud swung the boy back and forth as he spoke, the dog leaping to keep aiming licks at the human pendulum. Then, on the word "mongoose," he released him, and Genoes shot ten feet in the air, arms and legs flailing toward the corner of the garden.

Daine was about to shout in horror when the boy's flight slowed, then stopped as he was lowered to the ground as if by the gentlest of invisible giant hands. The moment he reached the floor, he was ambushed by a delighted dog. The boy's giggling and the dog's yapping as the two wrestled were, for Daine, a joy to hear.

Eliud turned to Kirstin, who quickly raised a warning finger. "I swear, I will bite you if you try that on me. If you want to speak to her alone, that is fine. I am more than capable of removing myself." She walked toward the tumbling mess of boy and dog, stooping to pick up a tiny kitten trotting at her side.

"There's a lot of pain there," Eliud said, watching the Archer go.

"For both. They've each lost people close to them the last few days."

For all his japery, the Pendragon had yet to meet Daine's

eyes. Now, finally, he turned to look at her, and she was struck by how tired he seemed. The clowning oaf from earlier had vanished to be replaced by a sombre face. She did not think she liked the change. "The years have not been kind, my Lord."

"Says the woman with a gaping wound in her back and her guts barely held in. What's that Goddess of yours playing at?" He made a quick gesture, and Daine felt her injuries heal instantly. "*Or* is *disembowelled chic* all the rage in the Capital nowadays? It's so hard keeping up with you fancy ladies and your endless fashions."

For the first time since she climbed out of the earth, Daine could take a proper breath. Her movement was more straightforward, no need to favour muscles that shrieked in outrage at every twitch. She was wise enough to realise the feeling had as much to do with the presence of the man in front of her as it did with any removal of pain. "My thanks, my Lord."

He dismissed her thanks with a wrinkle of his nose. "I mean it, Daine. After all this time, you turn up at my door, looking like a walking corpse with two heartsick children as your only companions. Has the Goddess turned her face from you?"

She felt her eyes blaze with the indignation of the Goddess. A voice not entirely her own escaped her lips. "Be mindful of your tone, Pendragon." And it was gone as quickly as it had surfaced.

"She's still spiky, I see."

"The Goddess has not abandoned me, my Lord. I still walk the Road."

He gestured to a bench beside his cottage, and the two sat. Despite all the unasked and unanswered questions, they fell into a brief, companionable silence. Genoes and the dog continued their rough-and-tumble game. Kirstin sat cross-legged, watching them, the kitten proud in her lap. Against the backdrop sound of the laughter and play, it was as if twenty years had vanished in an instant.

"I only see Josul. Are the other two hiding?"

He did not answer. When Daine looked over, tears ran down his face, and she quickly looked away. A chill entered the air, and the clouds darkened. "Casualties of my fiery fall from grace, my Lady."

She paused, thinking of the rumours around his ejection from the Capital. She knew it had been acrimonious. Even on the Road, she had heard tell of his confrontation with the King, but she had not understood blood to have been spilt. "I am sorry to hear that."

"Thank you." As quickly as his gloom had appeared, his expression cleared, and the sun burst through in the sky. "But it does little to dwell on the past. You have, I am sure, much to tell of the present. I can feel things stirring beyond my gate, and not all of it pleasant. What word do you bring me from the Road, Lady Darkhelm?"

As she recounted the previous week's events, Daine could not miss the thunderclouds that gathered above the cottage.

*

"Don't eat that." She tapped Genoes lightly on the hand as he reached to take hold of a steaming pie.

"What? Why?"

"Because she thinks, based on a memory fuddled by old age and her uncharitable disposition, that I am a terrible cook."

Genoes looked uneasily between the two of them and

then back at the plate of baked goods. "But they smell so good!"

She passed him a dish of fruit. "Take a pear. Much safer."

"So little faith, Darkhelm. That was always your trouble. Never could believe that people could change. Could improve. Gant was always saying that about you. That you believed you could only rely on the strength of your own arm and damn the rest of us for fools." Eliud leant back in his chair. The glint in his eye softened his words, but she felt the cut of truth nonetheless.

"Improved, have you? Well, if you eat one, so will I, my Lord." Daine picked up a slice of pie and tossed it to him, taking a smaller one for herself. "Go on. Take a bite."

Eliud looked dubiously at what he had in his hand. "Well, the truth of it is I have eaten already, my Lady. I am not sure I could fit in another mouthful." He put the slice on the table, as if worried it would explode and increased the width of his smile. "This feast is in your honour, after all. What host would I be if I reduced your fare? I eat like a bird nowadays. Age does terrible things to an appetite."

"Thought as much." And she tossed the pie back on the plate. Genoes snorted and took a piece of fruit.

"Can I ask you a question, my Lord?" Kirstin looked suspiciously at a bowl of stew that had unceremoniously been put in front of her.

"I am an open book, young Lady. Ask whatever you wish."

"Are you going to help? With what is going on in the village, I mean."

There was silence. Genoes looked up at the man

hopefully. Daine met the Pendragon's eye, interested in his response.

"What help do you think you require, Mistress Archer?"

Kirstin glanced at Daine for support. "There's going to be a rebellion. If the Trellecs get their way, this whole part of the West will break away from the Kingdom. You must want to help stop that?"

"I don't care about the rebellion. They killed Cenwyn!" The angry voice was Genoes's. "All he ever did was be kind and look after me, they destroyed his home and killed him!"

Eliud nodded, face crinkling in sympathy. "I can feel your pain, my boy. Can feel what he meant to you. For you" — he nodded at Kirstin — "the loss is different but no less painful. Yes, you are both in need of help." He stood and turned to gaze out of his window.

Rain lashed down, and the low rumbles of thunder, the backdrop to their meal thus far, felt like they had moved closer. With his back now to them, Eliud spoke softly. "But what help would you have me offer? The Lady Darkhelm has asked me for sanctuary. A place to stay, heal and think about her next move. I am glad to be of service. I may have little to offer that this world still wants, but a haven is within my gift. Likewise, my door is open to both of you as long as you need it."

Sudden lightning crashed in the sky, making the kitten nestled in Kirstin's lap cringe. Josul, sprawled under Genoes's chair, raised an ear, and then went back to softly snoring.

"But what you would have from me is something other than sanctuary." He turned around, and his eyes were filled with a strong emotion his audience could not discern. "You would seek vengeance, and that is a different matter."

"Justice, not vengeance, my Lord." Daine's taut tone was a match for his.

"But justice failed, my Lady. Did it not? Her chosen instrument itself was beaten down, interred, and then forced to flee. It was the failure of justice that led to rebellion, my Lady. Not the other way around." He raised a hand to forestall her fury. "I do not judge you, Darkhelm. That has never been my role, and I have no right to do so. But hear me, for I speak the truth. Should the West fall to rebellion and worse, that is no longer a matter of justice. The King will do what the King will do in the face of secession, and there will be no justice in that. The lad wants vengeance for the death of a man he loved. The girl wants those who led her brother to destruction to suffer the same. You? I think you want to crush the life out of those who made you feel fear."

Silence answered his words.

"You ask for my help because you seek slaughter. We all know the only way to pull things back from rebellion is to make a bloody example, to convince the bared teeth of the Throne to back down from the challenge. To forestall the violence to come. But you each want those who have wronged you to die in the course of it."

He paused and ran his hands across his face. The air in the room had become heavy with the weight of his words. "I have long retired from the world because I had supped full of death. I solemnly promised I would not involve myself in any more crimson causes. Twice now, Darkhelm, you have come to my door to ask me to break that vow. The first time, I accepted. But we were younger then, and neither of us fully knew the cost. Wiser now, can you truly ask it of me again?"

Daine felt all eyes on her. She knew, knew on a deeper level than she could ever share, the weight that rested on this man. They both had done terrible things because they had known they needed to be done. But it was her choice to walk the Road. He had chosen another path. She had no right to pull him along behind her again.

He was as fractured as the rest of them.

"My Lord. Eliud. I am sorry. We ask too much of you. The rebellion, nor those that drive it, are not your concern. We gratefully accept your offer of sanctuary and offer friendship in return."

The tension in the air dissipated as Eliud smiled. "A fine bargain, my Lady."

CHAPTER THIRTY-THREE

"Unformed"

Blood streamed down Eliud's face, his nose clearly broken, and his eyes stunned. Genoes gasped in horror at what he had done and backed away from the fallen man, shaking out his sore hand as he went. Kirstin and Daine exchanged glances, unsure how to react.

There was a moment of silence before a huge grin spread across the Pendragon's face and he laughed with genuine pleasure. "Now *that* is much more like it, my lad!"

*

"He worries me," Eliud had said the night before.

Both Kirstin and Genoes had taken themselves to their rooms, leaving the two old friends to sit around the table and talk. Josul snored at their feet and the kitten — Eliud had said she was called Savage — had insisted on accompanying Kirstin, loudly mewling until being allowed to follow. Daine could have sworn she heard a soft "thank you" from the cat when the girl's closed door cracked open to allow her entry.

If there had been tension from his refusal to help them against the Trellecs, it had quickly passed. It was hard to maintain bad humour in Eliud's presence; his wealth of outlandish stories — some involving Daine, much to her chagrin — were well-received. Likewise, neither Kirstin nor Genoes had ever seen someone use power so irreverently — juggling plates without touching them, casting his voice to various parts of the room and conjuring increasingly inappropriate items from behind ears. "You missed your calling as child's entertainer," Daine had noted, hearing the Goddess laughing softly at her words.

"I missed out on having any of my own. It feels good to make up for lost opportunities." His words, said lightly, had nevertheless affected them all. Genoes had moved to sit by Eliud's side for the rest of the evening.

"What is the nature of your concern?"

Eliud expression soured, as if tasting something bitter. "It's hard to explain." He picked up one of the uneaten pies and put it on the table between them. "Consider this delicious pie."

"Seriously?"

"Bear with me on this. Consider this delicious pie." He waved his hands around it, as if presenting it for inspection. "What is this?"

"It's a vile trap for the unprepared."

"Slurs against my talent aside, tell me what you see."

She played along, "I see a pie."

"Indeed. And we both have a shared understanding of what that means. This is a pie. If I were to show it to a hundred people, most of whom have a far more discerning palate that you possess, they would all tell me it was a pie. I could make use of the most arcane of my powers to investigate its essential being and it would remain, at its core, a pie."

"I don't see what this has to do with Genoes."

"What does the Goddess show you about him?"

Daine thought back to the few occasions she had been provided with visions about the boy. "Very little. It is as if he is hidden within fog. But that is not unusual. He is a child, after all."

He nodded thoughtfully. 'Hidden within fog is a good way of putting it.' He made a gesture and the pie's constitution changed. One moment, an unappetising pastry sat between them, and the next, a version of the same but now seemingly made up of mist. "Is this still a pie?"

"Sir, it's been a long few days. What's your point?"

"Let me speak plain. Everything has an essential nature. People, dogs" — Josul gave a contented sigh at being included "— even pies. No matter how someone seeks to disguise themselves, regardless of the trick they use to hide that essential nature, I should have the capacity, the <Truesight> to see them as they are."

"A handy Skill."

"And one that has saved more lives than I can count. But with Genoes, I can sense nothing. I see the boy in front of me and I know he is there. But it is as if he is as insubstantial as a cloud." He moved his hands through the pie and, while the shape wavered, it did not dissipate. "Should I have come across him in the palace, I would have assumed a powerful Assassin was stalking the King and was seeking to evade detection in a child's form."

"Sir, Genoes is a boy. He has no hidden powers."

"Does he not? You've told me of his unusual Strength, his Speed, his uncanny facility to <Dodge> He says he was able to sense your pain belowground. Likewise, from what Kirstin has shared, he should have died at her brother's hand. You are not an unobservant woman, Daine. All of these are signs he is so much more than a normal boy. That is, unless the Goddess wishes you to be ignorant."

She flushed at that. She knew what he said made sense. Genoes was extraordinary and yet she did not seem to be able to hold that idea in her head. Every time she tried to consider his abilities, those thoughts flew apart as if becoming lost in the fog.

"She's never influenced my mind before."

He raised an eyebrow. "And how would you know?"

She dipped her head in acknowledgement. "But what would be the point? He's just a boy."

"Daine, I sense we are going to have this conversation many times in coming days. If the Goddess does not wish you to consider the nature of Genoes too deeply, she must have her reasons and certainly has the power to keep you from doing so. I doubt there is much I can do to influence that, but I will try. What I say to you is that whatever sleeps in that room is much, much more than a boy. I do not think he is dangerous — at least not to us — but he is" — he moved his hands through the ethereal pie once more — "unformed."

"What do you suggest?"

"I think we should help him find out who, or what, he is."

*

"You want me to hit you in the face?"

"Yes."

"Why?"

"Because I'm a terrifying fiend from the Netherworld and you are defending the life of the beautiful princess. I am going to run toward the woman you are sworn to protect" — Savage cocked her head and meowed, unimpressed to be included in this mummery — "and you are going to beat me back."

Genoes looked to Kirstin and Daine for support. "I don't want to hurt you."

"Lad, and I mean this with all love, I am the Pendragon, Eliud Duskstrider. I held the Pass of Dornact alone for three days. I defeated the Demon Queen of H'jark armed with nothing but my natural charm and disarming smile. I have bestridden countless battlefields as a colossus and men have wept at my very approach."

"He knows he has tunic on back to front, right?" Kirstin whispered just loud enough for everyone to hear.

Eliud ignored her. "So, when I tell you to hit me in the face, please be assured that I do so secure in my confidence that I am probably going to survive the encounter."

Genoes clenched and unclenched his fists. "I don't like to hit people," he muttered.

And Daine was struck by a vision of a much older boy falling away, blood streaming, Genoes's face contorted in anger and then terror at what he had done.

"You won't hurt him, lad." She put her hands on his shoulders. "Trust us. He's twice as tough as me and three times as ugly. You could take an iron bar to him in his sleep, and he wouldn't stop snoring. Believe me, many have tried."

"An unnecessary slur. Boy, I'm coming to capture the princess."

Eliud advanced, on his knees, mud splattered upon his

trousers, toward Savage. Genoes half-heartedly moved between the two and offered a tentative slap toward the man. It did not land. The Pendragon had not blocked it, but his head had not been where Genoes had aimed.

"Pathetic human!" Eliud rasped. "I shall feast on this princess." And he kept shuffling forward.

Savage made a noise that, to everyone's ears, sounded uncannily like an unenthusiastic "help me, help me."

Genoes aimed a slap at Eliud once more, to miss again. He frowned and tried again. And again. Each time, the man's head moved, at the last moment, out of the way of the strike. "Human too slow. Will eat his princess."

This continued for several minutes. Daine could feel Genoes's growing frustration at the game, as well as the increasingly barbed nature of Eliud's commentary on his efforts. The boy was becoming distressed, not just at his failure to hit the Pendragon, but also from some of the words coming his way. She knew what Eliud was seeking to do, but it was becoming an unedifying spectacle. Kirstin, at her side, likewise shifted uneasily.

"He's being mean."

Daine thought back to some of her own training with Old Gant. "I'm afraid 'mean' is sometimes what we need to find out of what we are capable."

Genoes was breathing hard now; Eliud seemed entirely fresh.

"Foolish princess. Thinking such a pathetic human would protect her. Bet the human's own parents are disappointed in him."

At that, Genoes's eyes opened wide, and his fist flashed into the centre of Eliud's face, breaking his nose with an audible crack. The Pendragon was thrown back by the

impact to lie, for a moment, in the mud, before his bellow-
ing laugh was heard.

Savage sniffed and went back inside. "About time someone did that," she meowed.

CHAPTER THIRTY-FOUR

"Uneasy Allies"

An uneasy atmosphere had settled in and around Keep Trellec.

It was as if something in the very air were oppressive, a malevolent weight pressing down on the spirits of all who lived there. The feeling was so disconcerting that the Men-at-Arms had taken to patrolling the battlements in pairs, though none would be able to share a direct source of their overwhelming anxiety should you ask them. The Janes flitted hither and tither along corridors in groups, their constant chattering and uneasy mobbing more akin to starlings in the presence of a hawk than a functioning body of servants.

Indeed, no one dared to walk the Keep alone, no matter how highly they might be born. There were now too many fears of the dark, too many stories of screams in the night, and too many of those on the margins of social groups simply vanishing, never to be seen again.

The mood was becoming so morose, that those who worshipped the Dark God, and that number had swelled in recent years, began leaving increasingly elaborate offerings at His altar. After all, if any member of the pantheon could be bribed to turn their gaze to another, it would be He.

Moreover, despite the best efforts of the Healer — who seemed much more accepting of the use of, indeed openly advertising, her services of late — minor illnesses seemed to be rife among the Keep's occupants. Symptoms were nothing especially dire, but coughs, sneezes, and a general physical malaise seemed to be affecting everyone.

Most put it down to the stresses of knowing a political storm was coming — had it not, in reality, already arrived? — and seeking how best to weather it.

For all the confidence and bluster of Fion's speech to the village, there were, quite apart from whatever malign spirit was currently stalking the Keep, complex practicalities about the uprising that needed proper consideration and planning.

There had been an almost universally warm reply from the surrounding countryside to the call for a Great Council of the West. Whether this meeting would go as far as recommending formal secession remained to be seen. But there had not been such a gathering in many generations, so its mere existence was noteworthy enough.

Not everyone responded out of a genuine desire for change, to be sure, but the vanquishing of a Knight of the Road was persuasive enough of a motive to bring them together out of sheer naked self-interest.

And that was what made Daine's escape somewhat of a

fly in the ointment. That and the increasingly fractious attitude of the Lords of the High Houses, who had arrived in
the Hall of Keep Trellec on mass to beard Fion in his den.

"If I understand you right, sir, all we have to show for
the loss of my youngest son, several grievously wounded
Lordlings, the decimation of a company of prime pavise
crossbowmen and innumerable injured villagers . . . is a single dead Tailor?" Lord Geril's customary drawl was tight
with anger.

Fion shuffled uneasily in his seat. "Let us not dwell on
the negatives, my friend. Although once again, my Lord,
House Trellec offers sincere sympathy to you for your loss."

"I don't give a damn for your sympathies, Fion. Whoever
put a quarrel between my son's eyes did the world a service,
and we all know it. No tears are being shed in my household
for Veron's passing. Even Beth can see . . ." He paused as
if collecting himself before pressing on. "Sir, I tell you that
if circumstances were different, I'd be shaking the hand of
the Archer. And I know many will feel the same. My point
is not to dwell on what we have lost, but rather to highlight
that we are inviting the Western Nobility to a Great Council
to formalise secession from the Crown based on the prem-
ise that the threat of the Lady Darkhelm is at an end. And
that is, manifestly, not the case. Do you not think this may
cause comment, nay perhaps some resentment, when it becomes known?"

"Darkhelm is no threat to us."

At his words, all eyes turned to Drunnoc.

Aelric Geril could not stand this boy. He had enough
self-awareness not to blame Drunnoc entirely for what his
own son had turned into, but his influence had undoubtedly been a factor. Before the two had begun spending

considerable time together, Veron had been wild, but not —
and he hesitated to use the word — *evil*. He had witnessed
the change with growing dismay, unsure what he could do
to alter the descent. He knew now, had known at the time,
that his instinct to protect his boy from the consequence of
his actions had simply emboldened him to greater depths.

"Fion, I am unclear as to the benefits of the presence of
your boy and his — I am sorry, what is this young woman's
status?"

"Pernille is my friend, Lord Geril. And she is very welcome at this meeting." If Drunnoc was intimidated, he did
not show it.

Fion was unsure when control of things had begun slipping through his fingers. Everything seemed to have slotted
into place at the end of his speech to the village. Secession
was finally on the agenda, the Village Council was firmly
under this thumb, the Houses were uniting behind him, and
the iron grip of the Knights of the Road on the popular
consciousness had been lifted.

But, almost from that precise moment of triumph, it felt
like he had received a series of body blows.

First, that helpful riot at the Tailor's shop had run a
touch out of hand. While he was delighted to be rid of
that particularly self-righteous man, he had not anticipated
the damage to the other shops and buildings around his
home. A burning high street was not quite the projection
of a post-Tour utopia he sought to achieve. He had put
his Mage at the disposal of the Council for the rebuilding
effort, but a scorched-earth policy was not what had been
intended. He knew there were distinct rumblings about
how his Steward had riled up that crowd and, what is more,
there were several prominent people who could not be

accounted for in the aftermath. That comely young women made up a distinct majority of the missing was noteworthy. He feared Halcoth was fast becoming a liability.

Then, and perhaps most pressing of his concerns, the Lady Darkhelm has escaped. By itself, this was not a disaster — her claws had well and truly been clipped, after all — but there was a distinct difference in having her head on a spike when the Great Council assembled and instead describing her flight down a tunnel, crossbow bolts whirling past her. Both were spectacularly rare events, but he could not help but feel the latter was not quite what those attending in a few days would have in mind.

He glared at Lady Culloden, who met his gaze and glared right back. That alliance was shaky at best now. She blamed him for the loss of some of her most prized assets, he blamed her for her men not being as elite as she had claimed when insisting her forces should lead the charge. There was enough blame on both sides, but the fact of the matter was that the Darkhelm had slipped away. The slaughter of Veron and the maiming of a bunch of young jackals was neither here nor there. As the boy's own father noted, Veron's death was more a boon than anything else.

Finally, though, was the problem of Drunnoc and his new pet. That positive swell he felt toward his son in the immediate aftermath of his speech had long since faded away. Nothing specific had occurred to cause it, he knew. He just could not bring himself to feel easy in the boy's company.

And the Healer . . . He was not sure what the bond was there, but he had enough reports from his spies in the Keep to know nothing good was coming of it. People were going missing, not just those that the bloodlust around the riot could explain away. And these two seemed to be at the heart of it.

Although it was clear that whatever the two of them were up to, it was agreeing with the Healer. What little he knew of her was of being a shrewish, bitter little thing. But this vision of glowing health in front of him belied that image entirely. He did not think he had ever seen someone look so well. He could not imagine what threats Drunnoc had put in place to keep her out of Halcoth's orbit.

But all this was by the by. He could not allow internal worries to drain away the strength he had accrued in recent days. And that started with Lord Geril.

"In my own House, Aelric, I will choose whose presence has benefit and whose does not. Should you disagree, I am happy to accept your request to leave. And that goes for any of you who feel you would like to explore different paths than that to which we agreed. I have quite recent experience of not being able to trust the words of those around this table, and you will appreciate I am not anxious to repeat the experience. Fool me once, shame on me. Fool me twice, and there will be . . . repercussions."

The assorted Lords and Ladies in the room stayed wisely silent. For the time being, all the momentum was entirely with House Trellec and, certainly until the Great Council of the West, it would be foolish to move against them. However, there had already been informal discussions about how to change that reality. The importance of waiting for the perfect opportunity had been agreed upon by them all.

Fion pressed on with his theme. "Regardless of the final outcome, what should be clear to us all is that the Lady Darkhelm has stepped from the Road. We have rejected her right to have dominion over us and have driven her from our presence when she disputed our right to do so. That will be our message to our fellow Westerners, and we will invite them to share in that rejection. Do any of you fear they will not follow our lead? We were the spark, but the ground for this rebellion is both fertile and tinder-dry."

Trivian tutted at his mixed metaphor, and he saw a few others roll their eyes, Lord Michaeleas chief amongst them. That fat fool was going to have an accident in the near future, and as for his wife . . .

Was it too much to hope that she would support him in this? He remembered a time when he thought they shared his vision for a free West. It was one of the key reasons he had chosen her as his second wife. That and her dowry, of course. But, with some bitterness, he was coming to believe that it was just another in a lengthy line of examples of her telling him one thing while believing another. He missed having people around him whom he could trust.

"Do we have any idea where she may have gone?" a minor Lord — he did not think he knew his name, or at the very least cared — piped up.

"It is of little consequence. The Knight knows she will not find succour in any of the local villages. She is hurt, alone, and stripped of the tyrannical authority of her office. We were able to turn her from our walls while she had every advantage; what chance does she have now when we are united in our opposition? Why, I dare say we have heard the last of the Lady Darkhelm in the West."

And if anyone heard the clinking of glasses as the Lords of Misrule toasted this unwise tempting of fate, none around the table seemed keen to mention it.

CHAPTER THIRTY-FIVE

"Fools, Malcontents, and Monsters"

"So, in short, we're going blind into a meeting of fools, malcontents and monsters?" Taelsin Elm threw away the stack of reports he had been reviewing. They hit the edge of his desk and slid to the floor, spilling out a slew of handwritten notes.

His Secretary, Donal Assay, raised his eyebrow at such an uncharacteristic show of temper. If members of House Elm were known for anything, it was an ability to control their emotions. "I am sorry, sir, did you expect the first Lord to break cover over Western secession to be a perfect foil? If so, I heartily chastise myself for so failing in your political education. Although I must confess, I had not thought the area behind your ears to be quite so damp . . . "

"I was not seeking perfection, Donal, and my ears are perfectly dry, thank you very much. I just assumed that when everything for which we had planned came to pass, we wouldn't be following the lead of a bunch of lunatics and ne'er-do-wells." He gestured toward the pile of papers on the floor. "None of our agents has a good word to say about these Trellecs. Depending on whose account we give credit, they are either stupid or venal or, most worryingly of all, both." He raised a hand to forestall his Secretary interrupting him. "Which are both traits with which we can work, I understand. And if there were a House worth its name in that village, I would agree with you. But" — he waved his hands in despair at the notes — "you've read what we're working with! We will have one chance to free the West. One for, certainly, our lifetimes. And from the very outset, I sense our venture will be fatally flawed if it involves people like this. Let alone allows them to be the ones to call a Great Council of the West."

"And yet said Council has been called, my Lord. There is milk on the floor, but I would suggest we do not expend much energy weeping over how it came to be there. On the contrary, it behoves us to take advantage of the opportunity that presents itself, regardless of how palatable we find the instruments of that chance. Our allies will expect no less of us, and we cannot be certain that they will stay with our cause should we let this moment pass by without grasping it. And even if none of that was true, sir, we should remember that these 'lunatics' brought down a Knight of the Road."

Taelsin bit back an angry retort and nodded his head at that last point. Because, after all, was that not that singular fact the be-all and end-all?

He pushed himself free of his chair and moved to the window to look down on his City.

Swinford.

Once the largest, most powerful of the Western Cities. Now, tottering on the edge of abandonment, a pale shadow of its former glory. As far as his eyes could see, building after building told the story of that fall from grace. Disrepair, dereliction, and a profound lack of care marked each tenement, each business. Even the stained glass in the Church of Dawn was not safe from the depredations of time.

Oh, he spread his coin as liberally as he could, but it barely touched the walls of what was required to function, let alone restore to prior standards. So, while the needy could still shelter under the canopy of House Elm, it was becoming a threadbare tree.

While he knew this societal collapse had begun generations back and that he should not take the current state of the City as a personal slight, of course he did. He was the Mayor of Swinford, and that had used to mean something. Something of which to be so enormously proud.

Historians might lecture on the slow concentration of power to the Capital. The centralisation of resources into the hands of a select few. The disbanding of regional governments. The inexorable raising of taxes. The establishment of the Tours. These were all events from the distant past, but he felt the daily lash of each of those historic attacks as if they were happening anew.

Step by step, compromise by compromise, cities like Swinford had seen their spirits broken and their pride crushed. And now he was Mayor — did that title even mean anything anymore? —of a poor, reduced thing that squatted apologetically on the land. His father, and his grandfather, had been sure they could turn the tide of that descent. Had put such schemes in place and made such efforts to ensure a return to how things used to be.

That it all proved to be in vain against the complex machinations of the Crown had crushed them. As much as anything else, heartbreak had claimed them at the end.

As he pondered, Donal moved to his shoulder. "You know why it could never have been you to call the Council. There are those at court just waiting for the opportunity to have your head on Traitor's Hill. This way, as much as the actors are not ideal, you now have the cover you need. No one will look askance at House Elm attending a Council of the West — how could you be expected to do anything else? But no one will be able to say you called it with ill intent. And no one will be able to say what follows was down to you. So do not look this gift horse in the mouth because you dislike the smell of its breath."

He smiled at that. "Spilt milk and reeking gift horses? What pair of sparkling eyes has you in a such a metaphorical mind today?"

"Never you mind, sir. To return to the matter, the salient points remain the same. We needed the Council of the West to be called, and it has been. We wanted your name kept out of it, and you are clear on that score. And, beyond all the rest, we needed Daine Darkhelm not to be forced to choose a side."

"How on earth did this mob" — another disparaging gesture to the reports that littered the floor — "manage to bring her down?"

"I have two theories, sir. The first is that all things are possible under the sun. Knights of the Road are not immortal, and it is entirely possible, no matter how much it galls me to note, that House Trellec have simply been very lucky indeed."

Taelsin's thoughts turned to the grim figure of Daine

Orban. They had met several times, both when she was on Tour in Swinford and when he had been begging for some scrap or another from the Crown's table at the Capital. He liked her, liked her forthright manner. Unlike most at Court, you knew where you stood with the Lady Darkhelm.

Unfortunately, he knew that this aspect of her personality would be the one to set them against each other. She was loyal to the King. For that matter, so was he. To the man himself. It was against everything else around that decent soul that he chafed. When he was younger, he thought that if he could explain the issue correctly to his friend, all would be well. But he had learned to his cost the King was not the Crown. The tentacles choking the life out of his City were equally around the King's throat.

So, if there was no chance of genuine reform, Swinford, indeed the whole of the West, needed to be free before the collapsing kingdom dragged them all down. To achieve that, though, he did not need to have the Lady Darkhelm oppose him. Despite knowing that, he was still sorry to hear she might have been harmed.

There were precious few Knights of her quality still involved in the Tours. Her generation — the Golden Age, he had heard the Bards call it — was very nearly all gone. Indeed, should the reports of her demise be accurate, would anyone trained by Gallant Stonehand still be walking the Road? That was an alarming thought to add to a whole host of alarming thoughts.

He had always appreciated the even-handed way Daine had dispensed justice in his City, much as it grated on his independent spirit that he was required to allow such a thing as a Tour to take place.

She had passed through on her third Tour of his life-time — of course, he had been nothing but a baby on her first — a few months back. He thought she had looked tired and distracted when sounding her judgements. Truth be told, there was little to interest her in Swinford — he had long ensured that the local Constables were paid adequately to address any issues as they arose. He was certainly not naïve enough to think bribes did not cross palms, but not so bad anyone had any grave miscarriages of justice to bring to the attention of the Lady Darkhelm.

She had listened to those who brought their cases and, for the most part, dispensed precisely the justice he would have done in her shoes. She did nothing for self-aggrandisement and never overstepped the bounds of decency. In that, he knew other Mayors who were not so fortunate with the Knights who were forced upon them by this system.

Thus, if there had to be Tours — and with some good fortune, the time for such things was about to draw to a close — he would be happy to welcome Daine to his City every ten years.

Indeed, the thought of another being appointed in her stead, one with less respect for boundaries and restraint? Well, he would have grave concerns and nowhere to take such worries. 'Things fall apart,' he whispered, 'the centre cannot hold.'

"My Lord?"

"Forgive me, Donal. Wool-gathering. So, the first thought is that some harebrained scheme came good, and, for once, Daine Darkhelm could not come out the other side fighting. Perhaps. And your second theory?"

"That she is alive and well and preparing to express her distinct displeasure at this turn of events."

Taelsin pursed his lips. "Yes. That thought had crossed my mind. Does that change our plans?"

Donal smiled, and, with that expression, Taelsin recognised that whatever pair of sparkling eyes had caught the fancy of his Secretary was probably very happy with life right now. "Sadly, at the risk of returning to the realm of unwished-for metaphor, the barn door is open, and the horse has long fled. The Council of the West will convene in two days, and Swinford must be represented. To withhold our presence will be to strangle potential secession at birth. I know the sacrifices you and your family have made to lay the groundwork for Swinford to be free of the Crown. While not quite 'now or never,' such a confluence of events will unlikely happen again."

Taelsin pushed away from the window and returned to his chair. He set his feet on his desk and leaned backwards in a manner that, should his dear mother still be alive, would have led to a week of chastisement. His legs burned to think of it, and he quickly sat more appropriately. Donal smiled, knowing exactly what had passed through his master's mind.

"We have a narrow path to walk, then, Donal. On the one side, we have allies we neither like nor trust, but who have a cause to which we wish to lend our support. On the other, we have a corrupt and malign Court from whom we wish to liberate our people, but who are likely to be championed in this matter by a Knight of the Road we both like and trust but also hope has been horribly murdered."

"I am not sure I would quite use those words as a rallying call, but Sir expresses our current challenge with his customary aplomb."

CHAPTER THIRTY-SIX

"Return to the Road"

With a smile, Daine watched Eliud and Genoes play in the garden.

Of course, what Eliud was seeking to do was far more complex than simply "playing" with the boy. In the patterns of their games, she recognised many of the early training forms that Gant had so mercilessly drilled into her. Given a choice, she thought that, while she would much rather have had this gentle introduction to self-defence, she could see that Gant's approach would bring much faster results.

When someone was swinging an iron bar at you, your reflexes sharpened up much quicker than when it was a pillow.

"Ah, you got me!" Eliud shrieked as Genoes struck him a passing blow with the bright-pink cushion that was his chosen weapon. The Pendragon dramatically sunk to the floor, wailing briefly before his cries cut off with a desperate gurgle.

"He's good with him," Kirstin noted, idly stroking the head of Savage with her thumb. The kitten had not left the girl's side since they arrived.

"He is."

In a feat of necromantic brilliance, Eliud appeared to revive the moment Genoes turned his back and proceeded to throw his pillow at the boy's unprotected head. Genoes, without looking, swayed out of the way to let it sail past him. Then he turned and continued beating the older man. This tactic would have been an entirely solid strategy had not, with a twitch of his fingers, Eliud summoned the pillow to fly back to him, crashing into the back of the boy's head on the way and knocking him, face-first, to the floor.

"I am not sure it is that dignified for a man of his age and rank to perform a victory dance in these circumstances."

Daine snorted at Kirstin's dry tone. She liked this girl. She probably needed to review her opinion of Archers.

Eliud continued to dance around Genoes, the boy finding it hard to stand through the hail of soft furnishings that continued to crash into him, hurled by the Pendragon's magic. Soon, he was so thoroughly buried, that Josul was sent in to drag him clear.

"That Council is scheduled to take place tomorrow."

Daine's face betrayed no emotion at Kirstin's words. "It is."

Daine was impressed by the Archer's self-discipline as the silence stretched out. She could, just sitting next to her, feel the questions she was desperate to ask bubbling up inside. Then, finally, the dam burst.

"What are you planning to do about it?"

Daine turned to regard the girl. There were lines on her face that had no right to be there on someone so young. With what Daine had picked up about her family, she understood that Kirstin had needed to take on far too much too early. An executed father. That would leave its own scar in a small village. Would close doors to you before you even began. Then a mother who followed soon after. It would have been easy to break then, to run away and start anew. But she had accepted the charge to protect her brother when she was nothing but a child herself. And had held on to that role even when the Goddess told her to stand down.

All that to then watch him be crushed to death.

Daine knew the pain of that loss was hurting the girl. Or, rather, the relief she felt at Jak's death was causing her pain. Would bringing things out into the open help? Could the boil be lanced?

The Knight had resolved to speak when she felt a paw rest on her leg. Looking down, her eyes met Savage's, and she could swear the kitten shook its head. She then hopped up on Kirstin's shoulder and bunted her in that proprietary way that felines had. *Mine,* she seemed to be saying.

It spoke much as to how poorly Daine viewed her own counselling capacity that she was so relieved to have been usurped in that by a small furry companion.

"The Council of the West is entitled to meet," she noted evasively.

"The Trellecs are going to foment rebellion."

"They are."

"Aren't you the person who is supposed to stop that from happening?"

Daine closed her eyes and listened for a moment to the warring voices in her head. Gant was there, of course, all belligerent advice and gruff disparagement. *"Kill them until there's nothing left to kill, then find a Lich to raise them back up and kill them some more. Nothing settles an argument so well as blood running on the streets."* The presence of the Goddess was far more circumspect. From the little She was sharing, She wanted Daine exactly where she was right now. There was not quite a warning not to return to the village, but certainly something like disapproval whenever she thought about her next steps.

And in the middle of all that was her own voice. Eliud had been right to say she wanted revenge. Revenge for Cenwyn, for sure. Revenge for all those people forced to act against their will under the Steward's perverted Authority. Revenge for all those whose lives had been blinded by Drunnoc Trellec.

And yes, she thought the only way she would begin to find peace for what had happened to her belowground was for her to put her hands around someone's throat.

What worried her was that none of those voices — including her own — had any view on the West breaking away from the Kingdom.

Her duty was to walk the Road. First and foremost, and beyond everything else. She walked the Road, and she dispensed the Justice of the Goddess. But the Goddess wanted no part of what would come next in the village. Every hint, every vision, every suggestion made clear she should stay where she was.

But was there not an implicit compact that the Goddess's will was somehow aligned with the needs of the Crown? If news of this proposed Council of the West were to reach the King's ears, he would command her to ensure any suggestion of secession received a firm rebuff — *"heads on pikes is the only language some people understand,"* as Gant would put it. But if the Goddess did not see secession as unjust, where did that leave her?

And if secession was not unjust, what did that say about the Kingdom Daine served?

Kirstin was awaiting an answer. Daine could think of nothing to say but the truth. "Am I the person who is supposed to stop it happening? I don't know, lass. I just don't know anymore."

*

It was nightfall, and after Kirstin and Genoes had taken to bed, Daine and Eliud sat in silence.

Well, it would have been silence if Eliud had not insisted on singing fragments of a tune to which he could not quite remember all the words. She imagined he thought he was easing the tension that had settled on the group all afternoon after Daine and Kirstin had discussed the situation.

The truth was she was one more offbeat note from pulling his arm off and beating him to death with the wet end. Or a "stern warning," as Gant described that rather direct approach.

"He'll be safe here." His sudden words took her by surprise. "If you need to leave, I mean."

She did not answer him, not trusting her voice not to crack.

"He won't understand to begin with. But he's smart. He'll understand that you had no choice. That you have a path to follow, and it would be wrong to stop you from doing so."

"I think the Goddess wants me to stay."

He inclined his head and thought about that for a moment. "Interesting. Do you know why?"

Daine closed her eyes and tried to focus on her patron. With frustration, she wrestled with her perception of that presence before giving up and shaking her head. "It's nothing distinct. I can just feel Her approval when I think about being here and . . . worry, when I think about returning to the village."

"She's scared for you."

The idea made Daine laugh aloud. "I don't think you quite understand how our relationship works."

"So, tell me." His voice was soft, and when she glanced at him, she saw all traces of Eliud the buffoon were gone and replaced by the man who terrified so many — the Duskstrider.

She gave the question appropriate thought. How to explain the relationship in a way he could understand? "She doesn't feel that way about us. About any of us. The Knights of the Road have a job to do, and, if needed, we can call on Her for support, and She lends us aspects of Her power. We're not . . . we're not people for Her to care about. We're instruments of Her will. Having been with me so long, I don't doubt She would feel loss if I fell. But no more than we would feel at the passing of a pet."

A poor simile. She saw the grief at the memory of his slain dogs ignite on his face. Josul had chosen to bunk with Genoes, and the kitchen floor looked oddly empty without his snoring body. "You misjudge Her, Darkhelm. I think She would keep you safe. Would force you to accept that safety if She thought you could live with it. But She knows that is not to be your path. Whether you accept it or not. She cares about you. We all do."

The weight of those words was almost too much to bear.

"I don't want to go, Eliud."

The bleakness of her voice brought tears to his eyes.

"And I don't want you to leave, Daine. But I flatter myself that I know you well; maybe I'm one of the few people still above ground who can make that claim. If you are not present at the Council of the West to give answer to the Trellecs, it will eat away at you. No soul in the world would blame you for stepping off the Road and spending a season or two here with me. I could try to figure out what Genoes is, you could teach me to bake, and we could both try to make Kirstin laugh again. And I feel sure the Goddess would bless us as we went about it."

"But? "

"But one day, you will hear about someone who suffered because of what may be decided at that damned Council, and you will second-guess yourself each way to sunrise that you would have been able to stop that suffering if you were there. And that will break you. And I don't think anything would be able to put you back together again. I don't want you to leave, Daine Darkhelm, but if you stay here, it will just be a matter of time before you shatter. So, I say again, he will be safe here, and I wish you joy of the hunt."

Daine found herself standing, yet she did not remember moving. "And Kirstin?"

"I'll be coming with you." The Archer was in the doorway of her room, fully dressed for travel. She had fashioned a sling out of an old scarf, and Savage peeked out from its folds. "We can make it to the outskirts before the morn without pushing too hard. We'll be there around the time the others reach the village."

Daine felt such despair at that moment. She wondered if this was how Eliud felt when she came here so many years ago to persuade him to return to the Capital. She hoped not. She could not bear to think she had caused him such pain.

She barely met his eyes as she and Kirstin moved to the door.

"Daine?" She turned back to him. "Make sure you come back to us. We'll be waiting. And he will be safe."

She walked through the door without response.

Darkhelm walked the Road once more.

CHAPTER THIRTY-SEVEN

"Rising Temperatures"

It would be hard for an onlooker to believe that these many people were trying to descend on such an out-of-the-way place as the village. Nevertheless, it appeared that every hamlet, town, or City in the world had decided that it needed to be represented at the Great Council of the West and had, in consequence, sent every dignitary they possessed.

All along the Road, encampments of assorted sizes, shapes and complexities were springing up as far as the eye could see. Judging the press and scrum of travellers to be impassable, most people seemed to have decided that they were as close to their destination as they were likely to get. It added little to the chaos and confusion that most were simply choosing to unpack where they stood.

While the engineering around the construction of the Road was, at one time, the envy of the world, it would not be unfair to note that upkeep had not been a priority for recent monarchs. Thus, whereas there were indeed broad, well-maintained sections that could support the weight of so many people and horses, there were equally sizeable sections that were little more than mud tracks. The integrity of these particular parts was not improved by such an increase in traffic.

That only three people had so far been claimed by the rapidly formed quagmires was more due to luck than any sound judgement.

Things were little improved toward the head of the column. It appeared that chronology of arrival was the only form of precedence for a position in the fields surrounding the village. While it might have been hoped that the bigger, more prestigious delegations would be afforded space to build appropriately secure encampments, the reality was that options were somewhat more limited.

This explained why Donal Assay found himself in delicate negotiations with a man that, to his understanding — and he had sought to clarify the wording several times — was called "Red Kaul of "The Knook.""

"As I have explained, sir . . ." Donal tried once again.

"Ain't no sir." The small man, seemingly covered in moss and mud, spat a stream of green goo at Donal's feet.

"Quite. My apologies. As I have explained, Red Kaul, we would ask that you remove your . . . structure from this area of the field to allow for the establishment of the pavilion of Mayor Elm of Swinford. He has a sizeable retinue which would benefit from this more open position in a way, perhaps, your solitary mule and that fine-looking basket of apples does not truly require."

"Was here first." More green goo.

"Indeed, and the Mayor recognises the right of claim of . . . the Knook to this spot. However, should you be amenable to finding another position — and we have scoped out a smaller area with quite a lovely view of the river we think will be perfect for you — we have all manner of goods of which you may wish to avail yourself."

"Don't need nothing from no one. Here for the Council. Got here first." And with that, the small man tottered back toward his makeshift hut and basket of apples. His mule glared at Donal with an anger the Secretary had not believed such animals were capable of and then spat its own contribution to the slime on the ground.

There was a time, under a different Lord, when Donal would have simply ordered his men to remove this disgusting little man and his meagre possessions. Indeed, over his long life — and Donal Assay was considerably more ancient than may be thought — he had served a number of Lords who would have insisted that Red Kaul be a smear on the road for so much as daring to establish a camp before his betters had made their choice, let alone refusing to move on when requested. One or two of them would have taken such umbrage at the disrespect that generations unending of the dwellers of the Knook would have been executed, enslaved and — Donal had one particular Lord in mind — cannibalised.

There were moments when he looked back on those occasions as the good old days.

But no. That was unworthy of the new "him." He had chosen to enter the service of Taelsin Elm because he saw something in that man that spoke to the better angels of his mind. He had spent a not insignificant amount of time smoothing the passage through life for all manner of wastrel

Lords, and enough had been enough. The world was on the precipice of a momentous change — did not the calling of this Council make that clear? — and if it meant it was now to be viewed askance to murder the common-Classed, he supposed that was a price worth paying.

Sighing, he returned to where Taelsin sat on his horse and shook his head regretfully. "My apologies, sir. The delegation from the Knook is not for moving."

From his vantage point, Taelsin scanned the tumultuous scene along the Road. It was as if a vast, unwieldy travelling carnival had disgorged itself along this single dirt track, with hundreds of individual tents and hastily erected wooden structures crowded along it. He snorted; in many ways, that was a perfect description of the scene in front of him.

As he had feared, this debacle proved that the Trellecs were complete and utter morons.

A call had gone out for a Great Council of the West, and not a single arrangement had been put in place for what actually to do when all those people who were summoned arrived.

Had the reports he had received not been unanimous in their view that Fion Trellec was utterly sincere in his belief in secession, he would wonder if this whole thing was not a deliberate act of sabotage to the cause.

For the last few bells, bemused Lords had been arriving to find that there was, quite literally, no room within the village and none in the nearest of the surrounding fields. Instead, it seemed they were expected to camp out in the open on the approaching Road.

It would not be unfair to note the disappointment at these arrangements was leading to a number of regrettable incidents.

Taelsin judged he had witnessed more unnecessary injuries and death in the two-bell journey from Swinford than in the whole of his last military campaign. "Shambles" did not go anywhere near far enough.

"It occurs to me that, should I have been seeking to guide my fellows toward a momentous undertaking, I may have sought to ensure a good night's sleep before negotiations began. Maybe I would have extended some hospitality to smooth the frustrations of a hard journey. Perhaps, and I recognise I may be speaking out of turn here, I probably would have tried to avoid making *lifelong sworn enemies pitch a Goddess-cursed tent next to each other in the woods on a moonless night!*" Taelsin's voice increased to a frustrated shout on the last sentence, and Donal quickly sketched the confidentiality rune in the air to keep his Lord's explosion private.

"Quite. And if I could take this opportunity to note that while others can no longer hear you, your somewhat irritated gestures are very much on view. Shall we seek to grasp some positives from the situation? The more people who can work out their differences now, the more consensus we are likely to reach tomorrow. And, if we dare take further comfort from disaster, a little bird tells me that since a number of . . . accidents have befallen the Lords of Wroughton and of Bornbrook, and the survivors of those delegations will shortly be striking back for home. Providing we do not mind sluicing away some blood and burying some corpses, I think their former spot in yonder field would suit us very well as a base for operations."

Taelsin rubbed a hand over his face. He had such dreams about how the moment Swinford was freed from the Crown would play out. None of them included watching people fight over spots in the mud. "Yes, fine. Just get a camp set up and raise the strongest wards we have. With the mood out here, it will be a matter of time before we have a wholesale civil war."

The Historians would later write how three hundred delegations to the Great Council of the West arrived, all at once, outside a small village that had, seemingly, made no preparations. From the great cities such as Swinford right down to one-man fishing villages such as the Knook, ambassadors had been sent forth to hammer out the Kingdom's future.

And, as they would also write, tempers were already running high.

*

"I have never seen so many people in my life," Kirstin said, staring in wonder at the press of humanity that extended up and down the Road and left to right back into the woods. Savage, having tired of the sling on their journey, was now perched on her shoulder, eyes huge.

"It's a disaster waiting to happen." Daine shook her head in amazement. She had been attached to armies where just this sort of thing happened. In the heat of things, some inexperienced Noble found themselves in charge of thousands of men and gave all kinds of orders before those that actually understood how things worked had a chance to translate them into something practical. All kinds of nasty things could occur before some grizzled veteran of a Sergeant banged heads together and imposed proper order. Usually by killing the Noble issuing the orders.

However, while such things were not uncommon in the hustle and bustle of battle, how on earth had no one had the foresight to organise something more appropriately here? She had a low opinion of the Trellecs but had assumed some degree of organisational competence lurked in there somewhere. Yet, as far as she could see, not a single thing had been done to prepare for this vast immigration other than announce it and hope it all worked out for the best.

As she watched, two soldiers, each wearing different colours of one obscure House or another, escalated their argument from shouting into each other's faces to drawing swords with their fellows pitching in. The movement of so many people up and down the Road quickly hid the fight from her, but there were certainly going to be casualties there.

Such was the white-hot heat of tension radiating along the Road that Daine wondered if the reason for the Goddess's indifference to this Council, and the potential for secession, was that She foresaw this chaos degenerating into complete destruction. But there was no answer to that thought. If she were not thinking this about a deity, she would suggest that She had been in an almighty sulk from the moment they left the cottage.

"The way things are going, I will be astonished if there's anyone left alive tomorrow morning to actually speak at the Council. Come on, let's see what they've done with my room at the inn."

CHAPTER THIRTY-EIGHT

"Woe Betide Those That Cross the Line"

Nessa Acas, keeper of the only inn in the village, was a woman who knew her own mind.

She was unequivocal in her belief that there was right and there was wrong in this world, and woe betide anyone who crossed the line from one to the other. Possessing a sharp tongue and an even sharper right hook, with a Skill for lifting ale barrels one-handed, few in the village would seek to tangle with her. At least not twice.

She had known that her refusal to serve Drunnoc Trellec all those months back would have repercussions. Admittedly, she had expected that to take the form of some mild vandalism, perhaps a broken window here or there at worst. The attempted abduction and, presumably, murder of her youngest daughter had come as somewhat of an unwelcome surprise, but — as she had noted to Daine at the time — "boys will be boys." Particularly Trellec boys.

She had sent her Bella away to stay with a cousin the minute they left Lady Darkhelm's Court but, despite the consequences, still would not have acted in any other way. If you believed in right and wrong, you stuck to it even when it was easier not to.

Therefore, the last few hours had been quite enjoyable for a woman of a stubborn frame of mind when it came to all matters of politeness, etiquette, and appropriate behaviour. It was a rare day that she was able to give the "higher-ups," as she thought of them, a piece of her mind, so the constant succession of chinless wonders and their assorted hangers-on who had appeared to demand bed and board were proving to be a rich source of entertainment.

More than one Lord who had not managed to keep an acceptable tone when making their request for a room had left, if not quite in tears, then certainly redder-faced than they had been when they had entered. But, on the other hand, she felt the most satisfaction for the fate of one Lordling, who, having failed to take "no" for an an-swer in all sorts of ways, was currently seeking a Healer to help soothe the swelling on rather sensitive parts of his anatomy.

She was thus fully prepared, indeed delightedly expect-ant, for the next battle when the bell above the door tinkled once again.

"If you're here for a drink, sit yourself down, and one of the girls will see to you. If it's a room you want, we're full. If it's anything else, I ain't interested," she said, not looking up from the mug she was cleaning.

"Good evening, Mistress Acas."

Nessa's eyebrows rose at the voice, and she looked up to see the figures who had entered. The Lady Darkhelm and another younger woman she found familiar were walking toward her.

"My Lady!" She put down the mug and, wiping her hands on her apron, came round the bar to take the Knight in an embrace. "They said you had fallen from the Road."

Daine was somewhat taken aback by the woman's reaction. She had been civil enough with the Innkeeper in their limited interactions over the last few Tours, and, of course, there had been the business around her daughter, but nothing she would have expected to have caused such emotion. She stood awkwardly, unsure what to do with her hands, while she was hugged tightly.

Nessa finally released her and stood back, beaming up at the Knight.

"A momentary stumble but, as you can see, back to my feet."

"It does my heart good to know it."

The door tingled as another hopeful supplicant for the position of temporary lodger tried to enter. "We're closed!" Nessa bellowed, striding forward to push the startled woman backwards and out of the inn. Then she bolted the door and turned to look at the few solitary drinkers that still remained at this late hour. "Anyone seeing anything they may feel the need to share beyond these walls?"

"No, Nessa," was the choral reply.

"Rojer Untrack. I see you lurking over there. I get a visit from a Trellec tomorrow I'll know where it came from, you hear me?"

"Nothing from me, Nessa. I promise. Not after last time." The white-faced Farmer could not get the words out fast enough.

Nessa glared at him for a moment before ushering

Daine and Kirstin — "I ain't be holding with pets in here, so if I catch that thing without you about, I'm wringing its neck" — to an isolated corner and sat down opposite them.

"You know what's occurring? With the Council and all?"

"We do."

"Trellec's all puffed up after . . . well, what happened with you, and he's acting like he's the biggest dog in the yard. I'm sure you're here to take his balls and show him the error of his way. But, my Lady, there's some serious folk out there on the Road. Things are going to escalate and fast."

Daine nodded at the woman's words. The chaos churning on the Road would burn itself out tonight. For sure, there'd be more than a little bloodletting amongst the less major players — maybe even a few big blow-ups here as old scores were settled — but when the Council was called tomorrow morning, it would not be the fringe figures like Fion Trellec running the floor.

She'd seen the banners of Elm, Ironfort, Cliff Edge, and Felton out there. Good men and women. Lord and Ladies she'd met over the years and respected. Liked, even. "Serious folk," as Nessa had said. Not the type to be easily dissuaded from a path they had chosen. Nor ones to risk it all on the whim of the Trellecs.

Ah, Fion, she thought ruefully. *So, you think you're running this show? You're nothing more than a spark for embers long in the smouldering to ignite.*

"What are you going to do?" Daine was aware of three pairs of expectant eyes on her. Kirstin, eager to begin her bloody quest for vengeance; the Innkeeper looking forward to further tweaked noses amongst the Nobility; and Savage, who — well, who knew what that creature wanted.

She could walk over to Keep Trellec right now and put all of them to the sword. Of course, the existence of the Earth Mage caused some residual fear, but unless he was phenomenally talented, he would not be attempting a casting like the one that had used to entomb her for quite some time. That slaughter might slake a need within her, but would it change anything?

In fact, would not the execution of local Nobility play precisely into the broader narrative about the Crown and its Knights? She had presumed her sudden reappearance and a violent example made of the Trellecs would shatter the fledging confidence of those preaching secession. But, having witnessed the enormous numbers of attendees and seen Lords and Ladies of significant quality there, she could see that had been a naïve hope.

Of course, she could potentially go out on the Road tonight and stir up enough trouble that things would spiral out of control on their own. A few judicious slayings would turn that seething tension of uneasy alliances into full-scale madness. That was what Gant would have done in her shoes. It was what the King would order her to do if he knew of the situation.

But the Goddess did not want her to do that.

And she did not want to do that.

The eyes were still watching her. Awaiting an answer. She demurred from giving one. "Mistress Acas, may I ask what you have done with all my baggage?"

*

It turned out that when an Innkeeper knows her own mind, she needs to see a body before she is willing to believe a customer is dead.

"She paid hard coin for the month, and that room will

be hers for the month. Would be wrong to take money for it twice."

"Don't be stupid, woman. From what I hear, the Darkhelm is not coming back. You've got her gold, you get to keep her things, and I'll give twice the price myself for somewhere to sleep for a few hours. No one needs to know."

There was right, and there was wrong. And woe betide anyone who crossed the line from one to the other.

"And you broke his jaw?" Kirstin interrupted the story, wide-eyed, as they walked up the stairs toward Daine's room.

"You don't get to call me stupid in my own inn. Nor suggest I'm a grave-robbing thief." She fumbled with the keys at her belt and unlocked the door. It swung open, and Nessa shooed them inside. "It's all still exactly as you left it. Now, I'll leave you to it if there is nothing else."

The room was nothing to speak of. A bed, a chair, and a mirror propped against the wall. Daine had stayed in hundreds of these wayside inns' rooms throughout the years, and they were all much the same. In one corner were stacked three huge chests, each containing the few possessions she tended to bring with her on Tour. With ease, she lifted the top one and laid it on the floor, then did the same with the middle.

Opening the first chest, she removed a padded arming doublet and slipped it on before doing the same with a pair of arming hose.

Watching her, fascinated, Kirstin sat down on the edge of the bed. Savage, not remotely interested in observing a Knight of the Road gear for war, circled once or twice on the bed, stretched, and curled up in its centre.

Oblivious to her audience, from the same chest, Daine removed three chain mail items: a choker, mail sleeves and a long mail shirt that, once on, hung down to below her knees. With expert ease, betraying years of practice, she quickly added each of these on top of the doublet and hose. Then, satisfied with how they hung, she closed the lid and turned to the second, even larger, chest.

The first thing she removed was what looked like a pair of metal shoes. "Sabatons," Daine said in answer to Kirstin's confused look. "They're utterly useless. I don't think I've ever worn a pair that deflected anything. But I look ridiculous in the rest of this with bare feet."

She stepped into them, then took out and strapped on various polished metal armour pieces around her lower legs, knees, and thighs.

Finally, she removed the last two items from the second chest: a breastplate and a backplate. "That's about the limit of what I can do without a second pair of hands, I'm afraid. I'd welcome some assistance if you have a mind to it?"

Kirstin stood and helped, with great difficulty, the Knight buckle those two items around her torso. "You'll need to put your back into it, lass. Trust me, I don't break." Getting increasingly red-faced, Kirstin pulled as tightly as she could and then tied the shoulder armour to the laces on the doublet, following Daine's patient direction. Next followed metal plates over the upper and lower arms and elbows, each hanging from the shoulder attachment points.

Daine indicated the third chest. "Last one, lass. I will be set if you can get those out for me."

Kirstin knelt to open the final chest and removed two exceptionally heavy gauntlets, a sword wrapped up within a scabbard and finally . . . She suppressed a gasp at the last item. A vast, polished helmet of black iron.

Passed the items in turn, Daine slipped on the gauntlets and helped Kirstin buckle up the weapon belt around her waist.

Finally, she donned her Darkhelm.

"Been a while since I've had to have all this on. I appreciate your help." Her voice echoed through the metal.

The Archer was finding it hard to speak. While slowly building up the metal casing around Daine, she had not appreciated the power of the final impact. The figure standing in front of her was terrifying, and suddenly, she could well understand the plethora of songs that had grown up around such a sight.

Unaware of her impact on the girl, the Knight shifted awkwardly for a moment, muscle memory exploring the limits of reach and movement. Then she headed for the door. Kirstin went to follow, but Daine stopped and slowly turned.

"No. Not tonight. I know you have your own reasons for being back here. Of course I will support you against the Trellecs. But not tonight."

"Why all of this if you're not acting against them?"

"Folk need to see that there is still a Knight on this Road. I figure some out there are hoping that is no longer the case. I'm going to remind them."

CHAPTER THIRTY-NINE

"Theological Complexities"

When considering the nature of the pantheon that was worshipped across the Kingdom, it was easy to focus on the figure of the Goddess to the exclusion of all others. Indeed, such was the hold that the Knights of the Road held over the popular imagination — a situation encouraged by the not inconsiderable funds paid by Her worshippers to a succession of Bards — that the patron of these warriors dominated any and all liturgical discussions.

This situation had become so commonplace in the last century that, if asked about the existence of the Churches of Dawn, most people would confidently assert that these buildings had all been constructed in dedication to praising Her name.

The reality, of course, was far more complicated than this, but who in this world cared for an uncomfortable truth when easy lies were available?

Brother Evelyn, unusually sober for this time of the evening, carefully stepped through the various snoring bodies that had taken up temporary residence on his floor.

While Nessa may have been able to close the door of the inn to those seeking a bed for the night, there were, regrettably, theological complexities with him doing the same. That and, they realised, he was open to bribery for a spot in his pews, he now had a pleasantly jingling coin purse which would significantly upgrade the quality of his tippling in the near future.

He paused on his perambulations to regard the stained-glass depiction of the Goddess on the back wall. Sadly, it was not one of the images in his Church that received much attention. Here, She was represented not in Her modern likeness as a beautiful young woman, as was the most familiar icon worshipped of late, but in Her more traditional aspect as Mother.

He much preferred the maternal version of the Goddess. Her position in the broader pantheon made far more sense to his mind when She was worshipped in this manner. The fashion for calling Her the Goddess, in and of itself, appeared to raise Her above the other deities in a way he did not feel was appropriate nor consistent with the history of the Kingdom's gods. As the Mother of the Holy Family, She had a vital role, for sure, but that position was not to the exclusion of the others.

His eyes moved to the two figures depicted to Her right on the wall. Her eldest sons, the Lords of Misrule. As a child, he had been fascinated by these two perennially carousing young men. Indeed, he was self-aware enough to know that many of his current challenges with the demon drink came from that early attraction to the Lords and a willingness to seek to emulate Their example.

Nevertheless, it was too simplistic to view them as purely entities concerned with Luck, as so many nowadays did. The Brothers enjoyed Their games of chance, to be sure, but that interest was part of Their wider connection to and, indeed, Their personification of the forces of Chaos. To invoke the presence of the Lords of Misrule — in word, thought or deed — was not just to wish for their blessing when you cast some dice but to summon ungovernable powers that had the power to shatter fate itself. Not that anyone really saw them as having that potential anymore.

Traditionally, the role of the Goddess — when in her avatar as the Mother — was to restrain this potential and to direct Them toward more appropriate outlets for Their power. There were innumerable depictions of Mother and Unruly Sons in Churches across the Kingdom that explored countless iterations of this theme. Brother Evelyn was unsure when the tales of the Knights of the Road first began to supplant the stories of the Lords of Misrule, but he could see that this moment had radically transformed the power dynamic in the pantheon.

At some stage in the not-too-distant past, the Mother had withdrawn more and more from her role as a balance to Chaos and dedicated increasing energies to developing somewhat of a cult around the Knights of the Road. It appeared that through investing these warriors with elements of her power, with a strong emphasis on the delivery of Justice in opposition to the ravages of Chaos, the balance between the Mother and Her eldest sons was maintained, but in a significantly different, and fundamentally more human, manner.

Worship of the Lords of Misrule had almost entirely vanished from the Kingdom in the last fifty or sixty years. Instead, their power had become associated with that which the Knights opposed. After all, who would support the dragon against its slayer?

This change of focus had left a vacuum. And in that space, the figure depicted on Her left grew in prominence over the last thirty or so years. Even though he was sure all around him were asleep, Brother Evelyn drew a ward of sanctuary in the air when looking at the image of what the common folk called the Dark God.

In the version of Him on the wall, He was shown in His aspect of a small child, the Mother's youngest son. Evelyn knew that, in Churches less ancient than this, He was regularly depicted as a menacing hooded figure, all brooding, violent potential. A seething anger that could only find His expression through all that was terrible in the world. However, for Evelyn, and the countless secret worshipers like him, He was the embodiment of free choice.

If She was concerned with Order and Her eldest sons represented Chaos, then the Dark God was that which lay in between them. His existence represented the drive for complexity in the face of brutal simplicity. If all that existed was right and wrong, what space existed to be human? There was a need for the comfort of grey in a world that, of late, only accepted white and black.

The irony that, rather than seeing this as a middle ground, the Goddess seemed to be placing such ambiguity in direct opposition to Her will, was not lost on Brother Evelyn.

Was not much of the current political strife — he might be a drunkard, but he kept his ear to the ground when armies were on the march — due to a refusal to find any middle ground between the West and the Crown? No one in the West — at least no one of sound mind — wished for Chaos to reign. However, there was clearly a desire for something different from the stifling grip from the Capital.

The focus on the aspect of the Goddess, rather than on her as the Mother, and the wholesale collapse of the influence of the Lords of Misrule due to the Knights' success, meant that it was Her youngest son that seemed to have become Her key opposition.

And Brother Evelyn was not the only one of His worshippers uncomfortable with this dichotomy.

It troubled him that the Child, as he characterised his patron, was viewed with such terror by the populace. In his view, the world should not be divided into a war between Light and Dark with Chaos roaring in the background — the Goddess against the Dark God with the Lords playing Their games — but instead, all should be the result of a patient, loving Mother assisting Her children in finding Their own paths.

Of course — and his eyes flit upwards to the image that dominated the ceiling of the Church — that consideration of the nature of the world somewhat neglected the Father. Or rather, His perennial absence.

But there was enough woe in his world without spending time brooding on that particular issue within the pantheon.

Brother Evelyn reached the ladder that led up to his room and pulled himself upwards. He felt deflated. As he always did when reflecting on the world of gods and men.

There was something in his understanding of it all, of everyone's understanding of it, that was flawed. That humanity had sought to place a familial structure on these deities made sense, he supposed. But the pyramid of Father, Mother and Their Children was simply too simplistic an organisation for these powers. Yet the current movement to a monotheistic approach, the Goddess against the Dark God, was self-limiting in and of itself.

He reached the edge of his bed and closed his eyes as he lowered himself on it. He rarely prayed to the Child these days. He sensed that the wine-fuddled wishes of an old man held little interest for Him, particularly when those like the Trellec boy appealed to His darker instincts. However, with everything occurring in the world, he would feel remiss if, once more, he did not add his voice to those seeking change, but not wholesale war.

But while for Brother Evelyn, who moved from thought-ful prayer to dreamless sleep with his customary alacrity, Mother and Child were not in opposition, for the Goddess and the Dark God — entrenched in their newest aspects and unwilling to relinquish those positions — all the pieces were in place for the next stage of the game to begin.

And patient, peaceful negotiation was not on the agenda.

*

Eliud cracked open the door to check on Genoes. The boy was sleeping peacefully, Josul snoring on the bed beside him.

The Pendragon smiled and pulled the door gently shut behind him as he returned to the kitchen. For all his ridic-ulous appearance, the dog was a formidable power in his own right. Should anyone succeed in breaching the security of the cottage this night, they would quickly learn this to their terminal cost.

Wincing with effort — and then realising there was no one around to appreciate his pantomime of decrepitude — he moved his favourite chair to face the front door. Then, sat-isfied that he had a clear view, he sat in it, manifesting a mug of something hot and strong on the table next to him. It was the work of a further few moments to ensure all of his wards were as he wanted them.

Even without the comfort of the presence of Savage, he was sure there was little that could occur here tonight that would be beyond his capacity to repel. Although, of course, it was precisely that sort of arrogant thinking that had led him to be sitting alone in a cottage in the middle of nowhere in the first place. Frowning, Eliud added a few more esoteric defences to the windows and doors. He had promised Daine he would protect the boy, and he meant to keep that oath.

They would make an attempt tonight, of that he was sure.

Too much strength had been concentrated here of late, and there were powers that could not help but notice that. It stretched credibility that a gathering of a Knight of the Road, a Pendragon complete with his familiars, and a — whatever it turned out Genoes was — in one place would not cause significant ripples in the pond of the world. It would be wholly against the nature of those who cared about such things if they did not come to see how the situ-ation could be turned to their advantage.

Genoes, in particular, would be of interest to all the wrong sorts of forces in the world. So, they needed to be persuaded, firmly if not entirely politely, that the cost of gaining access to the boy would not be worth paying.

He wondered which of them was likely to try his pa-tience first.

CHAPTER FORTY

"Standing the Road"

The reaction of those camping outside the village to the sudden appearance of a Knight of the Road was less of a ripple of panic and more of a tidal wave.

To judge by the hullabaloo of trumpets, frenzied orders and hastily deployed defensive formations, it may have been thought that Daine had chosen to charge them rather than simply plant herself in the middle of the Road, both hands resting on the pommel of her sword, the tip pressed into the ground.

Half a bell earlier, there had been a brief cavalry sortie originating from within the village, apparently following orders to drive her from that position.

It had been less than successful.

"Damned fast, isn't she?" Donal remarked drily as the first of the galloping outriders reached the Knight and chopped down at what turned out to be entirely empty space.

"She's wearing heavy plate armour and dancing around them as if she's at a ball." Taelsin winced as that first horseman lost his head to a cut he did not see coming. "It's not just her Speed that will likely be problematic."

The second horseman to reach Daine showed quite some skill to avoid crashing into a bewildered, newly riderless horse. But unfortunately, that effort merely lined them up for the return swing from the Knight's sword, the top half of their torso tumbling to the floor.

The third and fourth horse riders, seemingly ignoring the carnage that had gone before, clung rather too confidently to their belief in the irresistible nature of a coordinated charge. The gathering crowd on the Road watched in appalled horror as Daine simply stood her ground and allowed the leading horse to crash into her — the snapping of equine bones causing more than a few episodes of vomiting in onlookers — catapulting its rider ten feet away to lie still.

The final rider of the group slashed downwards at the metallic monster that had so effortlessly despatched his peers and, for his trouble, was lifted from his saddle, pierced through by the point of an upthrusted sword. Then, with a dismissive flick of her wrist, the Knight shook the pinned body clear of her blade and resumed her position in the middle of the Road as if no casual slaughter had just occurred. The whole ill-conceived assault had taken less than twenty heartbeats.

For a moment, there was complete silence. Then blind panic set in among the onlookers. "I guess that answers the question of whether to believe the Trellecs' claims," Taelsin said, directing all his men into his pavilion.

Donal raised every ward he possessed, and some he probably should not, and grimaced. "I may suggest, sir, rumours of the Lady Darkhelm's demise seem to have been somewhat overstated."

*

The first figure to burst through Eliud's door instantly turned to ash. So did the second. And the thir

At that stage, there was a pause while the gathering crowd in his garden reconsidered their tactics.

"I feel I should note that in most cultures, it is considered rather rude to enter the house of another without so much as a bye or leave."

A smash from the window in Genoes's room, followed by a bloodcurdling roar from Josul, was the only response to his words from those outside.

"In case that outcome was a touch unclear, trying to sneak in the back way is likewise frowned upon in polite company."

There was a brief scuttling on the roof, followed by a wet-sounding explosion and the soft thudding noise of various body parts hitting the ground.

"I should point out that some of the trees out there get pretty indignant if you step on the grass. There's a sign warning you about that, after all. Ah, it sounds like some of you are finding that out firsthand for yourselves. Never you mind. I can wait while you regather yourselves."

Everything went quiet momentarily, and Eliud took a sip of his still-warm drink.

A tall, thin figure stepped into the open doorway and paused, careful not to cross the threshold. When Eliud saw it, the cup shook for a second in the Pendragon's hand.

"Ah. The Duskstrider." There was a reptilian hiss to the

voice. "They said it would not be you. That you would not be so stupid. Not again. I am so glad they were wrong."

With a flick of his finger, Eliud slammed the door shut. "Oh, my Lady Darkhelm. What have you got me involved in now?"

*

"She's just standing there."

"Probably enjoying the fresh air."

"Don't be facetious, my Lord. It's unbecoming."

"Actually, Donal, I think the fact we're hiding in a tent praying the big bad Knight of the Road won't descend on the camp to execute us all for treason is what is pretty darn unbecoming."

"The rare valid point."

Taelsin continued to pace his pavilion. The situation was close to becoming irrevocable. He was aware that a significant minority of those who had arrived for the Council of the West were busy preparing to leave. The shambles of the arrangements, coupled with the presence of Daine Darkhelm on the Road outside the village, had shaken already-fragile confidence in the endeavour.

Of course, the casual massacre of those horsemen had served as a poignant reminder for those who might doubt the efficacy of a Knight of the Road.

Damn those Trellecs. At every turn, they made it less and less likely there could be a successful outcome here. Their precipitate actions could be the death knell for the possibility of secession for generations.

Three hundred delegates had arrived to debate the future of the West, quarrelled amongst themselves for a few bells and now, potentially, would flee in panic with their tails between their legs now that a Knight of the Road had appeared. Such a narrative, reaffirming the power of the Crown, would be a devastating blow to independence.

He could not allow that to happen. Taelsin strode to the entrance of the tent and slipped outside. His men, taken aback by his sudden movement, hurried to follow. He turned, walking backwards for a moment. "No. You all stay here. I'm doing this alone."

"You're going to — sir, if I may?" Donal ran ahead to block his path and placed a hand on his chest to stop him. "Far be it from me to belittle your martial prowess, sir, but if you are planning to challenge a Knight of the Road to single combat, the words 'squashed like an ant' come to mind."

Taelsin shrugged off the hand and continued walking up the Road toward Daine. "I'm not going to fight her, Donal. I'm going to talk to her."

Donal kept pace with his master. "Sure. Because if there's one thing we all know about Daine Darkhelm, it is that she's a speak-first-brutally-dismember-later personality. All those stories about her lively conversation . . . I can see why you'd want to have a quick chat. Sir, will you stop!"

Taelsin paused, hearing the panic in his friend's voice. "Donal, I have to do something. Look at them." He turned and swept a hand toward the crowd of delegates. "They're all here —all of them, despite everything. Despite all the mistrust and all the history of betrayal, every major player in the West has brought themselves to the same place and at the same time to talk about our future. If we back down now, that's it. It's over. Who knows when we will get this momentum again? I can't allow this chance to just . . . just wilt away."

The Secretary took a breath to still his swirling emotions.

It had been long since he had liked the person he served. The prospect of any of his previous Lords confronting a Knight of the Road would barely have raised an eyebrow. The old Lord is dead; long live the new Lord. But Taelsin was different. While Donal cared not a jot for Western independence, Taelsin did, and that was enough for him. Certainly enough not to sit idly by while he lost his head.

"Sir, there is extraordinarily little I can do to mitigate the power of the Lady Darkhelm. If this conversation goes poorly, my only advice is to run and hope all that plate slows her down."

"Your faith in my negotiating powers is touching. Besides, I don't need to outrun Daine. I just need to be faster than you."

*

Daine watched, with amusement, as the two men approached her. Their bickering, she knew, hid a deep affection and loyalty of a type she rarely witnessed on Tour. She liked them both.

The younger man, Taelsin Elm, stopped and dipped a bow in her direction. "My Lady Darkhelm, it is good to see you well. We had heard troubling news."

She nodded a head in reply. "Thank you for your words, sir. Not sure all in that scrum feel similarly."

He grimaced. "You may be right, my Lady. Honest truth? As Mayor Elm, I feel nothing but dismay to see you here. Swinford would have you dead and gone. But as Taelsin, I smile at seeing a friend hale and hearty."

She did not reply.

"Can I be so bold as to ask you your intentions on this day, my Lady?"

"I am standing the Road, Lord Elm. There have been . . .

events in this village to which I will need to turn my attention." Donal and Taelsin could not help looking at the corpses lying around her. "The recent behaviour of the Manor Lord has raised the ire of the Goddess."

Donal jumped in. "Can I ask — and sorry to interrupt — what is your position on the Council of the West?"

She did not reply.

Taelsin pressed the issue. "My Lady, the Council of the West has been called, and we would meet to discuss various sundry matters. I feel I must note that the Crown has no jurisdiction over such a Council. Yet you appear to be seeking to intimidate us into cancelling the meeting."

"Why should you find my presence to be intimidating, Lord Elm? You have, in the past, welcomed me to your City, and, I may say, we have worked together to ensure justice was delivered. So, I am confused by your concern about me. Surely the Council of the West should be reassured that I stand by, ready to ensure your safety?"

"Safety?" Donal barked out a harsh laugh. "You stand in our path, geared for war, covered in the blood of your enemies. Do you expect us to believe you are not here to stop us from meeting? We are to, what, walk past you into the village to hold our Council, and you will do nothing to stop us?"

"I stand the Road, sir." Daine's voice suddenly boomed out, and all the delegates could hear it. "The Council of the West is under my protection. There will be no further violence this evening. Delegates will cease their petty squabbles, or they will answer to me. I will stand watch tonight, and you will hold your Council in the morning."

Taelsin cocked his head, mind racing at the implications of her words. "You know what we are here to discuss . . ."

"I know nothing, sir, beyond the fevered witterings of a Manor Lord who, come the morrow, will face the Justice of the Goddess. But I tell you, sir, for now, She has no interest in the content of your gathering."

Donal and Taelsin exchanged a glance. It was Donal that spoke first. "Sorry to press for clarity in this matter, my Lady, but, as you will appreciate, the potential slaughter or otherwise of a number of people requires we leave no ambiguity. You, that is, the Goddess, take no position on the Council of the West beyond guaranteeing our safety. Is there any matter we might discuss that would change that position?"

Daine turned her head to face Donal; he quailed back at the regard from the dark eyeless helmet. "I speak in truth, Secretary Assay, when I tell you that is an answer I do not know."

CHAPTER FORTY-ONE

"Holy Terror"

"Glass cannons. That's all they have found for me lately. Nothing more than glass cannons. Sure, you can throw out a punch, and the pretty lights are always helpful, but you lot fall to pieces as soon as anyone looks at you twice. More trouble than you are worth, if you ask me. Give me a proper soldier any day. Someone who will stand at your shoulder, hour after hour, and can hold a line when the cavalry comes charging. That's what this army needs, not fancy pants Mages."

He was aware of the rasping voice sounding out against the dark background of his pain. There was something wrong with . . . well, with everything. His whole face was a wall of agony, an intense itching across his eyes which, try as he might, would not seem to work. His mouth, which pulsed with pain to dwarf that around his eyes, was filled with a salty liquid. But he could not seem to spit it out.

With a movement that increased his pain even further, he opened his lips, which split as he did so, and let the blood spill out.

"Ah, so you're awake? Okay, I can respect that. Can't tell you the number of your lot that just gave up and died at this stage. Maybe they're right, and there's more about you than it looks. But that's what we're going to find out. Unlimited potential, they say. Hundreds of Skills. Bottomless mana pool, apparently. Don't you sound quite the prospect? Can't say I've been too impressed so far. You wet yourself when we took you."

He could not seem to focus on the words. His mouth kept filling with blood, no matter how much he let it drain. What had happened to him? He could not remember being attacked. Could not remember much about anything, really. Had some sort of great beast taken him? Was that how he had become so injured? He tried to raise his arms to explore the damage, but firm hands restrained him.

"Not yet, lad. It would be best if you listened to me, this is important. Do you hear me?"

His face was slapped, which caused new blossoms of agony. Panic overwhelmed him for a moment. He could not see, blood was filling his mouth, threatening to drown him — by the Goddess, had something happened to his tongue? — and he was being held down, so he could not move. He struggled to pull himself away.

"Stop!" The power of the voice broke through the pain, and he ceased his movement. "Boy, you are just a few minutes from dying. Let's get you up to speed so we're all clear. We cut out your tongue, so there will be no spoken spells. Cratun thought we should do the same with your eyes, and when you're lopping things off, it's sometimes hard to see where the line is, you ken what I'm saying? Your hands are in the basket over there, so no twirly finger stuff either."

He felt the lips of the speaker press against his ear. "We've tied tourniquets to your wrists, which is why you're still with us. In a second, I will tell the boys to untie them, and, well, at that point, you've got a choice. You can lay back and let it go. Have got to tell you, I wouldn't blame you. None of us would. A bunch of strange men kidnap me, blind me, cut out my tongue and lop off my hands, I ain't going to be feeling too chipper. Would probably call it a day for this world. But they tell me you're special."

The voice was barely a whisper. "If you've got as much power as they say, I ain't done anything you shouldn't be able to shrug off and ask for more. We've got enough glass cannons. Don't need any more, and I ain't wasting my time training another. Of course, no one's gonna be pleased that their new shiny Mage bled out on my floor, but they'll get over it. I might lose some sleep over tonight's work, but it won't be the first time, and Goddess knows it won't be the last. These boys? Well, I think they've enjoyed it more than I'd like, and I might need to do something about that. What I'm saying, though, is that the only one who won't get over this is you."

Through his pain and disorientation, he felt something loosen on his wrists, and then it was as if a wave of tiredness hit him. He could feel the blood stream from the stumps at the ends of his arms, and with it went all his energy and all his pain too. Then, finally, his entire body relaxed, and a soft darkness began to descend.

And then stopped as a flash of lightning tore through him.

No. Not today. Not like this. This was an unacceptable end.

He heard the men around him swear as that lightning arced around him and into them. Then, with an explosive rush, he felt his body rise from the floor and move to a vertical position, so he hovered in the air, blood flowing freely from his mouth and wrists.

But in a moment, instead of blood, it was lightning, and as it escaped his body, it reknitted and rebuilt lost flesh, muscle and bone. In seconds, he could see as this uncontrolled energy reconstructed his eyes, and he could make out the scene below his floating body. Two smoking skeletons lay around a vast pool of blood, the space within clearly marking where his body had lain. To the foot of the pool stood a man looking up at him with a smirk.

He hit that man with the most potent bursts of his lightning — blowing him backwards twenty feet. He swooped down, following him, all wounds healed, and hovered over the man as he started climbing back to his feet. He hit him with lightning bolts again and again and again until his hair was burned away, his clothes were aflame, and the very earth around him smouldered red with heat.

And then he stopped.

Because the man was laughing.

That shocked him so intensely that he settled himself back on the ground and walked toward the hideously burned figure on the ground who was laughing so heartily. What was left of the man looked up at his approach and grinned a ghastly grin, splitting the skin of his face clean open.

"Knew you had it in you, boy. You can always tell those with a bit of something about them. You're going to be one of the holy terrors of this world."

"What . . . who are you? Why did you do that to me?" He was aware that, even as they spoke, the terrible injuries of this man were healing just as quickly as his own had.

"They call me the Stonehand, those that know of me. I take soft metal and hammer it into something to be proud of. I think there's going to be a lot I can teach you. My friends call me Gant."

"Do you have many of those?"

"Now, now. We've had some spicy back-and-forth tonight. You lost some blood; I lost some hair. Nothing that neither of us couldn't afford to happen, and we're both the wiser for it. No need to add rudeness to it. What do I call you, boy?"

He thought for a moment. He had so many questions, but he guessed they could wait. "Eliud. You can call me Eliud."

He was six years old.

*

Seeing that figure in the doorway had transported Eliud back to that initial helplessness when Gant had taken him. It had been overwhelming, back then, to be in the presence of someone so much older and so much more powerful. Borelean, for that was its name, was certainly both of those.

But if Gant had taught him one thing over the years, it was that the only response to being afraid was to attack.

With a fluid charge, he stood and pulled open the cottage door, surprising the press of figures that had gathered on the other side. The only time he had seen the like of them was when a Fisherman had once proudly shown him the ugliest of his catches from when he once trawled the deeps. Nothing at his door looked like it should have been on the land, much less on two feet. A glowing sword of pure energy manifested in his hand, and he swung it through the nearest of them, who, somewhat improbably, exploded at the contact.

With a flick of his finger, he summoned a blast of air that forced the rest of them backwards. Bones, or what passed for bones in these creatures, snapped as they crashed into the garden fence.

There was a disconcerting shriek and thousands of hungry eyes turned his way. The snapping of their jaws and the hissing of their gills unnerved him for a moment. He suddenly felt very small and very alone in the face of such overwhelming power. But that fear did not have long to settle upon him as the host suddenly surged toward him. In response, Eliud threw out spell after spell, destroying anything within the garden that had no place being there.

Gant had been right all those years back: a bottomless mana pool was quite a thing. In the hands of someone who knew how to use it and was angry enough to forget about petty things like the structural integrity of the universe, nothing could stand in his way.

The forces arrayed against him, countless legions of beings that he simply erased from existence, melted away until just one remained. The tall, thin presence that had stood in his doorway. Borelean.

It was not a god, Eliud knew, but that did not lessen the danger he felt radiating from it. The form it had currently assumed was more human than reptile, but Eliud knew it had more in common, certainly in temperament, with a giant, ancient crocodile.

They had tangled before. Most recently, on the night that Eliud had left the Capital, vowing never to meddle in the games of the powerful again. The outcome had been inconclusive.

"Quite the temper tantrum, Duskstrider."

Eliud nodded in acknowledgement, and the sword vanished from his hand. "Trespassers always irritate me. You should have seen what I did to the last hawker who tried to sell me something door-to-door."

"You have something in there you should not. It tastes of power. I want it. We want it." Eliud noted his opponent's tongue flicked outwards on the word 'tastes.' For some reason, that disgusted him more than anything else he knew about this creature.

"I'd ask 'you and whose army?' but I guess I just killed them all, didn't I?"

"Always with the jokes. You were crying the last time we met. You ran as fast as those human legs of yours could carry you. We pitied you."

Eliud reignited the sword and held it low to his side. "I'd lost everything. There was nothing left for which I had to fight. My true victory was in not just letting you kill me. That's your error here. You remember how I was, the despair I felt, and think that is what I will always be. Because you are unchanging, you think we all must be."

"And you've found something for which to fight, have you, little Duskstrider? How delightful. Do you think that will be enough? Or will you weep again when I take them from you?"

A smile played on the Pendragon's face as he thought of a sleeping boy in his cottage; a dog, teeth bared, standing guard over him; a small kitten sat on the shoulder of a young Archer and a lonely Knight putting herself, so very unwillingly, in the middle of chaos.

"Why don't we find out?"

And the thunder rolled.

CHAPTER FORTY-TWO

"A Shattering"

"I'm sorry, what was the question?"

The atmosphere in Keep Trellec, already somewhat febrile following the announcement of the Council of West, was in danger of descending into dark chaos.

The preparations to accommodate the hundreds of Lords, and their retinues, who answered Fion's call had proved woefully inadequate. No one who had been party to the steady stream of frustrated messengers from the great Lords of the West could ignore that fact. All could see that, far from establishing House Trellec as the preeminent leaders of secession, the events of the last few hours had merely demonstrated a significant lack of logistical capacity. Moreover, no one could fail to recognise that any power House Trellec had gained through their purported removal of the Lady Darkhelm had begun to pall.

And that was before the reappearance of the Knight on the Road.

Gilles was dimly aware that people were angry with him. He just could not quite pin down why. His watery eyes fixed in confusion on Lord Trellec. "Have I done anything to displease, my Lord?"

Fion threw his cup of wine at the Steward, hitting him square on the chest. "You haven't done anything, Gilles! That's precisely the point. I am told no arrangements have been made to welcome our guests appropriately. No preparations, no order of precedence established, not even any accommodation prepared. This was our chance to show our peers our better selves, and we're showing ourselves to be nothing better than country bumpkins."

"That sounds appalling, my Lord. Who was charged with this task? They will feel the blunt end of my stick for their dereliction of duty." Gilles cast around the Hall, a ferocious expression on his face as he met the eyes of each of the Lords and Ladies arranged around the table.

"Dear Goddess," murmured Trivian.

Fion pressed his hands to his face in impotent rage. He had been so close. Finally, after all these years of contempt and derision, he would have been afforded the respect that was his due. He had spent several enjoyable hours imagining conversations with the Mayors and Lords. By the tone of some of the messages received, he would be surprised if they would still give him the time of day. So close and, when in touching distance of that prize, he found himself surrounded by wastrels and incompetents.

"Mage, tell me that, at the least, the Speaking Chamber is prepared?"

Boruld was startled at his name. He was watching the

Steward with a look of horrified disgust. He had quickly learned to fear this man and his power while also pitying him for the collapse of his mental faculties. To witness his rapid decline these last few days was appalling. How Lord Trellec had not acted to relieve him from his responsibilities and mitigate his control over others was beyond him.

"Yes, my Lord. The Chamber has been raised to your specifications." He paused, unsure how to continue but knowing the importance of clarity on this issue. "I should mention, though . . ."

"Spit it out, man." Fion's tolerance for old men was running thin. He included himself in that.

"The shaping of the Chamber has been extremely resource-heavy."

"Are you asking for more money, you grasping little worm?" Trivian had been seeking a safe outlet for her building rage and seemed to have settled on the Earth Mage.

"Not at all, Lady Trellec. I just wished to make clear that, as I have needed to make significant use of my mana, I am likely to be of little use should . . ." He paused again.

Trivian, in what was clearly a Trellec tradition, threw her goblet at him, missing and smashing against the wall. "Stop prevaricating. What is it that bothers you?"

"He is letting us know he will be no help against the Lady Darkhelm." Drunnoc's cold voice cut across the silence.

And with that, all thoughts turned, once more, to the terrifying figure standing in the centre of the Road. No one was clear on who had ordered the failed cavalry sortie — and that in itself was call for significant alarm — but all it had done was reinforce the precarious position in which they had found themselves.

"Lord Elm has said she will not stop the Council

meeting . . ." Lady Culloden's voice had lost some of its biting surety since the disaster in the tunnel. It was one thing to intellectually be aware of the prowess of a Knight of the Road and quite another to view the carnage wrought on what were previously thought to be elite soldiers. She was not confident that her pavise crossbowmen would re-take the field against Daine. And, having seen the bodies of those that had engaged the Knight belowground, she was not sure she blamed them.

"And what then, my Lady? Do we cram ourselves in Trellec's shiny new Speaking Chamber, and she enters to slaughter us all the moment we speak about secession? No. My House will have none of this." Lord Michaeleas hauled his considerable bulk to his feet. "Fion, it was a worthy idea, but as I've long advised you, this sort of thing is better left to others. Unfortunately, the Council has been called under false pretences. The Lady Darkhelm stands the Road, and I speak for many others around this table when I say we have lost confidence in your ability to manage this situation." He paused to clear his throat. "The failure to make appropri-ate arrangements for this crucial event has further . . . it's blasted hot in here . . . has further . . . well, it's shown that you . . ." More coughing. "My House will not . . . Goodness, I don't quite feel . . ."

In horrid fascination, the others in the Hall watched as the large man in front of them continued to melt away. But then they realised it was not sweat that poured from his brow, but rather, a far oiler substance. His fat was, quite literally, rendering in front of their eyes.

Boruld flicked his eyes toward the Healer — if that were what she could still be called any longer — and saw Pernille's eyes blazing with power. She was at the centre of whatever was happening to the unfortunate Lord. Well, at least as far as she was Drunnoc's instrument.

With a chilling sigh, Michaeleas collapsed back into his chair, less than a third of the man he had been before. A foul puddle spread out from the floor beneath him, reminding all of the smell of burning tallow.

No one spoke. That was the thing that struck the Earth Mage most strongly when he replayed this event in his mind that evening. These men and women had known this man for years. For sure, they may not have liked him, and some may actively have hated him, but it did not take personal affection to find what was happening here abhorrent. But no one raised their voices in opposition to this profane punishment.

They all watched as his life force was stripped from him as easily as butter heated in a pan.

Within moments — though Boruld was sure it felt longer to the Lord — all excess weight had been purged away, leaving a fragile stick figure absurdly swathed in oceans of cloth. Michaeleas's mouth opened and closed like a fish, eyes enormous in the sunken flesh of his face.

Fion cupped a hand to his ear. "I'm sorry, my Lord. I cannot quite hear you. Were you concerned about how House Trellec is managing this situation?" A low moan was the only sound that escaped newly thin lips. "No? Well, does anyone else have issues they wish to raise? Now would seem a suitable time to get everything into the open."

"What's that smell?" Gilles was sniffing the air. "Is someone cooking chicken?"

Silence. With a nod, Drunnoc indicated for a Man-at-Arms to remove the still-breathing husk of Michaeleas. Pernille stood and accompanied them out of the room, a disgustingly healthy sheen to her skin.

After a moment, Aelric Geril stood and brushed imaginary lint from his immaculate shoulder. "I think, my Lord, you have been clear you have this all in hand. House Geril looks forward to the morn and the Council of the West. We have confidence you have the matter of the Lady Darkhelm in hand." He began making his way to the doorway.

"We rejoice in your words, Lord Geril." Drunnoc's eyes were fixed on the back of the older man. "That gives us much confidence. Indeed, as I was saying to your daughter just this morning, considering your obvious fealty to us, it was thus astonishing that I heard House Geril was preparing to leave the village. She was most informative as to those arrangements. Eventually."

Lord Geril sagged slightly, momentarily, before continuing toward the exit. "My daughter often gets muddled about such things. Our House, as promised, will support you at the Council." He stopped and turned to face Drunnoc, unable to meet his eyes. "Can I expect Cecilia's return this evening?"

"I think it best you rationalise your expectations." Drunnoc smiled broadly.

Geril stood, as if stone, for a moment more before leaving the Hall.

After that, it was surprising how little objection remained toward the plans of the Trellecs.

*

It was the noise that woke Brother Evelyn: as if a thousand carts were colliding, repeatedly, just outside his door. He staggered to his feet and went down the ladder into the centre of the Church.

What was happening? Was the building collapsing down around him? He covered his ears to block out the worst of the cacophony. Then his arms fell to his sides in shock as he took in the sight before him.

The entirety of the glass wall was . . . reshaping. Familiar depictions of gods and goddesses, heroes and villains and noteworthy events in the Kingdom's history were collapsing in on themselves. But the glass was not breaking. Instead, it was reforming into new images.

But no, it was more than just that.

As new imagery appeared, the wall also appeared to split itself into two distinct sections.

On the side that Brother Evelyn felt instinctively drawn toward, he could make out the Goddess depicted in all three of her aspects. Likewise, he could see other faces with which he was familiar: the Lady Darkhelm geared for war, Lord Elm addressing a large crowd, that Earth Mage of the Trellecs raising a barrier to hold back attacking soldiers.

Other images were forming there that he could not place. A young woman, a cat sat on her shoulder, drew a bow. A man stood close to Lord Elm, weaving some sorts of protection runes in the sky. A gigantic dog of some silly breed guarded a threshold. An older man, surrounded by flashing lighting, battled a colossal serpent.

With an effort, his eyes moved to the opposite side of the wall, following the tail of that serpent. Again, he saw faces he recognised, their position on the wall seemingly in a direct challenge to those he had previously seen. Opposite the Goddess squatted imagery of the Dark God, and in the place of Lady Darkhelm was that devil spawn, Drunnoc Trellec, his father in the position held by Lord Elm. That reluctant Healer mirrored the Earth Mage, and Gilles Halcoth was there, so too various other faces he knew from the High Houses. On closer inspection — although

looking that carefully caused him to feel physically sick —
the serpent's tail seemed to sneak up and around a broken
version of the King.

To look on that side of the stained glass was to feel
violated, as if the light that came through were tainted
somehow.

Brother Evelyn sagged to the floor, the effort of trying
to comprehend what was happening too much for him. It
was as if the pantheon were reshaping. The Goddess and
the Dark God bringing their conflict into the open — with
their agents set against each other.

The thought was overwhelming.

So overwhelming was this notion, in fact, that it was
quite understandable why Brother Evelyn overlooked a
small figure, so ridiculously small, at the very centre of the
window, Unclassed and unaligned to any of the swirling
power around him.

CHAPTER FORTY-THREE

"Score One for an Unlimited Mana Pool

Eliud ran a hand across his face, clearing mud, blood and sweat from his vision. He could not think about the profound exhaustion spreading through him right now, he had other things to occupy his mind.

They seemed to have been fighting forever, although, it was likely that only a few seconds had passed. A downside of clashes between figures of such strength was that they tended to bend the rules of time and space somewhat.

He was slowly being worn down. He needed to try something different.

The sky above the cottage crackled with pulsing electricity. Eliud's purple eyes were suddenly ablaze with the power of storms. With a flick of his wrist, he activated several Skills in quick succession, commanding the heavens to open, summoning dark clouds that swirled menacingly above. Thunderous roars echoed across the countryside as lightning bolts danced and arced through the sky. Eliud channelled the raw energy, transforming it into a ball that crackled and fizzed in between his hands.

Borelean, having long since left its human aspect behind, coiled and writhed, scales shimmering with an iridescent sheen. Its massive body — it had chosen the form of a giant serpent, rather than the crocodile that Eliud had fought before — undulated with a sinister grace, its eyes glinting with an otherworldly intelligence.

"Getting tired, little human? Perhaps it would be best if I brought things to a conclusion?" The serpent hissed, venomous fumes escaping its gaping maw as it summoned its own brand of elemental power. The air grew heavy with anticipation as swirling vortexes formed around Borelean, drawing in dark clouds and gathering wind gusts.

Eliud's gaze narrowed as he sensed the serpent's impending assault.

"That old spell? You've tried that countless times before. What's the problem? Running out of tricks? We can take a break if you need to fix your makeup or anything like that?" With that, he thrust his hands forward, and with a mighty surge of power, he created a barrier of lightning, fending off the onslaught of wind and debris. The clash of forces was deafening, the world around the small cottage a tempest of raging elements.

"Always hiding behind the pretty lights. Did you not learn that was not enough before?" Borelean unleashed a tempest of its own, whipping up a cyclone that threatened to engulf everything in its path. The garden around the cottage was torn to pieces, ancient trees being ripped out of the earth by the summoned wind.

Suddenly, the serpent's fangs glinted with a malevolent

gleam as it launched itself toward Eliud, jaws wide open. Lightning swirled around Eliud as he leapt, and narrowly evaded the serpent's deadly strike.

As he soared through the air, Eliud raised his hands toward the swirling vortexes surrounding Borelean. Determination filled his eyes as he tapped into the full extent of his power. Thunder boomed, and lightning cascaded from the heavens, converging into a concentrated blast of pure electrical fury.

With a tremendous surge, Eliud directed the electrifying beam toward Borelean. The serpent recoiled, its massive form writhing in agony as lightning coursed through its body. The clash reached a crescendo, shaking the very foundations of the earth.

But despite all that, there was no victory here, Eliud knew.

On his own, he did not have enough raw power to destroy such a primordial being as Borelean. At least, not while ensuring he kept enough attention directed toward him to protect Genoes within the cottage.

However, he could be annoying enough that the serpent would decide to leave for less frustrating prey. Arcane energy gathered around him as he thought. Basically, he needed to find a way of irritating Borelean enough that it decided to flounce off. And if there was one thing he was good at, it was being annoying.

Eliud added an extra notch into beam striking the monster. "Ouch. That looks like it tickles."

With a hiss of rage, Borelean pulled on its deepest power reserves, unleashing a deluge of rain that cascaded from the sky. Sheets of water crashed down, obscuring vision and dousing Eliud's lightning magic. The ground around the cottage became a chaotic maelstrom, a clash of thunderous roars, foaming waves, and hum of power.

"Stupid child. Do you honestly think anyone cares if you make this stand? There's no one looking on approvingly at your oh-so-heroic actions. You waste yourself in this squalid part of the universe, and no one cares. Do you imagine your King weeps every night at not having you by his side? He has not thought of you in months. So, despite all your power, Pendragon, you face me alone again. I let you run last time, but not again. Give me what I seek, and I will leave you be."

"I mean, that's a tempting offer. What with no one caring about me and all, I guess I should just up and leave. After all, if there's one thing everyone says about Borelean, it is that you are a being that absolutely keeps its word. I can foresee no issue in giving you what you want. In no way does that outcome have a downside for me."

Eliud spooled through his reserves and channelled his magic, merging with the storm itself. His body sang with energy as he soared above the sea of rain Borelean had summoned.

From that height, he summoned lightning from the depths of the tempest, the bolts arcing and twisting around him in a display of sheer power. "Your army lies in pieces — and I mean that quite literally — around you. Your shrieking cries have been heard by anyone who might wish to take their chance to supplant you. And we both know that there's always a bigger snake out there. So, think about what you will do when one of them comes sniffing around. Don't you want to keep something in reserve to show them who is boss? Why don't we call it quits and give you a chance to take a breath?"

Borelean's only response was to retaliate with a deafening roar that shook the sky, sending shockwaves rippling through the ground and shattering the cottage's windows.

Undeterred, Eliud focused his energies on repairing the broken glass and conjuring a gigantic thundercloud. Bolts of electricity danced through the air, repeatedly striking Borelean's massive form. The serpent writhed in agony as the lightning coursed through its body, its scales hissing and smoking from the onslaught. But Borelean's resilience was unfathomable, and it continued its relentless advance.

"Okay, let's try Plan B, then". Eliud invoked ancient words of binding. With his voice carrying the weight of ages, he sought to ensnare the serpent in magical chains. The incantation reverberated in the air, and ethereal shackles wrapped around Borelean's gargantuan frame.

For a moment, victory seemed within Eliud's grasp. But Borelean, driven by primal fury, shattered the magical bindings with a single, mighty thrash of its body.

"Duskstrider, I grow tired of your insolence. You cannot bind that which is unbindable. You cannot hurt that which embodies pain itself. You are nothing in comparison to my might." The serpent lunged at the Mage with jaws gaping wide, teeth glistening in the sunlight.

Eliud's heart raced as he foresaw the downsides of being swallowed by this being.

Summoning all his remaining strength, Eliud cast a defensive shield, a shimmering barrier surrounding him with an impenetrable force. Borelean's immense jaws clamped down on the barrier; its fury was evident in the wicked glint in its eyes. The shield quivered under the serpent's assault, threatening to crumble.

And yet it held.

Aeons — or milliseconds — passed as the serpent sought to crush the barrier and Eliud poured more energy into its defence.

The eyes of the two met. Cold, reptilian stillness against resolute, purposeful humanity. If Borelean hoped the assault was wearing down its opponent, then the human winking at him dispelled that.

"Are we hugging? Is that what's going in? I should tell you, Borelean, I've never been with an ascended reptile before. Be gentle."

Suddenly the serpent returned to its vaguely human form. "So be it, little human. Keep your secret trinket of power. Just know that if I wished to take it from you this day, I would."

Eliud did not lower his defences. "Now, don't get in a sulk about it. I'm happy to keep exploring the issue if you're up for it?"

"Another time, little one."

And with that, Borelean vanished.

When he was quite sure it was not planning to return, Eliud sagged to the floor, his battered body sprawling across the cold, unforgiving mud. The air around him was heavy with the stench of blood and death. Borelean had not bothered to take the remains of its army with it. Well, at least it would be good for the flowers.

The battle had taken its toll on the exhausted Mage. While his magic remained undepleted — score one for an unlimited mana pool — every fibre of his being screamed in agony, each movement a symphony of pain.

With great effort, Eliud pushed himself into a sitting position, his body protesting with every agonizing inch. His robes were tattered and stained, and dark circles clung to his sunken eyes. It had been a long time since he had needed to push himself so hard. Since the last time he had fought Borelean, to be honest.

His trembling legs threatened to give way beneath him as he struggled to stand. For a moment, he felt the weight of Borelean's words settle on his shoulders, the burden of lives lost and shattered dreams, but he refused to succumb to despair. That was how the serpent had nearly defeated him before, after all.

Things were different now.

He forced himself upright with great determination, his legs unsteady yet resolute.

Eliud stumbled to lean against the remnants of a crumbling stone wall — he'd raised this himself with his own hands: no magic in its construction. He'd been so proud that day. And now look at it. It provided a meagre respite from the harsh reality that surrounded him. Collapsing against the dilapidated structure, he heaved a weary sigh, his body sinking again into the damp, moss-covered ground.

Time seemed to lose meaning as he closed his eyes, seeking solace in the darkness behind his lids. Images of his battles with Borelean, an endless loop of violence and destruction, replayed in his mind. Faces of friends and enemies blended, their expressions etched with anguish and despair. The weight of their lives, hopes, and dreams pressed heavily upon his conscience. Had he failed them by letting that monster escape again?

That was his arrogance speaking again. As if he had much choice.

He pulled all his energies into healing his wounds and found immediate relief from his myriad of injuries. The magic within him stirred, flickering like a dying ember but refusing to be extinguished. It surged within his body, knitting torn flesh and easing the ache of shattered bones. The pain subsided, replaced by a numbing calm that spread through his weary limbs. Sure, he might have an unlimited mana pool, but he could focus on only so many things at once. In his battles with Borelean — both scoring draws, he felt — that focus had been pushed to the limit. He would need to raise his game for the best of three decider.

With renewed determination, Eliud pushed himself upright once more. His steps were steady as he walked toward his cottage door, the garden returning itself to its idyllic state behind him. Within a few seconds, it was as if the devastation wrought by the battle with Borelean had never occurred.

CHAPTER FORTY-FOUR

"Morning Comes"

"Mind if I join you?

The flickering flames of a campfire danced in Daine's eyes, casting eerie shadows upon the face of the man approaching her. Taelsin's Secretary, Donal Assay. He had his arms in front of him, hands wide open, as if anxious to make clear he posed no threat.

Despite the uneasy detente that had fallen over the crowds outside the village, the air was heavy with the weight of the evening's events: the echoes of clashing swords and the scent of blood still lingered. Although no one had removed the riders' bodies that lay around her on the Road, there were no flies to be seen or heard. Daine recognised how intimidating she looked, but she had rarely found insects paid heed to that sort of thing. She assumed someone was keeping them at bay.

If she had to guess, she suspected the man approaching

of doing her that courtesy. She wondered why he was bothering.

"Master Secretary, good evening. I would not begrudge your company. If you have nowhere better to be, of course?"

He approached her hesitantly. Although a tall man, her height and bulk in her armour dwarfed him to a ridiculous degree. They stood awkwardly next to each other for some time: Daine staring at the silent camping Lords, Donal looking out into the dark.

Eventually, Donal broke the silence. "It occurred to me when we last spoke that you appeared to have things on your mind. I thought you might appreciate someone to talk with."

She did not reply.

Donal continued, taking the continued connection of his head to his body as tacit approval for his approach.

"I have lived a long time, my Lady. Don't let my handsome, youthful façade fool you. I have more years on my back than anyone else in the West. Maybe anyone in the Kingdom." He knew the eyeless helmet had turned his way, and those gauntlets had tightened on the longsword. He pressed onwards. "Nothing sinister, I assure you. I simply have a particular mix of talents that prolong life as long as I serve, wholly and completely, another."

"Your Class?" Daine's voice was clipped with tension.

"A unique one. In many ways, not dissimilar to one with which you may be familiar: Mentor. I knew your famous Stonehand in his youth. I doubt we would have called each other friends, but neither did we have cause for enmity."

"You did not answer my question."

"No, I did not. But, my Lady, if you grip the hilt of that

sword much tighter, it will snap. I tell you freely that I mean you no harm and let us be clear, even if I did, I doubt you have much to fear from me."

"Are you keeping the flies away?"

He frowned at the non sequitur. "If I say 'yes,' does that earn me a few more minutes of conversation before I flee for my life?"

She did not reply.

"As I was saying, and pardon me for a philosophical diversion here, during my long life, I have long pondered the concept of rulership. Is not our current system of government a delusion crafted to maintain the status quo, to justify the rule of the chosen few while suppressing the voice of the masses? But then, the right of the King to command has been a cornerstone of our society for centuries. Trust me, I can tell you that from personal experience. Indeed, that the ruler's authority is derived from the Goddess, granting them the legitimacy to govern is clearly central to your own role and purpose. The Goddess supports the Crown, and therefore you enact the wishes of the King. However, I must tell you that the interpretation and application of this view are, to my eyes, flawed."

Hidden within her helmet, Daine's eyes narrowed, searching for sincerity in Donal Assay's words. What he spoke flew close to her own thinking on the matter. "Flawed? How?"

"Who decides that the King possesses this divine right? Is it not merely a convenient tool used by those in power to maintain their grip on it? That the Goddess supports the King, and thus so do the Knights of the Road, has seemingly become a settled fact in this realm. The divine right of the King can be abused and manipulated to justify tyranny. And yet we must remember that the belief itself is not inherently flawed. It is how it is wielded that determines its righteousness or corruption."

"The King is a good man."

"The King, my Lady Darkhelm, is a weak man."

Her sword raised, its point held inches from Donal's heart. "Take care with your words, Master Whatever-You-Are."

"You could run me through, separate my limbs from my body, burn my corpse and spread my ashes to the corner of the world, and it would not change the fact that a weak man governs the realm. I don't doubt he has a good heart, but he is weakness personified."

Donal began counting on his fingers. "One. He sees his role as balancing the factions at Court. It is not. He should decorate the palace with heads on pikes. Again, trust me when I note that this approach is unfailingly successful in ending dissent. His failure to act to quell such squabbling simply emboldens it. Two. He sacrificed the support of the Duskstrider to try to maintain that balance. You do not expel your most powerful ally in an effort to keep other people happy. He is supposed to be our King, not a nursery schoolteacher. Three —"

"Sir, I would ask you to cease. You press too far." Her sword touched his breastbone.

"Why do you so fear my words, my Lady? We both know I say nothing that is not in your own mind. The very fact we" — he gestured to encompass the crowd on the Road — "are still alive demonstrates that. We are a group of people in open revolt against the Crown. Your duty was to slay us when we came within a sword's length. And yet here we stand."

"I am reconsidering my forbearance in the matter."

"No. No, you are not. I know a little of the Knights of the Road. I've had — entanglements — with a few of your forebears. The Goddess does not support our slaughter, does she?"

Daine slowly lowered her sword.

Donal took his reprieve from instant death to press onwards. "Secession is a complex matter, my Lady. It is a drastic measure, born out of desperation when the bond between ruler and subjects is severed. It should not be taken lightly, as it carries the weight of upheaval and potential chaos. But what if the ruler has failed their subjects, burdening them with suffering and hardship? What if their actions betray the very essence of their divine mandate? May that be why the Goddess asks you to stay your hand?"

Donal Assay's eyes softened, and he spoke with a touch of melancholy. "In such dire circumstances, Lady Darkhelm, the question of secession becomes a moral one. If a ruler's actions lead to the deterioration of the realm and the people's suffering, one may argue that they have forfeited their divine right. Yet, even then, the decision to secede must be made with caution, for the repercussions can be far-reaching. Caution is essential, but so is justice. When a ruler's grip becomes a chokehold, when they hoard power for their own survival in a courtly battle for dominance, the people have a right to reclaim their destiny, even if it means severing the ties that bind them to a tarnished throne. It is a path fraught with uncertainty and upheaval. But history has taught us that power can corrupt even the most noble of souls. If secession is the only way to restore justice and prosperity to the realm, then perhaps it is a path worth treading."

"You will say such tomorrow? At the Council?"

Donal smiled broadly. "They're not my words, my Lady. I've been listening to Taelsin make that argument for so long that I can quote him verbatim. I can even do an impression of the strange hand gestures he makes when he gets really into it."

A flicker of sorrow passed across Daine's face, imperceptible beneath the visor of her helmet. "There are evil people who want the chaos secession will bring. I cannot overlook that. They are like weeds in a garden, sir. They may be cut down, but their roots remain. The darkness within them festers, and soon they sprout anew, causing even greater harm."

"I am sure there are, my Lady. But Taelsin is not one of them. He believes the West must free itself and will spend his lifeblood to make that happen. To be clear, I could not care either way. Kingdoms rise and fall, and I have witnessed every version of this dance that can possibly be conceived. But he is a good man. I serve him with all my heart."

Lady Daine's grip tightened around the hilt of her sword once more, her voice filled with an undercurrent of sadness. "I wish it were that simple, sir. But this world we inhabit is not one of black and white, good and evil. It is a tapestry of greys, where even the noblest intentions can be twisted by the darkness that lurks within us all."

"And that is where we must differ, my Lady. I believe in good. Goddess knows I've seen enough and served enough evil in my time to tell the difference. He may be a pleasant enough man, but the King is weak, which is terrible for the realm. Taelsin would salvage something out of this, and I would support him in that endeavour. I flatter myself that my efforts in this matter will be of consequence."

"And if I stand against you?"

Donal shrugged. "We will die. Hundreds of us. Some of us will deserve it, and the world will be better for that. But others who had a positive role in the future will die, and I do not think you wish to be the cause of that. For a generation, the issue will not appear again. But during that time, things will continue to fall apart. There's something rotten at the heart of this realm. I know it. You know it. I believe the Goddess knows it. The West wants to be free. There is no tapestry of grey in that."

"Thank you for your conversation, sir. I wish you good night."

Donal nodded and started to step away. Turning his back on this nightmare figure of metal was an act of considerable courage. He had barely taken two steps when she called him back. "Sir?"

He turned, half expecting a sword thrust to the belly for his trouble. "My Lady?"

"Thank you for keeping the flies away."

"It is my pleasure."

She watched him walk back down the Road toward the pavilion, where the flag of House Elm flew in the soft breeze. She was running out of time to decide. The first streams of light from the East were reaching outwards.

The morning was coming.

CHAPTER FORTY-FIVE

"Just Following Orders"

"If we can't kill her, at least we can take out that turncoat Archer."

Nurkon supposed there was a certain cold logic to Lady Trivian's orders. If you could not strike to the heart of the matter, you took the wins where you can find them. That is, if you ignored such little things as "proportionate responses" or "appropriate use of resources in a crisis" or even "not making the situation a hundred times worse by prodding an angry bear."

However, they were where they were, and the order had been given, and if there was one thing you could say about Nurkon, it was that he followed orders. It was never personal. Always just following the orders.

That was how he found himself, just as the sun was coming up — and was not that a perfect time to try to attempt a murder — in a shadowed alley adjacent to the

Acas' inn where, if the rumour was to be believed, the Lady Darkhelm had left a companion.

To avoid risking Nessa's wrath, he would rather have tried to take the target anywhere else in the village. It did not do to get on the wrong side of that ferocious woman. But the girl had not left her room since the Knight had headed out to stand vigil on the Road, and he could not wait much longer. So given a choice between displeasing Lady Trivian or Nessa Acas, the former just edged it.

He looked at his two companions, their eyes fixed on the window of their target's room. They were both friends of Drunnoc, far too inexperienced for this sort of work. They knew only the joy of bullying, of being the loudest voice in the room, of having all eyes regard them fearfully. They were here because they knew Kirstin and wanted revenge for her "betrayal," as they saw it, of their master. But, just by wanting to do such a thing, they showed they had the wrong temperament for this.

Nurkon, a mountain of muscle and scars, sighed. His heavy hand clenched a wickedly serrated dagger, its edge glinting in the pale moonlight. He knew people looked at him and thought he was some sort of unstoppable monster. That was why Lady Trivian had picked him for this little misadventure, after all. No one really thought about whether anyone who was any good at this sort of thing would get injured quite so often. He was a useful tool; he had no illusions about that. But, as with any such tool, overuse tended to blunt the edge. He knew the day would soon arrive when a younger version of him would be Trivian's favourite, and where that left Nurkon was anyone's guess.

Beside him, Kesso, as he thought the lad was called, moved restlessly. He certainly looked the part, a lithe and shadowy figure, blending seamlessly with the murk. His eyes, like shards of ice, flickered with an unsettling intensity. Nurkon knew what was going through the boy's mind at the moment: he saw himself as the viper, swift and venomous, striking without mercy. A slender stiletto rested in his hand, a lethal whisper awaiting its target.

In reality, he was just a skinny lad with a too-thin dagger. Nurkon doubted such a flimsy thing would punch through a decent leather jerkin, let alone anything more substantial. Looking at the lack of muscle in the boy's arms, he figured he might even drop the blade out of exhaustion on his first stab. If it were not for the predatory leer on his face every time he spoke of Kirstin, Nurkon would have felt sorry for him being mixed up in this. As it was, he was determined to kill the Archer before the boy could "play with her," as he insisted on calling it.

Completing the trio was Sereth, and the less said about her, the better, Nurkon thought. He knew precisely why Trivian wanted this young woman out on this with him, and it had nothing to do with any ability with a sword. The rumour that Sereth had been warming Fion's bed of late had reached even his ears, and he had not needed Trivian's hastily scribbled note to have realised only two of them were to make it back this night. But, looking at Sereth's sweating face, he was sure she had few illusions as to what was coming.

So that was his team to murder an Archer whose only crime, as far as he could see it, was being a vulnerable proxy for Daine Darkhelm. Sure, he had done worse things in his time, but this would hardly be a memory he cherished.

The door to the inn before them stood as a gateway to darkness, a threshold that, he knew would unleash chaos and bloodshed once crossed. All the plans in the world mattered little once they went through that door. So, they waited, poised and patient, for the signal to unleash their mistress's wrath upon the unsuspecting occupant within.

It was time.

Nurkon's hand tightened around his dagger, his knuckles turning white. His gaze flickered to Kesso and Sereth, a silent command passing between them. They nodded, their eyes flashing with a shared understanding of what was occurring. The moment had come.

As one, they rose from their crouched positions, bodies tense with anticipation. Nurkon put a hand on Kesso's shoulder and pulled him back, stepping forward past him, his massive hand gripping the door handle. Damn the boy and his eagerness.

Nurkon's eyes narrowed, scanning the surroundings for any sign of danger. The girl was an Archer, after all. No knowing what sort of danger sense she may have. Finding no instant death awaiting them, he slowly turned the handle, the door swinging open with a soft creak.

The passage within revealed itself, bathed in a dim glow from the flickering candles. Nurkon could see the stairs leading the way to the girl's room. The three stepped forward; their movements were as silent as a sigh, their blades alive in the faint light.

But then, a stray cat darted across their path, tripping Nurkon and sending him sprawling onto the wooden floor with a resounding crash. The cat screeched and fled up the stairs, leaving behind a trail of chaos and overturned vases.

Kesso stifled a laugh, his eyes sparkling with amusement. Sereth, unable to contain herself, burst into giggles, clutching her sides as tears streamed down her face. Nurkon, his pride wounded — but it would not be the first time that had happened — grumbled about his bruised ego, struggling to regain his footing. He was supposed to be the one who knew what he was doing here — damned cat.

But amidst the laughter and confusion, the Assassins found a spark of grim determination. They surged forward toward the stairs, Kesso once more taking the lead, his blade dancing with deadly intent.

*

Kirstin readied herself, crossbow levelled at the door.

She had seen the trio set themselves up in the alley a few bells earlier and was quietly impressed by their patience. Nurkon's influence, she supposed. She did not dislike that huge man for all the foul deeds he undertook for House Trellec. His oft-muttered phrase 'nothing personal, just following "orders"' could be applied in every situation — be it throat-slitting or taking an extra serving at supper. He was not a good man, Kirstin had no illusions about that, but he was not terrible either.

The other two? Well, the less said about them, the better. Both of them things of Drunnoc's, and they were two who would have taken great delight in their mission this evening. Kesso, in particular, was one of the ones who had enjoyed tormenting Jak and was far too free with his wandering hands. Sereth saw herself as the next Lady Trellec, and that was all that needed to be said about her. Kirstin hoped it was she that came through the door first.

Kirstin placed a hand on the kitten pummelling her leg, stilling her and eliciting a low purr. She had rehearsed her moves here a hundred times. The door would crash open, and either all three would charge in, seeking to overwhelm any defence, or no one would, and they would hope to tease out her first shot. She had a plan for either assault but would much prefer the first. As well as the loaded crossbow she held toward the door, she had two smaller ones ready on the bed. Neither much use in the open, but in a cramped room such as this, they would be deadly.

Three assassins, three shots. Things would become more complicated if she needed any more than that. But she liked those odds.

A feline squall of displeasure from below signalled that the attack had begun. A quick glance at the alley showed that all three had moved into the inn. Kirstin was pleased with that; she had worried one would scale the wall and seek to come in through the window. But all was happening as she had anticipated.

The door broke as it was kicked in, and Kesso stood perfectly lit in the hallway. She wasted no time putting a bolt in the centre of his forehead. His look of surprise was comical as his body crumpled to block the door. Sereth followed and tripped over the unexpected barrier, which saved her from the shot from Kirstin's second crossbow, the quarrel missing high and sailing past the door.

Cursing, the Archer hurried forward to strike the girl's head with the crossbow's stock, shattering it and — at the very least — rendering her unconscious. However, it was the work of moments for her to have the third crossbow pointed at the open door.

But no third figure appeared.

A few seconds passed. "You still there, Nurkon?"

Silence.

Kirstin winced. Of all the ways this could have worked out, Nurkon being the one left healthy was not her favoured option.

Silence.

She was just considering a charge into the hallway when she was surprised by a smash of glass, and a vast figure crashed through the window, knocking Kirstin off her feet. The shock unleashed her final bolt, which flew harmlessly into the ceiling. They rolled over a few times before settling with Nurkon on top of Kirstin.

He pulled both her arms up roughly before pinning them to the floor with one hand, the other drawing his knife.

"Nothing personal, miss. Just following orders."

Kirstin closed her eyes as the blade descended. But no pain followed. Then, as quickly as his weight had fallen upon her, it was gone.

Kirstin scrambled upwards and looked around the room. The bodies of Kesso and Sereth still lay on the floor, but there was no sign of Nurkon, apart from his knife, which lay next to a very smug kitten.

"Meow," said Savage. And followed that up with an adorable burp.

CHAPTER FORTY-SIX

"A God with Mummy Issues"

Drunnoc had been in this field before. He was sure of it.

It stretched out before him, an idyllic landscape bathed in a pearlescent glow. The grass rustled gently under his foot as he pressed it downwards. The air carried a faint hint of wildflowers, their sweet fragrance mingling with the soft breeze that whispered through the leaves. Drunnoc imagined that for other this was a place of enchantment, where the boundaries between the mundane and the extraordinary blurred.

He was dreaming, he knew he was. And he had been in this dream before.

Birdsong filled the air, a chorus of melodies that danced on the wind. Colourful butterflies flitted from bloom to bloom, their delicate wings painting the air with splashes of vibrant hues. The sunlight filtered through the canopy overhead, casting dappled patterns on the ground below. It was as if the atmosphere were alive with magic, weaving a tapestry of wonder.

A butterfly landed on his bare arm, its wings fluttering as it settled. He watched it for a few moments, smiled, and then crushed it flat with a slap.

He set out toward what he instinctively knew was their meeting spot. As he walked deeper into the field, the air seemed to hum with otherworldly energy. The soft murmur of a nearby brook reached his ears, its pure waters meandering through the green expanse. The brook's gentle babble irritated his senses, its sparkling surface reflecting the sky above in a too-invasive manner.

As he ventured further, a subtle shift began to take place. The vibrant blooms turned pale, their petals losing their lustre. The birdsong morphed into discordant notes, a dissonant melody that sent shivers down their spines. The air grew heavy,

In the manner of dreams, time sped past in seconds before he stumbled upon a grove of ancient trees, their gnarled branches reaching out like skeletal arms. The oaks stood twisted and distorted. As Drunnoc looked, he could see grotesque faces in the bark lament his passing. The wind sighed mournfully through their leafless branches, a baleful dirge that echoed through the field. Shadows danced upon the ground. Their sinister movements mocking the fading light.

The soft grass had turned brittle and sharp, its blades now like razor-edged knives. The air grew stagnant, suffocating, as if a dark presence lurked beyond sight. Whispers, barely audible, teased at his ears, filled with fragmented promises and dark secrets.

Drunnoc took a moment to get his bearings. He was nearly there.

In the heart of the shadow version of this field, a circle of stones stood, ancient and weathered. Each stone bore markings, arcane symbols etched into their rough surfaces. The rocks radiated an oppressive aura, their presence a constant tug on his soul. The translucent barrier between dream and reality now felt impenetrable, trapping him in this realm.

That caused the boy little concern. He knew why he was here.

A hazy mist descended, enveloping the field in a shroud of darkness. Shadows elongated, taking on grotesque forms that writhed and twisted in the gloom. Unseen hands brushed against his skin, cold and clammy as if spectral fingers caressed his flesh. The whispers grew louder, a cacophony of tortured voices.

The wildlife became twisted abominations, their forms distorted and grotesque. Flowers withered into twisted thorns, their thistles dripping with venomous sap. The butterflies transformed into grotesque moths, their wings tattered and malformed, fluttering in erratic patterns.

He was nearly at his destination.

The field now revealed its true nature. The ground beneath his feet shifted, morphing into a labyrinth of treacherous pitfalls. The mist thickened, obscuring his vision. Desperate cries filled the air, mingling with the chorus of torment that echoed through the haunted trees.

"You found your way easily enough." The voice came from behind Drunnoc.

He did not turn; he had learned that the Dark God preferred not to be regarded directly. While he enjoyed undercutting the expectations of his friends and family, he had long known immortals had little patience for such games.

"It's hardly a journey to be forgotten."

He heard the rustling of the Dark God's cloak as if He were turning to look about. "She did not try to engage with you this time? I cannot find evidence of her presence, which is unusual."

Drunnoc thought back to the beautiful woman who had spoken to him the last time he was here. He recalled she had wanted something from him, but he had not wanted to give it to her. Then she had been driven off by the hidden figure behind him. No. She was not driven off. She had withdrawn rather than force a confrontation. Now that he thought on it, that was an important distinction.

"I came straight here. I didn't see her this time. I think" — Drunnoc could not say why he knew this, but he knew it for a certainty — "I think that was my chance to go with her. When I refused, she moved her attention elsewhere."

The Dark God snorted. "Never was a truer word uttered about my mother. 'Moved her attention elsewhere' once you disappointed her. 'Twas ever thus. Judgemental cow."

Not for the first time during his connection with this deity, Drunnoc felt moved to a pang of concern at what his friends would have called his god's "mummy issues." He really did feel the divine should be above such things. What hope was there for the rest of them if such thoughts plagued a god?

"Most of the pieces are now in place. You understand

the significance of the realignment of the window in the Church of Dawn?"

Drunnoc winced at the memory of Brother Evelyn's alcohol-fuelled ramblings about the breaking of the glass window.

"Not really. Does it matter?"

He felt the Dark God's cold regard prickle the back of his neck. "Be mindful of your tone, Lordling Trellec. There was a time I thought you were the one I was promised, but that is not the truth. You have had your uses, to be sure, but you are here because I have no better option. You are disposable. Your continued existence is at my whim. Do not allow the gifts I have granted you to close your eyes to your almost total irrelevance."

"I apologise, my Lord."

During the long silence that followed, Drunnoc likewise reflected that a god with exceptionally thin skin was also not an ideal focus for worship.

"The Church window unveils the powers at play in the world at a moment of crisis. As planned, many great beings are converging here, and there will be . . . conflict. I have done what I can to weigh the scales to your benefit, but the next moves will be yours. But the choices of the Unclassed will be key."

Drunnoc did not think the Dark God was speaking to him any longer.

"Borelean has overreached in seeking to kill the Duskstrider — that was always its flaw. But something drove it to act precipitously. I wonder what that was. It has slithered back to the King now, in any event. We must hope it has left Eliud in too bad a state to interfere with our plans."

The voice of the god was changing now as He spoke. Sometimes it was that of a young boy, at others, a peevish teenager, then a bitter old man. It was disconcerting.

"You failed and failed again to dispatch the Darkhelm. I should have expected no less. She was always Her favourite. It is no matter. This will not be a war won by raw strength alone. But you will need to be mindful of her in the coming days. Make use of the tools I have put at your disposal to negate her influence."

Drunnoc's thoughts flashed to Pernille, and a smile tugged at the corner of his mouth. He wondered how she would feel to have been described as a "tool."

"More of your followers have fallen this evening. They are insufficient for what will come if they cannot handle a solitary Archer. I have dispersed some gifts among those I find acceptable of notice. Spend their blood wisely. I do not wish them wasted."

Drunnoc could not say how, but it was as if he could feel the change in some of those he called friends. Skills multiplying. Bone density changing, mana pools darkening, wills turning to ice. He shrugged; they were never that close anyway.

"My final words to you, boy, and then I send you on your way. The Unclassed is out there. Somewhere. There is no victory for us while he remain unclaimed. But She does not have him yet either. You must ensure he dies if he cannot be won to our side. The Unclassed is everything. Do you understand?"

Drunnoc nodded his affirmation, and he felt the presence of the Dark God fade from this realm.

Almost instantly, the world began to heal. It was slow and arduous but determined.

Nature, resilient in essence, began reclaiming what had been lost. Tender shoots pushed through the cracked earth, breathing life into the desolate landscapes. The grass regained its softness and vitality, swaying gently in the breeze. Flowers, like colourful sentinels, bloomed defiantly, their vibrant hues injecting a much-needed touch of beauty into the world.

The air cleared its lungs and breathed anew. The songs of birds replaced the whispers that had plagued the haunted field, their melodies a chorus of rejuvenation. As a respite from the cacophony of despair, the gentle rustling of leaves carried a sense of calm,

The twisted trees straightened their trunks and stretched their branches toward the sky. Their canopy thickened, providing shelter and solace to those who sought protection beneath their boughs.

The stones that had radiated malevolence transformed, their symbols fading into obscurity. In their place, new carvings appeared, symbols of peace and unity.

And as the sun bathed the world in its warm embrace, casting a golden glow upon the rejuvenated land, it whispered of renewal. The healing continued a constant journey toward a brighter tomorrow.

Drunnoc felt like he wanted to vomit. If the Dark God was all teenage angst and unnecessary emotional outpourings of rage, this hopeful paternalism was as disgusting.

"I am sorry you find my love so wearying."

Drunnoc regarded the figure that had appeared before him. By his understanding of such things, she was a beautiful woman. He recognised others found value in that.

"He's already gone if you hoped to speak to him."

A shadow crossed her face. "He is not willing to hear

me. Until he is, any attempt to reconcile drives him to wider and wilder excess."

A rabbit hopped hesitantly around her feet and made its way toward Drunnoc, sniffing the earth with caution.

"What do you want from me?"

If she was shocked by his tone, the Goddess did not show it. "You may not be the Unclassed, but you do not have to serve him in this. You still have the power of choice. That is my gift to you."

Drunnoc looked into her eyes. He thought she was telling him the truth, as far as she understood it. But that was the problem with these gods, they were incapable of viewing the world in any other way than their own.

He looked down at the rabbit by his feet and back up to her. "Your gift to me? I do not want it. Nor do I need it. You are all the same. You think to awe us into submission. I may not agree with Him, but He does not pretend he is doing everything for my good. Your gift? I spit on your gift."

And he stamped down on the rabbit.

He awoke instantly, bathed in sweat, but with a triumphant smile on his face. Because while the Dark God might not know who the Unclassed was, Drunnoc had a very good idea.

CHAPTER FORTY-SEVEN

"Stain in the Mud"

I f the accommodation arrangements for the unexpected overnight stay had been somewhat taxing for those attending the Council of the West, they were nothing compared to the chaos of entering the village.

Of course, the smoothness of the operation had not been helped by the various Nobles needing to walk past a legendary warrior they were quite convinced was going to slaughter them at any moment, but, that detail aside, things were still not going well.

"I assume we are actually heading toward a destination?" Taelsin pressed his fingers to the bridge of his nose. "I mean, it would not be beyond expectation at this stage for us to simply walk through this blasted place and out the other side. Maybe into a midden?"

Taelsin and Donal had found themselves situated toward the back of the group seeking entry to the village.

This was not from any plan or design, but rather because a critical mass of Nobles had already started cramming their way past before members of House Elm recognised what was occurring.

"A huge Speaking Chamber, apparently. It is reported that the Trellecs have an Earth Mage of no little skill. I find that surprising."

"They had to get something right at some stage." Taelsin's eyes settled on the lone figure of Daine standing a short distance back from the mass of people trying to pass her as quickly as possible. "You have no further insight into her intentions?"

"I understand about as much of what motivates that extraordinary woman as she does, I suspect." Donal thought back to his conversation with the Knight a few hours before. "If it helps, she'd feel badly about beheading you."

"Not enough to stop her swinging the sword, though, of course?"

"No. But let us take our wins where we can, my Lord."

"From your mouth to the ears of the gods."

They watched in frustrated silence as the retainers of one minor House pressed too closely to that of another: harsh words, then blows, were exchanged. Initially, the moving column parted around their dispute, like a river redirecting around a rock. Then more people were dragged into the fray, leading to the whole procession to stumble to a halt.

"We are a rabble."

Donal was struck by the bitterness in his master's words. It was a tone he did not think he had heard before. "Sir?"

Taelsin gestured around him. "All this. It is a shambles. We're coming together to argue that those in the West should be free to govern ourselves, and we cannot take a walk in the morning air without it descending into chaos and bloodshed. Part of me thinks the Road Knight should simply put an end to it all. Put us out of our misery."

The two watched as blows led to drawn swords and a full-scale melee broke out. Those still seeking to move past the column sought to make room for the brawlers, but the quality of the Road leading to the village had been poor long before hundreds of pairs of feet had churned it up.

The sudden halt of progress had drawn the attention of Daine, who began slowly walking toward the fighting, drawing her sword, and rolling her shoulders.

Donal judged the distance was too far to get there ahead of her, but he started running nonetheless. Leaving Taelsin behind, he called back. "Be careful about what you wish, sir. It seems the gods are listening this day."

*

Despite all her formidable Strength, there was little to be done for the biting stiffness in her back that wearing all this armour caused. Daine knew there were Knights of the Road who were rarely out of their gear; they liked the impact it had on the villages as they passed through.

The awe. The terror.

Personally, she felt that anyone blessed with the powers of a Goddess, who also needed the extra psychological edge of being constantly encased in enough metal to sink a galley, was probably trying a little too hard. And obviously travelled with a dedicated masseuse.

The hours spent in full plate standing the Road that night had taken somewhat of a toll on Daine's good humour. She was thus already not in the best tempers when she saw some unnecessary pushing between groups of Nobles flare into something more violent.

"What part of 'no fighting' do these people not understand?" she muttered as she made her way toward the fracas.

As she walked, one of the benefits of all the armour became immediately apparent; few people wanted to stand in the way of several hundred pounds of metal moving toward them. For those who did not notice her approach, their fellows unceremoniously yanked them out of her way. Within a few moments, Daine was looking through a narrow alley between the parted crowd, where a small group of combatants was clashing with the ferocity of cornered animals.

It was clear that all sense had been lost. What had merely been a minor disagreement about stepping on someone's cloak had become something dark that only bloodshed could quell. Men-at-Arms, and not a few Nobles who should have known better, swung their weapons recklessly. Blades collided, bones snapped, and the air hummed with the scent of spilt blood. Daine took a moment more to survey the chaos before, with a shake of her head, she intervened.

"Enough of this foolishness!" she called, her voice booming through her helmet and carrying with it the weight of command. "If you keep flailing about in the mud like drunken pigs, I might mistake you for some. And trust me, I've seen pigs fight with more skill."

The combatants paused, their faces twisted in a mixture of surprise and anger. Then they realised who had spoken, and no little fear was injected into their expressions. In their bloodlust, they had seemingly forgotten the power of this lone figure.

"I was very clear," she continued, her voice sounding world-weary even to her own ears. "Until the Council convenes, all of you are under my protection. All of you. So, unless you want to test my displeasure, I suggest you put up your weapons, step back into line and keep walking up the Road."

A slight murmur of dissent rippled through both sides of the fight, a mixture of defiance and uncertainty. The Nobles within the group were well used to having their way through force and intimidation. They knew the cost of backing down — especially in full view of their peers — and none relished any loss of face. But, having said that, neither were any of them keen to push the forbearance of the Lady Darkhelm.

Just when it seemed the tension in the air would bleed away, one of the Men-at-Arms, a wiry man with a twisted grin, stepped forward, his blade dripping with fresh blood. He laughed, a grating sound that echoed through the crowd like a death knell.

"You think you can stop us, woman?" he taunted, his voice laced with arrogance. "You'll be nothing but a stain in the mud when we're through with you."

This would have made for quite the opening declaration of intent, had the speed with which the man's peers stepped away from him not been so impressive. Someone laughed. What had potentially been a bloody flashpoint between rival factions had now become something much more entertaining for the crowd.

In the silence following the man's words, Daine raised

her blade into a guard position and twirled it deftly in her hand.

"'A stain in the mud'? Really? That's what you want your final words to be?"

The wiry man's bravado wavered, his eyes flickering to where his fellows had stood by his side. It was one thing being the voice of a pack; it was quite another being a lone wolf.

Daine watched the man's eyes. He had made a mistake and needed to back out. But if he did, what would become of his position? People would remember this day. He could not turn tail . . . She pinpointed the precise moment he abandoned logic and reason and genuinely thought his best option was to attack.

The wiry man lunged at Daine in a blur of motion, his blade slashing through the air.

With a swift side step, she evaded the attack, her mailed fist crashing into his exposed flank. The crunch of bones made everyone wince as the man crumpled to the ground, clutching his side, his twisted grin replaced by a mask of agony. There was too much pain even to scream out.

Daine cast her eyes across the crowd, not making out anyone willing to meet her gaze. "I sense that might be the end of your entertainment. Now, be off with you."

The Secretary, Donal Assay, arrived and pushed his way forward, clearly out of breath. "Keep moving, you fools," he wheezed, "there's a seat in a Speaking Chamber up ahead with your name on it. There's nothing more to see here."

He looked down at the white-faced figure on the ground still unable to make a sound. "Otil Seetall, I might have guessed. Never could pass up the opportunity to irritate something bigger and better than you." He turned to Daine. "Thank you for leaving him alive, my Lady."

Daine shrugged. "I never like spilling blood before breakfast. He's known to you, then?"

Donal nodded. "Just your common or garden Western troublemaker. House Elm thanks you for your tolerance. We will ensure his master knows this could have gone differently. It is —"

The Secretary paused, a frown appearing on his face. "Not now, for the love of —"

The air around him shimmered, and a man in black appeared, plunging a knife into Donal. The blade darted in and out of the Secretary's chest, bright blood fountaining from the wounds.

The sudden eruption of chaos engulfed the still-pressing crowd, and people fell into the mud in their panic to escape. Gasps and screams rang out, melding with Donal's grunt of pain into a chorus of alarm.

Daine stepped forward, catching Donal as he fell and pulling him behind her, shielding him from further attack. She had no idea if the Secretary was still alive, but that could wait. She stood tall, her eyes aflame with determination, as the Assassin, knife flashing, descended upon her.

The attacker was good. Too good for the Trellecs to have kept him in reserve in their efforts to eliminate her. This was . . . something else. Something that Donal, in that last moment, seemed to sense.

The knife slid across her chest plate and bit into the gap under her armpit. Daine winced, then shifted her stance to protect that side. She recognised she was not well-suited to this matchup, slower than she would have liked in her plate armour, making it hard to pin her attacker down. For sure, she was only ever one blow away from victory, with sword or fist, but it was proving devilishly difficult to bring that advantage to bear.

The Assassin continued to move with astonishing fluidity in front of her. His strikes were swift, his blade constantly licking out toward the gaps in her armour. He was, of course, unwilling to clash blades with Daine's much heavier weapon, and she could feel his anxiety spike whenever it looked as if that would happen.

Taking advantage of that nervousness, her swings became thunderous; each blow was enough to fell a tree. Yet the Assassin, ever the predator, fought with equal skill, his every move a testament to his lethal finesse.

Daine's foot slipped momentarily. Donal's blood was pooling under her feet, staining the mud. The man in black darted forward, the blade tip piercing the soft spot between her helmet and chest plate.

It would have been a deadly strike against any other opponent, and she saw the flash of triumph in his eyes. Then that excitement was replaced with horror as he saw her fail to die. She cleaved through his torso with a resounding strike and rendered him in two.

Silence descended upon the field, broken only by the crowd's gasps.

Daine dropped to her knees — Goddess, her back ached — and put a hand on his chest to stem Donal's wounds. Any remaining doubts she had about the man's power disappeared, as she noted most of them were already healing.

"Not sure you truly needed my help there, Master Secretary," she said, helping him to his feet.

His jaw was clenched in pain. When had he been last so

beset? "Maybe not, my Lady. But hear me. Those things don't hunt on their own."

There was a shriek from the crowd, which drew Daine's attention away from those words. The dismembered body of the Assassin had dissolved into black smoke.

"We need to return to Lord Elm. I am afraid, my Lady, that the stakes here have risen again."

CHAPTER FORTY-EIGHT

"Council of the West"

"I suppose my frustration here is severalfold. Firstly, I may have thought the existence of a shadowy collective of assassins particularly concerned with eliminating you might have been mentioned at some time in the last decade? Just as an aside, you understand. I do not think it unfair of me to have assumed that such a thing may have come up over dinner, for example."

Donal opened his mouth to speak but shut it immediately on meeting Taelsin's eyes.

"Secondly, some may think, and I have to be inclined to agree with them here, that it would have been sensible for you to have appraised me of the full extent of your biography — including those significant capabilities you appear to have forgotten to mention — so that I could have factored those into the complex, nay I may term them 'labyrinthine,' planning that has occupied us both for the last few years.

I do not wish to diminish what you have done in support of our endeavour, but I wonder if we have quite made the most of — what did you say? — your thousands of years of experience? Finally, and I do not think I am wholly out of line here, I am feeling somewhat irked at you choosing to unburden yourself of all this quite valuable information right now when I should be LEADING A REBELLION AGAINST THE DAMNED KING!"

In many ways, Daine was pleased that Taelsin finally released the tension she had watched build up in the man over the last hour. She had helped Donal to the pavilion of House Elm, and they had been ushered inside. Donal quickly outlined his fairly remarkable history to which Taelsin had barely seemed to react. There were times for icy self-control and times for flinging tables. It was good that things seemed to have finally moved to stage two . . .

"And do not think just sitting there being all 'no master' and 'sorry my Lord' will help you get away with it! Trust me when I say I will find the most inventive, capricious, and entirely unreasonable punishment for these oversights. My mind, which some have described as the most brilliant in the West, will be dedicated to finding a way for you to make true recompense."

"Are you forgetting I wiped your backside when you were a babe in arms? I doubt there's anything more humiliating you can pile on me. Also, if you're still willing to accept my advice, I would probably dial down the whole 'rebellion against the King' spiel with a Knight of the Road sitting in front of you."

"Do not mind me, Lord Elm. I can put my helm back on if you want to shout at him some more. I can barely hear anything through that."

Taelsin glared at them both and momentarily looked as if he were going to explode into an even wilder expression of rage. Then, as if all the air had left him, he collapsed back into his seat and ran his hands through his hair.

"Take me through it all again, Donal. Let us start with the Order of Iskent and why they're quite so irritated with you."

*

Timing, as they say, is everything.

Should Donal Assay not have been attacked by his age-old adversaries at that moment, should the Lady Darkhelm not have been present to intervene, and should they not both have proceeded directly to the pavilion of House Elm — a pavilion warded with significant protections to prevent sound entering or escaping — then the upcoming course of events would have been very different.

As it was, the booming bell calling all stragglers to the Great Council of the West went unheeded by those three figures who could have been considered to be critical players in the upcoming drama.

*

As the final delegation members took their seats in the vast Speaking Chamber — Boruld had certainly completed a masterwork — all noted the absence of Taelsin and Daine.

That the Lady Darkhelm was not in attendance was a matter of profound relief for nearly everyone, but surprise that House Elm was not present tempered that. While everyone who had made the trek to the village saw themselves as crucial to the endeavour of secession, the majority were self-aware enough to know that the success of their venture rested on that impressive young man's shoulders.

There was indeed no one else that would be able to unite the disparate factions in the West. So the Council getting underway without him was . . . significant. The sound of a thousand schemes humming into life dominated the space.

Then the tolling of the bell ceased.

*

The cessation of the bell was Boruld's cue.

With great reluctance, he released the final spell he had prepared around this Chamber.

For all the challenges of his employment with the Trellecs, he genuinely loved what he had achieved in this latest work. Situated on the very edge of the village, the edifice rose in stark grandeur. Massive slabs of granite, hewn from the quarries by his will alone, were meticulously arranged to form a sanctuary of stone and sorcery.

Just walking through the Chamber's entrance had awed the crowd into silence; the colossal archway adorned with intricate carvings that spoke of forgotten histories had impressed everyone. None had passed by without feeling the weight of the responsibility they were embracing by crossing that threshold.

As the crowds had stepped into the heart of the space, the sounds of the world beyond had faded into oblivion. The walls, adorned with ancient symbols and enigmatic glyphs, whispered of a language long lost to mortal tongues. If asked, Boruld would have had to admit these mainly were meaningless doodles, but he liked the impression they gave of something truly esoteric taking place. Light filtered through narrow slits in the walls, casting ethereal patterns upon the artificially aged stone floor. The Earth Mage had encouraged tendrils of ivy to weave their way through the stonework there, to add a sense of age to a building that had not existed a week before.

A dais of polished obsidian stood in the centre of the Chamber, surrounded on all sides by banks and banks of seating. It appeared as if that platform were carved from the very heart of the earth, its black surface shimmering with a subtle luminescence. Upon the dais, Fion Trellec sat on a solitary throne of veined marble, an artefact of formidable craftsmanship that exuded an air of authority the occupant could not quite carry off on his own.

The sight of Lord Trellec sitting in such a manner was a cause of much discussion by the delegates. There was no desire to replace one monarch with another . . .

However, and this was something of which the Earth Mage was particularly proud, it was not the throne that commanded most of the attention. No, it was a towering pillar of rock, rising from the depths of the Chamber's core, stretching toward the heavens with an imposing presence, that was his real joy. Its rough and weathered surface bore the marks of a thousand secrets etched into its skin. Inscribed upon the pillar were countless runes pulsing with a gentle glow. They flickered and danced as if alive, echoing the wisdom he had embedded within.

It was these runes that Boruld now activated.

Within the confines of the giant Chamber, the Earth Mage communed with the very essence of his craft. He pushed back his concerns about the nature of the instructions the Trellecs had given and coaxed the dormant stone at the base of the entrance to awaken and bend to his will.

It rose and ultimately sealed the Chamber from the outside.

The Council of the West had begun.

*

Kirstin felt, rather than heard, the collision of stone that marked the sealing of the Chamber.

After the attempt on her life, she had reluctantly left the tavern in search of a more defensible position to await Daine's return. Savage rode on her shoulder and, while walking the village, the Archer tried very hard not to think about the implications of having the devourer of Nurkon sitting so close to her ear.

They eventually settled on a rooftop overlooking the crowds pouring into the newly raised Speaking Chamber. She was astonished at what had been achieved in constructing that building. Kirstin had met Boruld several times when living within the Keep and, honestly, had considered him underwhelming. Pleasant enough — which in Keep Trellec was unusual in and of itself — but, to all intents and purposes, rather nondescript. However, just as she was rapidly re-examining her thoughts around the lethality of the tiny kitten currently trying to pounce on a resistant beetle, so too did she think there was probably more to the Earth Mage than met her eye.

That thought gained significant momentum as she watched the entrance to the Speaking Chamber morph, shake and then simply vanish. In its place stood smooth stone, with no hint that anything other than solid rock had ever existed there.

"That is in no way a sinister development," Kirstin mused, pulling the kitten into her lap.

"Get Eliud."

Kirstin was halfway to her feet before her brain caught up with her body. "Savage? Did you just —"

"Meow?" the kitten replied.

Giving the cat a hard look, Kirstin set off toward the Duskstrider's cottage.

*

If the delegates were unhappy that Fion was occupying a throne in the middle of the Speaking Chamber, they were positively apoplectic when they realised they were being sealed in.

Only the appearance of Pernille next to Fion quieted the hundreds of voices raised in outraged anger. Or to be precise, it was the exercising of her burgeoning powers.

Every member of the delegation suddenly felt they had been awake for weeks. An intense lethargy washed over them as the erstwhile Healer syphoned away their life force. Slowly, all the upraised voices fell silent, and the most potent Nobles in the West, and all of their households, sat, panting as if exhausted, in their seats.

"Now, that level of noise seems much more appropriate to such an auspicious gathering," said Fion, his voice magnified so it boomed out across the Chamber. "That will be enough, Pernille." There was an audible intake of breath as all present suddenly found they could properly fill their lungs once more. The Healer glowed with stolen health.

"As you will have noticed, the entry to this Chamber has been sealed and will remain so throughout our deliberations. That is, of course, simply for our protection and for no nefarious reason whatsoever. We have weighty matters to discuss, and I know we will all speak so much the freer for not having to worry about outside interference."

From the glances exchanged between the Lords of the

West, it was not clear that these words of reassurance quite hit the mark.

"My Healer is present to ensure we are all properly cared for during this meeting. She has other . . . talents which will ensure no inappropriate behaviour gets out of hand. I am sure you all know of what I speak."

Flat expressions were his only response.

If the enmity of the entire room caused him a moment's concern, it did not show on Fion" beaming visage. "Now, with no further ado, I declare the Council of the West open. First order of business, the future of the West!"

CHAPTER FORTY-NINE

"Little Boys Throwing Stones"

In a somewhat undignified bundle, Eliud, along with Genoes and Josul, tumbled out of a portal that appeared in the woods on the outskirts of the village.

There was a brief moment while they rearranged themselves into good order before Genoes asked, "I do not want to be rude, sir, but was that supposed to happen? I had heard that portal travel was like walking through an open door. That was . . . not like that."

"Obviously, that slightly bumpier-than-expected ride was exactly as I intended. Nothing in this universe ever occurs without my express permission. You would do well to remember that, my boy." The grandeur of this statement was somewhat undercut by Josul urinating on Eliud's boots.

The Pendragon grimaced and released a jet of cleansing downwards from his index finger. "I will admit, though, it would appear that on this very limited occasion, I may have slightly miscalculated our destination. There seemed to be something in the way of our journey that 'shut the door' to continue your analogy. Either that, or . . ." He closed his eyes and quested outwards and into the village with his mana.

Genoes found and threw a stick for Josul to bound after, the oversized lapdog crushing several bushes under his comically large feet. He had done it three or four times before Eliud suddenly grabbed his arm and pulled him close, Josul taking up a guard position in front of him. "Incoming! Brace yourself."

Eliud thrust his arm upwards as he spoke, activating a series of shield Skills. They created a blast of energy that struck a colossal stone falling from the sky toward them. As his Skills hit the falling rock, they disintegrated it into thousands of tiny pieces, each crashing to the ground in a wide circle around them.

As the crescendo of impact faded away to silence, save Josul barking at a pebble that had dared fall too close, Eliud pursed his lips. "I don't know about either of you, but I'm sensing some fairly hostile vibes here." He looked back up at the sky and sighed. "Persistent fellow, whoever it is. Stay close."

He projected a broad purple shield above them with his cupped left hand and aimed with his right, his finger pointing to the sky. Eliud closed one eye, took careful aim down the length of his arm, and began blasting giant projectiles out of the air.

*

"So, while it may be argued that the Order itself was established with the sole purpose of, and I quote their Charter here, 'removing the Blight of Evil upon the Land,' I must note that quite some centuries have passed since I could truly be considered a 'blight' upon humanity. I was last bothered by one of their number back in the time of Empress Maud III, and that was quite a conclusive interaction. It thus strikes me as noteworthy that they have chosen this moment, a time of significant strife, to seek to re-emerge. Although . . ."

Taelsin glanced up as Donal's voice faded into silence. The Secretary had stood and turned to face toward the East. "Although what?" He looked over at the Knight and saw she was likewise standing and facing the same way. "What's happening? Daine? Donal? What's going on?"

"Power," they both said in unison.

"Power?"

"Someone's throwing around mana like they've heard the price is dropping tomorrow." Donal's knees suddenly gave way, and he pressed his hands to the sides of his head as if unseen hands were crushing his skull. "Whoever it is is pulling energy out of the very air! The power use is insane! Are the gods themselves clashing out there?"

Daine's smile was taut. "Don't let him hear you say that. His ego is big enough as it is."

*

Dranoth Strathen had not been a pleasant young man. His various misdeeds had regularly brought his mother and father to outraged tears. He had felt badly about that, of course, but not enough to actually to seek to do anything different. He had been an entirely creative follower of Drunnoc and Veron over the years, and with the latter picking up an arrow to the forehead, he had been viewed as the next in line.

As with so many young men in the village, the Dark

God had briefly thought little Lordling Strathen was the one he was promised. Indeed, long enough for his presence to have damaged the child's soul. Even then, though, Dranoth did not need to have turned out how he had. That had taken time, money, and a parental indulgence in casual immorality to achieve.

Thus, when the Dark God sought appropriate vessels to support Drunnoc's rise in the coming days, Dranoth was among the first to receive significant physical and metaphysical enhancements. As well as a hugely changed appearance, the list of Skills to which he now had access was astonishing. However, for all the power of the god that now flowed into the young man, it had needed to be harnessed to the personality of the shell around it.

That is how Dranoth Strathen, or what used to be Dranoth Stathen, found itself going toe-to-toe in a long-distance Mage battle with the Duskstrider, Eliud Villa. It was dimly aware of the voice of . . . something telling it to disengage. To not draw attention. To not risk the wrath of the Pendragon. To not open a new front in their war. But it was or had been Dranoth Strathen. And nobody had the right to tell it "no." Not when it had been human and certainly not when it knew it had access to all this delicious power.

Dragging its claws through the stone of Keep Trellec's parapet, it continued pulling down the giant rocks it had discovered in the thin air above the village and rained them downwards. Somewhere in that wood was an ant that had sought to defy it. And it needed squashing.

*

"STOP HIM!"

Drunnoc fell to his knees as his god's voice reverberated

through and around his head. He did not remember ever being affected this way before. Dreams? Visions? For sure. But this sort of sickening physical manifestation was an unwelcome surprise.

He was in the Keep, reviewing reports he had issued about the location of the boy he knew as "horserat." He was surprised to learn that the figure desired by his god was the skinny orphan he had so enjoyed tormenting when there was nothing more pressing to do. Surprised but entirely pleased. He would enjoy having a reason to return to that particular pastime.

Unlike everyone else in the Keep, he had elected not to attend the Council of the West. After all, his father would do what his father would do, and he did not need to be there to hold his hand.

Truthfully, he found his father's childlike need to manipulate secession somewhat embarrassing. Drunnoc had sought to outline the Dark God's broader desires for the world, but all Fion seemed to take from the discussion was that the deity did not oppose secession. He was a cockerel content with ruling the coop. Drunnoc saw himself far more like the dragon soaring in the sky above.

Nevertheless, with Pernille and Halcoth present, he thought the plan would likely proceed precisely as they had discussed. Let the old man have his day. He had even sent most of his newly altered "friends" to the Speaking Chamber, should extra power of persuasion be required.

Thus, when the pulsating head pain literally blew him off his chair, spilling papers around him, there was, thankfully, no one around to see him flounder.

"HE RISKS THE PENDRAGON'S NEUTRALITY. STOP HIM!"

Drunnoc's body did not seem to be his own as it was dragged upwards and started on the stairs toward the top of the Keep. He could feel his panic rising as his feet were unwillingly put one step in front of another. Step after step, his legs pumped upwards. As he was not in control, he felt bones in his toes and feet snap as they hit the stone steps in a rough approximation of running — like a child's puppet poorly controlled. Then he was through the open door where, through tear-filled eyes, he could see Dranoth perched, like a gargoyle, over the edge of the stone.

His erstwhile friend turned to look at him, frowning at his appearance and strange form of movement.

And then there was darkness and sudden awful pain, and then he did not feel much of anything anymore.

*

"I have to say, I'm impressed. It's not everyone that can command meteorites in this way. I mean, I can, obviously, but I'm me, and that's not a standard to which it is fair to hold anyone else. But that flaw aside, we're seeing a lot of heart here. A lot of determination. A lot of what Gant would call 'ignorant balls.' Not smart, but not without merit. I guess what I'm saying is that whoever this is, they're not absolutely terrible at throwing rocks around."

Genoes stared open-mouthed at Eliud, trying to pretend he was not perched on a tiny island of stable ground surrounded by a landscape of utter devastation. Beyond the little protected circle with the boy and the Duskstrider at its heart, the forest floor had dropped tens of feet into bedrock, with what foliage remained around them ablaze in unearthly fire.

"But there comes a time when, as diverting as playing 'shoot the big slow moving rock out of the sky' is, we have other things we will need to do. So, let's . . . Yes. Let's have that one . . . And, ah, found you. Let's play a new game. How about this one, my friend? Catch."

Eliud's eyes flashed purple.

*

Dranoth felt someone appear at the door of the Tower. It was Drunnoc, but he was moving oddly. It turned its head to see what had brought its Master all this way to the top of the Keep. He did not need to expose himself to danger in this way. Dranoth would be finished with whatever had tried to sneak its way into the village in a moment. Nothing could be left alive out there any longer.

Charitably, that distraction could be said to explain how it missed with one of the meteorites it was in the process of directing at that oddly resistant spot of power in the woods, and how the meteorite had slipped from its grip and, instead, began hurtling toward the Keep.

*

Taelsin, Daine and Donal stood just outside the Elm pavilion, staring at distant Keep Trellec. Despite the morning sunshine, the imposing building seemed almost entirely hidden within a shadow.

"My Lord, you remember discussing the strategic necessity of occupying Keep Trellec when we announced that the West seceded from the Kingdom?"

Taelsin glared at Donal's indiscreet words and glanced to see how Daine had reacted to them. Her expression had not changed, to his surprise, as she stared at the Keep. He looked its way again. That was odd. Was the shadow around it somehow getting bigger?

"I remember a theoretical discussion around securing the key strongholds in the West, Donal, yes. It's a powerful presence in this part of the West. We thought it best to keep all such buildings in our hands."

"Change of plan, sir."

And the Keep was obliterated.

CHAPTER FIFTY

"The Art of Persuasion"

The Council was not going especially well.

True, Fion reflected, it was difficult to argue that locking a large group of powerful Nobles within a large room, draining them of their life force to ensure compliance and then threatening to kill them all if they did not do precisely what you wanted was conducive to convivial debate.

Nevertheless, he did not feel anyone was really entering into the spirit of this momentous occasion. He had been speaking for close to a bell to very little response from the floor. He had carefully prepared any number of cunning arguments to gain favour for his side, but it seemed there was no interest in actual discussion.

With a sigh at the missed opportunity to further enhance his reputation for rhetorical flair, he brought the opening speech of the Council of the West to a close. "So,

I ask again, sirs, can we truly suggest the King has our best interests in his heart? He sits removed from us, unaware or uncaring of the plight of the West. He sends his minions to dispense 'justice,' but that is an imposition rather than a support. What do we gain from the relationship? I propose we seek to break with the Throne this very day."

If he expected applause, he was to be disappointed.

Hundreds of pairs of frightened eyes looked up, somewhat blankly, at Fion. Oddly, he did not feel the surge of triumph he would have anticipated from having so much control over those who had, for so long, scorned him and his vision. He remembered reading somewhere that it was better to be feared than loved. Right now, he'd settle for something closer to respect than whatever this was.

"Who would like to speak next? Lord Light, what news of the people of Tunnock? Will they abide the rule of the King further?"

A huge man with a red beard grimaced to hear his name and tottered to his feet. He felt utterly exhausted by whatever spell had been cast upon them. It was more than just physical tiredness, Goddess knew he was used enough to that feeling, but it was like there was a thick heavy fog across his mind. "Lord Trellec, the people of Tunnock are sympathetic to your words. We await hearing the thoughts of others before pledging ourselves to any course of action." He collapsed back into his chair.

"But I would hear your words, Lord Light. Kenryn, is it not. Can I call you Kenryn? We are all friends here, are we not? Fellow Westerners. Brothers in arms."

"Kenryn is fine." He waved a hand in a weak gesture of acceptance.

"Kenryn, for all our informal bonds of friendship, we

should maintain some decorum, at least. Please do stand when addressing the Council."

With an effort, Lord Light rose again. "My apologies, sir. Not feeling myself. There are others more suited to speaking before me. We note the absence of Taelsin Elm, I would hear his thoughts." He went to sit, but Fion raised a finger.

"Taelsin Elm. That is a name I have heard on many a lip over the last few days. The 'Saviour of the West,' I have heard him called. And yet, as you say, he is not here on this day. He is not in the Chamber. I say decisions are made by those that choose to show up. I care nothing for House Elm nor the failing city of Swinford. Let us focus on those of us that have chosen to accept the mantle of leadership. Would you agree, Kenryn?"

The big man swayed on his feet, trying to focus his thoughts. "Taelsin Elm has done right by my people, Lord Trellec. There is no stauncher believer in the rightness of the West ruling itself than he. I would ask —"

"He's not here, you great oaf!" Fion's shriek echoed round the chamber. "The gods-blessed sun shines out of his every orifice. He heals the weak and feeds hand-sliced apple to adorable rodents. He is surely the embodiment of every manly virtue. But the man is not here! He did not turn up. He has not sought to add his undoubted wisdom to this meeting. I will hear no more about him and I will not have my leadership of this Council disrespected in such a way."

Kenryn blinked, suddenly struggling to keep his eyes open. His head lolled on a neck seemingly not strong enough to bear its weight. His eyes met those of the woman standing near Fion. She was smiling at him. He did not feel it was a friendly smile. He felt like a mouse in the paws of a cat. "I meant no disrespect, my Lord."

Fion wiped some spittle from the corner of his mouth. "I do not accept your apology, Lord Light. I feel you represent a significant minority in this room who do not have the West's best interests at heart. It strikes me that there seems to be somewhat of a conspiracy developing to replace one absent, tyrant King with another. Would you use us, Lord Light, to help Taelsin Elm to a throne in the West?"

If anyone noted the irony of a man sitting on a throne on a giant dais castigating others for their unchecked ambition, no one felt in a position to make the point.

Kenryn's exhaustion was beyond his capacity to cope. He sank back into the chair, barely able to stay conscious. Deftly, Pernille kept pulling at the threads of his Stamina, exquisitely aware of just how close the whole tapestry of his life was to unravelling. He fouled himself as she removed yet more of his muscle control.

"You will stand when you address the Council, Lord Light." Kenryn made an incoherent noise in response. "One final time, sir. Stand when I address you, or I will have you and your people removed from this Chamber."

There was no response. There could not be. With a final tug on his life force, Pernille let the man slip into a coma. Trellec Men-At-Arms forced their way through the Chamber and dragged both he and his retainers out into the corridor. No one failed to miss the sudden surcease of their protestations once they were out of sight.

"Mark well my words, my Lords. My commitment to secession is absolute. I will not allow, this close to our moment of triumph, any backsliding on freedom for the West. I will not accept replacing one form of repression for another. Taelsin Elm will not rule my West, not while I have any breath left in me. Now . . ." Fion's whole demeanour changed, and he beamed out across the crowd. "I would like to hear from some others about anything that I said in my opening remarks or, indeed, anything else you feel pertinent to say."

There was a momentary pause while hundreds of powerful Nobles considered their best way to make it back to their towns and Cities alive. There was grudging respect for the audacity of Trellec's gambit here. Each and every one of them had done something similar in their time — perhaps not quite on this scale — but the fundamental principles were the same: gather people together, make an example, ask everyone to make a choice. All that mattered now was to make whatever insane pledge to secession Trellec wanted before releasing them, get back on the Road and then raise every single soldier they could to obliterate the village from existence and salt their fields.

If they played it right, they could even spin it to the King that they themselves had put down the seditious lunatic as a show of loyalty. That might buy them the sorts of concessions they could never hope to negotiate on their own. Yes, it did not take long for the collective minds of the West to see how they could turn this momentary discomfort to the advantage. They just needed to get reach home in one piece.

Lord Jarak, always slightly faster on the uptake than his fellows, and with significantly less shame, was the first to his feet. "My Lord," he said with a bow, "I may say I speak for many of my fellow Westerners when I note how deeply struck we have been by your words. We came here to debate the future of the West. But, having heard you so clearly make the case, I am unsure what possible response there could be in the negative. Your wit, your sagacity, your passion for this project is most clear, and I for one have been touched by it."

He went on in this vein for some time. Fion was dimly aware that he was being flattered outrageously, but he did not care one bit. For too long, he had been overlooked in the West, and while he did not believe a word of what Jarak was saying, it was lovely to hear it.

"And so, in conclusion, I suggest we all return to our people and make ready to announce formally establishing the West as a separate state."

"Oh, I think we can do better than that, Lord Jarak."

"My Lord?"

"Why wait until returning home? I think we should all swear at this very moment, in the presence of all the other Nobles of the West, to follow House Trellec's lead in the seceding from the Kingdom." Fion's beaming smile had taken on a somewhat too bright quality.

There were a few coughs and side glances. "Right now, my Lord?" Jarak tried to take back control of the situation. "Surely, we would be better to do such a thing from our own centres of power? To be able to send a strong message to the King of our intent."

"And what better way to do such a thing than with one voice? 'The Great Council of the West states we will follow House Trellec in removing ourselves from the Kingdom.' Who cannot make that pledge right now?"

Jarak caught several key Nobles nodding his way. They could work with that. In fact, the fool was giving them all the protection they needed to say it was not their idea. The King would be angry, of course, but they could all swear to the pressure they put under. It was Fion who would bear the brunt of that rage.

"My Lord, as a token of the respect we feel for you, I say that House Jarak will be happy to make such a pledge."

House after relieved House stood to acknowledge that they would make a similar pledge. It hardly seemed credible that, having them all at his mercy in this way, the fool would allow them to buy their freedom so cheaply.

Fion nodded happily. "Let us all stand and say the words together, then, in unison. To guarantee our comradeship and support in opposition to the Throne."

With rolling eyes, everyone in the Chamber stood and intoned the words, precisely as Fion had outlined them. When the last of the voices fell silent, Fion gestured to a much older man on the dais.

"Gilles, shall we see if that worked as intended?"

"Certainly, my Lord." The old man looked out over a sea of puzzled faces. "You will all sit."

And as one, every Noble in the West, somewhat to their surprise, sat down.

Fion beamed once more. "Excellent. This will be fun. Now, Gilles, let's see what else we can get them to do."

CHAPTER FIFTY-ONE

"Tears of a God"

She experiences everything — the past, the present and the future — all at once.

Her life is a waterfall of memories, experiences, hopes, and fears all looped together to form a never-ending stream of reality. She can, of course, pause the flowing torrent — stop and revel in any moment that took her fancy — but the current of time will soon sweep her up once again, and she will glide unmoored in its waters.

The entity known in this realm as "the Goddess" is alone in her verdant field. From where she stands, she observes the world through fractured, colourful prisms of light. Aeons roll past and return in seconds as if they are a constantly moving wall of stained glass, and throughout it all, she finds herself enraptured by the deeds of mortals.

She has always been, was, and would be fascinated by these short-lived creatures. So fragile and yet so resilient.

She blinked and saw them as they were now. They huddled in snow-flecked caves — small groups of stoic determination. Stone-tipped spears were their only defence against what awaited in the dark. Their fierceness appeals to her. The very least of all creation, and yet they do not meekly surrender to fate. She smiles and cannot resist providing them with a spark of fire, a mote of light that soon blossoms into the enfilade at Trellec Keep . . . but no.

Those events are millennia apart. And yet so tightly linked.

With the gift of fire, she becomes involved in the development of the civilisation of the cave-dwellers. Her love for them eclipses that for anything else she has crafted. In and over time, she gives them other gifts — immense Strength blooms in those who work upon the land and those that seek to defend others. There is quickness and Speed for those who hunt and seek in the forests. She bestows Wisdom on those who would unravel the world's secrets and take on the challenge of leading others out of the creeping darkness.

She gives and gives and gives a multitude of enhancements. She breaks herself into a myriad of Skill shards — all that she is, was and will be throughout time — to help the ones she favours to grow beyond the limits of what should be their mundane existence.

And they flourish.

Tears wet the corners of her eyes as, just as they thrive, their culture stagnates.

She was foolish in her sentimentality; she sees that now. Whenever "now" may be. These shining humans reach their endpoint too soon. Too quickly do they pass thresholds that should have cemented deep foundations in their struggle to overcome. In her careless love, she has borrowed from their future to fling open doors they should have needed the drive to break down.

As she watches, Woodcutters fell giant oaks with one swing, Fishermen haul whales from the sea with barely a grunt, and Mages — owners of the favourite of her gifts — solve every minor discomfort with scarcely a thought.

Sickness ends. Scarcity is removed. Want and need are now no more. But it is not the utopia for which she had planned. Variation in these people fails. She watches as infinite possible prisms of choices and directions darken and shatter. By custom or by design, stasis and apathy set in. There is no longer any need for innovation; there are no challenges in the world that her favoured people, with generation upon generation breeding in a moment, cannot overcome with minimum thought or effort.

Things fall apart. The centre cannot hold. Without inspiration, the world flattens. If everyone is a powerhouse, no one is.

She turns her face away from them and starts again. Ignoring the counsel of the rest of the pantheon, she designs a family of her own. She seeks to learn from her ongoing, upcoming failure and crafts two children representing the opposite of the dull consistency that plagues her people.

They embody Chaos. They bring Luck.

From the first, she ensures they exist outside her own stable river of time. And then she looses them, not cruelly, but with abiding love and hope for the future of her people. She charges her boys to release the world from the tyranny of her benign rule.

And they bring slaughter.

Their influence is profound. Just as her gift of fire leads to the transformation of the world, so does their injection of unconsidered chance back into time. Soon, now, later, her older boys, these "Lords of Misrule," have worshippers aplenty, and they challenge her as the most important influence upon the realm.

Her stable Classes, the work of which she was so proud, so ashamed, are suddenly evolving. No longer are families locked, generations unending, to their fate. The geniuses amongst her people grasp the significance and potential of chaotic evolution. They take these new sparks and shape them, crafting powers wholly unconnected to her river of time and influence.

And the world burns with energy anew.

In unguarded moments, she laments the cancerous growths she have released. Her people could have stayed forever trapped within the safe prison of her protection. But then she sees the new futures opened up by the interventions of the Lords and is pleased.

There can be no real joy without pain.

If she represents, represented stagnation, her oldest children brought unrestricted development. They broke what she sought to maintain, but they did so without malevolence. Steam does not care for the ice it melts. Their necessary interaction creates something new that neither can control.

But, of course, there remained her youngest child.

He, as should all children, strained against the road she had prepared for him. He chafed, he wandered, he explored. He rejected her and would not simply follow his older brothers on their own journeys of Chaos.

He wanted something of his own. He needed. He wanted. Oh, how he wanted.

Tears fall down the Goddess's face and then roll back up as she moves and shifts throughout time.

The Lords of Misrule spread through the land, breaking and reshaping the chains she had unintentionally laid upon her people. New and beautiful versions of her creations spring up everywhere she looks. Some thrive, and some die.

And that is as it should, must and will be.

She finds, found her own delight in these new people. In particular, she sought to involve herself with those who found a role in maintaining justice. With those whose hearts tore to see the cruelties that came with Chaos. Her love for these was, is, and will be as powerful as that for the cave-dwellers that first found her favour.

But her youngest?

He can find no joy in existence. He squats away from his brothers and her in a tiny, forgotten part of the world and plots. He seeks to influence, not in the way of his brothers — through chance and Chaos — or like his mother — through the gift of light — but through making all fear what lives in the darkness.

He encourages all that is anathema to her to grow within his domain. Those who live within the sphere of his influence are twisted into something that causes her despair. She wishes to take them into her arms and release them from the fear he pours into their lives. His malignance draws others — ones as ancient as her — to encourage him in his hatred.

And yet she loved, loves him fiercely. Where she can, she seeks to ensure her influence mitigates the damage done by his machinations. Ones she loves are destroyed and will be destroyed by putting themselves in between her youngest son and her.

She takes a fallen Tailor by the hand to lead him back to her heart.

She promises him a gift to ease her suffering and his anger. Whatever he desires, she will seek to meet. She explains that he does not need to twist and pervert the creations of his kin. He can have something of his own to guide and develop.

"A child. A child of my own. One untouched by any of you."

He feels her recoil at his need and curses her. Shadows of darkness spread across the land. New forms of claws and teeth flash from the night to swallow and consume.

To repair their relationship across existence, she makes what she now and then knows to be an unwise promise. He will have the opportunity to shape a creation of his own. But to find them, he must approach them in love, not hate.

He does not have the capacity for that. He is too angry to free himself from the 'truth' he has created about his existence and their relationship. He takes, and he takes, and he twists, and he destroys. He continues to inject darkness into his tiny part of existence until it is a lodestone for all who are evil in the world.

But she keeps her promise. She creates an Unclassed — one untouched by either her own gifts or those of the Lords of Misrule. This boy, for he grows to be a boy, has the capacity to become whatever he shall wish.

He is limitless.

He is without taint from light, chance or the dark.

Standing alone in her field of green, the Goddess sobbed and laughs. A moment was approaching that she could not see beyond. That was both wonderful and terrible. It had been so long and no time at all since there were new possibilities for her to experience.

Light and dark had converged in the domain of her youngest son, and the shadows spilt out from that conflict. There was a chance, of course, that this would be the end of all things. Her eldest awaited, agog, to inject their own elements of Chaos into the conflict.

The Goddess paused time and focused on a reuniting group in the shadow of a burning Keep. One of her most beloved, the Knight Daine. A Noble of whom she approved and his servant of whom she most certainly did not. A young Archer blessed by her sons and her companion who was not of this realm. The most powerful Mage alive, one who could one day stand at her side, and his dog, all that remained of the pack she had once gifted him.

And there, in the middle of them all, stood the Unclassed.

An innocent lamb amongst such wolves. And a lamb that could destroy them all with barely a bleat.

Yet, for all their power, such forces were arrayed against them.

And, for the first moment in millennia, she did not know what would happen next.

CHAPTER FIFTY-TWO

"Portal of Darkness"

"Your handiwork, I presume?"

"He started it."

"'He started it.' What are you? Five?"

"It's hardly my fault that whoever was in there enjoyed the sowing but not so much the reaping."

The reunited group observed, in silence, the smouldering pile of wreckage that was all that remained of Keep Trellec. "Tell me more about the new pacifistic 'you' that wouldn't come back here and help me maintain order because you'd killed too many people."

Eliud nodded in acknowledgement. "I admit I may have spoken too soon. Old habits. You know how it is."

In common with everyone in the village not ensconced in the Speaking Chamber, the various members of Daine's party had congregated in front of the rubble of the Keep. It was a muted reunion, with even Savage and

Josul greeting each other without much enthusiasm. Only Daine, picking up and pressing Genoes against her breast-plate so tightly he squirmed in protest, displayed anything close to emotion.

There was something about mounds of burning stone and giant ash clouds that put a dent in everyone's mood.

Sensing the interested onlookers, Donal bent and sketched a confidentiality rune in the soot beneath his feet. "I feel I should note that whatever the outcome of the Council of the West, the destruction of this Keep by an agent of the King will be seen as an act of war."

"What in the name of the Goddess are you?"

"Eliud —"

"No, seriously, Daine. Have you seen this guy's aura? He's drawing power from all the wrong places, if you know what I mean."

"My Secretary has a colourful past, Duskstrider. But I am assured that he's on our side. For now."

Eliud turned to Taelsin. "Mayor Elm, it's an honour. I've heard a lot about you. Of course, most of what the King had to say was how much he would welcome someone cru-cifying you above your own City walls. But I'm sure he says the same about me, so we're in rarefied company. I say, with sincerity, that it is good to see you well."

"You too, Lord Duskstrider. Rumours of your passing seem to have been exaggerated." Taelsin smiled over to-ward Daine. "Something the two of you have in common. Your enemies seem to be making a habit of not quite fin-ishing the job."

"With no little consequences," Kirstin said drily as a red-hot wall tumbled down to join its fellows at ground level. At a nod from Daine, the Archer ruffled Genoes's hair and drew him away from the discussions. Savage and Josul followed them, tracking the crowd for danger.

Once they were out of earshot, Donal took up his theme. "As lovely as all this is, can I return our attention to the unambiguous declaration of war that the Pendragon has just made against the West?"

"Pfft. Someone threw a rock at me; I threw it back. It's hardly worth making much fuss over."

"You destroyed a Keep."

"They started it. Not my fault that I finished it."

Donal let out a groan of frustration. Daine put a comforting hand on his shoulder. "He makes us all feel like that. You get used to it." The hand would have been more comforting had it not been a mailed fist. The Secretary staggered under the weight of it.

Taelsin stroked his chin at Donal's words. "My Lord Duskstrider, he does have a point. First, the King dispatches a Knight of the Road to dissuade a lawful meeting of the Council of the West. Then, when we brave Westerners refuse to be intimidated, he orders a preemptive strike on a village whose only crime is daring to play host. An act of brutal repression."

"Wars have been fought over less," Donal agreed. "When you put it like that, Mayor Elm, I find myself, as a loyal Westerner, not feeling bathed in the warm glow of my monarch's regard."

Eliud raised his hands in protest. "Anyone with the smallest knowledge of Court life knows I've been estranged from the King for years."

"And what better way to get back in his good graces than eliminating the threat of secession."

Eliud looked around for support. "N one is seriously

going to think I destroyed a castle in the backend of no-where in support of the King. I mean, that's ludicrous."

"The ways of the Duskstrider are strange and curious. Who is to know the motivations of one who has been known to battle with the gods themselves?"

"That was one time, and we both said sorry in the morning. Look, Master Secretary, or whatever you call yourself, someone tried to hurt those I protected, which went poorly for them. If there's a message in this, it's that the smart move is to leave me and mine alone. Anyone who wants to make a political point out of that can come and make it to my face, and I will disabuse them. Or incinerate them into their constituent parts. One of the two. Why is no one looking at me when I'm speaking?"

They were not looking because Josul was growling at a blackened arm that had thrust itself skyward out of the ruins of Keep Trellec.

The group backed away from the emerging creature as Savage's hackles went up, and she began hissing at a second clawed hand that appeared several feet away, scrabbling for freedom from the stone.

"What in the world —" Taelsin was thrust backwards by Daine, who drew her sword to stand between him and the emerging figures.

"Donal, Genoes, both of you get behind me. Mistress Archer, you too. I don't think there will be much for your skills here."

More and more of the shadowy creatures began springing up from the wreckage. There were close to twenty and rising in seconds.

"Don't be so sure, my Lady Darkhelm." Eliud touched Kirstin's quiver, and the arrows took on an unearthly glow.

"Be careful with these. They have quite a kick. I wouldn't want someone to accuse you of starting a war or anything like that."

The crowd had melted away as fast as it appeared, leaving the small group the only witnesses to the mass of things that were emerging from the ground.

There was no pause or discussion. The creatures, seemingly constructed of pure darkness, their forms shifting and contorting as they moved, flung themselves forward. There was just time for Donal to draw healing runes in the air and for Eliud to raise barriers of protection around Genoes and Taelsin, shrouding them in light before the battle commenced.

Kirstin nocked one of her newly enchanted arrows and let it fly toward the thing closest to her. It shimmered when a radiant light pierced it to the core. Letting out a howl of pain, it dissipated into nothingness for a moment to reappear far to the right of the growing pack of shadows.

The Archer frowned and followed its movement, firing repeatedly. With each strike, the creature dissolved to reappear, but — to her eyes — slightly less dark than before. She was dimly aware of Savage yowling and batting at something that had crept too close to her left, but she could not leave off her barrage on that first creature.

Eliud sought to occupy the middle swathe of attackers — a group of hundred or so and growing. How many of these things could there be? They stunk of some form of darkness he had not encountered before. But where there was darkness, let there now be light.

He forced swirling pillars of white energy into the heart of their pack, buffeting them and pushing them away from their intended target, Kirstin. He was pleased that Savage had taken up a guard position there; it allowed him to focus his attention elsewhere.

For while his mana pool might be unlimited, his powers of concentration were not. He could maintain a barrier around Taelsin, Genoes and Donal — although he was not sure that whatever it was that was pretending to be a Secretary really needed his protection — while also keeping half an eye on Kirstin and maintaining his own assault, but it was a mental stretch.

And he had not had a restful time the night before.

There was a reason the Pendragon preferred to fight alone and on a desolate plain. It was much easier when he could go all out without worrying about collateral damage amongst his allies or devastating civilian populations.

As if reading his thoughts, several of the shadowy figures in his line of fire blinked out of existence and reappeared in front of Taelsin, claws swinging in the air.

Daine drove a fist through one and sliced her sword through the second. With each swing, she carved her way through the monsters, severing their ethereal forms even as they reformed and resumed their assault elsewhere. Her sword clashed against the inky darkness, producing bright sparks of light with each collision.

"What are they?" Taelsin shouted at Donal, flinching as the Duskstrider's strange dog took a creature that had appeared close to Genoes. The boy looked on impassively as Josul ripped out its throat and shook it to pieces.

Donal's face was drenched in sweat, and he answered his master through clenched teeth. "They're not of this realm. Something, and I use the word 'thing' advisedly, is holding a portal open under all that rubble, and these things are flooding through. I'm trying to push it closed, but" — he licked his lips — "they're pushing back. I've only felt such strength in the presence of gods. This god . . . it's not benign. Believe me when I say I know of what I speak. I'm not sure I can keep this up."

"Is there anything I can do?"

The grimace turned into a smile. "How do you feel about prayer, my Lord?"

Kirstin's hail of arrows had finally taken down her first target, and she changed to the press of figures surrounding the Knight.

The number of attackers was growing with every passing second. Whatever Eliud had done to her quiver, it seemed that not only did it enhance their stopping power, but it also replenished their number. Thus, she was somewhat more profligate than normal.

"As fun as this is, I don't think unlimited arrows is going to cut it," she murmured to Savage, who had taken to — Kirstin thought the best word was "drinking" — the shadows that came too close.

To her sharp eyes, the majority of the new creatures seemed to be emerging from a glowing circle in the middle of what was left of the Keep. "What do you think, girl? Anything we can do about where they're coming from?"

Savage tilted her head to one side. "Portal. Open. Need. Close."

Kirstin paused for a moment and then, with a whole-body shake, chose to press on. "When this is over, we'll have to have a chat, me and you. Come on, let's go close the portal." Nocking and firing arrow after arrow with each step, she moved toward the heart of the darkness.

If asked to explain the sensation of crushing these shadows with his power, Eliud would have likened it to popping bubbles which simply reconstituted into more, smaller bubbles. He was not actually sure he was helping his fellows with what he was doing. Many of their number seemed to lose interest in him and seek easier prey amongst them.

He clapped his hands together, blasting all those besieging him away, and reached outwards with his mana to see how things fared.

He could feel Donal wrestling with . . . something. Whatever it was, it was trying to hold open a portal to this realm while Donal did his best to force it closed. He leant that strange man a portion — a significant portion, what in the world was that man? — and felt that struggle even up. If needed, he could intervene further, but he sensed the Secretary had other tricks to play.

He touched on his two oldest friends, Savage and Josul, and felt no alarm in their spirits. Their battles were hard-fought, but they had faced down much sterner opposition and would hold their own. Genoes was safe, that was the important thing.

Daine, well, she was more suited for this sort of combat than he was, remorselessly grinding the opposition down to dust. Or infinitesimal bubbles, if he did not want to mix his metaphors.

His mind scanned to Kirstin and felt determination in the young Archer. She was approaching the same portal with which Donal was wrestling. As Savage was with her, he did not feel he needed to worry overmuch. Indeed, a few of those arrows she was spending like water, if fired into the portal would probably end the whole thing. He wondered if she considered the mana cost of each of those strikes of pure light. Probably not. But hey, he was the battery with an infinite mana pool, right?

"They don't value you." It was a child's voice. Albeit a very old one. Like a grandfather's impression of a toddler. "Why spend your life helping them? You heard that ancient evil one. He sees what you did as an act of war. There is no love for you here. You belong on my side of the struggle. We could do remarkable things."

Eliud turned and struck the Dark God in the chest with a beam of lightning. The god was blown backwards, disappearing through a wall. The Duskstrider's face was taut. "I've been manipulated by beings far more cunning and subtle than you, my Lord. You might want to try offering me riches beyond imagining next. I think that's next on the list. That or fleshly pleasures. But you know, go with whatever you think best in the Evil Overlord handbook."

The Dark God reappeared to Eliud's left. His child's face was expressionless, but the eyes were haunted with pain. "So be it. Have it your way, Pendragon. Remember, I gave you a choice." And then vanished.

"'So be it'? What does that mean?"

Eliud looked around, sensing the number of shadows falling away. Kirstin stood above a portal of swirling darkness, launching arrow after arrow down into its maw, Savage perched on her shoulder looking out for any danger.

Donal seemed to have won his battle with the force seeking to tear a new hole in the fabric of existence, and was holding the door closed with little alarm. Even so, he lay in Taelsin's arms, the master trying to get water into the mouth of the servant. Daine rested on her sword, the shadows near her falling to pieces under Josul's frenzied attacks.

And Genoes . . .

Was not there.

Panic tore at Eliud's heart. "Where is he? What have you done with him? I order you to bring him back."

"But you've been manipulated by beings far more cunning and subtle than me. How could I have done anything without you knowing?" That strange old child's voice again echoed through Eliud's mind.

"You have my village. I have your child. I wonder which of us will feel the loss more keenly."

CHAPTER FIFTY-THREE

"Skipping Stones"

Genoes sat silently as the strange boy shouted and shrieked before him.

He thought "boy," but there was something not quite right about his appearance or voice. If Genoes concentrated, he could make out four or five different figures in the space that the one child occupied: each an older version than the last.

Young, innocent eyes were overlaid by ones that were burdened with ancient sadness. His skin was both fresh and smooth while at the same time lined and sagging away from the bones. In his anger, he paced around Genoes, upright and imperiously strutting while also being stooped and uncertain.

The overall effect, quite apart from the towering rage of the child, was chilling.

Genoes did not know where he was or how he had

come to be here. The last thing he could remember was the appearance of those shadow monsters from beneath Keep Trellec. Daine and Josul had moved to stand in front of him, and he had felt Eliud cast some sort of shield around him.

And then he was here. Wherever "here" was.

The boy — he had to think of him as a boy or that way madness lay — was furious. With all the different versions of his voice merging into one cacophony of hate, it was almost impossible for Genoes to make out the words.

In the end, he could stand it no longer. He stood and, with a deep breath, moved forward and folded him into a hug. He had fully expected the boy to turn his wrath his way and had hoped his improved control over <Dodge> — thanks to Eliud's somewhat idiosyncratic training — would save him.

The other boy stiffened at the contact, but he leaned into it rather than rejecting the comfort.

The two stood for a moment, and Genoes felt the child's shape stabilise into one body. When he released him and stood back, it was as if he were in the company of a wholly normal boy precisely of his age.

"I'm Genoes. What's your name?"

The boy tilted his head to one side, his dark hair falling forward almost to cover his eyes. He seemed puzzled and then to be lost in thought. Eventually, he answered, his voice without any of the reverberations of earlier. "I don't know. I don't think I was given one."

"Everyone has a name! What do people call you?"

"Dark One. Master. Lord."

Genoes burst out laughing, then stopped as he saw hurt swim into the boy's eyes. "Sorry. It's just that those aren't names. They're — sorry, do people really call you that? That's weird."

"Everyone is afraid of me. They act like I'm going to hurt them all the time."

"Do you?"

The boy did not answer.

Genoes bent and picked up a handful of stones from the ground. He still did not recognise where they were, but more details were starting to be fleshed out. As if, now that he was not so furious, the world around them felt it was safe to emerge.

He threw one of the stones into a pond that had shimmered into being a few steps to his right, trying to skim it across the surface. "Are you going to hurt me?"

The boy still did not answer, but his eyes keenly watched Genoes's game. After a few false starts, the stones started skipping over the surface. Once. Twice. Three times.

"Can I try?" The request was almost shy.

Genoes smiled and handed over the remaining stones, stooping to collect some more. "There's a trick to it. You need to —" He demonstrated the slingy action required. "Like that. They need to kiss the top of the water."

The Dark God started throwing stones — all, of course, sank without a trace. His eyes flared with dark energy after each failed attempt. When the fifth stone could not skim, he smashed both hands into fists. The water in the pond immediately boiled dry with a hiss of steam. "This is a stupid game!"

Genoes stopped himself from cowering away from that casual expression of overwhelming power. Young as he was, he had needed to adapt his behaviour to all sorts of people in the village — both good and bad — in order to survive. With all that experience, he sensed that should he show himself to be afraid of this boy, he would just become another one in a lengthy line of supplicants to that power. At the moment, the boy was unsure how to behave toward him — Genoes did not want to lose that advantage.

"Stop it! That's silly. You don't break things because you can't do them properly the first time. I won't play with you if you do that."

The Dark God's eyes flashed, and, for a moment, Genoes feared he had misread the situation. Then the flames died away, and the pool refilled. He picked up a stone and gave it to Genoes. "Show me again."

Genoes did.

It took a few more tries, but eventually, the boy managed to get one of his stones to bounce for a second time. The look of pure joy on his face was a remarkable sight.

At the very edge of the realm to which the Dark God had stolen Genoes away, a woman smiled to hear her child laugh.

*

Daine feared Eliud's rage would destroy the village.

Lightning spilt from the Pendragon, arching in uncontrolled bursts to strike the rubble around Keep Trellec. Two or three times, the spears of light were pulled into her armour, cracking her skin and burning away her hair. She was terrified of what would happen should one of the others be so struck.

"Eliud, calm down!"

He turned his head to face her, his eyes orbs of chaotic purple. "He took him!" Beams of energy shot out from him, smashing into a nearby building. Daine could only hope the occupants had long since left, as it was wholly vaporised.

"I know. But killing everyone around you is not going to bring him back!"

Those purple eyes held hers without flickering, and for a moment, she feared he was going to ignore her words and continue with the wanton destruction. But then he faced the sky, threw up his hands and roared. Huge bolts of lightning poured upwards from his hands, drowning the sky in light.

Donal quickly drew a shield rune to cover the group as hundreds of flash-fried birds started to rain down on them. Within moments, the top of the shield was wholly covered, and they could not see through it.

"I have to say, I did not have being killed, accidentally, by the Duskstrider on my dance card for today." Sweat was running down Donal's face as he kept drawing and redrawing the rune. The others watched the shield flicker and bend inwards under the weight of the falling bodies. "Although it would probably be higher up the list than being crushed to death by an avalanche of pigeons. I'm not sure how much longer I can hold this, ladies and gentlemen."

"Mine," Savage pronounced, looking hungrily upwards.

Kirstin and Donal shared a look, and then the Archer shrugged. "It's not like we have many other options."

"Indeed." And the shield failed.

No one who witnessed what happened next could quite agree about what they saw.

Donal swore the kitten opened a swirling portal above them that the birds simply vanished into. As for Taelsin, he said he saw a thousand tree branches thrust out from the ground around the cat, skewering what was falling and absorbing them back into the ground in an instant. Kirstin watched in astonishment as flurry after flurry of arrows flew from the cat's fur and obliterated the danger. Daine perhaps had the strangest version as she watched Savage's lower jaw detach and expand exponentially outwards, swallowing the dead animals' weight before they could be crushed by them.

In any event, they were all left looking at a very smugly satisfied kitten who purred and hopped back on Kirstin's shoulder. "Welcome."

"Is everyone okay?" An Eliud who seemed much more in control of his faculties was walking back toward them. "I'm sorry, I haven't lost control in that way since —"

"The Siege of Aven. Ten thousand dead after they executed the Crown Prince and had his body delivered to you in a barrel." Donal raised his hands in apology. "Sorry, I'm somewhat a connoisseur of your work. Big fan."

Eliud ignored him and addressed Daine. "I am so sorry, Lady Darkhelm. You placed the boy under my protection." He looked at the still-smouldering pile of Keep Trellec. "My presence here has bought nothing but disaster. I should have stayed away." Josul whined and rubbed against his master's leg. Eliud absentmindedly patted his head.

"My Lord, there will be time enough for recriminations later. For now, what news of the boy? Can you find Genoes?"

The Duskstrider shook his head. "He's still alive, I can tell you that much. But the Dark God has pulled him out of this world. I'll know when he brings Genoes back, but I do not have the skill to seek him into the realms of the gods. There are precious few that could. Your patron, certainly. The King, perhaps."

I will not interfere in this matter unless the boy is in danger. The Goddess's voice was uncharacteristically stern.

"The Goddess will not intercede. Would the King help?"

Eliud grimaced. "We hardly left on good terms. If I was left alive long enough to ask, maybe. And, of course, Borelean is at Court. That would complicate things."

Taelsin had been listening attentively. "What if you were to bring word of the West's secession? That would buy you some credit, no?"

Eliud considered. "Perhaps. But that would invite the King's wrath upon you months before he might be expected to hear the news. There's little chance your rebellion can succeed as it is; without time to consolidate, it will be over before it starts."

Donal nodded. "You speak true. But" — and he turned to look at the still sealed Speaking Chamber — "we must assume we have lost influence over the Council of the West. The Dark God is clearly supporting the Trellecs, and from what I understand, the Goddess seems unwilling to become involved either way. Likewise, let us not forget that the Order of Iskent has appeared in this part of the world. That says to me that there are unseen forces at play here. My reading is that the Lords of Misrule are poised to bring their own power to proceedings. The King's wrath, while unpleasant and potentially fatal, may prove to be the better of all the available evils."

Daine chimed in, "If you bring him news that the West had fallen, it may well go some way to heal your relationship. You can note that we have worked together and that we were both charged with protecting the boy. He's a father. He will find that hard to resist."

Their debate was halted as the bell above the entrance to the Speaking Chamber started to toll again.

It seemed the Trellecs had something to say.

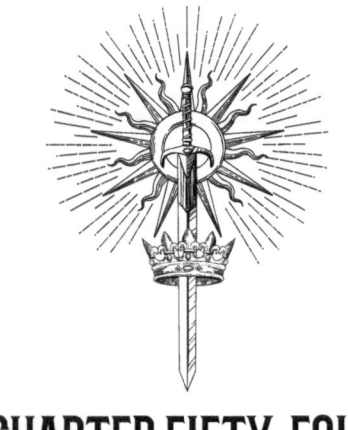

CHAPTER FIFTY-FOUR

"A Series of Poor Decisions"

It would be hard to determine what caused Fion Trellec the most rage.

Certainly, seeing the smoking remains of his home played a significant role. His mouth opened and closed several times as he took in the sight of smouldering, glowing rock at the moment of his greatest triumph. The construction of Keep Trellec had played such an essential part in his life that it defied comprehension that it had been simply removed. The colossal sum of money it had cost to construct over the last decade — consuming both his own fortune and the dowry of his second wife — had gone up in smoke in an instant.

His furious eyes shifted to the small group standing before it, and their identities likewise threw a not inconsiderable amount of fuel onto the fire of his anger.

Taelsin Elm. Eliud Villa. Daine Orban.

The Goddess could not have conjured a trio more likely to inflame his spirit. The "Saviour of the West" who had somehow contrived to escape Fion's wildly successful gambit in the Speaking Chamber. The Pendragon himself who, by the guilty expression on his face, was responsible for the destruction of Trellec Keep. And the Lady Darkhelm, who was both at the heart of his renaissance as a power in the West and one of the remaining critical threats to it.

When the entrance to the Speaking Chamber had been unsealed, he had expected — indeed, had paid well for — the acclamation of adoring crowds. Secession had, of course, been decided upon — under no small pressure from Gilles and Pernille — and the Council of the West had concluded by framing a Declaration of Independence that was sure to set a blaze under the King.

Thus, the paltry number of villagers who greeted him to hear this momentous news was the first spark for his wrath. After the last few days' logistical failures, he did not think he could cope with another disappointment; an idle part of him wondered if his son was responsible in some nefarious attempt to undermine him. As a response to this unwelcome thought, his eyes turned to where he imagined Drunnoc had sequestered himself away, and the column of smoke in the sky greeted him.

He stood in silence for a few moments, unable to see his way through to his next steps.

"My Lord, what would you have me do?"

He turned to Gilles, his most faithful, helpful, and unhinged servant. Who would have expected that his Skill would have proved quite so useful? The sight of the great Lords of the West clustered around this frail old man, like ducklings following their mother, eased his mood somewhat.

For sure, the Keep had played its part in his rise, but he had now reached the peak, and he did not need to be too concerned with what had helped the climb. He was destined for more extraordinary things now than anyone in this tragic little village could possibly conceive. Had not the Council of the West acclaimed him, unanimously, as the first Chancellor of their group of collected, free states? All the power he had wanted, but never thought was accessible, was now his.

He could have a hundred such Keeps made now.

In the face of the unity of the West, what could those three really achieve? The die was cast, the West was free, and the King's rule had been cast off.

Fion pointed at the small group already backing away from his presence and fleeing to the woods. "Drive them out. Kill them if you can; harry them from my sight if you cannot."

Gilles once more tapped into the power of his Class. He had been drawing on it almost constantly for the last few hours, and his head felt like it would soon explode. In support, Pernille put her hand on his shoulder and flooded him with stolen life force. His back straightened, and the voice that boomed from his mouth was as far away from the quiet, softly spoken old man that so many knew as it was possible to be.

"Kill them. All of them."

And the crowds, the greatest men and women of the West, howled like banshees and ran after the fleeing group.

*

"Ideas?" Daine was carrying Taelsin and Kirstin, one under each arm, as they fled the horde that continued to stream their way from the Speaking Chamber.

"You can't hurt them. They don't know what they're doing." Taelsin was doing a very creditable job of maintaining his dignity while being carried along like last week's linen.

"Can I just say I'm not settled on that course of action," Donal said. He was . . . the verb really was "flowing" alongside them. Daine, again, reflected that there was an awful lot still to unpick about Taelsin's Secretary. "If it's us or them, I'm perfectly comfortable with it being them."

Eliud hovered a little above them, ostensibly trying to identify a clear route away from the village. On hearing Taelsin's words, he adjusted his aim and fired a spread of lightning in front of the approaching crowd. It barely made them pause before they ran through the sparkling energy. Josul and Savage seemed to be keeping up with very little challenge. "Anyone know how far the reach of that damned Steward's <Authority> is? I can't remember anyone having this strong a sphere of control before — you can't usually make people act against the way they usually would."

Daine remembered the crowd that had attached them in Cenwyn's house. "He seems peculiarly gifted. I saw people — good people — completely crazed at his words. I've never seen anyone react to <Authority> like it."

"There's certainly something else there," Donal said. "Something dark, and it's powering him up. I can feel the pulse of its presence from here, but it has stayed back in the village, so I think it is likely we should be able to outrun this madness. Oh, that power is very nice, actually. Some sort of perverted Battle Healer. Maybe. But there are touches of something else there too. All spiky and forbidden. Quite lovely. If I were a few centuries younger, I could make a series of bad decisions with whoever has that particular Skill set, let me tell you." The pleasure in Donal's voice did not seem especially appropriate, considering the circumstances.

"I think we're reaching the edge of his influence. The majority of the crowd seem to be pausing," Eliud called from his position above them. "But there are other things still pursuing," he added. "They look like those shadows that were seeking to come through the portal. But different somehow. More solid." He paused and tasted their power. "There's a good five or six of them, but I'm struggling to keep track of them. I would suggest best we try not to engage them directly."

Daine felt the Goddess's reaction to Eliud's words. "The Goddess is horrified by them. We need to keep clear, if at all possible."

"I can support that," Donal chimed in. "There's dark and forbidden, which is always worth a dalliance, and then there's whatever is coming after us."

They ran on, the gap between them and those who pursued them from the village increasing.

*

Fion stood in the wreckage of his home. Little pockets of villagers had sprung up around the edges of the devastation.

"You see what they do?" he called out, not even sure who or what he was addressing.

"We suggest we would like freedom; they put parameters around that. We follow their rules; they change them. We gather to discuss things, and they do this."

He saw a few members of the crowd nod thoughtfully.

Some of the Council of the West who had been a little slow pursuing the small group out of the village were starting to filter back.

"You all know they sent the Darkhelm to dissuade us from our chosen, lawful path. And yet we would not be bowed by such intimidation. We came together. We spoke. We debated both sides of the issue, as was our right as free men and women. And, as we wrestled with that most weighty of purposes, they struck behind our backs."

He indicated the wreck of his home.

"You all saw the Pendragon himself. He brought down death and destruction to my own home. He killed my wife," *hopefully*, he thought, "and my son," *doubly hopefully*, "and removed most of my household. Had I not been in the Speaking Chamber, he would have undoubtedly murdered me too."

The grumbles in the crowd seemed sincere now. Gilles's power was long since spent, even allowing for the support offered by Pernille. Any response he was getting now was one that his words were owed. Yes, he was sure of it: no magically enhanced powers were in play. This was his own rhetorical power.

More and more Lords and their groups of retainers were filtering back from their helter-skelter pursuit — seemingly oblivious to their misuse within the Speaking Chamber.

"But, despite all this, I can proudly say that the Council of the West would not be swayed from our course. We would not allow ourselves to lose sight of our true purpose. We considered both sides of the argument and found that the West's future is no longer within this kingdom. Even before we saw this later outrage, we had decided to inform the King of our intention to secede, and he could do what he wished. Well, what else can he do but level our homes and kill our families? I say he has done that to me this day, and it changes nothing. Can any of you say any less than that?"

He raised his eyes to take in the growing crowd. "I say the West is now free."

The roar of the crowd was everything he had hoped it would be.

*

All but one of those strange, dark presences had abandoned their pursuit. The group had decided they would be wise to engage it before reaching Eliud's cottage. They had no way of knowing its skills or capacities, and there was no need to risk giving away that location if they did not need to.

"How long?" Kirstin had planted six of Eliud's enhanced arrows in the ground before her, and was covering the space in the woods from which they anticipated their attacker coming.

Eliud was hovering above the group, hands filled with dormant lightning. "A few minutes. I do not wish to alarm anyone, but it appears to be running through — and I mean through — the trees."

"Any thoughts on what we face, Lord Duskstrider?" Taelsin was acutely aware he had an extremely limited role to play in the upcoming confrontation. What was he going to do, diplomacy it to death? Donal had placed a series of runes around him, and Daine had given him a spare short sword. He could not help but feel that things would have to have gone very badly if it were needed.

"It's akin to what I dropped the meteorite on. Lots of borrowed power. This one feels more . . . physical."

"I can do physical." Daine had positioned herself well in

front of the rest of the group, flanked by Josul and Savage. She'd had worse allies by her side, she thought.

"Just so we're clear, Plan A is that the Lady Darkhelm holds it up on the edge of the clearing, and the rest of us hit it with everything we've got." Several glowing runes in the air next to Donal took on the appearance of open mouths with lots of teeth.

"Thirty seconds out. And Plan B?" Eliud rose a little higher in the air.

"Never does to overthink these things."

And it was upon them.

CHAPTER FIFTY-FIVE

"Big Fan of Your Work"

A giant black form with a bearlike muzzle exploded out of the woods, its speed as it barrelled toward them on all fours taking them by surprise. Even running like this, it was significantly taller than Daine, heavily muscled and with a width across its enormous shoulders to match. Although it carried no obvious weapon, its claws were wickedly curved, and its teeth flashed as it roared toward them.

Kirstin was able to get off one shot before the creature crashed into Daine, who had moved to put herself into its path. However, the arrow glanced off its slick, black carapace and disappeared to the side.

Daine met the charge with a shoulder barge, pushing the beast backwards before slashing toward it with her sword once, twice, missing both times. Its speed was astonishing, ducking beneath both blows with ease. In return, she took several fearsome blows from its forelegs. The last of these hit her head and sent her helmet flying, and the force of the impact snapped her jaw. She quickly jerked her head back and forth to clear her blurred vision, felt loosened teeth resettle with a click, and sought to re-engage, using the point of her longsword to keep the creature from closing the gap.

At the same time, Josul dived at its legs, seeking to hamstring it with his teeth, and was kicked unceremoniously away. He crashed to the ground, shook himself off and returned to Daine's side, yipping at the monster but not seeking to engage further. Savage, seeing the speed at which the dog was dispatched, stayed slightly further back, hissing ferociously.

Several lightning beams flew over Daine's shoulder, the second grazing her cheek, as Eliud tried to supply covering fire. Each of his efforts hit the creature square in the chest, but seemed to have no impact.

"Looks like no dice from me. Some sort of elemental resistance in the armour. Although is it armour, or the thing's skin? Anyone in the name of the Goddess know what it is?"

"I'm having no joy either," Kirstin added as her next flurry of shots bounced away. "It's like it's made of stone. Donal?"

The Secretary was staring with barely concealed horror at the thing that Daine was struggling to keep at bay. With each swing of its monstrous claws, the Knight of the Road was pushed further backwards, her armour screeching with each blow and her planted feet ploughing furrows in the earth.

"The Goddess would have nothing to do with such as

this." He gestured, and the two mouths he had summoned flew, teeth gnashing, to try to relieve some of the pressure on Daine. The mouths attached themselves to the neck of the beast and, for a moment, seemed to slow its relentless, brutal attack on the Knight. But then they each turned black and crumbled away to dust as if drained of their integrity.

"Well, that's suboptimal." Donal grimaced and started drawing something new on the ground." Buy me a bit more time; I think I will need to do something a touch injudicious."

Eliud dropped to the ground next to Daine and manifested a glowing sword in each hand. "Let's change it up. Pull back, my Lady. I'll take it from here."

Daine could not remember the last time she had retreated from a one-on-one foe, but she desperately needed the space Eliud offered her. She drove her sword forward, pushing the creature away, and quickly retreated as Eliud stepped into the breach.

Within moments, she could feel her wounds heal as the Goddess poured life force into her. That, in itself, was a call for alarm. Such direct engagement had been notably absent since arriving in the village. It said nothing good for their predicament that She chose to help now.

It seemed hardly the time to complain, though. There was a release of pressure as her fractured eye socket was repaired, and she took a few deep breaths, preparing herself to relieve the Duskstrider.

Although he fought with far more technical skill, he was faring no better than she in driving the monster back. Whereas Daine used the sword as a conduit for her immense strength, Eliud was elegant in attack, ambidextrously slashing and cutting intricate patterns that somehow made no impression on his opponent.

"There are three rules to fighting for you to remember, girl. First, every fight is over before it begins." She was suddenly back at Gant's school, spitting blood onto the sawdust. *"So, you go big, you go bold, and then you go home. Your job is to be so overwhelmingly terrifying that you scare the life out of them, and they back down. So, rule number two, you come up against someone who doesn't lose their lunch at the idea of fighting you once they've seen what you've got, you get out of there. I'm not wasting all this time on training you up for you to take on a god."*

Those words echoed around her skull as she watched the Duskstrider barely manage to hold the beast in place. Then he took a blow to the elbow, which made him drop one of his summoned blades. He swore and took again to the sky before it could press its advantage. "Sorry, my Lady, back to you."

Daine ran forward, dropping her own sword and tackling the creature to the floor, grabbing its forelegs and seeking to limit its mobility. Even through her plate mail, it was freezing cold to her touch, and she felt her skin blister as she tried to hold it tight.

Donal looked up, the complex rune he had drawn nearing completion. "Just a little longer. This will work. I think. Probably."

Daine was on the ground behind the beast, scrabbling to pin its arms and legs. Its movement was too frenzied, though, and it eventually was able to get enough space to crash the back of its head into the Knight's nose.

Momentarily stunned, Daine could not resist as the creature flipped over on top of her and drove several massive blows into her head.

She tried to bring her arms up in protection, but the rain of strikes was too overwhelming. She felt the ground beneath her give way under the force of the claws crashing into her.

"It's killing her!" Kirstin shrieked impotently as she fired arrow after arrow into the thing's back.

Sensing the immediate peril, Eliud sketched a portal in the air, dove down to pick the creature up, and then hurled it through. The shimmering light in the sky slammed shut when the dark creature vanished into it.

After the noise of the confrontation, the silence that now fell was disconcerting.

Eliud swooped next to the fallen Knight and poured healing force into her, reinflating a skull that had been wholly caved inwards by the assault. In moments, Daine's breathing settled and her eyes snapped open. "Where did it go?"

He shrugged. "No idea. I didn't have time for anything elegant. I just tore a hole and threw it in. But unless it happens to have some portal Skill of its own to return, we should be okay."

Daine sighed. "You had to say it, didn't you?"

A warning bark from Josul spun the group around as a dark portal opened just behind Donal, and the thing came careering back through.

Kirstin swung her bow like a bat to try to fend it off, but the wood snapped ineffectively off its head. She was slapped backwards, almost carelessly, to fall into a heap a distance back. Savage yowled and scampered over to her prone form, licking her head and mewling.

Eliud landed between the monster and Donal, fists blazing with purple fire as the two exchanged blows.

Taelsin had run to Daine's side and was helping her to her feet. "Surely the Duskstrider should be able to banish whatever this is?"

"He's holding back," Daine rasped, her tongue not quite fully regrown in her mouth.

"What? Why?"

Gant's final words, as he knocked her unconscious for the fiftieth time that day, came flooding back to her.

"Third rule of fighting, and this is the biggie. Don't tangle with the Duskstrider. Ever. You think gods are bad, you've never seen Eliud Villa in action. He spends his whole life trying to keep that power of his under control. When he loses his temper — well, that's when cities get levelled. Best-case scenario, he kills you. Worst, he kills everything around you and, you need to remember this, he won't mean to. He'll feel terrible about it. But there are cities you don't find on maps anymore where someone forgot rule number three."

Daine looked at Taelsin who winced as the bones in her face shifted back into place. "Don't make the mistake of thinking he's like us. He's not. I like him a lot, and I think he'd rather die than hurt us, but he's just too powerful. The only reason that creature is still alive is that he has not found a way to kill it that will not also kill all of us. He's holding back to be kind. I need to get back in there."

She took a few stumbling steps forward before her balance returned and she ran back toward the fighters.

She was about halfway there when Donal stood up, a sheepish look on his face, the newly empowered rune cycling his head like an incredibly dark rainbow.

"Okay, I'm going to cast this, and I want you all to remember that we're friends before I do it. I don't want this to be a looking-at-me-different-in-the-morning-after-we-take-things-too-far kind of deal."

The monster backhanded Eliud viciously and brought him to his knees. Daine was there to block the follow-up attack on her forearm, her bracer snapping with the impact. In return, she pummelled back with blows that would have brought down a castle wall.

The creature was momentarily stunned and stepped backwards. Then it reached out and put a massive hand around her throat before lifting her into the air.

"Donal, whatever it is, just do it!" Taelsin yelled.

Daine was hurled, like a ragdoll, out of sight into the woods, the sound of crashing branches marking her descent. Eliud watched her limp body fly away before turning back with purple fire leaking from his eyes.

"Hang on, my Lord. Let me cast this before we escalate things to a Lost-Continent-of-Szaba situation. Again, huge fan of your work, but it's best appreciated from a distance, I sense."

Donal was at Eliud's side, the hand on his shoulder and his calm voice, oddly, precisely what the moment needed.

He pointed toward the monster, slavering jaws inches from his face and spoke one word. "Unmade."

The rune that had been circling him leapt forward and struck the black armour of the creature. However, whereas everything else they had tried had failed to make an impact, the rune spread to envelop its giant body in seconds, everything beneath it turning into foul-smelling dust. The creature shrieked as it was, over the course of heartbeats, literally unmade.

Donal and Eliud watched the small pile of greasy dirt for a moment as if unsure the confrontation was over.

Eliud spoke first. "Was that one of the Dark Words of Ash?"

Donal cleared his throat and wrinkled his nose at the smell coming from the remains of the monster. "Maybe."

"I think I'm technically supposed to execute you just for knowing it, let alone using it. Probably should kill myself too, just for seeing it cast."

"Technically."

"Isn't there a whole Order dedicated to wiping out anyone with that knowledge?"

"There is. Some people don't let these things go."

Kirstin, Taelsin and Daine joined them, looking down at what remained of the creature. "Did you say six or seven of these things were chasing us away from the village?"

Eliud nodded. "Yes, the others turned back."

"Probably scared of us." Daine's voice was toneless.

"Yeah, we really showed him something," Kirstin added. "The fourth or fifth time it nearly killed one of us was quite a lesson to it."

Eliud turned to look back the way they had come, toward the village. "What is there that has access to this sort of power?"

CHAPTER FIFTY-SIX

"Obvious Metaphors"

Opening his eyes hurt.

Although "hurt" did not adequately explain the agony such a simple action had caused to reverberate around his face.

It felt as if his flesh had been stripped from his skin by a flaming torch and then, inexpertly, painted back on with boiling pitch.

Other parts of him hurt too, but he had only enough capacity to cope with one thing at a time.

So, the eyes it was.

What had occurred? He had a vague memory of urgently needing to stop something. Of running — or was it being dragged? — up the stairs to the roof of the Keep. Dranoth, or what used to be Dranoth, had been up there and casting some sort of spell. He needed to stop it before —

Then everything became somewhat of a blur.

He flickered his eyelids experimentally. The pain was still there, but pain was something to be managed.

Someone was shouting at him. He turned his head so his functioning ear was pointed in the right direction.

"I told you not to draw the Pendragon into our conflict, and what was the first thing you did? Had one of your idiots — one of your idiots that I wasted precious energy on upgrading their Class — try to bring down the sky on him!"

He understood that these words were intended as stinging criticism, but he did not have the strength to be hurt by mere words right now.

"You are fortunate he restrained himself adequately that the Keep was the only thing he destroyed." The voice — was it a child shouting at him? — went up several octaves. "Even I would hesitate before forcing a direct confrontation with Eliud Villa. He fought Borelean to a standstill! Do you not understand what that means!"

"Not really." The ball of agony that was Drunnoc Trellec managed to sneak those two words out of cracked lips. He felt he had been on the receiving end of enough of the Dark God's rants at this stage. He was sure death should come with some benefits.

"Of course you don't!" The child's voice shrieked at him now. But there was an odd bass rumble that suggested that more than one person — a much older one at that — was yelling too. "You don't understand anything. That's why you need to do exactly what I say! I have given you all the tools you need to achieve our purposes, and all you need to do is FOLLOW INSTRUCTIONS!"

He thought a hand slapped his face at those words, but everything hurt too much to make it out clearly.

"Your ineptitude has wasted one of my gifts in a fight

with a being so far above its abilities you may as well have thrown it into the sun, you drew the Pendragon into things such that his presence ensured my portal was closed before it was properly established, and a second of your followers I upgraded has just been eradicated outside of the village. At this stage, I must question whether there is any point in you at all!"

"I assume there must be, as you have, presumably, decided to bring me back from my fiery demise; the question, therefore, seems somewhat moot. Unless, of course, the purpose of my resurrection is so that you can give me the talking-to I so richly deserve. I must let you know, though, my father never found me an especially receptive pupil in such matters."

The silence in response was its own answer.

Although he could feel the pain start to lessen as the reknitting of his body continued, Drunnoc still could not move freely. He felt, though, on the edge of his vision, there was someone else near him.

"Who else is here? Is it Father?"

"Never you mind," the voice snapped. "I can invite anyone to my realm I choose. Should I want your prancing peacock of a father here, rest assured I could have him here in a moment."

Drunnoc's eyes now managed to focus on the area above him. He could see stormy skies and the occasional crash of lightning.

He idly wondered if all the gods' realms were such obvious metaphors. "I am the Dark God. See my stormy rage!I am the Goddess. Be dazzled at my green fertility. I am the God of the Ocean. Let's go for a swim."

He snorted, which led to a new blossom of pain in his

head; this caused him to turn to the side and, as he'd expected, he could make out a second figure standing next to the Dark God.

"The horserat. Interesting."

If the Dark God heard him, he gave no sign. "We cannot afford the loss of any more key pieces at this early stage of the game. I have supplemented the meagre forces you gathered together by upgrading the Class of eight of them; you have contrived to lose two already. You pitted an Equinox Warlock against the Duskstrider, which ended as well as could be expected. And I am unclear what brought down the Juggernaut, but it was entirely conclusive. There will be no more, so use the remaining six wisely."

Drunnoc was able to sit upright now.

"I do feel I should point out that I had nothing to do with what Dranoth was doing on the roof of the Keep — the first I knew of it was when you summoned me to stop him. Likewise, I was rather dead when whoever you turned into a — what was it? — a Juggernaut came to their own end."

"It was Marcus." A small voice came from behind the Dark God.

They both turned to face Genoes, who straightened defiantly. "It was Marcus who was turned into a Juggernaut. A friend of Lady Darkhelm's turned him into a pile of ash."

Genoes had been forced to watch the fight in the clearing. His heart had been in his mouth throughout, especially when the giant figure he found vaguely familiar quickly shrugged off so many of his friends' efforts to impede.

Judging by the Dark God's reaction, the old man who finally defeated him had said a very bad word indeed.

"Well, there's your problem." Drunnoc looked away from Genoes, not wanting to give him any more attention. "Marcus was a retriever in human form. Nothing would persuade him otherwise if he thought he was supposed to chase someone."

The Dark God made a noise in his throat that suggested a change in conversation would be wise.

Drunnoc obliged. "If the portal did not open, was the Council ended prematurely too?"

"No. Those who interfered with the portal were too late to stop your father's plan. The West has broken away from the Kingdom. Perhaps I put my faith in the competence of the wrong Trellec."

Drunnoc sensed he was supposed to be enraged by such a comment. It was an insight into the god's preoccupations that being compared slightingly to another was seen as a critical form of attack. He rolled his eyes.

"You will keep your regard on me!"

Drunnoc was pulled into the air by a gesture from the god — he hung limply as if suspended by a rope around his waist.

"As you proved yourself seemingly so incapable, let me outline your next steps. I will not do so again. The group aligned against us now will, by necessity, split. I have taken something they value" — the hood tilted toward Genoes — "they will not seek direct confrontation again until they recover it. The Pendragon will make that his mission. I will arrange how this is to be overseen. You are not, under any circumstances, to interfere. I hope I do not need to explain why that is so important?"

There was a silence, and then Drunnoc realised he was expected to answer. "No, my Lord. You do not need to explain why I should not seek to engage the man who destroyed my home and killed me without trying. He is all yours."

"Your father's success in breaking the West away from the Kingdom will now be a major distraction when they can least afford it. The Darkhelm will be pulled into addressing that rather than focusing too closely on us. She will either seek to warn the King or try to resolve it alongside her other new allies. You should ensure your father has all the support he needs to frustrate those efforts."

"Is there a particular goal there, or will general chaos be acceptable? My father . . . has limits."

"As long as he can keep the Darkhelm and, by extension, my mother distracted, I do not care what occurs in the West. Set the whole place on fire if that seems like it will fulfil that purpose."

A dark gleam entered Drunnoc's eyes at those words. Set it on fire? He could do a lot better than that.

"The only thing that remains," continued the Dark God, "is the whereabouts of the Unclassed. It will arise in or around your village, and you must seek to locate it."

It took a significant act of will for Drunnoc not to turn back to Genoes at that moment. If the Dark God could not see something literally under his nose, he was not going to assist. That was a significant trump card to be played on another day.

"We need to ensure either that the Unclassed chooses our cause or that they are removed before exercising their power on behalf of our enemies. The moment you identify them, you are to contact me; you understand?"

"Absolutely. The instant I find them, I will alert you."

Drunnoc was slowly lowered to the ground until he

stood facing the god. He was almost wholly healed now, with the burns fast fading away.

The hood of the figure before him dropped back, and once again, Drunnoc was shaken by how young, yet how old, the Dark God appeared.

"With the forces aligned against us split and each now pursuing their own agendas, we can now make use of our singular focus to achieve our goal."

"Which is?"

"Why, exactly what it has been since I first manifested to you. We will work together to bring about the death of the Goddess."

CHAPTER FIFTY-SEVEN

"A Blade of Ruin"

Daine sank awkwardly to the ground. Although her life-threatening wounds were largely gone, multiple minor tears and breaks were still healing. Josul waddled over to press up against her side in a comforting way; she scratched his head idly.

It seemed incredible, but it had been barely a week since she had entered the village. Not even that long since she had first encountered the Trellecs, and less again since she had met Genoes in Cenwyn's house.

Her depth of feeling toward all of them, the fallen Tailor included, seemed wholly out of line with the brevity of the relationships.

Her eyes scanned over what remained of their group. Of course, she'd known Eliud well before all of this, but she could sense the same pull of fierce protectiveness that linked the two of them reaching toward Taelsin, Donal and Kirstin.

After so many years alone, having these bonds tug at her felt wholly alien. But, perhaps, not in an unpleasant way.

Her mind, unbidden, returned to the evening before she had formalised her Class change to Knight of the Road.

Old Gant had come to see her as she was preparing for bed. She had thought it strange at the time, but now, with the benefit of experience, she felt she could recognise what he had sought to do that night.

He was not drunk; that was the first thing that had struck her as strange. For as long as she had been at his school, it had been his custom to drink himself into a stupor once classes were finished — indeed, he had been drinking more and more during sessions for the last few years.

"Big day tomorrow, girl." He had sat down opposite her, eyes roving anywhere around the room except on her face.

She was uncomfortable being alone with him like this.

His erratic behaviour was becoming increasingly terrifying for all those under his tutelage. His lucid moments were becoming very rare, and there was no reasoning with him when he became lost in his memories. While Daine, especially now that she had the attention of the Goddess, was robust enough to extricate herself from any unpleasantness relatively unharmed, others were not so lucky. At that very moment, the infirmary had three younger boys in it who Gant had attacked in the refrectory — apparently, he had taken them for "Imperial Assassins."

Quite what Empire he was raving about, no one had been able to uncover. The oldest of the boys had lost an arm.

Looking at him now, awkwardly opening and closing his hands, she wondered if he even remembered doing it.

"You're settled on that Class, then, girl?"

Daine had sighed and replied automatically. This had been their only topic of conversation for weeks. He obviously could not recall their hours going back and forth on the issue. Indeed, they'd walked this road so frequently that she could play her part without thinking.

They'd been going through the same arguments for some time when she realised he had said something that deviated from their established script.

"I'm sorry, sir. What did you say?"

He was crying, she saw with shock. Streams of water running unheeded down his cheeks to drip into his lap. It was the single most appalling thing she had ever seen in her life.

"It's not enough, you know. The killing."

She had not known what to say in response to that, but the old man continued as if she had replied.

"There's always someone else that needs removing. One last mission to make the realm safe. One final push to settle the matter. Peace is always just around the corner."

He took out the hip flask at his belt, unscrewed the top, but did not raise it to his lips. She had become so used to that gesture that his failure to complete the pattern was as disconcerting as the wet patches now forming on his tunic.

"And then they tell you, you're no use anymore. Of course, they don't put it like that, but everyone knows what you did, and it's embarrassing. Everyone's looking at you like you're a broken beast that needs to be put down or at least out to pasture. He changed my Class himself, you know? The King. One minute, I was the deadliest Blade of Ruin in the known world, and the next, a Mentor. A Goddess-damned teacher."

Daine had kept silent, somehow forcing the myriad of questions that leapt to her mind to stay down.

The potential for Class change was not hugely unusual — that was the point of this school, after all. But to change in adulthood? That was unheard of. And the King had the power to force that change? That had never been mentioned in any of her lessons.

But, even beyond all that, was Gant originally a Blade of Ruin? Even talking about that Class was considered taboo — the immense power bestowed upon those that held it was balanced by its corrupting influence on the soul.

She had heard tales of foreign despots who made use of schools like Gant's to force the children of prisoners into that Class — no free person would ever choose it of their own volition.

And Gant had been one of them?

The old man was speaking again, but not to her any longer. "I can still see them all, you know? Every one of them. You would think the faces would fade over time. But they don't. They just wait for you in the dark. I'd thought I could balance the books here. Pass on what I had learned to help keep all of you safe. So, you never had to make the choices I did, you know? But I'm just adding to it all, aren't I? Making monsters of my own to unleash on the world."

His face had turned to a snarl then, and she had felt her heartbeat thud in her chest.

"And you're one of the worst, you hear me, girl? Knight of the Goddess-damned Road. That's what you want to be? With everything you have. With everything I've taught you. You're going to use all that to be one of the King's bullies. Travelling the country and terrifying those who cannot fight back."

That had stung.

He was not the first to disparage her Class choice, but hitherto no one had been so explicit. "I will seek to dispense the Justice of the Goddess," she said.

"'Justice'? What does that bitch know about 'justice'? The first time you crush the skull of a bandit, see if She bothers to tell you why they chose to take to that life. See if She'll show you what road She forced them down that led them into your path. Justice. There's no such thing. There's no good or bad in this world, my dear, but thinking made it so."

He stood then, wiping the tears from his face. The angry look had gone, replaced by something far more terrible: this tyrant of a man, this demon who terrorised her every day of her childhood, was sorry for her.

She saw true empathy on his face, and she did not know what to do with that.

"Don't let her make you hard, Daine. We're not meant to be alone, no matter how jealous of relationships she may be. We're not built like that. There'll come a time you'll be finished with all this. She'll have used you up and moved on to someone else, and you will look around for people to share your twilight time with. It's them you'll want, not another quest for justice."

He'd left her then, and she'd thought little of that strange conversation. Just another one of those uncomfortable interactions with a man losing his mind.

That is, before now.

She stood and made her way back to the group. Taelsin and Eliud were in a heated debate. "I need to return to

Swinford, Lord Duskstrider. I have responsibilities there. If the Trellecs seek to hold the whole of the West, they will need my City."

"Did you not see what they've just sent against us? The West has fallen, Mayor Elm. All you can achieve by remaining here is your death. Heroically, for sure. But dead is dead. My Lady Darkhelm, talk sense into him."

They both turned to her. She said, "what's the disagreement?"

Taelsin spoke first. "He would portal us all to the King."

Daine raised her eyebrows, and Eliud hastily explained. "He will know where to look for Genoes. There's nothing to be gained from staying here. I would not slaughter thousands of Westerners battling the Trellecs, and I see no benefit from Mayor Elm staying to fall with his City."

"That's where we differ, my Lord. When the fall is all that is left, it matters a great deal."

Eliud made an exasperated noise and turned back to Daine. "Explain to him we'll be safer together. I can protect us from the King."

"Mayor Elm does not wish to be 'safe,' my Lord," Donal chimed in. "Some things are more important."

Daine nodded. "There is truth in that, my Lord."

Eliud's face collapsed into a frown. "My Lady, there is a boy out there that has been taken. Every moment we discuss our next steps, he remains in danger. I will go to the King to ask for his help. I cannot do that and protect you from the powers that are gathering here. I'm not going to have your deaths on my conscience."

Donal coughed discreetly. "I think we remember the defining moment of that last battle slightly differently."

Lightning crackled from Eliud's eyes. "And you don't

think using powers like that comes with a cost! There's a reason those spells are forbidden."

Donal's face remained impassive. "I paid that price long ago, my Lord."

Eliud looked around and saw the resolution on each face.

"You saw that thing. If you stay in the West and oppose the Trellecs without me, you are all going to die."

Daine rolled her shoulders, the last of her vertebrae slotting back into place. "Mayhap. But I would not leave those in the West to the Trellec's predations. Swinford is as good a place as any to hold a line. I'm with Mayor Elm."

The relief on Taelsin and Donal's faces was palpable. Eliud looked to Kirstin, who was palpably torn. "It's not that I don't care for the West. But" — she looked at Daine — "we need to find Genoes. He must be so scared."

Daine smiled back. "Then go to the Capital. The boy will need as many friendly faces as possible when you find him."

The Knight turned to Eliud and beckoned for him to follow her a short distance from the others. "I'm not finished here. Everything is telling me I need to stay and help marshal a resistance. I left Genoes in your care when I returned here, and I can think of no one I could trust more, nor anyone more able to find him and bring him back safe."

Eliud was shaking his head. "I don't want to make this choice. You or Genoes. I cannot keep you both safe."

"Life is not 'safe,' my Lord. You have already done far more for us than I could possibly have hoped when I came to your door."

"But if I fail?"

"Then there is no one — living or dead — that could

have succeeded. I will go with Mayor Elm to Swinford and do what I can to help. Once you have found Genoes, come join us in the City. I hear their bakers are second to none."

Eliud smiled at that. "I may learn some things."

"Where there's will, there's hope."

They hugged then. Had they ever been so intimate before? And then he was turning and walking back to the rest of the group.

"Archer, you're with me. Both of you, too." Savage jumped up onto Kirstin's shoulder, and Josul trotted to his side.

Eliud drew a door in the air that shimmered and then stabilised. They could see the domed buildings of the Capital through the haze.

"The moment I have him back, I'll return to you in Swinford. Try not to die before then." And with no further ado, he ushered his small group ahead of him, and the portal blinked out of existence.

Taelsin, Donal and Daine were left staring into an empty space. It was Donal that broke the silence.

"I've heard more rousing farewells than 'try not to die.' But then, I guess if you have the power to command the heavens, you probably don't need to bother developing stirring rhetoric. I, on the other hand . . ."

"Donal . . ."

"Shutting up, sir."

And the three made their way back to the Elm pavilion on the outskirts of the village.

CHAPTER FIFTY-EIGHT

"Chaos Will Reign"

"It is all a bit like the aftermath of a festival, is it not?" Fion mused. "So much planning. So much anticipation. So much expectation. And now it is all done with and over. What will we all do with ourselves?"

The crowd of Lords and Ladies following in his wake through the village streets exchanged nervous glances. Did this maniac expect an answer to his question? Was it even a question? Would responding be rewarded or punished? Were any of them brave enough to reply?

Fion, oblivious to the mounting concern behind him, pressed onwards. "I do not mind sharing that I feel a sense of profound relief, but also no little disappointment." He stopped to peer at the storefront of one of the few shops that had opened that day. "I mean, I truly do not know with what I shall occupy my time in the coming days." The trailing Lords, who had not seen that he had halted, bumped into the fellows before them. The sight would have been ridiculous were not the circumstances around this strange procession so sinister.

For most of the representatives from the West, the last few hours' events were somewhat of a haze. They could remember the beginning of the debate in the Speaking Chamber and were aware that they had elected to break away from the Kingdom. So far, so uncontroversial. That was why they had all gathered, after all.

Where they were increasingly unclear, however, was how they seemed to have elected Fion Trellec — a man most had never heard of before the last month, and for those that had, what they had heard was not good — as their first amongst equals. The way they were all following behind him now was quite undignified, and yet . . . they did not seem to be able to stop.

There were other, more troubling memories seeking to press their way forward through the murk of their collective subconscious. Visions of threats and foul deeds in the Speaking Chamber. Of an unrestrained, frantic pursuit through the woods that ended in confusion. Of terrible powers which they understood little being unleashed all around them.

Each could feel those memories bubbling below the surface, but it was as if a suffocating layer of . . . something was resting upon them. A restriction which denied access to those thoughts. A haze that, they were all sure, had much to do with the affable old man who walked at Trellec's side. But consideration there was for another time. The presence on the other side of Fion, the woman with the power to steal breath and pile on exhaustion, was one none wanted to provoke. Even through their unclear memories, the need to avoid her notice bellowed for attention.

Right now, for all of the Lords and Ladies of the West, the critical need, more than anything else, was to get back to their own towns and cities in one piece. To achieve that, they were clear that they needed to comply.

There would be a reckoning, of course there would be, but that was for a future when they were safe behind their own walls.

Fion was about to start his perambulations again — he did so like having all these great men and women following him around like ducklings — when his eyes rested on a familiar but unwelcome face approaching him.

"Drunnoc," he practically hissed. "I had thought you lost in the destruction of the Keep."

"An event that clearly caused you much angst." Drunnoc's voice had its characteristically flat tone, but there was something else there. An inflexion of amusement. Whatever it was, Fion did not like it.

"I am overjoyed, of course, to see you well. I don't suppose" — he smiled thinly — "your mother likewise survived?"

"If she did, I have not seen her." Dark shadows moved to stand behind Drunnoc. Fion remembered seeing these figures flitting around the Speaking Chamber. They reminded him of some of his son's friends, but twisted somehow. His eyes would not settle on them, as if his unconscious mind rebelled from observing them too closely.

Fion suddenly felt exposed. He glanced to his right and was reassured by the presence of his Steward. With Gilles at his side, he need fear little else. "Well, it is good to see you, boy. I was just explaining to these Lords how strange this morning feels. How liberating. All we have sought to achieve for so long has come to pass."

Drunnoc blinked slowly. The resemblance of his demeanour to a snake had never been more evident. Fion waited to see if he was going to respond, but no. His strange child just stood there, regarding him in that peculiar way of his. It was as if he did not quite grasp the momentous nature of the moment. This would not do; it would not do at all.

"The West is free, my boy. Free! Do you hear me? We've cast off the bonds of service that have bedevilled us for so long, and we can now look forward to a brighter future." He turned to the Lords that were clustered behind him. "Is that not true?"

There was a smattering of encouraging sounds. Fion looked at Gilles. "They do not sound quite as enthusiastic as I had hoped."

Gilles seemed surprised to be addressed, then turned to the crowd behind Fion. "I am sure they are delighted that your leadership has finally freed the West, my Lord."

The resulting cry of acclamation was everything Fion had hoped it would be. If anyone noticed several members of that crowd stagger, blood streaming from noses, it did not seem to be a profitable thing to remark upon.

"I wish you well of it, Father. I'm sure this outcome must be very gratifying for you. For my part, I am done with such petty concerns." Drunnoc turned, and his dark followers moved to leave with him, Pernille slipping from Fion's side to join them.

For all his desire to maintain proper decorum, Fion's customary anger when dealing with his son roared to the surface. "How dare you dismiss me so! You will not turn your back on me, do you hear?" Fion strode forward to grasp his son by the shoulder and pull him around. However, the second he made contact, he unleashed an unearthly shriek.

Lord Trellec backed away, holding his hand up to his face in wordless horror. What was left at the end of his arm was a smoking ruin, looking for all the world as if it had been held within a red-hot forge. Indeed, in the act of pulling his hand away, all the watchers could clearly see the skin that had welded itself to the surface of his son's jerkin.

Drunnoc turned and regarded his father for a moment. If he felt either pleasure or despair at seeing his father's pain, his face betrayed neither. After several long heartbeats, he gestured to Pernille. "Heal him."

A wave of life force poured from her to enter Fion, and his hand was immediately restored.

In the silence that followed, Drunnoc stepped forward, imposing himself upon his father's space. Fion stepped backwards, holding his hand in shock, regarding his son with wild eyes. "Father, I care so little for the events here I can hardly tell you. These are small things suitable only for small men. And you, my father, as one of the smallest, are well suited to these games. Have your West. Have your rebellion. I wish you all the joy of it you can clasp to your breast. For now — and only for now, I would have you hear — our paths align. My master" — and on that word, Drunnoc seemed to stumble for a moment — "would have chaos in the West, and your version of rule will certainly bring that. Play your silly little games but understand that, win or lose them, I care not at all."

Drunnoc paused. He wondered if he had ever said so many words to this man before in his life. He was sure not.

He turned to leave again, stopped, and looked at the Lords clustered behind Fion.

"You may think that when you leave this place and leave his control" — he nodded at Gilles, who positively quailed at the attention — "you will be able to ignore what has transpired here. I am sure many of you have already penned messages to the King, disassociating yourself from the day's event. Poor you. How the ghastly Trellecs have so manipulated you. However, let me make a little counterproposal."

Drunnoc gestured, and one of his followers darted forward to pull one of the Lords randomly from the crowd.

"What is your name, sir?" the boy asked, almost conversationally.

"J-J-J aneck Falian." The elderly man was being held off the ground by the scruff of his neck.

"From the Isle of Meridan? A lovely place at this time of year. Unusual wildlife, I hear. Well, Lord Falian, you will be pleased to hear that you are about to play an essential function in the rebellion of the West."

At a nod from Drunnoc, a dark follower, slowly and with obvious relish, pulled each of the screaming man's limbs from his body and casually tossed them, followed by the gushing torso, to the ground.

"I do not tend to give speeches," Drunnoc said, all eyes now fixed upon him. "I am not the wordsmith my father is. However, I want you to look at your fellow brother in rebellion and remember this. He did not die because I was angry with him. He did not disappoint me. He did not fail to live up to any promises. He is dead purely because I wanted to make a point. The West will rebel, and chaos will reign. I care not whether you follow my father's lead in this, but there will be no conciliation with the Throne. I have had this done to a blameless man because I wished it so. Imagine what I will see done to anyone who lets me down."

Satisfied at the reaction, he turned back to Fion. "I trust you will be having Boruld refashion our home? Pernille can lend him any life force he may need to have it done with alacrity. I would not wish to sleep on the streets this evening. I wish you a good morning."

Fion, still holding his hand as if it were burning, watched his son — was he truly his son any longer? — leave.

He looked back over the cowed Lords and barked at them. "You heard him. Stop hanging about me like an unpleasant smell. Don't you have homes to go to? We will be in touch."

With palpable relief, they scurried away as fast as they could.

"Is everything okay, my Lord?" Gilles was once more at Fion's side.

"Not at all, Gilles. Not at all. But that is not to say we cannot turn things to our advantage. Please send to Master Boruld. My son requires that he attend to his wishes immediately."

As they spoke, neither master nor servant noticed two figures tossing dice in an alleyway nearby. A close observer would have noted their facial similarities and known them as brothers; the game they were playing, though, did not seem to follow any obvious rules.

They watched everyone depart between throws.

"Each of these bright sparks of energy going separate ways," they thought, "like little chaotic streaks of life careering hither and tither with no set direction. How unknowable were their paths."

And They were well pleased.

EPILOGUE

Daine paused, then turned and took a few steps back down the Road.

Taelsin, noticing her absence, brought his horse up short and turned back to rejoin her, but Donal put his hands on his reins and quietly shook his head. "She'll catch us up when she is ready."

The short journey, thus far, had been uneventful. If any of the Lords that had attended the Great Council felt animosity toward the group from Swinford, they were in too much of a hurry to return to their own cities to make much of it.

Taelsin had sought to engage a few of those he knew better in discussion, but to little avail. All he could ascertain was that secession had been decided upon, the King had been informed, and fear — if not outright terror — of the Trellecs was rampant.

"Do you think she is going to be okay?" Taelsin's eyes were fixed on the broad back of the woman he had never imagined could be bested. The damage inflicted upon her by the creature in the woods had shaken a previously solid pillar of his worldview: up until a few bells ago, the only things he felt were certain in life were death, taxes, and victory for the Darkhelm.

Donal snorted. "I think you will find that woman is much more resilient than you suggest. The Stonehand himself trained her, if the rumours are to be believed. I imagine she took beatings like that before breakfast and twice again before bedtime."

"True, but that was a long time ago."

"My Lord, speaking for those of us for whom the words 'a long time ago' mean something quite different, I would respectfully disagree. I do not dismiss her recent pain, but rather suggest she has experienced worse before and doubtless expects to encounter the like again. It is her lot in life."

They rode on in silence for a few moments. "Just how old are you, Donal?"

"Old enough for it to be impolite to ask, my Lord."

*

She did not think she had ever before retraced her steps on the Road.

The journey back to Swinford, while strategically sound in the face of what was coming, was an admission of failure.

"Never retreat. Never negotiate. Never show them your back."

She'd lived her life by Gant's oft-repeated words, and it seemed a poor time to cut and run. There were people in that village who were going to suffer because she had been comprehensively outmanoeuvred.

Almost from that first moment in the Town Hall, the Trellecs had wrong footed her. She remembered Cenwyn's words in the inn that first evening: "You should have cut his thumbs off." Looking back now, she wished she had done that and much more.

How many people had died because she had stayed her hand?

You expect too much of yourself. The words of the Goddess reverberated in her mind. *These were the opening moves in a much bigger game. That you are alive at all is today's victory. Regroup, recover, and prepare for what is to come.*

She did not reply. There was not much to say to that.

The stream of people leaving the village had slowed to a crawl. Most of the Lords were now on their way, leaving the Trellecs free to continue with their machinations.

As she watched, giant blocks of stone continued to rise in the air, were shaped and then placed in situ in a growing tower. She knew the significance of such a working and was staggered at the power on display. Her heart skipped a beat thinking of that Earth Mage. Who would have thought he'd have such things in him?

It looked as if, in no time, Eliud's destruction of the Keep would be comprehensively undone.

That train of thought took her to Genoes, and again, the pang of failure was sharp. All the Tailor had asked of her was to protect that boy; now, she did not even know where he was.

But Eliud would find him. If there was one thing on which she could rely, it was that the Duskstrider would move heaven and earth to bring that boy home safe. They would see each other again in Mayor Elm's city.

She nodded her head once, twice, and then turned back up the Road.

She jogged quickly to rejoin Taelsin and Donal, smiling as she came into earshot of their squabbling.

"All okay?" Taelsin was doing a poor job at hiding his concern.

"No," she answered honestly. "But I will be."

She glanced again over her shoulder and then resolved not to look at the village again until she was returning to bring justice.

"I'll be back," she whispered under her breath. "That, I promise."

And they rode on to Swinford.

*

"Now, what you have to remember is that, around here, I'm kind of a big deal. So don't be intimidated if there's a certain amount of cheering at my presence. I'll still be the same Eliud you know and love; it's just that I will also be basking in the love and glorification of a grateful population."

If Kirstin's eyes had rolled much harder, she would have completed a full-body flip. When he prattled on like this, it was easy to forget that she stood next to one of the great powers of the world.

"In fact, it might be best if you addressed me as something like the All-High Great Duskstrider, too. Just to make sure you fit in with the general atmosphere of veneration." He regarded her critically for a moment. "Perhaps you should also stand in a permanent state of curtsey?"

Eliud was nervous, but was determined not to transmit it to Kirstin.

He had portalled them to one of the roads approaching the Capital, and they had joined the long procession of people seeking entrance. He'd briefly toyed, considering the urgency of his mission, with manifesting directly in the Throne Room. But, remembering his last conversation with the King, he had thought better of it.

Visions from that meeting flashed through his mind, and he reflexively bent to scratch Josul behind his ears. The dog whuffled in pleasure, but Eliud could sense the anxiety rolling off him in waves. The Pendragon was not the only one with bad memories of the Capital.

As they neared the front of the queue, he felt his restlessness soar.

"Although, now I think on it, once I reveal myself, it might be most appropriate for you to fully genuflect and perhaps follow me around on your hands and needs. You could even chant my name so that no one was unclear about who was approaching. That would establish the correct atmosphere, I think."

Kirstin met Savage's eyes, perched as she was on her shoulder. "How do you stand spending so much time with him? He is exhausting."

The kitten sniffed. "He feeds me."

"I've tasted his food. That seems like you are getting the poor end of the deal."

"And I think we need to put an end to this sort of irreverent backchat," Eliud said. "Should they overhear, the small folk might think you are failing to show appropriate respect toward someone they love unconditionally. I wouldn't want to be responsible for you being summarily executed by an angry mob."

As they spoke, they'd reached the front of the queue, and the guard on duty barely glanced their way.

"State your business."

Eliud pulled his hood slightly lower over his eyes. "Just your common or garden visit. I'm showing my daughter the sights."

"Papers."

Eliud retrieved a scroll from the inside of his cloak and passed it over. The guard barely glanced at it before handing it back.

"The rules for day visits are simple. Rule one: obey. Rule two: don't make anyone ask you anything twice. Rule three: don't test a guard's patience. You follow them, you're golden. Don't let the gates hit you on your way in."

Feeling more relieved than he had anticipated, Eliud ushered Kirstin in front of him.

"Thank you, kind sir."

But that relief was short-lived.

He had barely taken a step across the threshold of the Capital when the temperature dropped through the floor. "Ah, I worried this might happen." He pulled Kirstin behind him. "But never fret, I am sure whoever is on watch today will be a reasonable human."

"Eliud Duskstrider, as I live and breathe."

Eliud cursed and turned to look at the tall, dark-skinned figure that had appeared ahead of him. "Logan — sorry, I forgot the honorific you chose. It was something like Todgerfeeler, right?"

"Twilight."

"Yes, that was it. I'm sure I mentioned at the time, but that is one terrible name. I know they say that imitation is the sincerest form of flattery, but I am not sure you're inviting a fair comparison there. Dusk. Twilight. There are other states of light, you know. Logan 'Twilight.' Don't you think it says less 'behold my power' and more 'I dance for money'?"

"I had forgotten your legendary wit, my Lord. It remains, of course, a treat. However, you likewise seem to have forgotten you have been banished from the Capital. On pain of death, if I recall correctly?"

"I'm sure you are mistaken in that. 'Come back any time' were the King's last words to me."

Other hooded figures appeared behind the Mage, all with grim expressions. "I am afraid not, my Lord. The King has been clear as to what we are to do should you ever return." He raised his voice to boom out across the courtyard. "Brothers, as we have discussed, please. Lend me your power." A complex ritual circle started to form around Eliud.

Kirstin leaned in to whisper. "The veneration seems to be a touch slow to start. Would me curtseying help?"

"Probably not at this stage. Right now, I think the most diplomatic thing to do is let them have fun. We'd get off on the wrong foot if I started throwing lightning around. Don't worry; they are just casting a second-tier <Oblivion> ritual. Five, six hours of unconsciousness tops."

"Hours!"

"A day at most. I'll sort it all out once we're in front of the King."

And with that, the ritual was completed, and the small group fell silently to the floor.

Logan smiled thinly. "Gather them up and take them to Sky Keep. They've been preparing for a visit from the Duskstrider for some time."

The courtyard gradually cleared, save for a tall woman who was watching the proceedings with grey eyes.

Once the prone figures of Eliud and the others were carried out of sight, she pulled up her hood, whispering to herself as she did so. "Take care, my Lord. She'll need you by her side to overcome the approaching storm. For all our sakes, do not let her down."

And the Goddess stepped away from the realm.

If you enjoyed this book, please leave a review at your favorite online retailer's website!

Enthusiastic reviews from readers like you are incredibly helpful.

Thank you!

The adventure continues in . . .

TALES OF SHATTERED GLASS
BOOK 2: STONEHAND

ABOUT THE AUTHOR

BardLyre hails from the Midlands where they teach English. When not writing or teaching they can usually be found in the library. They own more books than is strictly necessary.

Visit BardLyre on Patreon for exclusive content:
https://patreon.com/BardLyre577

Discover more epic fantasy and LitRPG at
www.nefhousepublishing.com

NEF HOUSE PUBLISHING